实用商务英语写作

Practical English Writing for Business

安 然　孙继红　编著

国防工业出版社
·北京·

内容简介

本书将求职写作、日常办公写作、商务报告、合同协议、商务社交信函、外贸函电、电子沟通等各种可能遇到的国际商务写作任务全面融合,既介绍写作理论知识、业务技巧,又提供例证;书中总结出标准模式、范文、常用词汇和句型,并配有很有操作性的技巧训练,同时编入合同及各种单证。

本书可作为大专院校相关专业商务英语写作教材,也可作为从事商贸工作人员的参考用书及商务英语等级考试的指导用书。

图书在版编目(CIP)数据

实用商务英语写作/安然,孙继红编著. —北京:国防工业出版社,2008.6

ISBN 978-7-118-05707-2

Ⅰ.实... Ⅱ.①安...②孙... Ⅲ.商务-英语-写作 Ⅳ.H315

中国版本图书馆 CIP 数据核字(2008)第 060199 号

※

国防工業出版社 出版发行

(北京市海淀区紫竹院南路 23 号 邮政编码 100044)

腾飞印务有限公司印刷

新华书店经售

*

开本 787×1092 1/16 **印张** 18¼ **字数** 418 千字

2008 年 6 月第 1 版第 1 次印刷 **印数** 1—5000 册 **定价** 29.00 元

国防书店:(010)68428422 发行邮购:(010)68414474

发行传真:(010)68411535 发行业务:(010)68472764

前　言

中国经济的全球化使得中外商贸活动日益频繁，以英语作为载体的商务沟通，在商务活动中发挥着重要作用。国际商务的新发展，也对国际商务人才提出新要求，即急需具有商务写作能力的高素质应用型人才。然而从我们对毕业生和从业人员的调查发现，他们大多缺乏这方面能力。其原因一方面在于相关人员教授或学习方法不对，另一方面也因为缺乏合适的指导性教材。目前市场上的教材往往将商务写作内容割裂开来，只针对外贸函电或商务书信等研究，而没有英文商务写作完整的介绍，使读者缺乏全面认识和掌握；有的教材片面注重提供范文和例句，对于写作方法和商务活动背景很少介绍，使读者不能灵活、准确地应用写作进行商务沟通；有的教材内容陈腐，误导了读者；有的教材只重语言研究，而不能将内容和实际工作需要结合，学生学习后，还是不知道具体工作时如何使用。于是，针对现有教材的不理想状况，我们决定编写这本书。

本教材将求职写作、日常办公写作、商务报告、合同协议、商务社交信函、外贸函电、电子沟通等各种可能遇到的国际商务写作任务全面融合，内容设置系统、实用、创新；既介绍写作理论知识、业务技巧，又提供例证，充分贯彻了理论和实践紧密结合的原则，全面提升写作水平。书中总结出标准模式、范文、常用词汇和句型，行文现代、先进，有代表性；并配有操作性强的技巧训练，巩固写作技能；同时编入合同及各种单证，还附有常用商务英语词汇，将训练基础英语技能和商务工作有机结合起来。

本教材共十章。第一章是商务写作的基本原则，主要阐述有效商务写作的标准，如何构建清楚的句子和段落，以实现成功的写作。第二章求职英文写作，从其重要性开始论述，并根据西方实际，分别给予了简历、求职信和跟进的致谢信的写作指导和例文。第三章是日常办公公文，首先从理论上对便函、时间表、通知和海报、证明信、介绍信、便条和账单的写作方法加以阐述，然后提供实例。第四章报告写作，介绍了写作步骤、要素，并具体分析了较短的非正式报告和正式的长篇报告。第五章对比分析了合同和协议，介绍了撰写方法。第六章和第七章是商务社交信函，首先阐述了规范格式和风格，之后具体论述邀请函、道歉信、感谢信、卡片、表扬信、恭贺信、慰问信和推荐信的写作方法。第八章和第九章论述了外贸函电，根据实际业务顺序分别介绍了建立商务关系、询盘、发盘、还盘、接受订单和谢绝订单、包装、运输、支付方式、保险、投诉和索赔的写法。第十章是有关电子商务写作。

本书可作为大专院校相关专业商务英语写作教材，还可作为从事国际商贸工作人员的参考用书及商务英语等级考试的指导用书。

由于作者水平有限，书中难免有疏漏和不足之处，恳请广大读者及专家提出批评和指正。

编 者

2008 年 3 月

Contents

Chapter One An Introduction to Business Writing ······ 1

1.1 An Overview of Business Writing ······ 1
1.2 Criteria for Effective Business Writing ······ 1
1.2.1 Consideration ······ 1
1.2.2 Clarity ······ 3
1.2.3 Conciseness ······ 3
1.2.4 Concreteness ······ 5
1.2.5 Correctness ······ 5
1.2.6 Completeness ······ 5
1.2.7 Courtesy ······ 6
1.3 Construction of Effective Sentences and Paragraphs ······ 6
1.3.1 Construction of Effective Sentences ······ 7
1.3.2 Construction of Effective Paragraph ······ 12

Chapter Two English Writing of Employment ······ 18

Section One Business Writing ······ 18
2.1 Introduction ······ 18
2.2 Professional Resumes ······ 18
2.2.1 Introduction to Professional Resumes ······ 18
2.2.2 Structure of a Resume ······ 19
2.2.3 Format ······ 23
2.2.4 Sample Resumes ······ 23
2.3 Cover Letters ······ 31
2.3.1 What is a Cover Letter? ······ 31
2.3.2 Structure ······ 31
2.3.3 Format ······ 32
2.3.4 Sample Cover Letters ······ 34
2.4 Thank You Letters ······ 40
2.4.1 About Thank You Letter ······ 40
2.4.2 Samples of Thank You Letters ······ 41

Section Two Language Handbook 43
Useful Words and Expressions 43
Useful Sentences 47
Exercises 51

Chapter Three Office Daily Routines 53

Section One Business Writing 53
3.1 Introduction 53
3.2 General information and Samples of Office Daily Routines 53
3.2.1 Memos 53
3.2.2 Schedules 60
3.2.3 Notices and Posters 61
3.2.4 Certificates 65
3.2.5 Letters of Introduction 66
3.2.6 Notes and Bills 68
Section Two Language Handbook 71
Useful Words and Expressions 71
Useful Sentences 71
Exercises 72

Chapter Four Business Reports 75

Section One Business Writing 75
4.1 What is a Business Report? 75
4.2 Steps of Writing a Business Report 75
4.2.1 Determine the Scope of the Report 76
4.2.2 Determine the Scope of the Report 76
4.2.3 Consider Your Audience 76
4.2.4 Gather Your Information 77
4.2.5 Analyze Your Information 78
4.2.6 Determine the Solution 78
4.2.7 Use Graphics and Illustrations 79
4.2.8 Organize Your Report 89
4.3 Elements of Effective Business Reports 89
4.3.1 Accuracy 90
4.3.2 Objective 90
4.4 Short Business Reports 91
4.5 A Standard Format of Long Business Reports 91

4.6 Samples of Business Reports ········ 97
Section Two Language Handbook ········ 106
Useful Words and Expressions ········ 106
Useful Sentences ········ 107
Exercises ········ 109

Chapter Five Contracts and Agreements ········ 111

Section One Business Writing ········ 111
5.1 Introduction ········ 111
5.1.1 What is Contract? ········ 111
5.1.2 What is Agreement? ········ 111
5.1.3 Difference between Contract and Agreement ········ 111
5.2 General information and Samples of Contracts and Agreements ········ 112
5.2.1 Structure of Contract ········ 112
5.2.2 The Verbal Characteristics of Contracts ········ 122
5.2.3 Samples of Contracts and Agreements ········ 124
Section Two Language Handbook ········ 138
Useful Words and Expressions ········ 138
Useful Sentences ········ 140
Exercises ········ 141

Chapter Six Business Social Correspondence (Ⅰ) ········ 143

Section One Business Writing ········ 143
6.1 Introduction ········ 143
6.2 Formats ········ 143
6.3 Styles ········ 148
6.4 Punctuation Styles ········ 149
6.5 Business Social Correspondence in Details ········ 150
6.5.1 Letters of Invitation ········ 150
6.5.2 Letters of Apologies ········ 156
6.5.3 Letters of Thanks ········ 159
6.5.4 Card Writing ········ 162
Section Two Language Handbook ········ 165
Useful Words and Expressions ········ 165
Useful Sentences ········ 166
Exercises ········ 168

Chapter Seven Business Social Correspondence (Ⅱ) ······ 170

Section One Business Writing ······ 170

7.1 Letters of Praise and Appreciation ······ 170

7.2 Congratulation Letter ······ 172

7.3 Condolence Letters ······ 176

7.4 Letters of Recommendation ······ 178

Section Two Language Handbook ······ 182

Useful Words and Expressions ······ 182

Useful Sentences ······ 182

Exercises ······ 183

Chapter Eight Trade Correspondence (Ⅰ) ······ 185

Section One Business Writing ······ 185

8.1 Introduction ······ 185

8.2 General Information and Samples of Trade Correspondence ······ 185

8.2.1 Establishing Business Relations ······ 185

8.2.2 Inquiries ······ 188

8.2.3 Offers ······ 191

8.2.4 Counteroffers ······ 195

8.2.5 Acceptance, Orders and Declining Orders ······ 197

Section Two Language Handbook ······ 200

Useful Words and Expressions ······ 200

Useful Sentences ······ 202

Exercises ······ 209

Chapter Nine Trade Correspondence (Ⅱ) ······ 215

Section One Business Writing ······ 215

9.1 Packing and Shipment ······ 215

9.1.1 Packing ······ 215

9.1.2 Shipment ······ 217

9.2 Terms of Payment ······ 219

9.3 Insurance ······ 227

9.4 Complaints, Claims and Settlements ······ 228

Section Two Language Handbook ······ 231

Useful Words and Expressions ······ 231

Useful Sentences ······ 237

Exercises ········· 238

Chapter Ten Netiquette in Business Communication ········· 242

Section One Business Writing ········· 242
10.1 Introduction ········· 242
10.2 Netiquette in Details ········· 242
Section Two Language Handbook ········· 246
Useful Words and Expressions ········· 246
Useful Sentences ········· 247
Exercises ········· 249

Appendix ········· 251

1. Sales Contract ········· 251
2. Sales Confirmation ········· 253
3. Certificate of Origin ········· 254
4. Commercial Invoice ········· 255
5. Praforma Invoice ········· 256
6. Bill of Lading ········· 257
7. Draft ········· 258
8. Inspection Certificate ········· 259
9. Packing List ········· 260
10. Collection Order ········· 261
11. Letter of Credit, Irrevocable Documentary ········· 262
12. Marine Cargo Transportation Insurance Policy ········· 264
13. English Abbreviations in Business ········· 265

References ········· 282

Chapter One

An Introduction to Business Writing

1.1 An Overview of Business Writing

Written applications must be made to fill staff vacancies. Every business produces paperwork. A prospective business needs to convey various kinds of business information to its employees, clients, trading partners and funding bodies in order to operate the business and to promote products and services. Business writing serves to pass on information, to express ideas, to exchange feelings and to deal with social business.

Successful (Good) Business Communication can realize two goals, i.e., the receiver interprets the message as the sender intended it; it achieves the sender's purposes. At every stage, fluent, error-free writing can give a big advantage. Good writing will be used in different contexts to develop businessmen or to expand the business. Therefore, it is necessary for people who engage in foreign affairs to have a good command of the linguistic features and writing techniques in practical English writing.

1.2 Criteria for Effective Business Writing

Effective writing for business must comply with seven criteria, to be considerate, clear, concise, concrete, correct, complete and curtest. It should realize three functions: to inform; to influence; to entertain.

1.2.1 Consideration

The interrelationship between the sender and receiver profoundly affects communicative effectiveness. Consideration means that the writer prepares the writing with the readers in mind. You should take the following into consideration:

(1) Identify the audience. Determine the size and composition of the audience.

(2) Analyze the audience's desires, problem, circumstance, emotions.

(3) Analyze the audience's possible reaction.

(4) Determine the audience's level of understanding.

(5) Analyze the audience's needs. (informational, motivational, emotional, practical needs)

To indicate you are considerate, you can use the following:

1. Focus on "You" Instead of "I" and "We"

Your readers are usually more concerned about themselves than about you. They are more interested in your writing when they see the pronoun "you" rather than "I, we". You-Viewpoint is a technique for building goodwill in letters. It involves being friendly and treating people in the way that they like to be treated.

1) "I" or "We" Oriented

I am happy to tell you...

We are pleased to have your new account.

We make Willet razor in three weights-light, medium and heavy.

We have shipped the two dozen Crown desk sets you ordered.

We require that you sigh the sales slip before we will charge to your account.

2) "You" Viewpoint

You will be happy to know...

Your new charge account is now open for your convenience.

Willett makes razors for you in three weights—light, medium and heavy.

Your two dozen desk sets should reach you with this letter.

For your protection, you are charged only after you have signed the sales slip.

2. Make Your Writing Interesting and Beneficial to Your Readers

Whenever possible, show your readers what benefits they will get from your writing. They will be more likely to respond favorably and do according to your suggestions if they see that the benefits are worth the effort and cost, for example:

To emphasize the positive means stressing what can be done instead of what cannot be done and focusing on ideas your readers can view favorably. By making clear what you call or will do, you often indirectly make clear what you cannot do without using a single negative word, for example:

(1) "We allow 2 percent discount for cash payment. We won't be able to send you the brochure this month." (Worse)

(2) "You earn 2% discount when you pay cash. We will send you the brochure next month." (Better)

3. Apply Integrity and Ethics

To be truly considerate, you need also apply integrity—high moral standards, personal honor, truthfulness, sincerity—to your writing. Ethics is concerned with what is right human conduct. Codes of ethics provide standards enabling us to determine the fundamental distinction between right or wrong human behavior. An honest business person needs a strong conscience as well as knowledge of communication principles. There are also some other requirements leading to successful business writing, in addition to the essential ones mentioned above which are unique to business writing to some extent. When these requirements are reached, they can help you express your ideas clearly and persuasively.

1.2.2 Clarity

Clarity means your purpose and the words are clear to your readers so that the receivers can interpret your words with the same meaning you have in mind. But it is difficult for you to accomplish the goal because individual experiences are never identical and each person's mind is a unique filter.

Here are some suggestions to help make your messages clear:

1. Choose Proper, Short and Familiar Words

Choose proper words to make the messages easy to understand, e.g.:

(1) As to the steamers sailing from Hong Kong to San Francisco, we have bimonthly direct services. (Worse)

We have two direct sailings every month from Hong Kong to San Francisco. (Better)

(2) We have semimonthly direct sailing from Hong Kong to San Francisco. (Better)

(3) We have a direct sailing from Hong Kong to San Francisco. (Better)

Choose short and familiar words to make the messages easy to understand, e.g.: better say "after", "use", "show", instead of "subsequently", "utilize", "disclose".

2. Make Idea Clear

Put one idea in a sentence, put one topic in a paragraph, and put one subject in a letter.

3. Use Short Sentences

Short sentences lead to clear meaning and easy understanding. The average sentence length is about 17–20 words. You can use sentences containing 3–40 words. If there are more than 40 or 50 words in a sentence. You can consider rewriting it into more than one sentence.

4. Have Paragraphs of Suitable Length

In business writing, it is suitable for paragraphs to contain 7–8 lines. If a paragraph is too long, it may make the main idea unclear and lead to a loose structure. If a paragraph is too short, your reader may be impressed that your topic is not adequately supported.

1.2.3 Conciseness

Conciseness means to write the fewest possible words without sacrificing completeness and courtesy. A concise message saves time and expense for both sender and receiver. Conciseness contributes to emphasis. By eliminating unnecessary words, you help make important ideas stand out. To achieve conciseness, try to observe the following suggestions:

1. Shorten or Omit Words or Expressions

As few words as possible should be used to give complete, and clear meanings. If possible, a word should be used instead of a phrase, a phrase instead of a clause, a clause instead of a sentence, and a sentence instead of a paragraph.

1) **Avoid Cluttering Phrases**

Cluttering Phrases	Shorter Substitutions
at the present time	now
for the purpose of	for
for the reason that	since, because
in the near future	soon
in view of the fact that	since, because
prior to the start	before
a draft in the amount of $1000-	a draft for $1000

2) **Eliminate Surplus Words**

With Surplus Words	Eliminate Surplus Words
There are five rules that should be observed.	Five rules should be observed.
In the period between June and August they found the error.	Between June and August they found the error.
His performance was good enough to enable him to qualify for the promotion.	His performance was good enough to qualify for the promotion.
It came at a time when we were busy.	It came when we were busy.
Leather depreciates in value slowly.	Leather depreciates slowly.
We will ship these shoes at a later date.	We will ship these shoes later.
As a matter of interest, I am interested in learning your plan.	I am interested in learning your plan.

However, the process of condensing should not be carried so far that the message becomes general and loses its original meaning.

2. Include Only Relevant Facts

The effective concise message should omit not only unnecessary wordy expressions but also irrelevant material. To make sure you include only relevant facts, you should, first, stick to the purpose of your writing; second, omit information obvious to your reader; third, avoid unnecessary background material or explanations, excessive adjectives, pompous words, and gushy politeness.

3. Avoid Unnecessary Repetition

Sometimes repetition is necessary for emphasis. But if the same thing is said several times without reason, the message be comes boring. The following are three ways to prevent unnecessary repetition: First, use a shorter name after you have mentioned the long one once. For example, use "China Telecom" to indicate "China Telecommunications Company" when the latter one has been mentioned before. Second, use pronouns and initials rather than repeating long names. For instance, instead of "First Automobile Works" again and again. use "it" or "FAW ". Third, get rid of all needless repetition of phrases and sentences.

1.2.4 Concreteness

The writing should be specific, definite and vivid rather than vague, general and abstract.

Abstract	**Concrete**
a significant loss	a 53 percent loss
in the near future	by Thursday noon
light in weight	feather light
the majority	70 percent

1.2.5 Correctness

Business writing should be correct in grammar, punctuation, spelling, information, figures, etc.

Wrong Sentences	**Correct Sentences**
My research report in business communication took a long time to prepare. And turned out badly.	My research report in business communication took a long time to prepare and then turned out badly. (Fragment)
Profits were down in 1998, the Board blamed the recession.	Profits were down in 1998. The Board blamed the recession. (Comma splice)
Employees want to keep their jobs they will work hard for promotions.	Employees want to keep their jobs. They will work hard for promotions. (Run-on sentence)

1.2.6 Completeness

Your business writing is complete when it contains all the necessary information and data the reader needs. An incomplete message may result in increased communication costs, loss of goodwill, sales, and valued customers, cost of returning goods, and wasted time.

Keeping the following guidelines in mind will help you achieve completeness:

1. Make All Points Detailed

Evidence must be precisely stated. The significance of the facts in relation to the problem must be shown. The treatment of each section of the article must be complete or the reader may misunderstand that particular section. The analysis is a basis for the conclusions, and the conclusions are a basis for the recommendations.

2. Answer All Questions Asked

If you need to reply to an inquiry containing one or more questions, answer all questions clearly stated and implied. If you have no information on a particular question, you must say so clearly, instead of omitting an answer. If you have unfavorable information in answer one or more questions, handle our reply tactfully.

1.2.7 Courtesy

Business writing should be polite, sincere, tactful, thoughtful and appreciative

1. Singling Out Your Reader

Letters that appear to be written for one reader tend to make the reader feel important and appreciated. To single out your reader in a letter, you should write for his particular situation, e.g.:

We look forward to hearing from you. (Worse)

We look forward to the possibility of sending our executives to you in the years ahead. (Better)

2. Using the Reader's Names

Using the reader's names makes him or her feel important, e.g.:

"Mrs. Wilson, you haven't used your charge account in the last six months, and we are getting concerned about you. Will you do us a favor? Write and tell us what happened or, better still, come in and let us serve you again."

3. Avoiding Anger (Sarcasm, Insults, and Exclamations)

Angry Words

We cannot understand your negligence.

We will not tolerate this condition.

Your careless attitude has caused us a loss in sales.

We have had it!

4. Response in Time

To response in time shows the courtesy, e.g.:

We have received with many thanks your letter of 20 May, and we take the pleasure of sending you our latest catalog. We wish to draw your attention to a special offer which we have made in it.

You will be particularly interested in a special offer on page 5 of the latest catalog enclosed, which you requested in your letter of 20 May.

1.3 Construction of Effective Sentences and Paragraphs

Effective sentence and paragraph construction is vital both in terms of making writing easy to understand and helping us control the pace and impact of the writing.

1.3.1 Construction of Effective Sentences

You will be able to construct clear sentences and paragraphs by emphasizing unity, coherence, conciseness, and emphasis as you pay attention to grammar, choice of words, and punctuations.

1. Unity

Unity demands that every word and phrase should be relevant to one idea, and help produce one desired effect. In other words, a sentence cannot contain two parts that express two different ideas.

For example:

(1) Helen Keller wrote a total of eleven books, authored numerous articles and died in 1968.

There is no error in (1) except that it lacks unity because the two coordinated clauses are unrelated to each other. The sentence can be improved in either of the following ways:

(2) Helen Keller wrote a total of eleven books, and authored numerous articles. She died in 1968.

(3) Helen Keller, who wrote a total of eleven books, and authored numerous articles, died in 1968.

In Example (2), the two sentences each expresses one idea. In Example (3), the main clause expresses the main idea, and the attributive clause only serves to modify the subject. So in both cases, the unity principle is followed strictly.

Wordiness also violates the principle of unity. For example:

(1) There are many people who attended the conference.

(2) Many people attended the conference.

Sentence (1) is too wordy to destroy the unity. The revised (2) sentence without unnecessary words is better.

2. Coherence

Coherence influences the readers' perception of the writing. Sentences lead to readers' conviction only when the words are properly connected and their relationship is clear. Coherence is product of many different factors, which combine to make every sentence and every phrase contribute to the meaning of the whole piece. To achieve coherence, we can resort to parallelism and consistency in voice, mood and person.

1) Parallelism

Parallelism is for clarity and emphasis for a sentence. It can be achieved mainly by parallel constructions and g correlative conjunction.

Example for parallel constructions:

(1) I like having a cup of coffee and reading an interesting novel on Sunday.

(2) It is said that there is going to be a thunderstorm and that we'd better stay at home.

Example for correlative conjunction:

(1) Both illustrated catalogues and price list are enclosed for your convenience.

(2) Shakespeare was not only a writer but also an actor.

2) Consistency

A good piece of writing needs to maintain consistency in context, mood, subject and voice.

To achieve consistency in context, link one sentence to the next, consider the following techniques:

(1) **Repetition.** In sentence B (the second of any two sentences), repeat a word from sentence A.

(2) **Synonym.** If direct repetition is too obvious, use a synonym of the word you wish to repeat. This strategy is called 'elegant variation'.

(3) **Antonym.** Using the 'opposite' word, an antonym, can also create sentence cohesion, since in language antonyms actually share more elements of meaning than you might imagine.

(4) **Pro-forms.** Use a pronoun, pro-verb, or another pro-form to make explicit reference back to a form mentioned earlier.

(5) **Collocation.** Use a commonly paired or expected or highly probable word to connect one sentence to another.

(6) **Enumeration.** Use overt markers of sequence to highlight the connection between ideas. This system has many advantages: (a) it can link ideas that are otherwise completely unconnected, (b) it looks formal and distinctive, and (c) it promotes a second method of sentence cohesion, discussed in (7) below.

(7) **Transitions.** Use a conjunction or conjunctive adverb to link sentences with particular logical relationships.

a. **Identity.** Indicates sameness.

that is, that is to say, in other words, ...

b. **Opposition.** Indicates a contrast.

but, yet, however, nevertheless, still, though, although, whereas, in contrast, rather, ...

c. **Addition.** Indicates continuation.

and, too, also, furthermore, moreover, in addition, besides, in the same way, again, another, similarly, a similar, the same, ...

d. **Cause and effect.** Indicates the consequent connection.

therefore, so, consequently, as a consequence, thus, as a result, hence, it follows that, because, since, for, ...

e. **Indefinites.** Indicates a logical connection of an unspecified type.

in fact, indeed, now, ...

f. **Concession.** Indicates a willingness to consider the other side.

admittedly, I admit, true, I grant, of course, naturally, some believe, some people believe, it has been claimed that, once it was believed, there are those who would say,...

g. **Exemplification.** Indicates a shift from a more general or abstract idea to a more specific or concrete idea.

for example, for instance, after all, an illustration of, even, indeed, in fact, it is true, of course, specifically, to be specific, that is, to illustrate, truly,...

English verbs have three moods—the indicative, the subjunctive and imperative. Usually, a sentence is not composed of different moods without a good reason. For example:

(1) Analyze the project, and you write a report on its practicability. (Worse)

(2) Analyze the project and write a report on its practicability. (Better)

(3) He proposed that she read something worthwhile, and she practices more. (Worse)

(4) He proposed that she read something worthwhile and practice more. (Better)

Unnecessary shifts in subjects and voices often make sentences awkward, e.g.:

(1) After I handed out the prints, my note book was left in the meeting room. (Worse)

(2) After I handed out the prints, I remembered that I had left my note book in the room. (Better)

(3) Some thoughts and theories were put forward, and people carry out many experiments. (Worse)

(4) Some thoughts and theories were put forward, and many experiments are carried out. (Better)

3. Conciseness

Conciseness refers to the absence of superfluous words in writing and emphasis on short sentences.

1) Economizing on Words

Economizing on word generally means seeking shorter ways of saying things. Once you try to economize, you will probably find that your present writing is wasteful and that some words and combinations of words have more efficient, one-word equivalents.

The camera sells for a price of US$ 200.

By means of this device we are able to make it.

The close proximity of these two incidents is that they both happened at a time when others are busy.

We approached about this at a meeting held in the city of London during the time between June and July.

2) Avoid Long Sentences

Long sentences are nearly always harder to understand than short ones. That's because they either contain more sub-clauses—so the main, controlling subject and verb are harder to find—or because they contain a list of multiple elements.

As a general rule, anything over 30 words is a long sentence. Take a second look at any sentence that long and see if there is a way of breaking it more effectively.

Example 1

"The evolution of business information and communications technology and the client/server model has left enterprises with multiple systems and legacy applications deployed across incompatible IT platforms, making it difficult to integrate applications for mutual collaboration and benefit."

This sentence is 37 words long at the moment. It becomes complex around the move to the second clause. By making this a separate sentence, it becomes far easier for the reader to follow the argument.

Rewritten Example 1

"The evolution of business information and communications technology and the client/server model has left enterprises with multiple systems and legacy applications deployed across incompatible IT platforms. The result is that companies face real problems when it comes to integrating applications for mutual collaboration and benefit."

An alternative way to break sentences is to use punctuation such as commas, semi-colons and colons. Each of these punctuation marks has a slightly different purpose, but all of them serve to increase the clarity of sentences.

(1) Commas are the most flexible of all punctuation marks and have three main uses: to join elements of a sentence together, to isolate elements of a sentence that are not part of the main clause, and to denote a list.

Firstly, there is nothing to stop a comma being used before "and", but it should only do so if it is joining two elements together.

Secondly, use of the comma, to isolate elements of a sentence, is particularly valuable for relative clauses. When you use commas in this way, which is something that happens quite frequently, they normally come in pairs. They act as a kind of bracket at each end of the clause.

Thirdly, commas are used to separate items in a list. The comma should be used instead of a semi-colon, unless the items listed involve commas too.

(2) Semi-colons have two core purposes: joining two sentences together as one, and separating items in a list when one or more items have a comma in it.

(3) A colon should be used to introduce an explanation, example or list, as in the definition above.

Example 2

"The UK business telecoms market is a busy one: packed with numerous telecom providers fighting for your attention. That's why, at Cable & Wireless, we're focussed on straight-talking; and delivering real value."

This example highlights incorrect uses of the colon and semi-colon as well as a potentially unnecessary pair of commas. In the first sentence, the colon breaks the sentence abruptly. It could be argued that it explains the statement in the first half, but in fact the second half is merely a continuation of the first point. In the second sentence the semi-colon again breaks copy unnecessarily; the reader is expecting a second sentence, but all that is provided is a short phrase. The commas that place "at Cable & Wireless" in a kind of parentheses are also not strictly necessary.

Rewritten Example 2

> "The UK business telecoms market is a busy one, packed with numerous telecom providers fighting for your attention. That's why at Cable & Wireless we're focused on straight-talking and delivering real value."

4. Emphasis

An English sentence usually consists of several parts, which are not equal in their value. One part of it receives more emphasis that the rest since it carried the most important information. The following are the common ways to emphasize a particular element of a sentence:

1) Positioning

The most emphatic position in a sentence is generally the end, where the new information normally occurs. The second emphatic position is the beginning since it meets the eye first. The middle position is the least emphatic one. Study the following examples:

(1) The president, with the support of the whole nations, decided to take actions against terrorists.

(2) With the support of the whole nation, the president decided to take actions against terrorist.

(3) The meeting will be put off, he said.

(4) The meeting, he said, will be put off.

In sentence,(2) the phrase "with the support of the whole nation" obviously gives the reader a much deeper impression. The "he said" part is deemphasized in sentence (4).

2) Parallel Structure

The use of parallel structures in sentences can help achieve emphasis also. Very often the paralleled parts are almost equal in length. For example:

My degree, my work experience, and ability to complete complicated projects qualify me for the job. (Worse)

My degree, my work experience, and my ability to complete complicated projects qualify me for the job. (Better)

- Prepared weekly field payroll
- Material purchasing, expediting, and returning
- Recording OSHA regulated documentation
- Change orders

- Maintained hard copies of field documentation(Worse)
- Prepared weekly field payroll
- Handled material purchasing, expediting, and returning
- Recorded OSHA regulated documentation
- Processed change orders
- Maintained hard copies of field documentation(Better)

1.3.2 Construction of Effective Paragraph

A paragraph is a cluster of sentences. The simplest explanation of how to use paragraphs effectively is to work on the theory that each paragraph should convey a single thought. A series of paragraphs make up an entire composition. Each paragraph is an important part of the whole, a key link in the train of thought. Designing paragraphs requires the ability to organize and relate information.

1. Elements of a Paragraph

Paragraphs vary widely in length and form. You can communicate effectively in one short paragraph or in pages of lengthy paragraphs, depending on your purpose, your audience, and your message, the typical paragraph contains three basic elements: a topic sentence, supporting sentences that develop the topic, and connections between sentences. The following examples are well written paragraphs with all three parts.

2. Creating a Topic Sentence

The topic sentence expresses the main point in a paragraph. You may create your topic sentence by considering the details or examples you will discuss. What unifies these examples? What do your examples have in common? Reach a conclusion and write that "conclusion" first.

1) Purposes of Topic Sentences

(1) To state the main point of a paragraph;

(2) Relates the paragraph to the essay's thesis;

(3) Defines the scope of the paragraph itself.

2) Placement of Topic Sentences

(1) Often appear as the first or second sentences of a paragraph;

(2) Rarely appear at the end of the paragraph.

3. Supporting a Topic Sentence with Details

To support a topic sentence, consider some of the possible ways that provide details. To develop a paragraph, use one or more of these:

1) Illustration

When you develop a paragraph by illustration, you give examples that demonstrate the general idea, for example:

Rural workers opportunities of residence, education, health care and other security benefits are largely deprived, thus block their possibility of improve their income. For example, if a child without Beijing hukou wants to go to the elementary school and middle school in Beijing, he has to pay a large amount of money. Or even if he is willing to pay, the school may don't like to accept non local students.

2) Comparison and Contrast

Similarities or differences among thoughts often provide a strong basis for paragraph development. Here is an example:

On the other hand, Bergsten and Noland (1993) state that most Japanese firms in semiconductor industry have a clear preference towards VI relative to their US counterparts. In the automobile industry, on the other hand, the US and European automakers are substantially more vertically integrated than Japanese automakers (GM and Daimler Benz reached about 50% while Toyota was around 20%, according to an OECD study) (Nagaoka and Goto, 1997). In comparison, the Japanese 'Keiretu' is indeed quite open to the entry of new upstream firms although it is a long run relationship between auto part suppliers and the automakers and sometimes involves ownership stake, because the automakers pursue a 'multiple vendor policy' and often procure parts from new suppliers when they develop new models.

3) Cause and Effect

When you develop a paragraph using the cause and effect technique, you focus on the reasons. Cause/effect paragraphs generally follow basic paragraph format. That is, they begin with a topic sentence and this sentence is followed by specific supporting details. For example, if the topic sentence introduces an effect, the supporting sentences all describe causes. Here is an example:

In recent decades, cities have grown so large that now about 50% of the Earth's population lives in urban areas. There are several reasons for this occurrence. First, the increasing industrialization of the nineteenth century resulted in the creation of many factory jobs, which tended to be located in cities. These jobs, with their promise of a better material life, attracted many people from rural areas. Second, there were many schools established to educate the children of the new factory laborers. The promise of a better education persuaded many families to leave farming communities and move to the cities. Finally, as the cities grew, people established places of leisure, entertainment, and culture, such as sports stadiums, theaters, and museums. For many people, these facilities made city life appear more interesting than life on the farm, and therefore drew them away from rural communities

4) Define Your Terms

To define the terms is to explain exactly the meaning of a particular word or idea or to describe something correctly and thoroughly, and to say what standards, limits, qualities etc it has that make it different from other things, for example:

Habit formation is a relatively new field in economics, since it considers the influence of the individual's past experience on the current decision while the new classical or traditional economic theory just consider the current situation when make a current decision. Weder (2000) estimated the impact of habit formation on busyness cycle and found that the habit formation can't deduce the fluctuation in a stochastic environment.

5) Quotation

Quotation is a sentence or phrase from a book, speech etc which you repeat in a speech or piece of writing because it supports the idea, for example:

Not only did the rural workers are discriminated in material benefits of the social security system, but also they are mentally discriminate. They are lack of safety and stability, so they usually seek for short-term behavior, as Fan (2005) stated, "Because temporary migrants lack permanent resident status, their calculations tend to focus on short-term monetary gains rather than long-term investment of human capital", which further deprive their opportunity of getting higher paid jobs, and thus decrease their income.

6) Classification

Paragraphs developed by classification show how a general idea is broken into specific categories, for example:

Generally speaking, there are three modes for firms to step out into the world market, that is, Greenland investment, merging and acquisition (M&A)1, and exporting. During the recent years, there is a fade for Chinese firms to conduct merging and acquisition to compete in the international arena.

4. Connections between Sentences

A good paragraph has unity: All the sentences have a relationship to one another and to the main idea. The connection between sentences in a paragraph can be shown in several ways, but principally by the use of transitional words and phrases. Transitional words and phrases may be conjunctions, such as and, but, and however, or explanatory expressions, such as for instance, on the other hand, and so on. Transitional words and phrases act as signals. They give directions. They tell where the paragraph is going. In this sense, transitional words and phrases also act to hold sentences together, achieving unity.

Here are some of the most commonly used connecting words and phrases and the purposes they serve.

Purpose	**Connecting Word/Phrase**
to add another idea	furthermore, in addition, also, moreover, likewise, similarly
to arrange ideas in order time	first, finally, meanwhile, eventually, next, subsequently, ultimately, at the same time
to add an illustration explanation	for example, for instance, in other words
to conclude or sum up	hence, therefore, thus, accordingly, in brief, in conclusion, consequently
to connect two contrasting ideas; to differentiate ideas	on the other hand, however, yet, conversely, nonetheless, nevertheless, rather, although, on the contrary
to emphasize or confirm	indeed, naturally, of course, certainly, undoubtedly, admittedly, plainly

Additionally, the logical development chosen for the paragraph can be made very clear to the reader by the words used to connect one sentence to the next. These words are often referred to as logical connectives because they make clear not only the order but also the meaning of the writing.

Each organizational pattern has its own logical connectives. Order of importance may be emphasized with transitional words and expressions such as first, a second factor, equally important, furthermore, of major concern, finally, least important, and most important. Transitional expressions such as equally, similarly, just as, however, on the other hand, despite, and otherwise may be used to emphasize comparison or contrast. Words particularly suited to writing about causes and effects are as a result, because, consequently, and therefore.

5. Types of Paragraphs

In terms of positions and functions, paragraphs can be classified into three: the opening paragraph, the body paragraph and the concluding paragraph.

1) Writing a Strong Opening Paragraph

Your first job in writing any letter is to gain your reader's attention. It's an important principle of effective writing to put the most important information first. Your opening paragraph is both the headline and the lead for the message that follows in the rest of the letter.

Make your first paragraph do something other than just referring to known information—so plunge straight into your message and don't waste your reader's time. For example, you could

- answer a question
- ask a question
- explain an action taken
- express pleasure or regret
- give information

As the opening paragraph sets the tone for your letter, try to avoid using tired phrases that are wordy, give little information and create a formal and impersonal tone. Using the classic business-speak opening of Further to... almost guarantees the rest of the letter will be a typical, long-winded, standard piece of business writing.

2) Writing a Supporting Body Paragraph

Body paragraph or paragraphs are those in the middle of a writing that serve to develop the theme or main idea. They discuss, substantiate, and support the main idea proposed in the opening paragraph through various ways, including illustration, comparison, contrast, and definition, etc.

3) Writing a Strong Concluding Paragraph

In a longer letter the last paragraph can summarize the key points or repeat the key message. If some action is needed, explain what you want the reader to do or what you will do.

6. Ways of Arranging Information within or between Paragraphs

- order of time (chronology)
- order of space (descriptions of a location or scene)
- order of climax (building toward a conclusion)
- order of importance (from least to most important or from most to least important)

In summary, writing can be composed of three types of paragraphs. A good opening paragraph should arouse the reader's interest in reading more and focus on the main idea of the whole essay. The body paragraph should be the development of the opening. The concluding paragraph is almost as important as the opening one. It not only summarizes the main points of the whole essay but also echoes the opening paragraph.

7. Sample Writing

Example 1: Offer to Special Order Merchandise Not in Stock

Dear Sirs:

[Opening paragraph]

After checking with all of our other stores in the area, I regret to inform you that I have been unable to locate another item requested for you.

[Body paragraph]

If you would like me to place a special order, I would be most happy to do so. Normally, it takes between four to six weeks to receive merchandise ordered in this manner. If this is your desire, please call me at your convenience at 666 - 666.

[Concluding paragraph]

On behalf of our firm I would like to thank you for shopping at our store and if there is any way that we can be of further assistance to you, please let us know.

Example 2: Executive Summary

[Opening paragraph]

For the past eighteen months, the Satellite Products laboratory has been developing a system that will permit the companies with large fleets of trucks to communicate directly with their drivers. This communication is intended to take place at any time through a satellite link.

[Body paragraph]

During the week of May 18, 1999, we tested our concepts for the first time, using the ATS-6 satellite and five trucks that were driven over an eleven-state region. All trucks carried our prototype mobile radios.

More than 91% of the 25,000 data transmissions were successful. In addition, over 98% of the voice transmissions were judged to be of commercial quality with exceptional clarity. The most important factor limiting the success of the transmissions (8.5% of the total data transmissions and 1.7% of the voice transmissions) was movement outside the satellites broadcast footprint. Other factors include the obstruction of the line of sight between the truck and the satellite by highway overpasses, mountains and hills, trees, and buildings.

[Concluding paragraph]

Overall, the test demonstrated the soundness of the prototype design. Our work on it should continue as rapidly as possible. We recommend the following actions: Develop a new antenna designed specifically for use in communications between satellites and mobile radios. Explore the configuration of satellites needed to provide thorough footprint coverage for the 48 contiguous states, Alaska, and Southern Canada at a elevation of 25 or more.

Chapter Two
English Writing of Employment

Section One Business Writing

2.1 Introduction

To have a job maybe is not so difficult, but it is not easy to have an ideal job. It is a complicated process that involves many writing jobs together with some other efforts such as information collection, personal analysis and designing and interviewing. Generally speaking, the process of employments always includes the following links: self-analysis, job search, application, interviewing and acceptance. A successful application process for a job needs three kinds of writing: professional resumes, cover letters and thank you letters.

2.2 Professional Resumes

2.2.1 Introduction to Professional Resumes

A resume or curriculum vitae (c. v.) is a summary of one's qualifications. An effective resume is the foundation of every successful job campaign. The resume is a written presentation meant to impress a prospective employer with one's skills, education, and experience. Ninety-four percent of all interviews today require a resume. When you respond to a job advertisement, many other people are also answering the advertisement. An outstanding resume is critical if you want your resume to stand out from the pack. Keep in mind that a good resume alone won't get you a job; however, it can help you get an interview and influence an employer's perception of your skills and potential for a particular kind of work. The point of creating and submitting a resume is to get called in for an interview. A strong resume will allow you to remain at the top of the consideration pile while the unqualified sludge sinks to the bottom. Once you are called in for a personal interview, you can sell yourself, add colorful anecdotes, and complete the package.

The formats of resumes can vary as writer intend. However, a professional resume should present the following principles:

(1) Actively market your skills, abilities and excellence;

(2) Put the employer's concerned information in the first place;

(3) Detail your achievements and results;

(4) Emphasize outstanding information instead of the common;

(5) Keep coherent and balanced;

(6) Considerate the employers' requirement.

2.2.2 Structure of a Resume

A resume is a brief overview of Personal Information, Job Objective, Education, Work Experience, and Core Competencies or Transferable skills. The optional parts include Part-time Jobs, Activities, Technical Qualifications, Special Skills, Publications, Patents, Accomplishments, Languages, Travel, Hobbies and Interests, and References/Referees. These should be inserted at suitable and logical places.

1. Personal Information

Personal Information includes Full Name, Address, Telephone Number, Date of Birth. Among other headings that may be added are Permanent Domicile, Marital Status, Gender, Height, Weight, Health, Photo(if need)etc. In some developed countries, such factors as height, weight, sex, and marital status, etc. should not be listed on the resume. They are irrelevant and cannot legally be considered in employment decision. The situation depends in China. You can decide whether or not put such data in the resume. The style is free. It can be written in forms, in sentences or the mixed.

1) Full Name

Unlike Chinese, Westerners put family name at the end as last name instead of at the beginning. The acceptable type for the name of "李扬"are seven: (a) Yang LI (b) YANG LI (c)·Yang Li (d) Yang Li (e) Li, Yang (f) Li Yang (g) LI Yang. The second type is the standard and prevailing writing method in foreign companies. The forth type is convenient for recruiters; To avoid misunderstanding, you may either put a comma after the surname as the fifth—Li, Yang—or capitalize every letter of it like the seventh—LI Yang.

In case of two or more given names, there are four writing methods: 1)Xiao-feng 2)Xiao-Feng 3)Xiaofeng 4)Xiao Feng. We suggest the third the most for it is the most convenient and explicit.

2) Address

If you like, you can write both your business or temporary address and your home address. The post code is put between the names of city and the nation. For example:

Temporary address: Room 212 Building 111

Tsinghua University, Beijing 100084 China (until Dec. 31, 2007)

3) Telephone Number

(1) To be "user friendly",put district telephone number at the front, e.g. (86-0411).

(2) The blank comes between the bracket after the district number and the telephone number e.g.(86 – 010) 6666 – 2222. This is the fixed style of English writing.

(3) (O) or (W) is put after your office telephone number and (H), your home telephone number.

(4) Put a "-"between eight numbers, such like 6666-2266. Such will be easy to read and dial.

(5) The mobile phone number should comply with the "4-3-4 rule", e.g. "1111-135-1234".

4) Marital Status

Put Single or Married (no/two children).

Example 1

Position Desired:	HR Manager
Name: ×××	Sex: Male/Female
Date of Birth: June 2, 1975	Address: ×××, China
Marital Status: Single/Married	Post Code: 100001
Height: 1.70m	Weight: 50 kg
Health: Excellent	E-mail Address: 123456@sohu.com
Tel: (86-010) 6666-2222	Mobile phone: 1111-555-3333
Homepage: http://www.sohu.com/~1	
Current Annual Salary: 50,000 RMB	

2. Job Objective

Decide what type of job you will be applying for. This can become your objective statement, should you decide to use one in the first line of the profile section of your resume to give your reader a general idea of your area of expertise.

Objectives are not required on a resume, and often the cover letter is the best place to personalize your objective for each job opening. There is nothing wrong with using an objective statement on a resume, however, provided it doesn't limit your job choices. As an alternative, you can alter individual resumes with personalized objectives that reflect the actual job title for which you are applying. Just make sure that the rest of your information is still relevant to the new objective, though.

Never write an objective statement that is not precise. You should name the position you want so specifically that, if a janitor came by and knocked over all the stacks of sorted resumes on a hiring manager's desk, he could put yours back in its right stack without even thinking about it. That means saying, "A marketing management position with an aggressive international consumer goods manufacturer" instead of "A position which utilizes my education and experience to mutual benefit."

3. Education

If you are a recent college graduate and have little relevant experience, then your education section will be placed at the top of your resume. As you gain more experience, your education almost always gravitates to the bottom.

If you participated in college activities or received any honors or completed any notable projects that relate directly to your target job, this is the place to list them.

Showing high school education and activities on a resume is only appropriate when you are under 20 and have no education or training beyond high school. Once you have completed either college courses or specialized technical training, drop your high school information altogether.

Continuing education shows that you care about life-long learning and self-development, so think about any relevant training since your formal education was completed. Relevant is the key word here. Always look at your resume from the perspective of a potential employer. Don't waste space by listing training that is not directly or indirectly related to your target job.

Basic details about your education, including college location (city and state), degree, date of graduation (or expected graduation), major, related course work and (possibly) G.P.A. Most college students do not need to include information about secondary school, but it is important to summarize education attained through community colleges, other colleges (i.e., transfer credits), and specialized training programs.

The popular style is that schools should be listed in reverse chronological order (usually starting from the year when you entered the highest college or when you got your last degree).

Example 1

2002 till present	Yale University, New Haven, CT, U.S.
	M.A. East Asian Studies, expected to be received June 2005
1998 – 2002	Beijing University, Beijing, China
	B.A., Major: History

Example 2

1990 – 1991	TRAINING, INC., Boston, U.S.
	An office careers training program in bookkeeping, typing, reception, word processing, and office procedures
1987 – 1990	ST. JOSEPH'S ACADEMY, Portland, Maine, U.S.
	High School Diploma

Example 3

May 2001	California State University, Fullerton
	Master of Business Administration degree with a finance specialty
April 2001.	Certified in Financial Management
October 1999.	Certified Management Accounting
May 1994.	CPA candidate, passed the entire CPA Exam
May 1993	Bachelor of Arts degree with concentration in Accounting

4. Work Experience

Work experience is brief summaries of principle employment to date. Start with your current (or most recent) position and work backward. Include all employment relevant to your career objective in any way. Internships and cooperative experience can be listed either under employment or under education.

Provide the name of the employer, the employer's location, your job title, dates of employment, and simple verb phrases to summarize your main activities on the job. When ever possible quantify and qualify data with specific details and statistics that illustrate your potential.

Whichever way you choose, be sure that the items under such headings as work experience, awards and publications follow the same order.

5. Core Competencies or Transferable Skills

Once a recruiter understands your focus, he/she will want to know if you have the required core competencies or transferable skills to accomplish the job. A thorough research of employer job descriptions will help you identify the core competencies your resume must feature.

You'll capture and hold recruiter attention by including only those core competencies relating specifically to your focus. Be careful not to muddy up your personal marketing message by including extraneous skills. If you remember the all-important rule of relevancy, you'll go a long way toward keeping the reader's attention on your key skills.

6. Optional Parts

1) Activities

List all major activities and awards as well as any skills that are relevant to your career objective. These can show leadership, organization, critical thinking, teamwork, self-management, initiative and influencing others.

2) Accomplishments

With record-high resume response to job openings, recruiters need good, solid reasons to recommend you for consideration over the mountain of other candidates. Clear, concisely stated accomplishments are the best way to distinguish yourself from your competition. For optimum impact, write accomplishments that illustrate the strength of your core competencies, transferable skills and focus. An accomplishment is only valuable to your resume if it promotes the skills your target employers are looking for. Remember the rule of relevancy as you craft each of your accomplishment statements.

3) Languages

Language levels are the easiest to be test in interviews. Therefore, be sure to tell the truth in your resumes. The proficiency degrees rank from the most fluent to the worst in the following ways: "Native speaker of", "Fluent in", "... as working language", "Some knowledge of".

If you have passed some English tests, put the results in this part, e.g.: "Passed Cambridge BEC Preliminary".

4) References/Referees

They are people who know you and can offer information or recommendation. The normal number of references is two or three, and it is imperative that you obtain their permission before using their names. In addition to names of your references, provide also their positions, full business addresses, and telephone numbers.

Prof. Tan Yonggang (Chairman)
Department of Foreign Literature
Modern University
Baoyiyan, Wuchang
Hubei, 430062, P. R.C.
Telephone: 611999 Ext. 565

7. Typing, Typography, Paper, and Font

Remember to keep all information on the resume concise and clear. A one-page resume is best, although people with extensive experience or advanced degrees may have to use two pages. Be scrupulously careful when you proofread; some employers will refuse to consider candidates who submit resumes with spelling or typographical errors.

As for the specification of paper, the standard paper size is 29. 7cm long and 21cm wide; it weights around 80g or 100g.

The font of Times New Roman or Palatino is suggested. The font of Harvard Business School is "Palatino preferred, Times New Roman acceptable".

2.2.3 Format

There are several standard formats for resumes. Chronological format of the resume briefly summarizes candidate's employment history. Functional portion of the resume focuses on candidate's unique qualifications, skills, and accomplishments. Some people might prefer to use a Functional Format to call attention to particular skill areas. Besides, some resumes have the mixed styles of the two formats. The organization of the resume can be adapted as necessary to emphasize an individual's most outstanding characteristics.

The following present four commonly used resume formats: the Chronological, the Functional and the Combination—Chronological and Functional

2.2.4 Sample Resumes

1. Chronological Sample Resume

Example 1

Melody Cantata

Campus	**Home**
123 Handel Hall	1812 Overture Ave.
Westminster College	Frederick, MD 21701
New Wilmington, PA 16172	(301) 555-1212

(724) 555-1234   melody@earthweb. com

cantatam@westminster. edu

Education

Westminster College, New Wilmington, PA   December 2000

Bachelor of Music Education

Cumulative GPA: 3.35/4.0

Certification

Pennsylvania certification   December 2000

National Teacher Examination qualified   December 2000

Pre-professional Skills Test qualified   May 2000

Experience

Stephen Foster High School, Sharon, PA   Spring 2000

Student teacher

Taught music theory and music appreciation classes and assisted with chorale and glee club

Harmony Elementary School, Frederick, MD   Summer 1999

Enrichment program leader

Led summer music program for children in grades 1 through 6

Woody Guthrie Middle School, New Wilmington,   Spring 1999

PA Student observer

Observed music teacher work with music classes, band, and chorus two mornings a week. Assisted with music-related activities.

Performance Background

Chamber Singers, Westminster College,   Fall 1998-present

New Wilmington, PA

First soprano in select group of singers that performs nationwide

Symphony Orchestra, Westminster College,   Fall 1999-present

New Wilmington, PA

Principal violin

Second violin

Adult Choir, St. Cecilia's Catholic Church,   Fall 1997 – Spring 1999

Frederick, MD

First soprano and soloist   1997 – present

Example 2

Haley Storm

hstorm100@psu. edu

Current Address
32-F Snowdrift Lane
State College, PA 1111
(814) 555-2222

Home Address
212 Sunrise Road
Tempe, AZ 88888
(480) 555-1111

Objective: An entry-level position in radar and satellite imagery analysis that would utilize my analytical and communications skills.

Education: Bachelor of Science Degree in Meteorology — Expected May 2001
The Pennsylvania State University
University Park, PA

Research/ Employment Experience:

ORISE Student — Summer 2000
National Weather Service, Silver Spring, MD
National Oceanic and Atmospheric Administration
Office of Hydrology
- Generated gridded radar-derived rainfall climatologies for radars in the West Gulf River Forecasting Centers.
- Results are being used to generate real-time map coverage for precipitation for the West Gulf regions.

SOARS Protege — Summer 1999
National Center of Atmospheric Research, Boulder CO
University Corporation for Atmospheric Research
Mesoscale and Microscale Meteorology Division
- Analyzed the relationship between cold cloud tops and maximum radar return in three different types of Mesoscale Convective Systems that occurred in May 1998.
- Utilized analytical and communication skills for the presentation of scientific result in colloquy.

Research Assistant, Department of Meteorology — Summer 1998
The Pennsylvania State University
Assisted Dr. Ray Van Allen in NASA-funded project.
- Researched and analyzed the 1982-83 and 1986-87 El Nino and the 1988 summer drought.

Campus Weather Service — Fall 1997-Spring 1998
The Pennsylvania State University

	• Collected data from UNIX workstations and other specialized computers to forecast the weather.
	• Researched, forecast, and narrated live weather broadcasts for radio stations.
Computer Skills:	Working knowledge of C programming and UNIX Working knowledge of Microsoft Office Suite and Corel Wordperfect
Conference Presentation:	"The Relationship Between Cold Cloud Tops and Maximum Radar Return in Three Different Types of Mesoscale Convective Systems that Occurred in May 1998" (poster) SACNAS National Conference — Spring 1999
Honors:	Weatherly-Flood Scholarship — 1997-present Galen Raines Scholarship — 2000 Women in Science and Engineering Student Leadership Conference — Spring 1998
Activities:	Support, Survival, and Success Mentor — 1997-1999 University Choir — 1998-1999 Intramural Basketball — 1997-present

2. The Functional Sample Resume

Example 1: Applying for Accounting

Adam Wright

Campus Address	Permanent Address
444 Grant St.	111 Banks Ave.
Bowling Green, OH 43403	Elyria, OH 44000
111-555-1040	000-555-9999
×××××@bgsu. edu	×××××@fastmail. com

Education

B.S. in Accounting, Bowling Green State University — Expected May 2001
3.4 cumulative GPA, 3.6 major GPA

A.A.S. in Accounting, Lorain County Community College — May 1996
3.7 cumulative GPA, 3.9 major GPA, Dean's List all semesters

Relevant Course Work

Financial Accounting	Auditing	Effective Business Writing
Managerial Accounting	Federal Taxation	Speech Communications
Cost Accounting	Corporate Finance	Information Systems

Work Experience

Junior Accountant, Homanick Inc., Akron, Ohio September 2000-present

Handle monthly journal entries; analyze sales/marketing monthly expenses and sales representatives' gross receipts; create spreadsheets; handle special projects.

Accounting Intern, Burry and Associates, Akron, Ohio May-August 2000

Reviewed and corrected accounting entries, assisted with financial planning input and analysis, and generated reports. Accounting corrections revealed nearly $50,000 in unpaid bills and mislaid funds.

Billing Coordinator, Corpora Corp., Elyria, Ohio June 1996-August 1999

Handled collections on more than 500 past due accounts; reconciled payment discrepancies; resolved client billing and eligibility issues.

Crew Leader, Michael's Muffins, Elyria, Ohio June 1994-May 1996

Supervised crew of seven workers and managed bakery's daily operations.

Computer Skills

MS Excel	MS Access	MS Word	MS Internet Explorer
MS Powerpoint			

Example 2: Resume for Culinary Arts/Hospitality

CHRISTOPHER BACON

4 Buttermilk Court

Poughkeepsie, NY 12666

OBJECTIVE

A position in catering, event planning, or convention services.

HIGHLIGHTS

- Three years experience operating own catering business.
- Educated in culinary arts and communications.
- Experience planning dinners and other events.
- Good communications skills, particularly in promoting or selling an idea.

RELEVANT SKILLS AND EXPERIENCE

Sales and Promotion

- Helped prepare promotional materials for clients of public relations firm.
- Conceived and implemented promotional campaign for Culinary Institute of America (CIA) externship program with culinary magazines and journals.
- "Pitched" vacation packages for country inn and resort in New York State.

Catering and Event Planning

- Operated successful catering business for groups of up to 75 people.
- Created custom-designed menus for all clients.
- Arranged dinners, luncheons, and receptions at public relations firm.

Organization and Leadership

- Secured financial support of Cook & Baker Corp. and services of Art Center at SUNY-Cortland for development of promotional materials for fundraiser.
- Assisted chef-instructors with course presentations for CIA's Continuing Education Division.
- Served as group leader and student council member at CIA.

Catering and Event Planning

- Helped prepare promotional materials for clients of public relations firm.
- Conceived and implemented promotional campaign for Culinary Institute of America (CIA) externship program with culinary magazines and journals.
- "Pitched" vacation packages for country inn and resort in New York State.

WORK HISTORY

- Test kitchen extern, Good Taste magazine, New York, NY — Spring 2000
- Cooking extern, Mama Rosa's Gourmet Market, Fishkill, NY — Fall 2000
- Caterer, self-employed, Albany, NY, and Poughkeepsie, NY — 1995-1999
- Administrative assistant, Colby & Gruyere Public Relations, Albany, NY — 1993-1995
- Promotions intern, Strawberry Fields Farms, New Paltz, NY — Summer 1992
- Line cook, The Cider Press Tavern, Cortland, NY — 1991-1992

• Server, Applejack's Cafe, Cortland, NY 1989-1991

EDUCATION

• Associate in Occupational Studies, Culinary Arts, The Culinary Institute of America, Hyde Park Spring 2001

• B. A., English, State University of New York at Cortland, Cortland, NY Spring 1993

3. The Sample Resume of the Combination Format—Chronological and Functional

Example 1: Resume for the Inexperienced

Room 222 Building 333
Tsinghua University, Beijing 100084
(010) 2222222222 Email: ×××××@tsinghua. edu. com

Zheng Yan

Objective

To obtain a challenging position as a software engineer with an emphasis in software design and development.

Education

1997.9-2000.6 Dept. of Automation, Graduate School of Tsinghua University, M. E.
1993.9-1997.7 Dept. of Automation, Beijing Institute of Technology, B. E.

Academic Main Courses

Mathematics
Advanced Mathematics Probability and Statistics Linear Algebra
Engineering Mathematics Numerical Algorithm Operational Algorithm
Functional Analysis Linear and Nonlinear Programming
Electronics and Computer
Circuit Principal Data Structures Digital Electronics
Artificial Intelligence Computer Local Area Network

Computer Abilities

Skilled in use of Sun, HTML, CGI, Perl, Visual Interdev, and SQL software

English Skills

Have a good command of both spoken and written English. Past CET-6, TOEFL:623; GRE: 2213

Scholarships and Awards

1999.3 Guanghua First-class Scholarship for graduate
1998.11 Metal Machining Practice Award
1997.4 Academic Progress Award

Qualifications

General business knowledge relating to financial, healthcare
Have a passion for the Internet, and an abundance of common sense

Example 2: Resume for the Experienced

RESUME

Personal Information:

Family Name: Wang Given Name: Bin
Date of Birth: July 12, 1971 Birth Place: Beijing
Sex: Male Marital Status: Unmarried
Telephone: (010) 62771234
E-mail: career@sohu.com

Work Experience:

Nov. 1998- present CCIDE Inc, as a director of software development and web publishing. Organized and attended trade shows (Comdex 99).

Summer of 1997 BIT Company as a technician, designed various web sites. Designed and maintained the web site of our division independently from s electing suitable materials, content editing to designing web page by FrontPage, Photoshop and Java as well.

Education:

1991 - August 1996 Dept. of Automation, Tsinghua University, B.E.

Achievements & Activities:

President and Founder of the Costumer Committee
Established the organization as a member of BIT
President of Communications for the Marketing Association
Representative in the Student Association

Computer Abilities:

Skilled in use of HTML, CGI, JavaScript, Perl, Visual Interdev, Distributed Objects, CORBA, C, C++, PL/I and SQL software

English Skills:

Have a good command of both spoken and written English. Past CET-6, TOEFL:623; GRE: 2213

Others:

Aggressive, independent and be able to work under a dynamic environment. Have coordination skills, teamwork spirit. Studious nature and dedication are my greatest strengths.

In today's extremely competitive job market, employers rely heavily on recruiter to screen out the crowd of applicants. Allow them to present you as one of their best candidates by letting your resume present your best abilities.

2.3 Cover Letters

2.3.1 What is a Cover Letter?

A cover letter is a document sent with your resume to provide additional information on your skills and experience. A cover letter typical provides detailed information on why you are qualified for the job you are applying for. Effective cover letters explain the reasons for your interest in the specific organization and identify your most relevant skills or experiences.

Job searching specialists and career counselors recommend that job applicants write a customized resume cover letter to accompany each resume sent to an employer. As an employer, a customized resume cover letter matters, for The employers is seeking the resume and resume cover letter that describe the candidate who will best fill their position. A thoughtful resume cover letter tells that the candidate took the time to customize his application to fit their needs. Perhaps the applicant with a superior resume cover letter will make a superior employee.

A well-written, carefully typed, error-free resume cover letter should immediately set the application apart from the average application they receive.

2.3.2 Structure

To be effective, your cover letter should follow the basic format of a typical business letter and should address three general issues:

- first Paragraph—why you are writing
- middle Paragraphs—what you have to offer
- concluding Paragraph—how you will follow-up

1. Why You Are Writing?

In some cases, you may have been referred to a potential employer by a friend or acquaintance. Be sure to mention this mutual contact, by name, up front since it is likely to encourage your reader to keep reading!

If you are writing in response to a job posting, indicate where you learned of the position and the title of the position. More importantly, express your enthusiasm and the likely match between your credentials and the position's qualifications.

If you are writing a prospecting letter, in which you inquire about possible job openings-state your specific job objective. Since this type of letter is unsolicited, it is even more important to capture the reader's attention.

If you are writing a networking letter to approach an individual for information, make your request clear.

2. What You Have To Offer?

In responding to an advertisement, refer specifically to the qualifications listed and illustrate how your particular abilities and experiences relate to the position for which you are applying. In a prospecting letter express your potential to fulfill the employer's needs rather than focus on what the employer can offer you. You can do this by giving evidence that you have researched the organization thoroughly and that you possess skills used within that organization.

Emphasize your achievements and problem-solving skills. Show how your education and work skills are transferable, and thus relevant, to the position for which you are applying.

3. How You Will Follow Up?

Close by reiterating your interest in the job and letting the employer know how they can reach you and include your phone number and/or email address. Or bid directly for the job interview or informational interview and indicate that you will follow-up with a telephone call to set up an appointment at a mutually convenient time. Be sure to make the call within the time frame indicated.

In some instances, an employer may explicitly prohibit phone calls or you may be responding to a "blind want-ad" which precludes you from this follow-up. Unless this is the case, make your best effort to reach the organization. At the very least, you should confirm that your materials were received and that your application is complete.

If you are applying from outside the employer's geographic area you may want to indicate if you'll be in town during a certain time frame (this makes it easier for the employer to agree to meet with you).

In conclusion, you may indicate that your references are available on request. Also, if you have a portfolio or writing samples to support your qualifications, state their availability.

2.3.3 Format

As for the format of a cover letter, sample cover letter format guidelines are given below:

Example

PARTS OF A COVER LETTER	SAMPLE LETTER
HEADING	Your Mailing Address City, State Zip Code Today's Date (4 "Return"s or "Enter"s on Keyboard)
INSIDE ADDRESS	Employer's Name Job Title Business Name Business Address City, State Zip Code
SALUTATION	Dear (Mr. /Mrs. /Ms.) (Use the name of the person that will read the letter):
INTRODUCTORY PARAGRAPH Tell why you are writing.	In response to the February 24th advertisement in the Bangor Daily News, I have enclosed my resume for the Receptionist position.
1ST MAIN PARAGRAPH Describe your qualifications. Sell your skills and knowledge. Tell why you are interested in the company or college. Point out any related experience you have.	I have two years of prior work experience as a receptionist with XYZ Telecommunications. My work has involved answering ten incoming lines and greeting customers in a fast-paced office setting. I have also been responsible for all incoming and outgoing mail, as well as purchase orders. I am very detail oriented and able to handle multiple tasks simultaneously.
2ND MAIN PARAGRAPH Continue to describe qualifications. Highlight relevant training or classes that relate to the job or major for which you are applying.	I am currently completing an Associate Degree in Executive Administrative Assistant at Northern Maine Technical College. In completing this program, I have gained valuable experience in several computer programs including Microsoft Word, Excel, and Access. Additionally, my training has provided me with the skills to reach my goal of office management.
CLOSING PARAGRAPH Close by thanking the reader and requesting an interview.	I welcome the opportunity to discuss my qualifications with you in person. I can be reached at (207) 555-1234. Thank you for your time and consideration.
COMPLIMENTARY CLOSE	Sincerely,
SIGNATURE	(4 "Return"s or "Enter"s on Keyboard)
NAME	Joe Doe

ENCLOSURE This indicates that you have enclosed other items (resume, transcripts, etc.) for the reader to see.	Enclosure

2.3.4 Sample Cover Letters

Cover letters generally fall into one of two categories: **Letter of Application:** applying for a specific, advertised opening; **Letter of Inquiry:** expressing interest in an organization, but you are not certain if there are current openings. See the following sample cover letters of these two types:

Example 1: Letter of Application, Hard Copy Version

E-2 Apartment Heights Dr.
Blacksburg, VA 24060
(540) 555-0101
abcd@vt.edu
February 22, 2007
Dr. Michael Jr. Rhodes
Principal, Wolftrap Elementary School
1205 Beulah Road
Vienna, VA 22182
Dear Dr. Rhodes:

I enjoyed our conversation on February 18th at the Family and Child Development seminar on teaching young children and appreciated your personal input about helping children attend school for the first time. This letter is to follow-up about the Fourth Grade Teacher position as discussed at the seminar. I will be completing my Bachelor of Science Degree in Family and Child Development with a concentration in Early Childhood Education at Virginia Tech in May of 2007, and will be available for employment at that time.

The teacher preparation program at Virginia Tech includes a full academic year of student teaching. Last semester I taught second grade and this semester, fourth grade. These valuable experiences have afforded me the opportunity to:

develop lesson plans on a wide range of topics and varying levels of academic ability, work with emotionally and physically challenged students in a total inclusion program, observe and participate in effective classroom management approaches, assist with parent-teacher conferences, and complete In-Service sessions on diversity, math and reading skills, and community relations.

Through my early childhood education courses I have had the opportunity to work in a private day care facility, Rainbow Riders Childcare Center, and in Virginia Tech's Child Development Laboratory. Both these facilities are NAEYC accredited and adhere to the highest standards. At both locations, my responsibilities included leading small and large group activities, helping with lunches and snacks, and implementing appropriate activities. Both experiences also provided me with extensive exposure to the implementation of developmentally appropriate activities and materials.

I look forward to putting my knowledge and experience into practice in the public school system. Next week I will be in Vienna, and I plan to call you then to answer any questions that you may have. I can be reached before then at (540) 555 - 7670. Thank you for your consideratinon.

Sincerely,

(handwritten signature)

Donna Harrington

Enclosure

Example 2: Letter of Application, E-mail Version

April 14, 2006

Mr. William Jackson

Employment Manager

Acme Pharmaceutical Corporation

13764 Jefferson Parkway

Roanoke, VA 24019

jackson@acmepharmaceutical. com

Dear Mr. Jackson:

From your company's web site I learned about your need for a sales representative for the Virginia, Maryland, and North Carolina areas. I am very interested in this position with Acme Pharmaceuticals, and believe that my education and employment background are appropriate for the position.

While working toward my master's degree, I was employed as a sales representative with a small dairy foods firm. I increased my sales volume and profit margin appreciably while at Farmer's Foods, and I would like to repeat that success in the pharmaceutical industry. I have a strong academic background in biology and marketing, and think that I could apply my combination of knowledge and experience to the health industry. I will complete my master's degree in marketing in mid-May and will be available to begin employment in early June.

Enclosed is a copy of my resume, which more fully details my qualifications for the position.

I look forward to talking with you regarding sales opportunities with Acme Pharmaceuticals. Within the next week I will contact you to confirm that you received my email and resume and to answer any questions you may have.

Thank you for your consideration.

Sincerely,

Lynn A. Johnson

5542 Hunt Club Lane, #1

Blacksburg, VA 24060

(540) 555-8082

lajohnson@vt. edu

Resume attached as MS Word document (assuming company web site instructed applicants to do this)

Example 3: Letter of Application, E-mail Version

March 14, 2008

Ms. Charlene Prince

Director of Personnel

Large National Bank Corporation

Roanoke, VA 24040

cprince@largebank.com

Dear Ms. Prince:

As I indicated in our telephone conversation yesterday, I would like to apply for the marketing research position you advertised in the March 12th edition of the Roanoke Times and World News. With my undergraduate research background, my training in psychology and sociology, and my work experience, I believe I could make a valuable contribution to Large National Bank Corporation in this position.

In May I will complete my Bachelor of Science in Psychology with a minor in Sociology from Virginia Polytechnic Institute and State University. As part of the requirements for this degree, I am involved in a senior marketing research project that has given me experience interviewing and surveying research subjects and assisting with the analysis of the data collected. I also have completed a course in statistics and research methods.

In addition to academic work, my experience also includes working part-time as a bookkeeper in a small independent bookstore with an annual budget of approximately $150,000. Because of the small size of this business, I have been exposed to and participated in most aspects of managing a business, including advertising and marketing. As the bookkeeper, I produced monthly sales reports that allow the owner/buyer to project seasonal inventory needs. I also assisted with the development of ideas for special promotional events and calculated book sales proceeds after each event in order to evaluate its success.

I believe that the combination of my business experience and social science research training is well-suited to the marketing research position you described. I have enclosed a copy of my resume with additional information about my qualifications. Thank you for your consideration. I look forward to receiving your reply.

Sincerely,

Jessica Lawrence

250 Prices Fork Road

Blacksburg, VA 24060

(540) 555-1234

jessica.lawrence@vt.edu

Resume text included in email below and attached as MS Word document

Example 4: Letter of Application, Hard Copy Version

1000 Terrace View Apts.
Blacksburg, VA 2000
(540) 555-4444
××××××××@vt.edu

March 25, 2005

Mr. John Wilson
Personnel Director
Anderson Construction Company
3333 Rockville Pike
Rockville, MD 11111

Dear Mr. Wilson:

I read in the March 24th Washington Post classified section of your need for a Civil Engineer or Building Construction graduate for one of your Washington, DC, area sites. I will be returning to the Washington area after graduation in May and believe that I have the necessary credentials for the project.

I have worked at various levels in the construction industry every summer since the 8th grade. As you can see from my resume, I worked several summers as a general laborer, gradually moved up to a carpenter, and last summer I worked as assistant construction manager on a 100 million dollar job.

In addition to this practical experience, I will complete requirements for my Building Construction degree in May. As you may know, Virginia Tech in one of the few universities in the country that offers such a specialized degree for the construction industry. I am confident that my Building Construction degree, along with my years of construction industry experience, make me an excellent candidate for your job. The Anderson Construction Company projects are familiar to me, and my aspiration is to work for a company that has your excellent reputation. I would welcome the opportunity to interview with you. I will be in the Washington area during the week of April 12th and would be available to speak with you at that time. In the next week to ten days I will contact you to answer any questions you may have.

Thank you for your consideration.

Sincerely,

(handwritten signature)
Steve Mason
Enclosure

Example 5: Letter of Inquiry about Employment Possibilities, E-mail Version

December 12, 2007

Mr. Robert Burns
President, Template Division
MEGATEK Corporation
9845 Technical Way
Arlington, VA 22207
burns@megatek.com

Dear Mr. Burns:

I learned of MEGATEK through online research using the CareerSearch database through Career Services at Virginia Tech where I am completing my Master's degree in Mechanical Engineering. From my research on your web site, I believe there would be a good fit between my skills and interests and your needs. I am interested in a software engineering position upon completion of my degree in May 2008.

As a graduate student, I am one of six members on a software development team where we are writing a computer aided aircraft design program for NASA. My responsibilities include designing, coding, and testing of a graphical portion of the program which requires the use of GIARO for graphics input and output. I have a strong background in computer aided design, software development, and engineering, and believe that these skills would benefit the designing and manufacturing aspects of Template software. Enclosed is my resume which further outlines my qualifications.

My qualifications make me well suited to the projects areas in which your division of MEGATEK is expanding efforts. I would appreciate the opportunity to discuss a position with you, and will contact you in a week or ten days to answer any questions you may have and to see if you need any other information from me such as a company application form or transcripts. Thank you for your consideration.

Sincerely,
William Stevens
123 Ascot Lane
Blacksburg, VA 24060
(540) 555-2556
WStevens@vt.edu

Resume attached as MS Word document

Example 6: Letter of Inquiry about Internship Opportunities, Hard Copy Version

2343 Blankinship Road
Blacksburg, VA 24060
(540) 555-2233
StacyLeeGimble@vt. edu

January 12, 2006
Ms. Sylvia Range
Special Programs Assistant
Marion County Family Court Wilderness Challenge
303 Center Street
Marion, VA 24560
Dear Ms. Range:

I am a junior at Virginia Tech, working toward my bachelor's degree in family and child development. I am seeking an internship for this summer 2006, and while researching opportunities in the field of criminal justice and law, I found that your program works with juvenile delinquents. I am writing to inquire about possible internship opportunities with the Marion County Family Court Wilderness Challenge.

My work background and coursework have supplied me with many skills and an understanding of dealing with the adolescent community; for example:

I worked as a hotline assistant for a local intervention center. I counseled teenagers about personal concerns and referred them, when necessary, to appropriate professional services for additional help.

I have been active at my university as a resident hall assistant, which requires me to establish rapport with fifty residents and advise them on personal matters, as well as university policies. In addition, I develop social and educational programs and activities each semester for up to 200 participants.

My enclosed resume provides additional details about my background.

I will be in the Marion area during my Spring break, March 6 - March 10. I will call you next week to see if it would be possible to meet with you in early March to discuss your program.

Thank you for your consideration.

Sincerely,
(handwritten signature)
Stacy Lee Gimble
Encl.

Example 7: Letten of Inquiry about Information Seeking, Hard Copy Version

23 Roanoke Street
Blacksburg, VA 24060
(540) 555-1123
email: K. Walker@vt. edu

October 23, 2006

Mr. James G. Webb
Delon Hampton & Associates
800 K Street, N. W., Suite 720
Washington, DC 20001-8000

Dear Mr. Webb:

I will be graduating from Virginia Tech with a Bachelor's degree in Architecture in May 2007, and am researching employment opportunities in the Washington area. I obtained your name from VT CareerLink, Career Services' Alumni database. I very much appreciate your volunteering to help students with job search information, and I hope that your schedule will permit you to provide me with some advice. I am particularly interested in historic preservation and understand that your firm does work in this area. I am also interested in learning how the architects in your firm began their careers. My resume is enclosed simply to give you some information about my background and project work.

I will call you in two weeks to arrange a time to speak to you by telephone or perhaps visit your office if that would be convenient. I will be in the Washington area during the week of November 21. I very much appreciate your time and consideration of my request, and I look forward to talking with you.

Sincerely,
(handwritten signature)
Kristen Walker
Encl.

2.4 Thank You Letters

2.4.1 About Thank You Letter

Don't underestimate the power of a thank you letter. Also called a follow-up letter, it may be the deciding factor in your favor, especially when there are other candidates with your qualifications applying for the same job. Immediately after a round of interviews, always send a thank you letter to each of your interviewers by fax, mail or email.

Most interviewers expect you to send thank you letters. It's also an effective interviewing strategy. For example, it:

(1) Shows that your are courteous, knowledgeable and professional;

(2) Demonstrates your written communication skills;

(3) Helps to make you stand out in the minds of the interviewers;

(4) Elevates you above competing candidates who didn't bother to write them;

(5) Gives you an opportunity to reinforce your good points;

(6) Allows your to include something important you forgot to mention during your interview;

(7) Confirms your understanding of topics discussed and helps to avoid misunderstanding.

Thank you letters can be letters of job acceptance and job rejection. Or it is simply a letter after interview to show your courtesy. Comparatively, the acceptance letter is a simple and pleasant letter to write. In the first paragraph, thank the company for the offer and directly accept the position. Next, restate the contract provisions as you understand them. These are points that you and your contact at the company have discussed in relation to your employment. They may include salary, location, benefits, or any other items. Restate any instructions you were given in their acceptance letter to you. These might include the date that your will begin working, the salary discussed, or the hours you would be working. It is extremely important to restate these details because they provide documentation of an understanding between you and the company before an actual contract is signed. Finally, end with a statement of your happiness at the opportunity to join the company. Be thankful and courteous, watching your tone so as not to sound too overconfident.

2.4.2 Samples of Thank You Letters

Example 1: Follow-up Letter to Information Seeking Meeting, E-mail Version

November 30, 2006

Mr. James G. Webb
Delon Hampton & Associates
800 K Street, N.W., Suite 720
Washington, DC 20001-8000
webb@delon.com

Dear Mr. Webb:

Thank you so much for taking time from your busy schedule to meet with me last Tuesday. It was very helpful to me to learn so much about the current projects of Delon Hampton & Associates and the career paths of several of your staff. I appreciate your reviewing my portfolio and encouraging my career plans. I also enjoyed meeting Beth Ormond, and am glad to have her suggestions on how I can make the most productive use of my last semester in college.

Based on what I learned from my visit to your firm and other research I have done, I am very interested in being considered for employment with your firm in the future. I will be available to begin work after I graduate in May 2003. As you saw from my portfolio, I have developed strong skills in the area of historical documentation and this is a good match for the types of projects in which your firm specializes. I have enclosed a copy of my resume to serve as a reminder of my background, some of which I discussed with you when we met.

During the next few months I will stay in contact with you in hopes that there may be an opportunity to join your firm. Thank you again for your generous help.

Sincerely,
Kristin Walker
23 Roanoke Street
Blacksburg, VA 24060
(540) 555-1111
KWalker@vt.edu

Example 2: Follow-up Letter to a Job Application

Mr. George Gilhooley
XYZ Company
88 Delaware Road
Hatfield, CA 08888

Date

Dear Mr. Gilhooley,

I submitted a letter of application and a resume earlier this month for the programmer position advertised in the Times Union. To date, I have not heard from your office. I would like to confirm receipt of my application and reiterate my interest in the job.

I am very interested in working at XYZ Company and I believe my skills and experience would be an ideal match for this position.

If necessary, I would be glad to resend my application materials or to provide any further information you might need regarding my candidacy. I can be reached at (555)555 - 5555 or jdoe@abcd.com. I look forward to hearing from you.

Thank you for your consideration.

Sincerely,
(handwritten signature)
Jane Doe

Example 3: Thank You Letter for a Career/Job Fair

3000 Last Tree Lane
DeLand, FL 32720
333 - 555 - 0000

Mr. Gary Barnett
Aerial Communications, Inc.
3777 W. MLK Jr. Blvd.
Tampa, FL 33333

Dear Mr. Barnett,

Thank you for taking the time to meet with me at the Central Florida Career Fair today. I certainly appreciate your time and attention in the midst of so many students seeking jobs.

You were extremely thorough in explaining Aerial's customer service and marketing trainee program. Now that I have a better idea of what the position entails, I am even more sure that I would be an asset to your team and to Aerial.

My solid education from Stetson University's Marketing Department and the fact that I have worked my way through college show a work ethic and determination, two qualities you said were important to success at Aerial.

I look forward to an opportunity to visit Aerial's Tampa office and speak to you further about the trainee program. I will contact you next week to arrange an appointment.

Thank you again for your time and consideration.

Sincerely,
Chandwritten signature Steve Mason

Section Two Language Handbook

Useful Words and Expressions

1. Personal Data 个人资料

date of birth 出生日期
birth place 出生地点
native place 籍贯
autonomous region 自治区
prefecture 专区
nationality 民族,国籍
citizenship 国籍
current address /present address 目前地址

permanent address 永久地址
postal code 邮政编码
marital status 婚姻状况
lane 胡同,巷
district 区
ID card No. 身份证号码
date of availability 可到职时间

2. Objectives 应聘职位

career objective 职业目标
employment objective 工作目标
position wanted 希望职位
job objective 工作目标
position applied for 申请职位
position sought 谋求职位
position desired 希望职位

3. Educational Background 教育程度

curriculum 课程
major 主修
minor 副修
social practice 社会实践
part-time jobs 业余工作
refresher course 进修课程
extracurricular activities 体育活动
recreational activities 娱乐活动
academic activities 学术活动
social activities 社会活动
student council 学生会
post doctorate 博士后
doctor (Ph. D) 博士
master 硕士
bachelor 学士
abroad student 留学生
intern 实习生
the national higher education exams for self-taught adults 成人高考
second Bachelor's degree 第二学位
double degree; two Bachelor's degrees 双学位
credit; academic credit 学分
credit hours 学时
this year's graduates 应届毕业生

on-job doctorate 在职博士生
on-job postgraduates 在职研究生
upgrade from junior college student to university student; students with the diploma of junior college try to obtain the undergraduate diplomat through self-taught study 专升本

4. Tests 考试

College English Test(CET)大学英语等级考试
Test for English Majors(TEM)英语专业学生等级考试
Public English Test System(PETS)全国英语等级考试
Cambridge Business English Certificate(BEC) 剑桥商务英语证书
Test of English as a Foreign Language(TOEFL)托福
International English Language Testing System(IELTS)雅思
Test of English for International Communication(TOEIC)托业
Graduate Record Examination(GRE)美国研究生入学考试
National Computer Rank Examination(NCRE)全国计算机等级考试
Japanese Language Proficiency Test(JLPT)国际日语能力考试
Graduate Management Admission Test(GMAT)国外工商管理硕士入学考试
National Matriculation Test(NMT)高考
self-study examination 自学考试
entrance exams for postgraduate schools 研究生入学考试

5. Work Experience 工作经历

work experience / work history/ occupational history /employment history 工作经历
position / job title 职位
second job 第二职业
achievements 工作成就,业绩
administer 管理
assist 辅助
accomplish 完成(任务等)
behave / performance 表现
conduct/ execute/ handle/ deal with 经营,处理
be promoted to /be proposed as 被提名为,被推荐为

6. Awards 获奖

rewards 奖励
scholarship 奖学金
excellent leader 优秀干部
merit student; three good student(good in study, attitude and health) 三好学生
excellent League member 优秀团员
advanced worker 先进工作者
working model 劳动模范
excellent Party member 优秀党员

7. Personalities 个人品质

adaptable 适应性强的
amiable 和蔼可亲的
analytical 善于分析的
apprehensive 有理解力的
candid 正直的
competent 能胜任的
cooperative 有合作精神的
creative 富创造力的
efficient 有效率的
energetic 精力充沛的
enthusiastic 充满热情的
expressive 善于表达
faithful 守信的,忠诚的
frugal 俭朴的
generous 宽宏大量的
genteel 有教养的
hard-working / industrious 勤奋的
hearty 精神饱满的
ingenious 有独创性的
initiative 首创精神
intelligent 理解力强的
liberal 心胸宽大的
logical 条理分明的
motivated 目的明确的
original 有独创性的
painstaking 辛勤的,苦干的,刻苦的
precise 一丝不苟的
purposeful 意志坚强的
steady 踏实的

8. Demission 离职

for more specialized work 为更专门的工作
for prospects of promotion 为晋升的前途
for higher responsibility 为更高层次的工作责任
for wider experience 为扩大工作经验
due to close-down of company 由于公司倒闭
due to expiry of employment 由于雇佣期满
sought a better job 找到了更好的工作
to look for a more challenging opportunity 找一个更有挑战性的工作机会

9. Section Names 部门名称

Personnel Department 人事部

Human Resource Department 人力资源部

Sales Department 营销部

Product Development Department 产品开发部

Public Relations Department 公关部

Marketing Department 市场部

Finance Department 财会部

Purchasing(Procurement) Department 采购部

After-sale Service Department 售后服务部

Quality Control Department 质量控制部

10. Job Titles 职位名称

Chairman of the Board 董事长

President (Am E.) 总裁

Executive Vice-President 执行副总裁

Managing Director 行政董事

Executive Manager, General Manager 总经理

Section Manager 部门经理,科长

Sales Manager 销售经理

Assistant Manager 助理经理(副经理)

Sales Representative 销售代表

Supervisor 总管

executive 高中级管理人员

Useful Sentences

1. Stating Your Job Objective 说明应聘职位

A responsible administrative position which will provide challenge and freedom where I can bring my initiative and creativity into full play.

负责管理的职位,该职位将提供挑战和自由,使我能充分发挥我的进取精神及创造能力。

An executive assistant position utilizing interests, training and experience in office administration.

行政助理职位,能运用办公室管理方面的兴趣、训练与经验。

A position in management training programs with the eventual goal of participating in the management rank of marketing.

管理培训计划方面的职务,最终目标在参与市场管理层。

An entry-level position in sales. Eventual goal: manager of marketing department.

销售方面的初级职位。最终目标:销售部门的经理。

A position requiring analytical skills in the financial or investment field.

财务或投资领域需运用分析技巧的职务。

To begin as an accounting trainee and eventually become a manager.

从当会计见习开始,最后成为经理。

An entry-level position responsible for computer programming.

负责计算机程序设计的初级职务。

Administrative assistant to an executive where shorthand and typing skills will be assets.

高级管理人员的行政助理:可用上速记和打字技能。

A position which will utilize my educational background in biology, with prospects of promotion.

谋求能运用我在生物学方面的学识,并有晋升前途的职务。

Responsible managerial position in human resources.

人力资源方面负责管理的职务。

A position in Foreign Trade Department, with opportunities for advancement to management position in the department.

外贸部门的职位,有机会晋升到该部门的经理职务。

An administrative secretarial position where communication skills and a pleasant attitude toward people will be assets.

行政秘书的职务,用得上交际技巧和与人为善的态度。

Looking for a position as a computer programmer with a medium-sized firm.

谋求一家中型公司的计算机程序员职位。

To serve as sales promoter in a multinational corporation with a view to promotion in position and assignment in parent company's branch abroad.

担任多国公司的推销员,期望在职位上有晋升并能有分派到母公司的海外分公司去工作。

2. Stating Your Education 说明教育程度

Useful Courses for English Teaching include: Psychology, Teaching Methodology, Phonetics, Rhetoric, Grammar, Composition.

对英语教学有用课程包括心理学、教学方法论、语音学、修辞学、语法、写作。

Specialized courses pertaining to Foreign Trade: Marketing principles, International Marketing, Practical English Correspondence and Telecommunications, Foreign Exchange, Business English.

和外贸相关的专门课程:市场学原理、国际营销学、实用英文函电、外汇兑换、商务英语。

Academic Preparation for Management:

Management: Principles of Management, Organization Theory, Behavioral Science.

Communication: Business Communication, Personnel Management, Human Relations.

Marketing: Marketing Theory, Sales Management.

大学时为管理所做的学术准备:

管理学:管理学原理、组织理论、行为学。

交际学:商务交际、人事管理、人际关系。

市场学:市场学理论、营销管理。

Curriculum included: Signal processing, 88; Systems and Control, 92; Electric Energy Systems, 92; Solid-state Electronics, 88; Communications, 94.

课程包括:信号处理,88 分;系统控制,92 分;电力能源系统,92 分;固体电子学,88 分;通信,94 分。

Major courses contributing to Management Qualification: Management, Accounting, Economics, Marketing, Sociology.

对管理资格有帮助的主要课程:管理学、会计学、经济学、市场学、社会学。

Courses completed: History of mass communication, 88; China's communication history, 92; Media research, 90; Public opinion, 92; Conceptual analysis, 88; Content analysis, 90; Advertising, 92; New media technology, 94.

所修课程:大众传播史,88 分;中国传播史,92 分;媒体研究,90 分;舆论学,92 分;概念分析,88 分;内容分析,90 分;广告学,92 分;新媒体方法,94 分。

Courses in industrial designs and related field: Dynamic systems, evaluation and management of designs, systems control, ergonomics, tensile structures, structural analysis, computer-aided design, applied mechanics.

工业设计及其相关领域的课程:动力系统、设计评估与管理、系统控制、人类工程学、张力结构、结构分析、计算机辅助设计、应用力学。

Majored in Banking. Courses covered are as follows:

Banking operations, 89; banking and computers, 90; loans, 92; letters of credit, 90; savings, 88; foreign exchange, 92; telegraphic transfers, 90; remittances, 94; financial systems in the west, 92.

主修金融学。涉及的课程有如下几门:银行业务,89 分;银行与计算机,90 分;贷款,92 分;信用证,90 分;储蓄,88 分;外汇兑换,92 分;电汇,90 分;汇款,94 分;西方金融制度,92 分。

3. Stating Your Work Experience 说明工作经历

In addition to ordinary sales activities and management of department, responsible for recruiting and training of sales staff members.

除了销售活动和部门管理之外,还负责招聘与训练销售人员。

Assistant to the General Manager of Shenzhen Petrochemical Industrial Corporation Ltd. Handled the itinerary schedule of the general manager. Met clients as a representative of the corporation. Helped to negotiate a $5,000,000 deal for the corporation.

深圳市石油化工集团股份有限公司总经理助理。安排总经理的出差旅行计划时间表。作为公司代表接见客户。协助公司谈成了一笔 500 万美元的交易。

Secretary to president of Silverlion Group Corporation Ltd. Responsibilities: Receiving visitors, scheduling meetings, taking and typing dictation, writing routine letters and reports.

银利来集团有限公司董事长秘书。职责:接待访客、安排会议、笔录并打字、书写日常信函及报告。

Public relations girl at Guangzhou Holiday Inn. Fulltime in summers, part-time during school.

在广州假日酒店当公关小姐。暑期全职,上课时间兼职。

Assistant to manager of accounting department of a joint venture enterprise. Analyzed data and relevant financial statistics, and produced monthly financial statements.

一家合资企业会计部门经理的助理。分析数据及相关财务统计数字,而且提出每月的财务报告。

Worked 21 hours weekly as a salesgirl at the bookstore of Shenzhen University. Earned 45% of college expenses.

在深圳大学书店当售货员,每周工作21小时,赚了大学费用的45%。

Production manager: Initiated quality control resulting in a reduction in working hours by 20% while increasing productivity by 25%.

生产部经理:引入质量控制,使得工作时数减少了20%,而生产力则提高了25%。

4. Stating Your Qualifications 说明任职资格

University major in computer science, three years of part-time work in a computer software company.

在大学主修计算机科学,在计算机软件公司兼职三年。

Educational background in business administration with major in secretarial science and two summers of full-time work experience. Working knowledge of all common office fascility.

有工商管理的学历,主修秘书学,两年暑假的全职工作经验。对办公室所有常用设备有运用知识。

Four years of experience in marketing, in addition to a bachelor's degree in management with major in marketing. Like to be challenged with a responsible job.

除了主修市场学的管理学学士学位,还有四年的市场营销经验。喜欢迎战责任重大的工作。

Ability to organize marketing campaigns and to supervise employees. Effective communication abilities and public relations skills.

具有组织市场活动和督导员工的能力,并具备有效的交际能力和公关技巧。

Three years of successful job experience ranging from sales responsibilities to management of marketing department. Adaptable, versatile, industrious.

三年的成功工作经验,范围从销售职责到市场部门的管理,适应性强、善变通、勤奋。

Special training in accounting at Guangdong College of Commerce and three years of practical experience in accounting environment. Enjoy working with people. Responsible and reliable.

在广东商学院接受会计方面的专门培训,并有三年在会计部门的实际经验,喜欢和别人一同工作,负责可靠。

Work experience in personnel affairs in a foreign capital enterprise coupled with educational background specialized in personnel management. Maintain good human relations.

外资企业人事事务的工作经验，加上人事管理的专门学历背景，能保持良好的人际关系。

Good university education with Japanese as my major combined with practical experience in translating business documents. Worked as an interpreter in Japan for a Chinese investigation group for three months.

良好的大学教育，主修日语，加上翻译商务文件的实际经验。为中国考察团在日本当过三个月的译员。

Exercises

Ⅰ. Questions

1. Why is a successful resume important?
2. What are the imperative contents in an English resume?
3. What are the optional data in an English resume?
4. State in details the way one writes the personal information.
5. Should people write awards when they have in their resumes?
6. What types of Resume Formats are there? What are their features?
7. What terms do you know when you introduce your education?
8. Can you tell your work experience in English?

Ⅱ. Translation

Write a resume in English according to the following personal information.

个人基本资料

姓　名	出生日期 1984-10-23
性　别 女	婚姻状况 未婚
身　高 162cm	体　重 52kg

求职意向描述

应聘岗位 商务/贸易/国际业务/英语翻译/文秘/高级文员

岗位描述 进出口业务员

工作经验 0 年

期望月薪 2000 元

教育背景

毕业学校 西南财经大学	最高学历 本科
专　业 对外贸易	电脑水平 良好
外语语种 英语	外语水平 优秀

工作简历

2005年5月	兼职商场促销员
2004年10月	兼职公司策划
2003年5月	数学家庭教师

个人能力及自我评价

自我评价

性格开朗、稳重、有活力,待人热情、真诚。工作认真负责,积极主动,能吃苦耐劳。有较强的交际能力、组织能力、实际动手能力和团体协作精神,能迅速地适应各种环境,并融合其中。

英语技能

具备较强的英语听、说、读、写、译等能力;擅长撰写和回复英文商业信函,熟练运用网络查阅相关英文资料,并能及时予以翻译。

计算机技能

熟悉办公室软件的操作;精通办公自动化,熟练操作 Windows XP,能独立操作并及时高效地完成日常办公文档的编辑工作。

Ⅲ. Prepare a Resume for Yourself

Chapter Three

Office Daily Routines

Section One Business Writing

3.1 Introduction

More often than not, business writings are just writings of the office daily routines. The most common, and of course, the most important one, is memo/memorandum. Other daily routines include schedules, notices and posters, certificates letters of introduction, notes and bill.

3.2 General information and Samples of Office Daily Routines

3.2.1 Memos

Like business letters, memos are frequently used in office for different purposes. They are usually brief and direct. So we can say that only the most necessary and specific information can be expressed in memo.

Memos can be written in different forms. But usually, they are composed by five parts: to whom, from whom, date, subject and body. Many companies use pre-printed forms that can be easily used.

Memorandum

Date: (date sent)

To: (name of receiver, and title, if necessary)

From: (name of sender, and title, if necessary)

Subject: (concise phrase describing the most important ideas)

Text of the memo

The segments of the memo should be allocated in the following manner:

- Header: 1/8 of the memo
- Opening, Context and Task: 1/4 of the memo
- Summary, Discussion Segment: 1/2 of the memo
- Closing Segment, Necessary Attachments: 1/8 of the memo

This is a suggested distribution of the material to make writing memos easier. Not all memos will be the same and the structure can change as you see necessary. Different organizations may have different formatting procedures, so be flexible in adapting your writing skills.

1. Memos and Letters

Memos and letters are the two most common types of business communication. Memos resemble letters in that they communicate information and are commonly used in the world of business writing. However, memos differ from letters in several important ways:

(1) Memos are almost always used within an organization;

(2) Memos are usually unceremonious in style;

(3) Memos are normally used for non-sensitive communication (communication to which the reader will not have an emotional reaction);

(4) Memos are short and to-the-point;

(5) Memos have a direct style;

(6) Memos do not have a salutation;

(7) Memos do not have a complimentary closing;

(8) Memos have a specific format that is very different from a business letter.

2. Parts of a Memo

Standard memos are divided into segments to organize the information and to help achieve the writer's purpose.

3. Heading Segment

Be specific and concise in your subject line. For example, "Clothes" as a subject line could mean anything from a dress code update to a production issue. Instead use something like, "Fall Clothes Line Promotion."

4. Opening Segment

The purpose of a memo is usually found in the opening paragraph and includes: the purpose of the memo, the context and problem, and the specific assignment or task. Before indulging the reader with details and the context, give the reader a brief overview of what the memo will be about. Choosing how specific your introduction will be depends on your memo plan style. The more direct the memo plan, the more explicit the introduction should be. Including the purpose of the memo will help clarify the reason the audience should read this document. The introduction should be brief, and should be approximately the length of a short paragraph.

5. Context

The context is the event, circumstance, or background of the problem you are solving.

You may use a paragraph or a few sentences to establish the background and state the problem. Oftentimes it is sufficient to use the opening of a sentence to completely explain the context, such as, "Through market research and analysis..."

6. Task Segment

One essential portion of a memo is the task statement where you should describe what you are doing to help solve the problem. If the action was requested, your task may be indicated by a sentence opening like, "You asked that I look at..." If you want to explain your intentions, you might say, "To determine the best method of promoting the new fall line, I will..."

Include only as much information as is needed by the decision-makers in the context, but be convincing that a real problem exists. Do no ramble on with insignificant details. If you are having trouble putting the task into words, consider whether you have clarified the situation. You may need to do more planning before you're ready to write your memo. Make sure your purpose-statement forecast divides your subject into the most important topics that the decision-maker needs.

7. Summary Segment

If your memo is longer than a page, you may want to include a separate summary segment. However, this section not necessary for short memos and should not take up a significant amount of space. This segment provides a brief statement of the key recommendations you have reached. These will help your reader understand the key points of the memo immediately. This segment may also include references to methods and sources you have used in your research.

8. Discussion Segments

The discussion segments are the longest portions of the memo, and are the parts in which you include all the details that support your ideas. Begin with the information that is most important. This may mean that you will start with key findings or recommendations. Start with your most general information and move to your specific or supporting facts. (Be sure to use the same format when including details: strongest to weakest.) The discussion segments include the supporting ideas, facts, and research that back up your argument in the memo. Include strong points and evidence to persuade the reader to follow your recommended actions. If this section is inadequate, the memo will not be as effective as it could be.

9. Closing Segment

After the reader has absorbed all of your information, you want to close with a courteous ending that states what action you want your reader to take. Make sure you consider how the reader will benefit from the desired actions and how you can make those actions easier. For example, you might say, "I will be glad to discuss this recommendation with you during our Tuesday trip to the spa and follow through on any decisions you make."

10. Necessary Attachments

Make sure you document your findings or provide detailed information whenever necessary. You can do this by attaching lists, graphs, tables, etc. at the end of your memo. Be sure to refer to your attachments in your memo and add a notation about what is attached below your closing, like this:

Attached: Focus Group Results, January- May 2007

If a memo continues to a second page, on the second page, across the top, put the name of the person to whom the memo is sent flush with the left margin, the page number in the center, and the date at the right margin.

Here is a sample:

Jason MacGruder	2	Donna Shaw

Example 1

MEMO

To: Project Planning Dept. From: General Manager

Date: Jan. 5

Subject: Aqua Warm BV

I have looked though our records of the work that we did at Perfecta Ltd. The heating system was checked three times before it was turned on. We are absolutely sure that explosion is not our responsibility.

I suggest, therefore, that Perfecta writes to Aqua Warm to claim compensation.

Please write to Perfecta (address: 61 Bath Road, Worester, England WR 5 3AB) and explain our position.

(From: Business Communications (7th ed). William C. Himstreet & Wayne Murlin Baty, 1984)

Example 2

Data Guys, Inc.

Memorandum

Date: December 13, 1996

To: Annette T. Califero

From: Kyle B. Abrams

Subject: A Low-Cost Way to Reduce Energy Use

As you requested, I've investigated low-cost ways to reduce our energy use. Reducing the building temperature on weekends is a change that we could make immediately, that would cost nothing, and that would cut our energy use by about 6%.

The Energy Savings from a Lower Weekend Temperature

Lowering the temperature from 68 degrees to 60 degrees from 8 p.m. Friday evening to 4 a.m. Monday morning could cut our total consumption by 6%. It is not feasible to lower the temperature on week nights because a great many staff members work late; the cleaning crew also is on duty from 6 p.m. to midnight. Turning the temperature down for only four hours would not result in a significant heat saving.

Turning the heat back up at 4 p.m. will allow the building temperature to be back to 68 degrees by 9 a.m. Our furnace already has computerized controls that can be set to automatically lower and raise the temperature.

How a Lower Temperature Would Affect Employees

A survey of employees shows that only 7 people use the building every weekend or almost every weekend. Eighteen percent of our staff has worked at least one weekend day in the last two months; 52% say they "occasionally" come in on weekends. People who come in for an hour or less on weekends could cope with the lower temperature just by wearing warm clothes. However, most people would find 60 degrees too cool for extended work. Employees who work regularly on weekends might want to install space heaters.

Action Needed to Implement the Change

Would you also like me to check into the cost of buying a dozen portable space heaters? Providing them would allow us to choose units that our wiring can handle and would be a nice gesture towards employees who give up their weekends to work. I could have a report to you in two weeks.

We can begin saying energy immediately. Just authorize the lower temperature, and I'll see that the controls are reset for this weekend.

(From: Business Communications (7th ed). William C. Himstreet & Wayne Murlin Baty, 1984)

Example 3

A Moment In the Sun Tanning Salons

Memo

Date: December 14, 1998

To: T.R. Soleau

From: Ray Ban

Re: Marketing Plan Review

As you requested, the Marketing Plan Review process has been established and is ready to be put in motion.

Initial meetings with all divisions, salons, and marketing & sales staff have been scheduled to begin early next month and will continue until March. Here is the schedule for the meetings:

Southwest	Century City Hotel, Los Angeles	Jan. 3 to 7
Northwest	Raddison Hotel, Portland	Jan. 15 – 19
West	Sheraton Stratford Hotel, Boise	Feb. 1 – 4
Midwest	Chicago Carlton Hotel, Chicago	Feb. 10 – 14
South	Atlanta Belle Hotel, Atlanta	Feb. 20 – 24
Northeast	Central Park Central Hotel, New York	March 5 – 9
Southeast	New Century Hotel, Tampa	March 15 – 19

Attendees will discuss the new marketing plan and give their opinions. In particular, we are anxious to have the following questions answered:

* Will the plan work in all areas?
* Are any regional adjustments needed?
* How does each region react to our new image?
* What is each region's gut-level reaction to the plan?

I have prepared a 16 page questionnaire to be distributed at the meetings. Hopefully, we will receive input for everyone. I've attached a copy of the questionnaire.

Thus far, Harry Hampton and I are scheduled to attend all of the meetings. However, I think it would be advisable to have a substitute available if Harry or I find ourselves ill or otherwise unable to travel.

Please let me know if you have any questions.

Attachment: Questionnaire

Example 4

To: All members of staff, Northern Branch
From: K. L. J.
Date: 5 December 1994
Subject: PERSONAL COMPUTERS

The board urgently requires feedback on our experience with PCs in Northern Branch. I need to know, for my report:

1. What you personally use your PC for and your reasons for doing this. If you are doing working that was formerly done by other staff, please justify this.
2. What software you use, Please name the programs.
3. How many hours per day you spend actually using it.
4. How your PC has not come up to your expectations.
5. What unanticipated uses you have found for your PC, that others may want to share.

Please Fax this information directly to me by 5 p. m. on Wednesday 7 December. If you have any questions, please contact my assistant, Jane Simmonds, who will visit you on Tuesday, 6 December. Thank you for your help.

Example 5

MEMORANDUM

To: Heads of factories Subject: Trip by GM
From: Office of the GM.
Date: Feb. 1

Below are details of the factories that the general Manager will visit. In each one, the GM would like to speak to all members of the Production Dept. Please inform each factory and them to cancel all other appointment.

March 8 Kuala Lumpur
March 9 Singapore
March 10 Singapore
March 11 Jakarta

Example 6

To: Mr. Brown manager of operations

From: Betty Green Supervisor

Subject: comments on the "punch in" system

Date: September 21

This is further to your memo dated back to June 12, 2006, in which you proposed that the employees adopt the "punch in" system.

I fully agree with you that we should take measures to increase the productivity and that we would a tighter control over the employees if the "punch in" system is adopted. However, honestly speaking, I don't think that adopting a tighter system will increase productivity. The most effective way to increase productivity, in my opinion, is to give the employees more incentives to work. I think we could further discuss other possibility of achieving this goal.

Your consideration of this suggestion would be highly appreciated.

Yours sincerely,

Betty Green

3.2.2 Schedules

Schedules can be daily work plans, weekly (monthly and yearly) schedules, appointment schedules and schedules of activities. It can be written in a pre-printed table of simply written on time sequences.

Example 1: Daily Work Plan

MANATEE COMMUNITY COLLEGE PROFESSIONAL STAFF DUTY SCHEDULE

NAME:	Mike Mears		SEMESTER:		Spring, 2002	
DEPARTMENT/CAMPUS		Math / Bradenton	OFFICE #	19-115	EXT#	65267

Example 2: Weekly Work Plan

	Monday	Tuesday	Wednesday	Thursday	Friday
9:00					
9:30					
10:00					
10:30					
11:00					
11:30					
12:00					
12:30					
1:00					
1:30					

2:00					
2:30					
3:00					
3:30					
4:00					
4:30					
5:00					
Hours	7	6	7	6	7

Example 3: Weekly Work Plan

Employee:	Week of:
Department:	Attention:
Week's Objectives:	Week's Accomplishment:

Example 4: Appointment Schedules

Date: ____________

For: Department:

Time	With whom	Nature of Appointment	Comments
9:00 a.m.			
12:00 noon			
2:00 p.m.			

Example 5: Activities Schedule

Events of National Day's Celebration with Foreign Teachers 2005

Listed below are some of the main events to be arranged during the 2005 National Day celebration session:

1. ethnic culture show of Tengtou Village
2. A Sea Shore Barbecue
3. Two hours' Night Tout on the Sanjiang River of Ningbo by Tourist Yacht
4. Karaoke Party with Students

3.2.3 Notices and Posters

Generally, a notice or an announcement tells that something will happen in the near future of announces that something has already happened. Since its content must be dispersed to a lot of people, it is usually written in form letter. This may lead to being stereotyped and dull in writing. The best way for writing an announcement or a notice is to strive for clarity, correctness, conciseness, concreteness, courtesy and completeness.

Example 1: Notice for a Dismissal of an Employment

Dear Mr. Yin:

I regret to inform you of a very difficult decision regarding your future employment at the Company of Jin Chen. After careful consideration and review of current positions held within the company, and after an extensive analysis of the budget, it has been determined it is in the best interest of the company to eliminate the position of sales representative. Your last day of work is June 15, 2000.

We appreciate the contributions you have made while at the company and would like to assist you in this time of transition by offering the enclosed information packet. If I can be of further assistance to you, please do not hesitate to contact me at 5555-3333.

Sincerely,

Enclosure

Example 2: Notice of Removal

Dear Sirs:

We are happy to inform you that owing to steady growth of our firm in the past years and in view of facilitating business expansion, we have decided to move our office at 114 Xinhua Street to the following address:

Dalian Trading Co. Ltd.
Tian Tian Building
Room 301
55 Tianyi Road
Dalian, Liaoning, China

The office phone number will remain the same. We wish you to continue patronizing us in the years to come.

Yours truly,

Example 3: Notice for Rent and Sale

Dear Sir or Madam:

We now have Lan-tian Apartments for rent and sale. The detailed information is as follows:

- Luxurious apartments with good furniture
- By the north gate of the Beijing Workers' Stadium near the first embassy district
- Sizes range from 80 square meters - 200 square meters

You can contact Miss Lily for more information about the apartments. Hotline number is 6666-5555.

Sincerely yours,

Example 4: Meeting Announcement

The College Commission of Academic Research

NOTICE

All professors and associate professors are requested to meet in the University Conference Room on Wednesday (Oct. 10) at 1:00 p.m. to discuss questions of international academic exchanges.

Oct. 8, 1998

Example 5: Notice about a Lecture

NOTICE

All Are Warmly Welcome

Under the auspices of the Teaching Affairs Section

A report will be given on

Contemporary American Economy

By

Visiting American Prof. Green

In

The Reading Room of the Library

On Thursday, Nov. 20, 2000, at 2:00 p.m.

Nov. 18, 2000

Example 6: Posters

Here presents some general guidelines that would apply to most posters.

First, the title of an effective poster should quickly orient the audience.
Second, the poster should quickly orient the audience to the subject and purpose.
Third, the specific sections such as the results should be easy to locate on the poster.
Fourth, you should design the individual sections of a poster so that they can be quickly read.

Example 7: Poster of Goods Auction

Good News

Winter Clearance Sales

All the good on show are sold at 20% discount. Please examine and choose them carefully before you pay. There will be no placement or refunding. You have been warned in advance. You are welcome to make your choice.

The Wonder Shop

Example 8: Poster of Activities

Friendly Basketball Match

All Are Welcome

Organized by the Students' Union of our school, a friendly basketball match will be held between No. 3 Middle School team and ours on the basketball court on Saturday, June 5, 1993 at 4 p.m.

The School Students' Union

Tuesday, June 1

Example 9: Poster of Activities

This Week's Film

Name: Modern Time

Time: 7 p.m. Saturday, April 10

Place: The meeting hall

Fare: One Yuan

Ticket office: The school gate house

Example 10: Poster of an Academic Lecture

Learned Report to Be Given

Under the auspices of the Students' Union
a lecture will be given
on
Essential English Grammar
by Prof. David Lipman
in the auditorium
on Wednesday, June 10, 1998 at 2 p.m.

June 8, 1989

3.2.4 Certificates

Certificate is one of the most frequently used office writing. It is usually used to prove people's identity or something of a specific person. Certificates have many types, such as certificate of one's identity, working experiences, education, health situation, financial status, etc. More often than not, "certificate" will appear in the title and it often uses "To whom it may concern" as the addressing term. Usually it starts with "This is to certify that...". The content of certificates should be brief and objective. Writer's signature and title or the stamp of the writer's organization are needed in the end.

Example 1: Identity Certificate

IDENTITY CERTIFICATE

This is to certify that Mr. Li Wenbin, Male, age 30, is an employeer in Xin Hua Company, Tianyu Building, Room 301, 55 Tianyi Road, Dalian city, Liaoning province, China.

Zhang Jia
Chief Manager
Xin Hua Company

Example 2: Doctor's Certificate

Doctor's Certificate

June 18, 2000

This is to certify that the patient, Mr. Tomas, male, aged 41, was admitted into our hospital on June 9, 2000, for suffering from acute appendicitis. After immediate operation and ten days of treatment, he has got complete recovery and will be discharged on June 19, 2000. It is suggested that he rest for one week at home before resuming his work.

Jack Hopkins
Surgeon-in-charge

Example 3: Education Certificate

Certificate

(90) Lu Zi, No. 1130

This is to certificate that Mr. Wang Chong holds a diploma issued to him in July, 2002 by Shannan University (Diploma No. 068) and that we have carefully checked the seal of the University and the signature by President Zhao Yong.

Jinan Notary Public Office
Shannan Province
the People's Republic of China
Notary: Wang Fang

May 2, 2000

3.2.5 Letters of Introduction

Letters of introduction refer to those short letters to introduce a person of business purpose (of other purposes as well). A letter of introduction is used to write to a connection to refer a candidate for employment or to request career assistance. Another type of letter of introduction is used to write to someone introducing yourself and asking them to refer you to a job opportunity or requesting assistance with a job search.

Example 1: Letter of Introduction for Business

To Whom It May Concern

The bearer of this letter, Mr. Zhang Wen, an engineer for Haier, is entrusted with the task of helping you to get familiar with our products newly bought by your company. Please favor him with an interview.

Faithfully yours,
John Smith
Sales Manager

Example 2: Letter of Introduction for Business

Dear Sir or Madam:

As introductions, I represent a Chapter of the Construction Specifications Institute, a national organization devoted to improving communications among and between all the parties that are involved in the design, construction or operation of any facility. Our membership includes, architects, engineers, constructors, representatives of product suppliers and manufacturers, code enforcement officials, facility managers, faculty members, geotechnical professionals, and any other profession related to the design, construction and operation of facilities as well as students. Our organization has developed several documents that have become default standards in our industry such as the Uniform Drawing System (UDS) which is the basis for much of the National CAD Standard, Master Format used for organizing project specifications and cost estimating and Section Format used to organize individual specification sections. We have also developed three major "Certification Programs" that are recognized across the industry.

Our organization would like to assist you or any other faculty members in your program to help your students better understand some of the issues they will face after graduation and move into their chosen career. We expect some of these issues you are not able to accommodate within the confines of the academic schedule. We believe the diverse background and occupations of our membership as well as the knowledge they have gained through experience may be a source of information that you might be able to utilize in either curricular or extracurricular activities.

We are extremely flexible in our activities as they relate to today's students. In our view, the options may ranges from bring our member's actual experience into one of your classes to a more informal non-class activity where our Chapter might provide snacks and soft drinks to those that attend.

I would like to set up a meeting at your convenience to discuss possible ways that our Chapter might help prepare your students for their future careers. I plan on calling you on July 1 to set up an appointment, or if this is not convenient, you can reach me at 0411-5555.

Our Chapter looks forward to working with you to help make your students, transition into their careers as easy as possible.

Sincerely,

Example 3: Letter of Introduction for Employment

Dear Bob:

I'm writing to introduce you to Janice Dolan. I know Janice through the Brandon Theater Group, where, as you know, I am the technical director. Janice and I worked together on several local theater projects.

Janice is interested in relocating to the San Francisco area in the near future and would appreciate any recommendations you could offer her for conducting a job search for a theater position and any help you can provide with the logistics of relocating to California.

I've attached her resume for your review and you can contact her at janicedolan@email. com or 555-555-5555. Thank you in advance for any assistance you can provide.

Sincerely

Example 4: Self-introduction Letter for Employment

Dear Sir or Madam:

I am a friend of Janice Dolan and she encouraged me to forward my resume to you. I know Janice through the Brandon Theater Group, where I am the technical director. We worked together on several local theater projects.

I'm interested in relocating to the San Francisco area in the near future.

I would appreciate any recommendations you can offer for conducting a job search for a theater position, finding job leads, and any help you can provide with the logistics of relocating to California.

My resume is attached. Most of my theatrical experience is in lighting and projection design, however I have worked at most backstage areas during my career.

Thank you for your consideration. I look forward to hearing from you.

Sincerely

3.2.6 Notes and Bills

Notes are common in office daily writing. Notes are short letters written for various purposes. Compared with a letter, a note is simpler in form and often informal or colloquial in language. In a note, the following may be omitted:

- the addresses of the addressee and the addresser
- the word "Dear" in the salutation
- the complementary close
- the year in date

Example 1: Daily Work

Feb. 27, 2003

To: All Staff

Recommended for all staff to know we should use phones, because we have received so many complaints from our customers. The following are some recommended telephone procedure:

1. Do not leave the phone to ting too long before answering.
2. Answering calls politely, instead of just saying "hello".
3. Let colleague know the transfer and how long the call will be when transferring calls.
4. Take down messages including date; time, caller's name and number.

Example 2: Daily work

Nov. 21, 2003

To: Mr. Jim Asano

Massage:

May I have you permission to take twenty brochures and three sample printers with me when visiting Softcell who have expressed an interest in our printers. I will come to collect them at 8 am on Thursday morning.

Rose Rivers

Example 3: Call Message

To: Mr. Schofield:

Message:

Mr. Reter Schulz called from Vienna, wanted you to call him today before 4 pm or any time tomorrow on 014569924.

Message taken by: J. B. K.

Example 4: Postpone the Meeting

Miss Liu,

I've got an urgent meeting today. Please contact the applicants to postpone the interviews till further notice.

DS

Example 5: Ask a Leave

To: Mr. Slater

I am sorry to tell that I won't be able to go to the office today due to a sudden dizziness. So I have to ask for a day's sick leave.

David Tao

Example 6: Arrange a Job

To: Mr. Richardson

Please send a letter to Naves Limon in C.R.

Find out:

Are they satisfied with the order?

Can we provide any after sales advice?

R.R.

Example 7: Bills

Bills are usually concerned with the receiving and payout in daily business.

Cyber Internet Services, Inc. — CyberBill

1838 Lancaster Dr. NE Salem, OR 97301

Contact Name — Date: Nov 04, 1996

Contact Address — Due: Dec 01, 1996

City, St. Zip — Bill ID: 00483346265

Product	Item Description	From	To	Ext Price
Int Pkg	username	10/1/96	11/1/96	$19.95
Int Pkg	username	11/1/96	12/1/96	$19.95

Total This Bill: $39.90

Payments Processed Since: 9/20/96

Date	Pmt Type	Reference	Comments	Amount
10/8/96	Check	#157		$5.00
10/8/96	Visa	Failed	Invalid Account	$0.00
10/10/96	Visa	Approved	Authorization ID	$24.90

Total Payments: #12 $29.90

* * Thank You * *

ACCOUNT SUMMARY

Previous Billing: $78.35

Payments: - $29.90

Balance Forward: $48.45
Total This Bill: $39.90
===========
TOTAL: $88.35
DUE

Please Forward a Check to:
Cyber Internet Services, Inc. - Accounts Receivable
1838 Lancaster Dr. NE
Salem, OR 97301
Payable to: Cyber Internet Services, Inc.

Section Two　Language Handbook

Useful Words and Expressions

memo 便函
schedule 日程表
poster 海报
certificate 证明
notice 通知
note 便条
bill 账单
letters of introduction 介绍信
according to/ in accordance with/ under/ subject to/ as provided in 依据
hereof/ hereto/ herein/ hereby/ hereinafter/ hereunder/ whereby/ whereas/鉴于
because of / on account of/ due to/ attribute to/ by virtue of 因为
undertake to/ represent and warrant/ guarantee/ warrant 保证
be obliged to do sth. / have the obligation to do sth. / shall/ be responsible / liable for 有义务做某事
effect 完成

Useful Sentences

I have several proposals for cutting down the cost.
关于降低成本我有几个建议。
In response to your request for... I have to inform you that we can not approve it.
对于你……的请求,我不得不告诉你我们不能批准。
This is further to your memo dated June 6, 2006, in which you proposed that employ-

ees adopt the "punch in" system.

回复你2006年6月6日关于员工实行打卡考勤制度的备忘录。

I believe these changes will decrease the product cost.

我相信这些改革会降低成本的。

Please let me know your response to these suggestions. 我想知道你对这些建议的看法。

Please feel free to contact me if you need further information. 如果需要更多信息请随时与我联系。

I highly appreciate your considerations to these proposals. 我期待你能考虑一下这些建议。

Through market research and analysis, it has been discovered that the proposed advertising media for the new lines need to be changed.

经过市场调查和分析,发现针对新产品建议的广告媒体需要更换。

Findings from surveys of target consumers have made it apparent that we need to update our promoting efforts。

调查目标客户发现,显然我们有必要更新促销手段。

By focusing on marketing efforts, we will be able to maximize the profits of our products.

通过加强营销,我们才能扩大产品的收益。

At that time, you were notified that you would be able to take another product without charge.

届时,我方将通知你可免费获取另一产品。

Thank you for your letter of 2 November, requesting a reference for Sun Computers Ltd.

感谢您11月2日的来函,咨询关于太阳有限公司的情况。

This is to certify that Mr. Thomas was a competent employee when he worked with us.

兹证明托马斯先生在我公司就职时表现出色。

This is to certificate that Mr. Zhao Hai holds a bachelor degree issued to him in July, 2000 by Beijing University.

兹证明赵海先生于2000年获得北京大学授予的学士学位。

This is to introduce Mr. Frank, our new marketing specialist who will be in London from April 5 to mid April on business.

现向您推荐我们的市场专家弗兰克先生。他将因公务在4月5日到4月中旬期间停留伦敦。

We shall appreciate any help you can give Mr. Jones and will always be happy to reciprocate.

我们将非常感谢您向琼斯先生提供的任何帮助,并非常高兴施以回报。

Exercises

Ⅰ. Translate the Following Memo into English

日期:2005年9月3日

致:市场部全体职员

自:市场部经理
事由:年度秋游

今年的秋游安排在9月10日星期日进行。我们将在这一天参观西湖。上午9点大型客车将从办公楼的门口出发。愿意参加秋游者请最迟于9月6日(星期三)告诉我。如车上有空余座位,可以提供给职员的亲属或朋友。市场部职员的游园花销、午餐费、交通费由公司承担,亲属、朋友等则由本人承担除交通费以外一切费用。

客车将在晚上6点从西湖公园入口处返回。希望各位能按时返回。祝旅行愉快!

Ⅱ. Write a Memo

Write a memo of a director meeting on 8 September. You are a chief manager and you should let all the heads of the company know about the meeting decisions on annual bonus. Meeting decisions are as follows:

(1) 给全体员工发奖金,奖金将于2008年1月初发放。
(2) 销售人员的奖金根据2007年的全年销售额而定。
(3) 企划部人员在销售期间工作时间长,业绩突出,其部门职员奖金为2007年全年工资的50%。
(4) 其他部门的奖金根据绩效考核结果,分15个级别发放。

Ⅲ. Write a Schedule

You, the staff in the training department of a Sino-American joint venture, have arranged a series of training courses especially for the new recruits as SAP staff. Analyze the proper courses offered, and create a schedule using your imagination and deduction. Your schedule should include a series of courses, regular study hours, break periods, and the need to observe the schedule.

Ⅳ. Notices

Write a Notice:

(1) To announce a meeting/party / football match/ talk;
(2) To give information about a bus tour to the Great Wall/ some scenic spot/ place of historic interest.

Ⅴ. Certificates

Write a Certificate for Mr. White who will represent your company to attend a conference.

Ⅵ. Notes

Write a note to a foreign expert:

(1) Making an appointment to discuss the outline of your paper with him/her;

(2) Asking him/her to a party to celebrate the Mid-Autumn Festival;

(3) Apologizing for not being able to hand in your paper on time;

Write a note to a foreign friend:

(1) Asking him/her to go to a Peking Opera;

(2) Apologizing for not being able to keep an appointment;

(3) Thanking him/her for a small gift.

Note that the style and tone you use for notes in the above situations should be somewhat different—the former is more formal and the latter, rather informal.

Chapter Four

Business Reports

Section One Business Writing

4.1 What is a Business Report?

Business and industry often demand reports. Simply stated, a business report conveys information to assist in decision-making. They may be proposals, progress reports, trip reports, completion reports, investigation reports, feasibility studies, or evaluation reports. As the names indicate, these reports are diverse in focus and aim, and differ in structure. However, one goal of all reports is the same: to communicate information to an audience. Some reports might present the actual solution to solve a business problem; other reports might record historical information that will be useful to assist in future decision making. Either way, information is being "reported" that will be useful in making decisions.

Generally speaking, reports are used in the following occasions:

To say how a task or project is progressing (information or memo report);

To say that a task or project is finished (information/memo/research findings);

To provide routine information—administration, sales figures (information/memo/manuals and instructions);

After an accident or incident (information/memo/recommendation report/evaluation);

After a conference, meeting, presentation (information/memo/recommendation report);

To examine a problem (memo/recommendation report/evaluation report)

Business report can be presented in different forms. They may be long (usu. more than 10 pages) or short, formal or informal, public or private, business routine or reported on special occasions. Some companies require daily or weekly while others require only monthly or even annual report is quite enough.

4.2 Steps of Writing a Business Report

In all areas of business, report writing is a principal means of turning thoughts into reality. The ability to express yourself is the key to gaining recognition within your organization; success in persuading others often determines whether you reach your career goals.

By following a simple, seven-step process, you can ensure that your reports reflect the four "C's" of good reports:

- clear thinking
- complete information
- concisely presented
- correctly stated

4.2.1 Determine the Scope of the Report

The first thing to think about is that why you are writing a report and then decide the scope of your report. The scope should not be too general or too vague. It is defined by the most needed and most important factors to the topic of the report. You need to limit the amount of information you will gather to the most relevant and persuadable. For example, factors to be studied to determine ways to improve employee morale might include:

- salaries
- fringe benefits
- work assignments
- work hours
- evaluation procedures

You could study many other factors relative to improving employee morale. Some may be important, and you may want to consider them later. For any one report, however, a reasonable scope must be clearly defined by determining what factors will be included.

4.2.2 Determine the Scope of the Report

Why are you writing the report? Who will read it? The best way to begin is to fill in two statements that reflect a goal and an audience: "I am writing this report to (a reason, such as recommending a performance review system). The people who will act on this report are (an individual or specific group, most of whom you can name, such as Executive Committee)."

Your opening statement is your vision for the entire report; it is the goal you will strive to reach. The best statements will be clear, concise, and descriptive. Just like the old advertising contest, keep the length to 25 words or less.

4.2.3 Consider Your Audience

Always consider your reader or readers. Unlike letters and memos, reports usually have a far wider distribution. Job for a report is to make it easy for the readers. In order to make reading your report easier, think in terms of the reader. Some audience's consideration includes:

- education level
- position in the organization
- knowledge of your topic or area
- possible reaction

- age, gender
- schedule
- economics
- values
- experiences

Some false assumptions commonly made regarding audiences are:

(1) The person who will fist read or edit the report is the audience;

(2) The audience is a group of specialists in the field;

(3) The audience is familiar with the subject of the report;

(4) The audience has time to read the entire report;

(5) The audience has a strong interest in the subject of the report;

(6) The author will always be available to discuss the report.

To avoid making these false assumptions, writers should identify everyone who might read the report; characterize those readers according to their professional training, position in the organization, and personal traits; and determine how and when the reader might use the report. Audiences are basically of three kinds:

Primary	People who have to act or make decisions on the basis of the report
Secondary	People affected by actions of the primary audiences would take in response to the report
Immediate	People responsible for evaluating the report and getting it to the right people

Additional questions to ask regarding your audience are:

(1) How much background will the audience need?

(2) Do you need to define any terms you are using?

(3) What language level will be most appropriate for your readers?

(4) How many and what kind of visual aids should you use?

(5) What will the audience expect from your report?

(6) Does the reader prefer everything given in detail or merely a brief presentation that touches upon the highlights?

4.2.4 Gather Your Information

The key to the success of a report is information. Information you gather can be of two types: secondary and primary. Secondary is information gathered and recorded by others. Primary is information you gather and record yourself.

	Sources	Caution
Primary	Books, internet, reports, newspapers, magazines, pamphlets and journals, etc.	Information may be inaccurate, out of date, or biased.
Secondary	Questionnaires, surveys, observations, experiments, historical information, and raw data	Information must be gathered carefully to ensure it its accurate and bias free.

Use a variety of tools including review of existing reports, records, and test results and your own tests, observations, interviews, and surveys.

How much information should you gather? In general, you want to ask key questions any good reporter would ask: who, what, where, when, why, and how. They will help you focus your research and ensure that the information is germane to your subject.

The point is to be complete—but not necessarily exhaustive. In many areas today, new information is coming faster and thicker every day. Waiting for a bit more data may not help management make the key decisions it must reach with your assistance.

You must also be accurate—nothing destroys your credibility faster than a few loose facts.

4.2.5 Analyze Your Information

Once you have your information, you must process it in a meaningful way. Use charting, outlining, mindmapping, and other tools to help you think through and arrange the data. Look for gaps in logic or facts and decide how to bridge them. You may find you need a bit more research to fill in. Don't let small obstacles keep you from developing as many findings as possible while you look to complete your research.

If you find that you need much more information, consider suggesting areas for future research rather than postponing the report far beyond your original deadline. In most cases, timely information is more important than encyclopedic data.

4.2.6 Determine the Solution

Based on your analysis, you will then be ready to offer a solution (or solutions) to the problem you have been studying. Make sure, however, that a solution is even requested. Depending on your position in the organization and the particular business study, a solution may NOT be requested in the report. Your purpose would then be to present the objective facts. These facts would be used by someone else to determining the best solution.

If you create recommendations in a report, let your recommendations flow naturally from your conclusions. To this point, you have identified the issue, whether an ongoing problem or a new business opportunity; analyzed it; and thought through a series of conclusions. What action should be taken?

Your recommendations should include:

Actions: Consistent with your initial definition or problem statement.

Options: The reader should consider if your recommendations are not followed.

A schedule: For implementing your solution, including dates and who is responsible.

For a reality check, discuss your recommendations with your boss or a co-worker. If your report is likely to be controversial, make sure that at least one senior manager knows about it and the courses of action you are considering.

4.2.7 Use Graphics and Illustrations

1. Why Employ Use Graphics?

Graphics, of course, are not required as part of a business report. However, since your goal in a business report is to convey information clearly to the reader, a graphic can often be clearer than text.

Reason 1: Graphics simplify ideas

Graphics present a message in an economical manner using less space than would be needed to provide the same information in the text. Graphics can help them cut through technical details and grasp basic ideas and thus save readers' time. A quick look at the graphics is much better than reading hundred words of text.

Reason 2: Graphics reinforce ideas

When a point really needs emphasis, create a graphic. For example, you might draw a map to show where computer terminals will be located within a building, or use a pie chart to show how a budget will be spent, or include a drawing that indicates how to operate a VCR. In all three cases, the graphics would reinforce points made in the accompanying text.

Reason 3: Graphics create interest

Graphics can be used to entice readers into the text, just as they engage readers' interest in magazines and journals. If your customers have three reports on their desks and must quickly decide which one to read first, they probably will pick up the one with an engaging picture or chart on the cover page.

Reason 4: Graphics are universal

Some people wrongly associate the growing importance of graphics with today's reliance on television and other popular media—as if graphics pander to less-intellectual instincts. While visual media such as television obviously rely on pictures, the fact is that graphics have been mankind's universal language since cave drawings.

2. Types of Graphics Used

Among the many types, there are 8 types which are often used in technical writing:

- pie charts
- bar charts
- line charts
- schedule charts
- flow charts
- organization charts
- technical drawings
- tables
- others (pictograms, maps, photographs)

3. Specific Guidelines for the Graphics

1) Pie Charts

Pie charts create a visual representation that helps readers understand the relationships and meanings of numbers. Pie charts are especially useful in representing proportions, percents, and fractions.

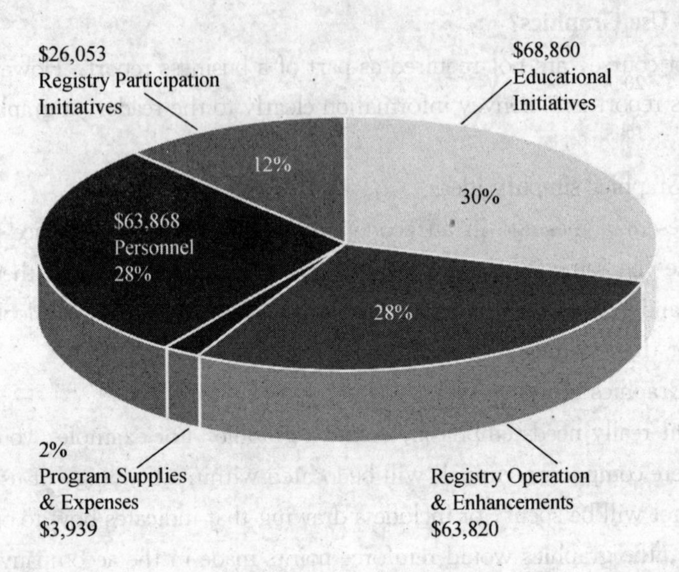

Pie Charts Guidelines:

(1) Use no more than 10 divisions.

To make pie charts work well, limit the number of pie pieces to no more than 10. In fact, the fewer, the better.

(2) Move clockwise from 12:00, form largest to smaller wedge.

Readers prefer pie charts oriented like a clock—with the first wedge starting at 12:00. Move from largest to smallest wedge to provide a convenient organizing principle.

(3) Use pie charts especially for percentages and money.

Pie charts catch the readers' eyes best when they represent items divisible by 100, as with percentages and dollars.

(4) Be creative, but stay simple

- shading a wedge
- removing a wedge from the main pie
- placing related pie charts in a three-dimensional drawing

Graphics software can create these and other variations for you.

(5) Draw and label carefully.

The most common pie charts errors are: Wedge sizes do not correspond to percentages or money amounts and pie sizes are too small to accommodate the information placed in them.

2) Bar Charts

Bar charts provide a simple, effective way of representing different quantities so that they can be compared at a glance.

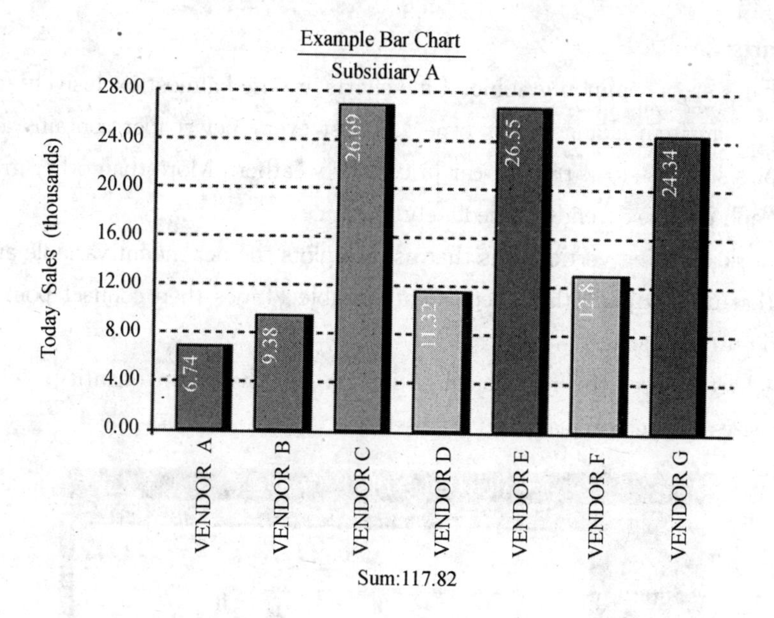

Bar Charts Guidelines:

(1) Use a limited number of bars.

The maximum bar number can vary according to chart size. Bar charts begin to break down when there are so many bars that information is not easily grasped.

(2) Show comparisons clearly.

Bar lengths should be varied enough to show comparisons quickly and clearly. Avoid using bars that are too close in length, for then readers must study the chart before understanding it. Such a chart lacks immediate visual impact.

(3) Keep bar widths equal and adjust space between bars carefully.

While bar length varies, bar width must remain constant.

As for distance between the bars, following are three options:

Option A: use no space when there are close comparisons or many bars, so that differences are easier to grasp.

Option B: use equal space, but less than bar width when bar height differences are great enough to be seen in spite of the distance between bars.

Option C: use variable space when gaps between some bars are needed to reflect gaps in the data.

(4) Carefully arrange the order of bars.

The arrangement of bars is what reveals meaning to readers. Here are tow common approaches:

Sequential: used when the progress of the bars shows a trend.

Ascending or descending order: used when you want to make a point by the rising or falling of the bars, from the lowest to the highest.

3) Line Charts

Line charts are a common graphic. Line charts are used almost exclusively to show how the quantity of an item changes over time. Almost every newspaper contains a few charts covering topics such as stock trends, car prices, or weather. More than other graphics, line charts telegraph complex trends immediately.

They work by using vertical axis that usually plots the dependent variable and the horizontal axis that usually plots the independent variable. Lines then connect points that have been plotted on the chart.

A line chart focuses the readers' attention on the change in quantity, whereas a bar chart emphasizes the actual quantities themselves.

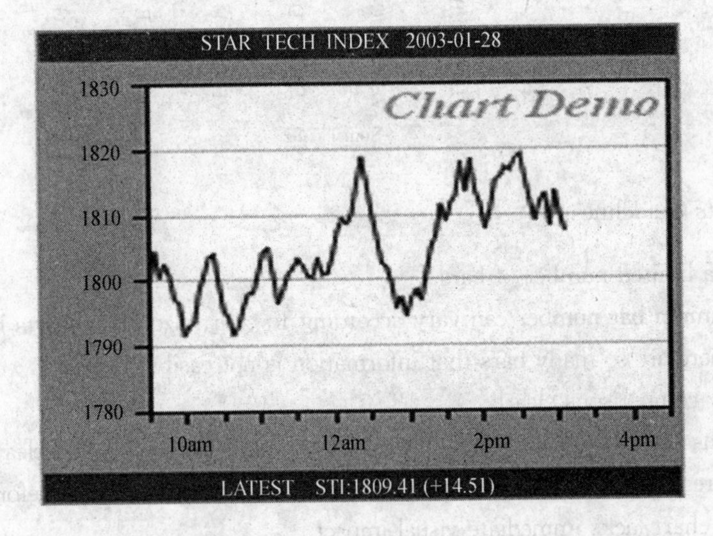

Line Charts Guidelines:

(1) Use line charts for trends.

(2) Locate line charts with care.

Given their strong impact, line charts can be especially useful as attention-grabbers. Consider placing them on cover pages to engage readers' interest in the document at the beginning of sections that describe trends in conclusion to reinforce a major point your document.

(3) Strive for accuracy and clarity.

Here are some specific suggestions to keep your line charts accurate and clear:

- start all scales from zero to eliminate the possible confusion of breaks in amounts
- select a vertical-to-horizontal ration for axis lengths that is pleasing to the eye
- use shading under the line when it will make the chart more readable

(4) Don't place numbers on the chart itself.

Line charts derive their main effect from the simplicity of lines that show trends. Avoid cluttering the chart with a lot of numbers that only detract from the visual impact.

(5) Use multiple lines with care.

Use no more than four or five lines on a single chart. If you place too many lines on one chart, however, you run the risk of confusing the reader with too much data.

4) Schedule Charts

Users can display calendars as charts with tasks and schedule their tasks within the charts. Many documents, especially proposals and feasibility studies, include a schedule chart that show readers when certain activities will be accomplished. The schedule chart usually highlights tasks and times already mentioned in the text. It includes:

- vertical axis, which lists the various parts of the project, in sequential order
- horizontal axis, which registers the appropriate time units
- horizontal bar lines (separate markers/milestone), which show the starting and ending times for each task

Monday	Tuesday	Wednesday	Thursday	Friday
Lay down rough animation	Tweak animation	Create smoke effect	Setup lighing and rendering Render out all layers and passes	Composite soene together

Schedule Charts Guidelines:

(1) Include only main activities.

Keep readers focused on no more than 15 main activities.

(2) List activities in sequence, starting at the top of the chart.

List activities from the top to the bottom of the vertical axis. Thus the readers' eyes move from the top left to the bottom right of the page, the most natural flow for most readers.

(3) Run labels in the same direction.

If readers have to turn the chart sideways to read labels, they may lose interest.

(4) Be realistic about the schedule.

Be realistic about the likely time something can be done. Your managers and clients understand delays caused by weather, equipment breakdowns, and other unforeseen events. However, they be charitable about schedule errors than result from sloppy planning.

5) Flow Charts

A flow chart, as its name suggests, traces the stage of a procedure or a process, which tells a story about a process, usually by stringing together a series of boxes and other shapes that represent separate activities.

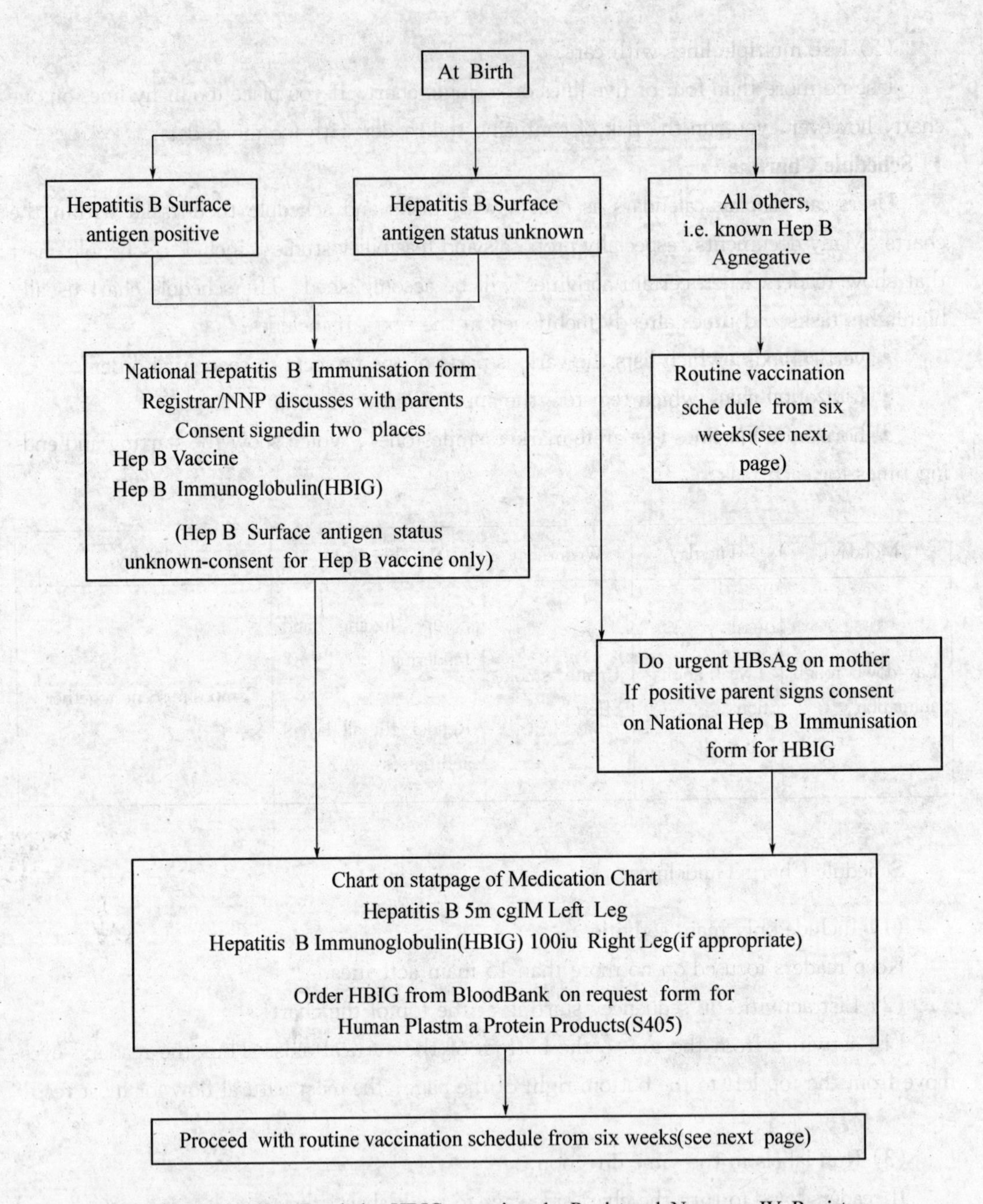
At Birth
Hepatitis B Surface antigen positive
Hepatitis B Surface antigen status unknown
All others, i.e. known Hep B Agnegative
National Hepatitis B Immunisation form
Registrar/NNP discusses with parents
Consent signedin two places
Hep B Vaccine
Hep B Immunoglobulin(HBIG)
(Hep B Surface antigen status unknown-consent for Hep B vaccine only)
Routine vaccination sche dule from six weeks(see next page)
Do urgent HBsAg on mother
If positive parent signs consent on National Hep B Immunisation form for HBIG
Chart on statpage of Medication Chart
Hepatitis B 5m cgIM Left Leg
Hepatitis B Immunoglobulin(HBIG) 100iu Right Leg(if appropriate)
Order HBIG from BloodBank on request form for
Human Plastm a Protein Products(S405)
Proceed with routine vaccination schedule from six weeks(see next page)
Both the Hep Band the HBIG are given by Registered Nurse on IV Register.

Flow Charts Guidelines:

(1) Present only overviews.

Readers usually want flowcharts to give them only a capsule version of the process, not all the details.

(2) Limit the number of shapes.

Flowcharts rely on rectangles and other shapes to relate a process in effect to tell a story. Different shapes represent different types of activities. For the sake of clarity and simplicity, limit the number of different shapes in your flowchart.

(3) Provide a legend when necessary.

Simple flow charts often need no legend. When charts get more complex, however, include a legend that identifies the meaning of each shape used.

(4) Run the sequence from top to bottom of from left to right.

(5) Label all shapes clearly.

The best approach is to write the label inside the shape.

6) Organization Charts

Organization charts, also known as organizational charts, are tree diagrams that illustrate the relationships among personnel, departments, or divisions in an organization and displays the structure of organization, its departments and work groups.

They are drawn as either horizontal or vertical trees with labeled geometric shapes representing staff or business units.

There are three different types of organizational chart:

(1) Hierarchical—describe the hierarchy of the organizational structure.

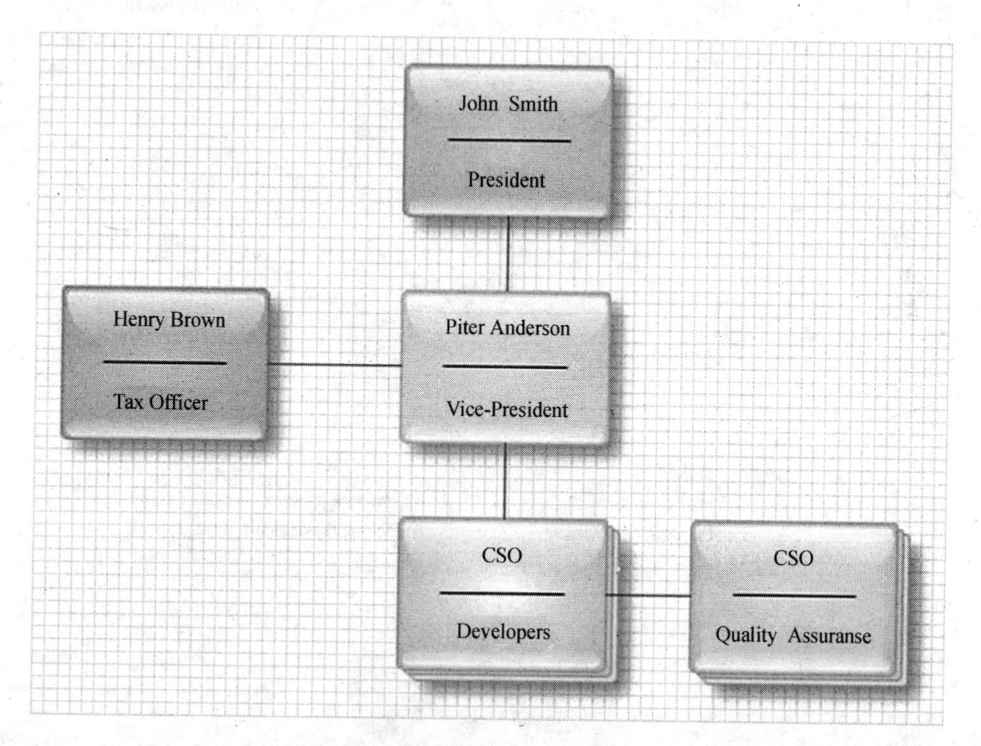

(2) Matrix—divide the structure of the organization by types of works. All the employees, engaged in work of the same type belong to the same array, regardless their position in the hierarchy.

(3) Flat—oriented to working processes. They describe the manufacturing path of the product.

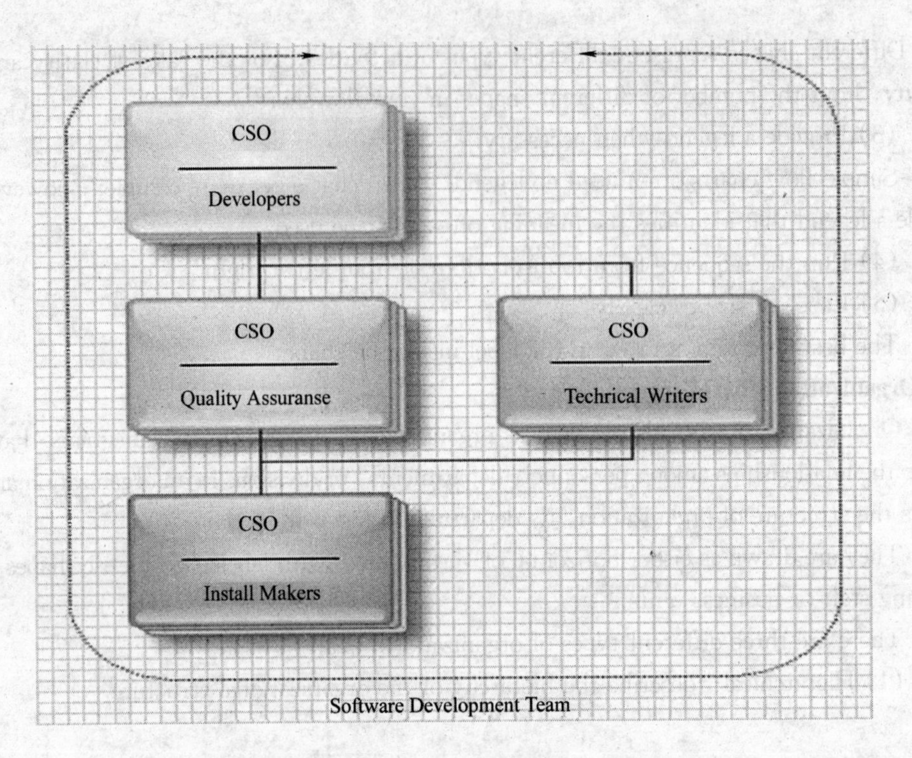
CSO
Developers
CSO
Quality Assuranse
CSO
Techrical Writers
CSO
Install Makers
Software Development Team

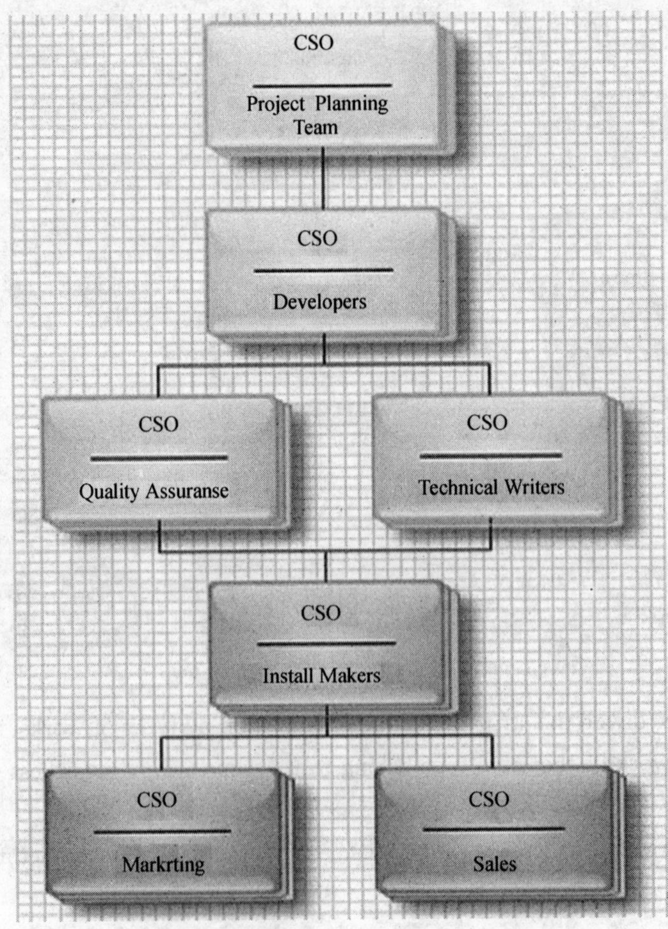
CSO
Project Planning Team
CSO
Developers
CSO
Quality Assuranse
CSO
Technical Writers
CSO
Install Makers
CSO
Markrting
CSO
Sales

Organization Charts Guidelines:

(1) Use the linear "boxes" approach to emphasize high-level positions.

(2) Connect boxes with solid or dotted lines.

Solid lines show direct reporting relationships; dotted lines show indirect or staff relationships.

(3) Use a circular design to emphasize mid-level and low-level positions.

This arrangement of concentric circles gives more visibility to workers outside upper management. These are often the technical workers most deeply involved in the details of a projects.

(4) Use varied shaped carefully.

Organization charts can use different shapes to indicate different levels or types of jobs. However, you should be convinced this approach is needed to convey meaning to the readers.

7) Technical Drawings

Technical drawings are important tools of companies that produce or use technical products. These drawings can accompany documents such as instructions, reports, sales order and proposals.

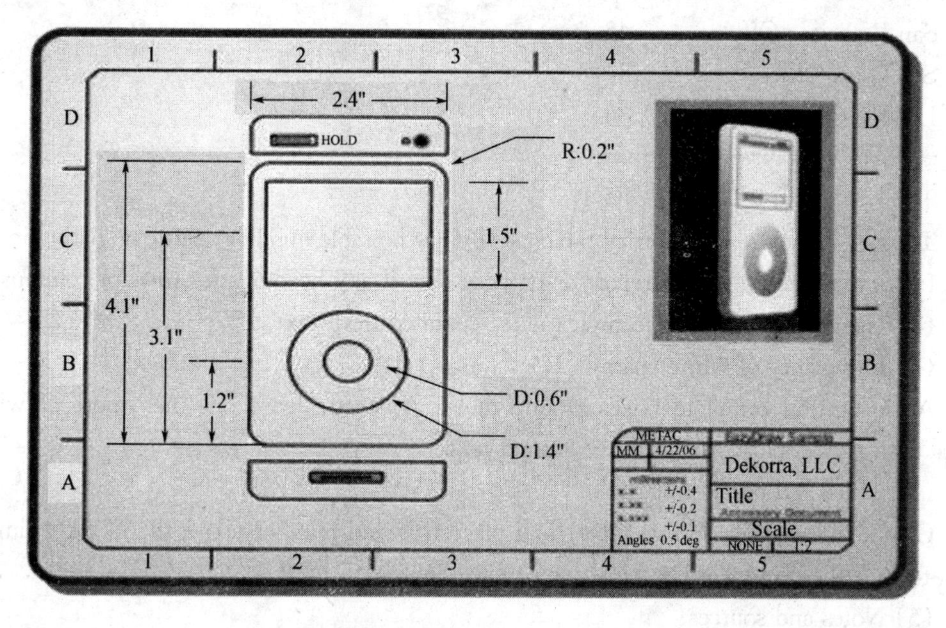

8) Tables

Tables easily convey large amount of information, especially quantitative data, and then proved the only means of showing several variables for a number of items

Tables are classified as either formal or informal:

(1) **Informal Tables**: Limited data arranged in the form of either rows or columns.

(2) **Formal Tables**: Data arranged in a grid, always with both horizontal rows and vertical columns.

City	Country	Population(million)
Mumbai (Bombay)	India	12
Sao Paulo	Brazil	10.5
Seoul	South Korea	10
Karachi	Pakistan	9.8
Delhi	India	9.8
Shanghai	China	9.2
Jakarta	Indonesia	9.1
Mexico City	Mexico	8.5
Istanbul	Turkey	8.1

Tables Guidelines:

(1) Use informal tables as extension of text, for example:

Our project in Alberta, Canada, will involve engineers, technicians, and salespeople from three offices, in these numbers:

San Francisco Office	45
St. Louis Office	34
London Office	6
Total	85

Thus, you may se an informal table usually has no table number or title no listing in the list of illustrations in a formal report or proposal few if any headings for rows or columns.

(2) Use formal tables for complex data separated from text.

(3) Use plenty of white spaces.

Avoid putting complete boxes around tables. Instead, leave one inch more of white space than you would normally leave around text.

(4) Titles and numberings:

Give a title to each formal table, and place title and number above the table. Number each table if the document contains two or more tables.

(5) Notes and sources:

Place any necessary footnotes below the table. Place any source references below the footnotes.

4. How to Relate the Graphics to the Written Text?

The graphics are part of the report, not a supplement. Work the graphic into the flow of your text.

(1) Place the graphic within the text immediately after the paragraph in which the graphic is first mentioned.

(2) Refer to each graphic by its figure number.

(3) Interpret the information found in the graphic within the text material. Textual material should not merely repeat what can be seen in the graph or table.

4.2.8 Organize Your Report

When you have got your topic, your information and your decision, it's time to get your report on paper (or on your hard drive). Before actually writing, organize your information into an outline form. You can formulate an outline for your report by choosing the major and supporting ideas, developing the details and eliminating the unnecessary ideas you've gathered. This outline becomes the basic structure of your report.

(1) Inductive order—moving from know to unknown:

- orientation (introduction)
- facts (perhaps including their analysis)
- summary or conclusion
- recommendation

(2) Deductive order—start with conclusions, then present supporting facts and analysis, often preferred for short reports.

(3) Chronological order—combine with one of the above, but list facts in chronological order.

(4) Organization by division:

- division by time period (e.g., quarter)
- division by place (e.g., sales region)
- division by quantity (e.g. sales by categories of amounts)
- division by conceptual factors (e.g., worker availability, transportation facilities, etc.)

But no matter what organization you follow, the following requirements have to be fulfilled:

- define the project or problem
- give the background
- give the supporting data
- state your conclusions and recommendations

Before preparing the report for final release, ask someone who has not seen it before to look it over. If possible, have two or three people to review your report. Request specific types of feedback such as checking for logic and consistency or for tone and readability.

4.3 Elements of Effective Business Reports

The most important elements of business reports are accuracy and objectivity. After the overall outline and rough draft of the report, we need to start the "polishing". In presenting information, an effective business report should be accurate and objective.

4.3.1 Accuracy

Accuracy in a business report includes accuracy of information and that of writing. Since the information is used to make decisions, inaccurate information can lead to inaccurate decisions. Therefore, make sure your facts are right. The accuracy of any report depends upon the correctness of the data that was gathered to prepare it. Use reliable sources and be accurate in reporting all information.

When you have a logical, accurate draft, ensure that your report creates the best impression by editing it to:

(1) Eliminate unnecessary words.

(2) Use specific words, not vague terms.

(3) Use jargon only if your audience understands it.

(4) Check your grammar and punctuation.

The accuracy of writing depends on accuracy in writing mechanics (spelling, punctuation and grammar) and accuracy in wring style. To avoid wring style errors, use precise words and terms that are not likely to be misinterpreted by the reader.

Vague Terms	Specific Terms
increase largely	increase of $ 10,000 annually
a great loss	20% loss
the plan implemented soon	the plan implemented in June and July, 2007

4.3.2 Objective

In writing, objectivity means presenting materials free from personal feelings or prejudice. You can achieve objectivity though the following techniques:

1. Make a Distinction between Facts and Opinions

Minimize unsupported judgments and inferences. For example:

A surveyed employee complained the employees in his company were forced to work over time quite often. While this information is valuable for your report, it should be included an opinion rather than a fact before you can prove it to be truth.

2. Reporting All Pertinent Information

Present both positive and negative aspects. For example:

You are reporting on effects of your company's experimental flex-time system for work hours. Look for both benefits and problems resulting from the system. If you enjoy the new system and want to see it become a permanent arrangement, it may be difficult for you present a fair-minded view of the negative aspects. However, your credibility as a writer and the value of your report depends upon your objectivity.

3. Using Bias-free Language

Avoid emotional terms, such as "amazing", "tremendous", etc. For example:

The collectors achieved an outstanding response rate of 50 percent.

The collectors achieved a response rate of 50 percent.

4. Using Impersonal Style

Avoid interjecting a personal note, which might weaken a report by making it seem merely a statement of one person's opinion and beliefs. For example:

I compared the qualities of three word processors.

Qualities of three word processors were compared.

Generally, a good report:

- is about one clearly defined subject
- is accurate and up to date
- includes everything the reader needs to know
- omits irrelevant information
- is easy to read and understand
- is clearly presented
- follows the required format
- is written in a concise and simple style
- is well organised and logical in its structure
- does not contain too much jargon or technical detail

4.4 Short Business Reports

This style is mostly likely a typical report, perhaps called essay or thesis which we learned in middle school. It should include:

Summary: For a short report, it is probably one paragraph that summarizes or introduces the report. It should sufficiently overview the report so that an executive gets the main ideas and conclusions of your report.

Introduction: An introduction paragraph, including a statement of purpose for the report.

Text: The length of the body of the report will be determined by necessity to convey the analysis and conclusions. Headings and subheadings are frequently used to ease the reading.

Conclusions: A conclusion paragraph responds to the report's purpose and how the report has achieved it.

4.5 A Standard Format of Long Business Reports

Companies may have standard format for reports, or you may have to decide the content and format yourself. Generally, the typical components of a business report are:

- Title Page

- Letter of Authorization
- Letter of Transmittal
- Table of Contents
- Abstract/Summary/Synopsis
- Introduction
- Background
- Body or Findings
- Conclusions
- Recommendations
- Bibliography
- Attachments/Appendices

1. Title Page

In a short report this may simply be the front cover. In a long one, Table of Contents and so on. The essential information here is your name, the title of the project, and the date. Be aware of any other information. The title of a report can be a statement of the subject. An effective title is informative but reasonably short. Ornamental or misleading titles may annoy readers.

2. Letter of Authorization

This letter comes from the person who authorized the report and should state the purpose of the report and its significance to the company and/or recipients.

3. Letter of Transmittal

This letter is usually in memo format and contains the author's name, a list of everyone who should receive a copy of the report as well as the date when the report is sent. This can be used as a check list for distribution.

4. Table of Contents

For page numbers, use lowercase Roman numerals (i, ii, iii) for the letter of authorization, letter of transmittal and synopsis. All other sections should be numbered with Arabic numerals (1,2,3).

5. Abstract/Summary/Synopsis

This section states the report in miniature. It summarizes the whole report in a one half to one page. It might be useful to think in terms of writing one sentence to summarize each of the traditional report divisions: objective, method, discussion, conclusions. Emphasize the problem, the purpose and the analysis of the results (including recommendations). Avoid the temptation to copy a whole paragraph from elsewhere in your report and make it do double duty. Since the abstract condenses and emphasizes the most important elements of the whole report, you cannot write it until you have completed the report.

Some people, especially senior managers, may not read anything else so write as if it were a stand-alone document. It isn't but for some people it might as well be. Keep it brief and free from jargon so that anyone can understand it and get the main points.

There are two types of abstracts: informational and descriptive.

1) Informational Abstracts

- communicate contents of reports
- include purpose, methods, scope, results, conclusions, and recommendations
- highlight essential points
- are short-from a paragraph to a page or two, depending upon the length of the report (10% or less of the report)
- allow readers to decide whether they want to read the report

2) Descriptive Abstracts

- tell what the report contains
- include purpose, methods, scope, but NOT results, conclusions, and recommendations
- are always very short—usually under 100 words
- introduce subject to readers, who must then read the report to learn study results

3) Qualities of a Good Abstract

- an effective abstract
- uses one or more well-developed paragraphs, which are unified, coherent, concise, and able to stand alone
- uses an introduction-body-conclusion structure in which the parts of the report are discussed in order: purpose, findings, conclusions, recommendations
- follows strictly the chronology of the report
- provides logical connections between material included
- adds no new information but simply summarizes the report

Remember, the abstract should be a precise and specific summary—give details. A technical document is not a mystery novel—give your conclusion right away. Support it later.

Too general	This report considers three energy sources and recommends the best one.
Specific & detailed	This report compares nuclear plants, fossil fuels, and solar generators, in order to determine which energy source will best meet the nation's needs. The criteria for comparison were the economic, social, and environmental effects of each alternative. The study concludes that nuclear energy is the best of these options, because North America is not self-sufficient in fossil fuels, and solar power is currently too unreliable for industrial use. Although nuclear plants are potentially very dangerous, nuclear energy is still the best short-term solution.

6. Introduction

The introduction provides the background information needed for the rest of your report to be understood. It is usually half to three-quarters of a page in length. The purpose of the introduction is to set the context for your report, provide sufficient background information for the reader to be able to follow the information presented, and inform the reader about how that information will be presented.

The introduction includes:

- the background to the topic of your report to set your work in its broad context
- a clear statement of the purpose of the report, usually to present the results of your research, investigation, or design
- a clear statement of the aims of the project
- technical background necessary to understand the report; e. g. theory or assumptions
- a brief outline of the structure of the report if appropriate (this would not be necessary in a short report)

Example 1

(Introduction from a report entitled "A Review of Greenhouse Gas Reduction Actions and Opportunities: the Current Status of the Kyoto Protocol".)

The greenhouse effect is a natural phenomenon that keeps the earth's surface warm. Greenhouse gases trap heat from solar radiation, analogous to the way glass panes trap heat in a greenhouse. Due to increasing greenhouse gas emissions from human activities, the greenhouse effect has been significantly augmented, causing a rise in the earth's surface temperature. This temperature rise has led to climate change, causing frequent natural disasters. This has generated increasing awareness of the importance of reducing greenhouse gas emissions through international and domestic initiatives. (contextual background)

The aims of this project are to examine the Kyoto Protocol and the effect it would have on participating countries. Another aim is to investigate actions already taken by three industrialized countries, namely Australia, the United States, and Canada. (aims)

Example 2

(Introduction from a report entitled "Preliminary Design of a Bridge". In this report, two alternative designs are presented and evaluated according to the given criteria, and then the better design selected.)

A dual carriageway bridge with two traffic lanes in each direction is to be constructed on the Calder Freeway crossing Slaty Creek in the Shire of Macedon Ranges in Victoria. The bridge is to span 125 metres between man-made compacted fill embankments, and is approximately 15 metres above the river surface, with a grade of 0.056 m/m. (technical background/assumptions)

This report presents two possible concept designs for the bridge. (purpose of report) In evaluating these designs, the following criteria are considered: construction method, construction and maintenance costs, possible disruption to traffic during construction, the durability and the aesthetics of the bridge.

The two conceptual designs are presented in the form of sketches of the elevations and cross-sections of the structures. (content structure)

Use the introduction to provide the reader with any background information which the reader will need before you can launch into the body of your paper. You may have to define the terms used in stating the subject and provide background such as theory or history of the subject. For example, the purpose statement quoted above might warrant some explanation of daylight trawling or even of the commercial shrimp industry. Avoid the tendency to use the introduction merely to fill space with sweeping statements that are unrelated to the specific purpose of your report.

7. Background

If the introduction requires a large amount of supporting information, such as a review of literature or a description of a process, then the background material should form its own section. This section may include a review of previous research, or formulas the reader needs to understand the problem. In an academic report, it is also the point where you can show your comprehension of the problem.

8. Body or Findings

This section is the most important part of your report. It takes many forms and may have subheadings of its own. Its basic components are methods, findings (or results), and evaluation (or analysis). In a progress report, the methods and findings may dominate; a final report should emphasize evaluation.

Before you begin writing, ask the journalist's questions: who? when? where? what? why? how? The last three in particular will help you focus analysis. Beyond asking these simple questions, you also need to make decisions such as: How do you interpret the data? What is the significance of your findings?

9. Conclusion

The conclusions section provides an effective ending to your report. The content should relate directly to the aims of the project as stated in the introduction, and sum up the essential features of your work. This section:

- states whether you have achieved your aims
- gives a brief summary of the key findings or information in your report
- highlights the major outcomes of your investigation and their significance.

The conclusions should relate to the aims of the work:

Example 1

(1) **Aim:** The aim of this project is to design a mobile phone tower.

(2) **Conclusions:** In this report, a design for a mobile phone tower has been presented. The key features of the tower are... It was found that...

Example 2

(1) **Aim:** The aim of this investigation is to analyse the bus delays at the intersection of the bus loop and Wellington Road at Monash University.

(2) **Conclusions:** In this report, bus delays were analysed. It was found that... Based on these findings, it is recommended that...

Example 3

(Conclusions from a report entitled "Preliminary Design of a Bridge".)

Two designs for the bridge to be constructed on the Calder Freeway across Slaty Creek have been presented and discussed in this report. Design 1 is a super-T beam bridge and Design 2 is a simple composite I girder bridge. Both designs incorporate round piers on piled foundations, which are used because the soil conditions are unknown and possibly unstable. Design 2 has some advantages because it is made of steel and thus has longer spans and fewer piers. (key features)

However, Design 1 is clearly the better design. This design requires minimal formwork in the construction of its concrete deck, it is relatively easy to erect and it maintains stability during transportation and construction. In addition, it is cheaper to build and more durable. (outcome)

10. Recommendations

What actions does the report call for? The recommendations should be clearly connected to the results of the rest of the report. You may need to make those connections explicit at this point—your reader should not have to guess at what you mean. This section may also include plans for how further research should proceed. In professional writing, this section often comes immediately after the introduction.

11. Bibliography

Bibliography is a list of writings referred to or considered by an author in preparing a particular report. It is a list of works, including books, journals and essays, on a particular subject, with the description and identification of authorship, the editions, dates of issue, and the publisher of the material.

12. Attachments/Appendices

These will include references and may include appendices. Any research that you refer to in the report must also appear in a list of references at the end of the work so that an interested reader can follow up your work. Since the format for references varies across engineering, consult your instructor, or check a style manual for the field.

Appendices may include raw data, calculations, graphs, and other quantitative materials that were part of the research, but would be distracting to the report itself. Refer to each appendix at the appropriate point (or points) in your report. In industry, a company profile and profile of the professionals involved in a project might also appear as appendices.

As a guide, if some detail is essential to your argument then include it in the main body, if it merely supports the argument then it could go in an appendix.

The above describes the general components for a business report, which you can adapt to the needs of specific assignments. Bear in mind that a format, however helpful, cannot replace clear thinking and strategic writing. You still need to organize your ideas carefully and express them coherently. Be precise and concise.

4.6 Samples of Business Reports

Example 1

Audit Report

To: The Board of Directors (or Shareholders) of ABC Company Ltd.:

We have audited the accompanying balance sheet of ABC Co., Ltd. ("the Company") as of December 31, 2002, and the related statements of income and cash flows for the year then ended. These financial statements are the responsibility of the Company's management. Our responsibility is to express an audit opinion on these financial statements based on our audit.

We conducted our audit in accordance with the Independent Auditing Standards for Certified Public Accountants. Those Standards require that we plan and perform the audit to obtain reasonable assurance about whether the financial statements are free of material misstatement. An audit includes examining, on a test basis, evidence supporting the amounts and disclosures in the financial statements. An audit also includes assessing the accounting principles used and significant estimates made by management, as well as evaluating the overall financial statement presentation. We believe that our audit provides a reasonable basis for our opinion.

The accompanying balance sheet at December 31, 2002 includes project service fees receivable of RMB17, 309,667 and other long-term receivables of RMB160, 599,155. These amounts are owing by one of the joint venture investors of the Company and certain business partners of that investor. As described in Notes 5 and 6 to the financial statements, there is uncertainty about the collectibility of these receivables. Because the ability of the debtors to repay these receivables is dependent upon the success of future operations of certain projects and upon the ability of the debtors to comply with the terms of their agreements with the Company, it is not possible to estimate the amount which ultimately will be collected. Provision for loss relating to the project service fees receivable has been made at approximately 3% of the year-end balance, and no provision is made for other long-term receivables.

In our opinion, except for the possible effects of the uncertainty about the collectibility of the project service fees and other long-term receivables, the financial statements referred above give a true and fair view (or are presented fairly, in all material respects,) the financial position as of December 31, 2002, and the results of its operations and its cash flows for the years then ended in accordance with the requirements of both the Accounting Standard for Business Enterprises and other relevant financial and accounting laws and regulations promulgated by the State.

The accompanying financial statements have been prepared assuming that the Company will continue as a going concern. However, as explained in Note 10 to the financial statements, the Company has been unable to negotiate an extension of its borrowings with its foreign joint venture investor beyond December 31, 2003. Further, as described above, there is uncertainty about the collectibility of project service fees receivable and other long-term receivables. Because of this uncertainty, and without the continued financial support of the foreign investor, there is substantial doubt that the Company will be able to continue as a going concern beyond 2003. Consequently, adjustments may be required to the recorded asset amounts. The financial statements do not include any adjustments that might result from the outcome of this uncertainty.

- Certified Public Accountant: Lili
- Certified Public Accountant: Zhang Hua
- Certified Public Accountants (name and stamp of the firm)
- Beijing, People's Republic of China February 26, 2003

Example 2

2004 – 2005 Annual Report on China's Wool Textile Market

Report Summary

The report sums up the development of the global and Chinese wool textile markets in 2004. Through accurate data and full elaboration, it describes the structure of China's wool textile market and features of the demand-supply relationship from various angles. Meanwhile, it examines competition between enterprises in different market segments, presenting assessment of leading players' competitiveness.

The report especially points out the following: With the recovery of the world economy and wool textile garments regaining popularity, the European and American wool textile markets gradually recovered in 2004. In the first half of the year, China's wool textile industry continued to maintain a good growth momentum, witnessing big year-on-year rises in production and sales and notable improvement in operational quality. On the whole, the industry was a market of perfect competition. But there was a very high degree of concentration in some production departments like worsted woolen piece goods. It is forecast that with the abolition of the world textile quota system, Chinese wool textile enterprises will increase their investment and expand their production. For a certain period of time, there will be not much change to a market structure of high competition. Integration between the upstream and downstream industries will become a new development trend of China's wool textile industry. Chinese wool textile enterprises should greatly improve the quality of wool, pay attention to brand and intellectual property protection, and seize the opportunities that come with the lifting of world textile quotas in 2005 to accelerate their growth.

After analyzing major factors affecting the development of China's wool textile market from 2005-2009, the report presents qualitative and quantitative forecast of the development trend of the market. Finally, it provides development strategy and recommendations for leading enterprises and growing enterprises respectively.

Report Outline

Ⅰ. Overview of the Global Wool Textile Market in 2004

(Ⅰ) Development Status

(Ⅱ) Basic Characteristics

(Ⅲ) Overview of Development in Major Countries and Regions

1. Australia

2. New Zealand

3. India

4. Italy

Ⅱ. Size and Structure of China's Wool Textile Market in 2004

(Ⅰ) Market Size

1. Overall Size and Growth Rate

2. Monthly Industry growth and Market Situation

(Ⅱ) Segmented Product Structure

1. By Type of Raw Wool Material

2. By Finished Product Variety

(Ⅲ) Market Structure

1. Market Concentration

2. Brand Structure

Ⅲ. Analysis of Supply & Demand in China's Wool Textile Market in 2004

(Ⅰ) Demand Analysis

(Ⅱ) Supply Analysis

(Ⅲ) Analysis of Market Features

Ⅳ. Competition Situation in China's Wool Textile Market in 2004 & Assessment of Leading Players' Competitiveness

(Ⅰ) Analysis of Competition Situation

1. Market Competition Situation

2. Means of Competition

(Ⅱ) Assessment of Market Competitiveness

1. Comparison of Competitive Players

2. Brief Introduction to Leading Players

(Ⅲ) Assessment of Growing Players' Competitiveness

1. Market Opportunities and Risks

2. Distribution of Growing Players

3. Assessment of Growing Players' Competitiveness

Ⅴ. Factors Affecting the Development of China's Wool Textile Market from 2005 to 2009

(Ⅰ) Favorable Factors

(Ⅱ) Unfavorable Factors

Ⅵ. Analysis of Development Trend of China's Wool Textile Market from 2005 to 2009

(Ⅰ) Development Trend of Products

(Ⅱ) Development Trend of Channels

(Ⅲ) Development Trend of Prices

(Ⅳ) Trend of User Demand

Ⅶ. Forecast of China's Wool Textile Market from 2005 to 2009

(Ⅰ) Forecast of Market Size

(Ⅱ) Forecast of Market Structure

Ⅷ. Recommendations

Report Specifications

(Ⅰ) Objective of Report

(Ⅱ) Research Scope

(Ⅲ) Survey Region

(Ⅳ) Data Source

(Ⅴ) Research Approaches

(Ⅵ) General Definition

(Ⅶ) Market Definition

(Ⅷ) Evaluation Index System of Competitiveness

(Ⅸ) Forecasting Model

(Ⅹ) Special Specifications

(Ⅺ) Research Object

Example 3

State of Minnesota

(Project Name) Project

Monthly Status Report (Example)

Project Name: Example Project　　　　Reporting Period: November, 2004

Project Manager: Name, Title

Project Owner: Name, Title

Project Sponsor: Name, Title

Overall Status: Yellow

	Green (Controlled)	Yellow (Caution)	Red (Critical)	Reason for Deviation
Budget	☐ ☒ ☐	☐ ☐ ☐	☐ ☐ ☐	
Schedule	☐ ☐ ☐	☐ ☒ ☐	☐ ☐ ☐	Deliverable XYZ delayed
Scope	☐ ☐ ☐	☐ ☐ ☒	☐ ☐ ☐	External project deliverable strategy being redefined

Comments

Definition of the XYZ deliverable needs to be finalized. Content is currently being generated. This important deliverable will need to be reviewed and updated for high quality.

Issue Status

A strategy needs to be established and agreed upon relative to responding to requests for information associated with the project. This issue is being worked.

***Change Status*:**

XYZ deliverable due date changing from 3/7/2005 to 3/21/2005.

***Risk Status*:**

Risk: There is risk that the project accomplishments could lose their impact and the needed momentum for the follow-on effort could be minimized if a transition plan to the next phase is not defined and executed.

Mitigation: The following two activities are being initiated:

(1) A communications plan is being developed and executed to support the involvement of the Governor's office and related legislative sponsorship.

(2) A program portfolio for the follow-on effort is being generated. A transition work plan will capture the recommendations of the project. Follow-on project initiatives will be developed based on the recommendations of the project.

Budget

Budget Status as of 10/31/2004

Expense	Original Budget	Current Budget	Spent to Date	Est. to Complete	Current Forecast	Variance
Labor						
Internal	3,659,200	3,732,800	3,585,600	147,200	3,732,800	0
External	2,500,000	2,500,000	2,125,000	375,000	2,500,000	0

Budget Status as of 10/31/2004

Expense	Original Budget	Current Budget	Spent to Date	Est. to Complete	Current Forecast	Variance
Hardware					0	0
Software					0	0
Other					0	0
Total	$ 6,159,200	$ 6,232,800	$ 5,710,600	$ 522,200	$ 6,232,800	$ 0

Budgetary Comments

(1) Burden rate of $ 100 per hour assumed for internal resources.

(2) Spent to date is estimated based on a linier prorated over time algorithm.

(3) Internal budget does not include steering committee member resources.

(4) Increase in internal current budget is due to two additional weeks of deliverable generation.

(5) Internal budget includes state resources deployed on the effort.

Scheduled Milestones / Deliverables

Milestone	Approved Schedule	Current Forecast	Actual	Status
Start Project	6/1/2004		6/1/2004	Complete
Vendor RFP posted	6/19/2004		6/19/2004	Complete
Vendor selected	7/21/2004		8/8/2004	Complete
Vendor contract awarded	9/1/2004		9/25/2004	Complete
Program resources identified		9/9/2004		Complete
Steering Committee identified				Complete
Phase I kick-off	10/8/2004	10/13/2004	10/13/2004	Complete
Communications Plan available	10/10/2004		10/10/2004	Accepted
Activity completed	12/8/2004		12/8/2004	Complete
Activity completed	12/8/2004			Complete
Activity completed	12/8/2004	12/15/2004	12/15/2004	Complete
DEF Deliverable available	12/29/2004		12/29/2004	Accepted

Milestone	Approved Schedule	Current Forecast	Actual	Status
GHI Deliverable available	12/29/2004		120/29/2004	Accepted
Phase II kick-off meeting	1/1/2005		1/1/2005	Complete
Phase III kick-off meeting	1/6/2005		1/6/2005	Complete
JKL Deliverable available	2/3/2005	2/17/2005		In Review
XYZ Deliverable available	3/7/2005	3/21/2005		Redefined
Records Retention Plan executed	3/30/2005			Yellow
Project complete	3/31/2005			Green
Note: Bold milestones are key external project deliverable				

Accomplishments & Plans

Accomplishments during this Reporting Period:

(1) Continued to execute the communications plan.

(2) Held several steering committee meetings. Reviewed and approved deliverable.

(3) Subcommittee of the Steering Committee evaluated and categorized recommendations and opportunities.

(4) Developed a work plan to schedule final update, review and acceptance of the project deliverable.

Plans for the Next Reporting Period:

(1) Develop, review and accept the XYZ deliverable.

(2) Review, update and accept all the vendor deliverable.

(3) Organize and archive all project materials.

(4) Execute the Records Retention plan.

(5) Start to initiate a transitional communications plan and program portfolio for the next steps that can be handed off to the program office that will be recommended by the project.

(6) Continue to maintain the project control practices—steering committee meetings, status reporting, issues management, change control, work plan, budget management, document management and risk management.

Project Description

This section contains a brief description of the business need that drives the project. The project will accomplish the following activities to support this vision:

- broad description of activity
- broad description of activity

Project Definition

Business Objectives	• Providing modern, comprehensive and user-friendly electronic access to government program. • Decreasing the administrative cost of providing the service while increasing the quality and efficiency.
Scope	• Identify business transactions performed by the program, documented in the form of a current business process model. • Identify information requirements of the business transactions performed by the program, documented in the form of a data flow diagram. • Identify technologies used by the program, documented in the form of a current technology model. • Identify potential opportunities to improve efficiency and effectiveness through the use of streamlined processes.
Assumptions	• The program's resources meet the requirements (skills, experience and time commitment) specified in the "Roles and Responsibilities" and "State FTEs" attachments to the Statement of Work. • Existing procedural and system documentation for all in-scope businesses and systems will be available to the project team very early in the project. • The approach to this project is based on the vendor's methodology for organizational performance enhancement. • It will be the State's responsibility to review, verify, and confirm the accuracy of the data provided to the project team by each agency.
Dependencies	• The Governor's budget process • Constraints governed by the Data Practices Act • Constraints inherent in an aggressive project schedule

Report Summary

The report sums up the development of the global and Chinese men's wear markets in 2004. Through accurate data and full elaboration, it presents from various angles the structure of China's audio-video products market, features of the demand-supply relationship and pattern of competition between leading vendors in different market segments. Meanwhile, it examines competition between enterprises in different market segments, presenting assessment of leading players' competitiveness.

The report especially points out the following: Despite a small rise in sales volume, sales revenue in China's men's wear market nevertheless grew significantly in 2004. Currently, domestic brands have taken a notable lead in the market, while foreign high-class men's wear brands have increased their investment in the Chinese market, leading to intensified competition. After 2005, with changes in the market environment both at home and abroad, brand will become the key for men's wear to maintain vitality. Leisure-style men's wear will continue to be in a rising trend in the next few years. Promoted by various government policies, the rural market will bring a new space for men's wear consumption.

After analyzing major factors affecting the development of China's men's wear market from 2005-2009, the report presents qualitative and quantitative forecast of the development trend of the market. Finally, it provides pertinent development strategy and recommendations for leading enterprises and growing enterprises respectively.

Report Outline

Ⅰ. Overview of the Global Men's Wear Market in 2004

(Ⅰ) Development Status

(Ⅱ) Basic Characteristics

(Ⅲ) Overview of Development in Major Countries and Regions

1. U.S.

2. Italy

3. Germany

4. Russia

Ⅱ. Size and Structure of China's Men's Wear Market in 2004

(Ⅰ) Market Situation and Characteristics

(Ⅱ) Market Size

(Ⅲ) Market Structure

1. Regional Structure

2. Product Structure

3. Brand Structure

Ⅲ. Analysis of Supply & Demand in China's Men's Wear Market in 2004

(Ⅰ) Analysis of Market-Related Industries

1. Analysis of the Textile Raw Materials Industry

2. Analysis of the Clothing Fabric Industry

3. Analysis of the Supplementary Clothing Materials Industry

(Ⅱ) Analysis of Consumers' Demand

1. Overall Characteristics of Men's Wear Consumption in China

2. Analysis of Men's Wear Consumption Habits in China

3. Analysis of Factors Men's Wear Consumption in China

(Ⅲ) Analysis of Vendors' Supply

1. Number and Distribution of Men's Wear Vendors in China

2. Variety and Structure of Men's Wear Supply in China

3. Price Structure of Men's Wear Supply in China

Ⅳ. Competition Situation in China's Men's Wear Market in 2004 & Assessment of Leading Players' Competitiveness

(Ⅰ) Analysis of Competition Situation in China's Men's Wear Market
1. Regional Competition Situation
2. Competition Situation in Key Cities
3. Situation of Competition Between Western-Style Clothes Brands
4. Situation of Competition Between Shirt Brands
(Ⅱ) Assessment of Leading Players' Competitiveness
1. Youngor Group
2. Shanshan Group
3. Romon
4. Baoxiniao Group
Ⅴ. Factors Affecting the Development of China's Men's' Wear Market from 2005 to 2009
(Ⅰ) Favorable Factors
(Ⅱ) Unfavorable Factors
Ⅵ. Analysis of Development Trend of China's Men's Wear Market from 2005 to 2009
Ⅶ. Forecast of China's Men's Wear Market from 2005 to 2009
(Ⅰ) Forecast of Market Size
1. Forecast of Demand in the Western-Style Clothes Market
2. Forecast of Demand in the Shirt Market
(Ⅱ) Forecast of Market Structure
Ⅷ. Recommendations
(Ⅰ) Product Strategy
(Ⅱ) Pricing Strategy
(Ⅲ) Competitiveness Strategy

Report Specifications

(Ⅰ) Objective of Report
(Ⅱ) Research Scope
(Ⅲ) Survey Region
(Ⅳ) Data Source
(Ⅴ) Research Approaches
(Ⅵ) General Definition
(Ⅶ) Market Definition
(Ⅷ) Evaluation Index System of Competitiveness
(Ⅸ) Forecasting Model
(Ⅹ) Special Specifications
(Ⅺ) Research Object

Section Two Language Handbook

Useful Words and Expressions

preliminaries 篇首

texts 本文
acknowledge 谢词
title 封面
letter of Authorization 授权书
letter of Transmittal 传递函/提交信
contents 目录
abstract/summary/synopsis 提要
background 背景
introduction 引言
review 回顾
body or Findings 正文
conclusions 结论
recommendations 建议
references/ Bibliography 参考书目
attachments/Appendices 附录资料

Useful Sentences

1. Purpose 目的

the purpose/ objective/ aim of this report is to... 本报告的目的是……
to analyze... 分析……
to assess or estimate... 估计……
to descibe some features of... 描述……的一些特征
to deal with problems of... 处理……问题
to evaluate... 评估……
to explore two aspects of... 探索……的两个方面
to focus on... 关注……
to investigate... 调查……
to present information on... 提供关于……的信息
to recommend... 建议……
to study... 研究……

2. Overview 总论

This report includes a discussion of the facts of the investigation, conclusions, and recommendations.

本报告包括对适时的调查、结论和建议。

This proposal recommends a solution and provides budget and time schedule figures.

本建议书特提出一个解决方案,并提供预算和时间安排。

This project is specifically oriented towards investigating the relationship between...

本项目旨在专门调查……之间的关系。

The major finds of the present study can be summarized as follows:...

目前研究项目的主要结果可以总结为以下几点：……

3. Review 回顾

The progress that has been reported up to this point includes the following: ...

迄今为止已经汇报过的进度如下：……

In May, we completed the following steps per the project plan authorized in February: ...

至五月份，我们完成了根据2月份上级计划规定的以下工作：……

Since the last progress report was prepared, the following have been completed: ...

上次报告提交后，又完成了以下工作：……

Surveys were conducted among...

在……中间进行了若干次调查。

Questionaries were distributed to... for their completion at the end of a 2-month preiod.

我们向……分发了问卷并要求在两个月内填写完毕。

A meeting was held involving...

我们召开了一次有……参加的会议。

4. Problem Analysis 问题分析

... has not lived up to the aims and goals it was supposed to achieved.

……尚未达到预期的目标。

There is another problem which has to be solved.

还有一个必须要解决的问题。

In the past several months, a number of orgnizational problems had surfaced: ...

在过去的几个月中出现了一些组织管理上的问题：……

5. Conclusions 结论

We'll conclude by saying...

我们的结论是：……

In view of the above, we find...

鉴于此，我们认为……

Thus it is proved that...

由此可见……

The following conclusions are based on the results of the investgation: ...

根据调查结果，我们得出如下结论：……

6. Recommendations 建议

It is hereby recommended that...

兹建议……

The following recommendations are offered: ...

现提出如下建议：……

One possible solution to the problem of... is to do...

解决……问题的一个途径也许是……

On the basis of these findings, I recommend that...
基于这些调查结果,我建议……
In view of the favorable feedback, we strongly recommend that the company...
考虑到良好的反馈,我们强烈恳求公司……
We suggest that... be... If this is not possible, we recommend that...
我们建议……如果不能实行,我们建议……

Exercises

1. For this assignment, you are the HR staff of a software company. Right now, the most of the employees in the company are at their twenties. Some of them find themselves very hard to be punctual for work. Think over this problem and write a report to the management to offer a solution. The report can include the current situation, the reason, the solutions and the prospective results.
2. Select one of the following topics and plan an analytical report. Your report should have first - and second-level headings.
   a. The gym for the employees in the company is always crowed. Find the solutions.
   b. Security is threatened when night-shift employees prop open the backdoor late at night so that they can get more fresh air. Offer the alternatives.
   c. Where should the company install additional pay phones to be used by all the employees?
3. Wal-Mart Stores, Inc. is an American public corporation that runs a chain of large, discount department stores. As the assistant consultant, make a feasibility research report for the opening of Wal-Mart Stores in your near area.
4. You have been asked by a new Web start-up company to help them to decide the best form of business organization. This new enterprise involves two married women. Should they incorporate, consider a limited liability arrangement, or a partnership? What effect would each have on their income taxes? Advise them on the best choice, given their circumstances.
5. In a recent meeting, managers and supervisors for the bank where you work expressed concerns about employees' customer-service skills. Moreover, they wonder whether a specific set of procedures should be established—especially for new employees. They have asked you to investigate the customer service practices at other local banks to determine what skills should be emphasized and what procedures—if any—should be adopted.
6. Your company's managers haven't been satisfied lately with the quality of some new employees. They believe that the hiring process may be the reason, and they've asked the HR department to recommend a set of criteria for cover letters and resumes. You have been chosen for the job. You will accomplish this through interviews with and surveys of recruiters from companies similar to yours.
7. To be sure, both telemarketing and sales letters have taken a lot of heat recently. Howev-

er, your boss is convinced that one or the other will boost your company's sales. He's asked you to assess the pros and cons of each from both the standpoint of the customer and the company. He's particularly interested in the legal liabilities associated with each one. Ultimately, he wants you to decide which one is the most favorable.

8. You have been asked by a new Web start-up company to help them to decide the best way to market its product. While advertising on the Web is certainly one option, the company's partners want to know about alternatives like the local newspaper, magazines, and even the local business-to-business directory. Certainly, cost is an issue; but the main concern is getting the best exposure for a reasonable price.
9. A hot new trend in today's workplace is "telecommuting". Your boss has had several employees ask her about the possibility of performing work—at least part time—at home. Your boss isn't convinced that telecommuting is in her best interest, so she asks you to write a report that analyzes the pros and cons of this form of employment. Consider what jobs are ideal for telecommuting, what the employment statistics reveal, and how it affects both businesses and employees.
10. Many companies are touting the benefits of various forms of employee participation in management decisions. An example of this is self-managed project teams. You've been asked to investigate the most popular methods. What criteria should be established to evaluate these methods? After you've evaluated each method, provide your recommendation for the best one.

Chapter Five

Contracts and Agreements

Section One Business Writing

5.1 Introduction

5.1.1 What is Contract?

The second article of China's Contract Laws (1999) defines the contract as: A contact in this Law refers to an agreement establishing, modifying and terminating the civil rights and obligations between subjects of equal footing, that is, between natural persons, legal persons or other organizations.

Steven H. Gifts's "Law Dictionary" defines the contract to be "contract is a promise, or a set of promises, for breach of which the law gives remedy, or the performance of which the law in some way recognize as a duty."

L. B Curzon, in his "A Dictionary of Law", defines the contract as: "Contract is a legally binding agreement."

There is a common concept from the above definitions that "Contract is an agreement". A contract can be said to be "An agreement which binds the parties concerned" or "An agreement which is enforceable by law", or contracts are promises that the law will enforce.

5.1.2 What is Agreement?

L. B. Curzon defines agreement as: "A consensus of mind, or evidence of such consensus, in spoke or written form, relating to anything done or to be done."

"Law Dictionary" defines agreement in two ways: one is: "A concord of understanding and intention between two or more parties with respect to the effect upon their relative rights and duties, of certain past or future facts or performance."

The other is: "The consent of two or more persons concurring respecting the transmission of some property, right or benefits, with the view of contacting an obligation, a mutual obligation."

5.1.3 Difference between Contract and Agreement

A contract has a few main elements, including the agreement, the purpose, the intention to establish legal relationship and the ability to perform.

L. B Curzon mentioned in his work—"A Diction of Law": Contract generally involves:

- offer and absolute and unqualified acceptance
- consensus ad idem
- intention to create legal relations
- genuineness of consent
- contractual capacity of the parties
- legality of object
- possibility of performance
- certainty of terms
- valuable consideration

"Law Dictionary" explains: Although often used as synonyms with "contract", agreement is a broader term, e.g. an agreement might lack an essential element of a contact.

In real practice, an agreement is not necessarily bound by provisions, while the contract cannot be without the necessary provisions. Some contracts list them separately as General Provisions.

The twelfth article in China's Contract Law (1999) stipulates eight general provisions:

- title or name and domicile of the parities
- contract object
- quantity
- quality
- price or remuneration
- time limit, place and method of performance
- liability for breach of contract
- methods to settle disputes

Therefore, contracts and agreements are not interchangeable despite their similarities because different scopes contract tends to be used to mean a binding or formal agreement. Only those agreements that comply with the requirements of contract and are enforceable by law can be called contracts.

5.2 General information and Samples of Contracts and Agreements

5.2.1 Structure of Contract

Contracts are used to stipulate the relative parties' rights and obligations and are the base on which the disputes are prevented from and solved. Contracts in English are written precisely and deliberately. They have a long history and contain profound legal implication.

Contracts in Chinese have names and start with the concerned parties' names, addresses. Then comes the body. The end is combined with the concerned parties' stamps, signature, positions and the date to sign.

English contracts' structures depend on the types. The general contracts contain the following: the Head, Habendum, Attestation, Schedule and the End.

1. The Preamble

Contracts start with preambles. The Preamble clarifies the name of the contract, the contract number, the signing date and place, the concerned parties' full names, the registered places and contact method, the preface which includes the basic situation of each party, the purposes and the principles of the contract and definition of the addressed terms of the parties involved in the contract.

2. The Name of the Contract

The name of the contract should state the feature of the contract, e.g.:

Consulting Contract on Beer Market Research in Hubei Province

Joint Venture Contract on... Thermal Power Company

Confidentiality Agreement with Employees

Know-how Contract for...

Besides, the Original or Copy are put on the upper right.

3. Contract Number

The contract number is usually made up of the year, the code of the company and the division, e.g., 03CMEC, DA006. "03" refers to the year of 2003; "CMEC" is China Machinery Export Company; "DA" stands for Depart A; "006" means the sixth document.

4. The Address of the Parties

Example:

The legal addresses of the parties of this contract:...

5. Definition of the Parties

In order to state easily, the parts who sign the contract can be referred to by each brief names or "Party A" and "Party B", even "Party C", "Party D" and the like when more parties are involved in the contract.

Example 1

This JOINT VENTURE AGREEMENT ("AGREEMENT") is made as of June 3, 1998, by and between E * TRADE GROUP, INC., a Delaware corporation ("E * TRADE"), and SOFTBANK CORP., a Japanese corporation ("SOFTBANK"). E * TRADE and SOFTBANK are hereunder also referred to collectively as the "PARTIES" and individually as a "PARTY".

Example 2

THIS DEVELOPMENT AND SUPPLY AGREEMENT (the "Agreement") is entered into and is effective as of June 30, 1995 (the "Effective Date"), by and between JetFax, Inc., a corporation duly organized and existing under the laws of Delaware, U.S.A. with its principal place of business at 1376 Willow Road, Menlo Park, California 94025 ("JetFax"), and Samsung Electronics Corporation, a corporation duly organized and existing under the laws of the Republic of Korea, having its principal place of business at 20th Floor, Severance Building, 84-11, 5-Ka, Namdaemoon-Ro, Chung-Ku, Seoul, Korea ("Samsung").

6. The preface

1) Background of the Contract

(1) Background of Each Party(such as the occupation of each):

Example 1

AMD engages through its Communication Products Division ("CPD") in the design, development, manufacture and sale of telecommunication products for public communications infrastructure systems, customer premise equipment and cordless telephony applications.

Example 2

This JOINT VENTURE AGREEMENT is made as of June 3, 1998, by and between TRADE GROUP, INC., a Delaware corporation ("TRADE"), and SOFTBANK CORP., a Japanese corporation ("SOFTBANK"). TRADE and SOFTBANK are hereinafter also referred to collectively as the "PARTIES" and individually as a "PARTY".

(2) Purpose of the Contract:

Example 1

The Parties desire to form a joint venture to provide online securities trading services to residents of Japan on the terms and subject to the conditions set forth herein.

Example 2

The parties intend to share revenues generated by the Health Category, as well as revenues generated by similar activities conducted by McKesson using the AvantGo software on behalf of McKesson's customers, but do not intend to share revenues arising from the operations of their respective core businesses.

(3) Background of the Contract:

Example 1

This Agreement is being executed and delivered simultaneously with the execution and delivery of the Agreement and Plan of Merger dated December 13, 1999 (the "Merger Agreement") among Union Oil, the Company, Sub and Titan.

Example 2

Pursuant to a Stockholders Agreement entered into simultaneously with the execution and delivery of this Agreement, Union Oil will have the right to nominate certain persons ("Designees") to serve on the board of directors of the Company following the Merger. Certain of the designees may be directors of or employed by Union Oil or companies in which Union Oil has an interest, other than the Company and its subsidiaries.

2) Each Party's Intention to Sign the Contract

Example 1

NOW THEREFORE, IN CONSIDERATION OF the mutual promises and covenants set forth in this Agreement, the Parties agree as follows:

Example 2

NOW THEREFORE, for valuable consideration, the receipt and adequacy of which are hereby acknowledged, the Parties hereby agree as follows:

Example 3

This contract is signed by and between the Buyer and the Seller, according to the terms and conditions stipulated below.

7. Habendum

The Habendum is the main body of a contact, including each party's responsibilities, rights, obligations and other agreement. The habendums vary from each other in content due to the various types of contracts, for example, an international sales contract's habendum has:

- commodity and Specifications
- quality
- quantity
- price
- time of Shipment
- insurance
- packing
- shipping Mark
- guarantee of Quality
- inspection and Claims
- terms of Payment
- terms of Shipment
- force Majeure
- late Delivery and Penalty
- arbitration

While the complete Habendum contains the following:

- definition
- representations and Warranties
- conditions Precedent
- limited Liability or Limitation of Liability

- non-disclosure or No Publicity
- termination
- headings
- validity of the Contract
- waiver
- amendment or Modification
- assignment or Successors and Assignment
- notice
- governing Law or Applicable Law
- dispute Resolution
- severability or Survival of Terms
- no other relation
- force Majeure
- entire Agreement
- execution by Fax
- language
- counterparts
- ambiguities
- currency

8. Definition

This clause is to define some terms in the contract to ensure the constant meanings and avoid discrepancy. These terms are categorized into two types. One is common words in English contract, such as "Affiliate and Financial Statements". Another is words with special meanings in the particular contracts.

Example

> As used in this Contract, the following terms shall have the following meanings (such meanings as necessary to be equally applicable to both the singular and plural forms of the terms defined):
>
> "Contract" means this Contract, all written amendments, modifications and supplements hereto, all Scope Change Orders, and the Appendices hereto which by this reference are incorporated herein:
>
> "Application for Payment" shall have the meaning set forth in Section 4.2 hereof.

9. Representations and Warranties

This clause is to represent some basic facts and promise its truth, which is the premise of the contract to be signed and affected. It contains mainly: Organization, Standing and Qualification; Capitalization; Due Authorization; Liabilities; Status of Proprietary Assets; Title to Properties and Assets; Material Contracts and Obligations; Litigation and Arbitration; Compliance with Laws; Governmental Consents; Compliance with Other Instruments and Agreements and Disclosure.

10. Attestation

Example

BEFORE ME, a Notary Public in and for said County, personally appeared Timothy J. Gunter and Daniel L. Webb, known to me to be the person(s) who, as Secretary and Assistant Secretary, respectively, of INDUSTRIAL DEVELOPMENTS INTERNATIONAL, INC., the corporation which executed the foregoing instrument in its capacity as Landlord, signed the same, and acknowledged to me that they did so sign said instrument in the name and upon behalf of said corporation as officers of said corporation, that the same is their free act and deed as such officers, respectively, and they were duly authorized thereunto by its board of directors; and that the seal affixed to said instrument is the corporate seal of said corporation.

IN TESTIMONY WHEREOF, I have hereunto subscribed my name, and affixed my official seal, this 15th day of March, 1999.

11. The End

The end contains the expiry date, the law complied with, the parties' signatures and the remarks.

Example

This Contract shall come into effect after signature by the both parties. This Contract is made out in two original copies, one copy to be held by each party.

12. Structure Samples

The following are the structure samples of Singapore, U.S.A, Hong Kong and Japan.

Example 1: Singapore

Agreement

THIS AGREEMENT is made the 9th day of August, 2001 between LUCKY INTERNATIONAL LTD, a company incorporated in Singapore and having its registered office at Telek Blongar Rise, Singapore 19569 (hereinafter called "The Company") of the part and JACK Wong (NRIC No. ________/A) of 108 Orchar Road, Singapore 01688 (hereinafter called "The Manager") of the other part.

WHEREAS:

1. The company is engaged in IT business and requires a person with the necessary qualifications and experience to manage its business.

2. ...

NOW IT IS HEREBY AGREED as follows:

1. The company shall employ the Manager and the Manager shall serve the Company as manager of the Company's IT business for a period of two years commencing on 1st day of September.

2. …

IN WITNESS WHEREOF, the parties hereto have set their hand the day and year first above written.

THE SCHEDULE ABOVE REFERRED TO

Duties of Manger

1. To manage, maintain and promote the business of the Company.

2.

3.

SIGNED by Roger Tan

For and on behalf of LUCKY INTERANTIONAL LTD.

In the presence of

SIGNED by TERESA WONG

In the presence of

Singaporean common contract contains 5 parts:

(1) Parties

It mainly introduces each party's names, registered country and place, post code and the abbreviated names in the contract.

The common opening structure is:

THIS AGREEMENT is made the – – – – – – – – – ________ day of ________ (month), ________ (year) between A ________ (hereinafter called "The Company") of the part and B ________, (hereinafter called "The Manager") of the other part.

(2) Recital

It is begun with WHEREAS to state the cause for the parties to sign the contract.

(3) Habendum

Habendum stipulates each party's rights and obligations. The ending paragraph is:

IN WITNESS WHEREOF, the parties hereto have set their hand the day and year first above written.

This paragraph is used like "to certify with each signature and stamp" in Chinese contract.

(4) Schedule or Addendum

Schedule or addendum is the necessary supplement to the provisions in the contracts. It is not necessarily involved in every contract.

(5) Attestation

If the concerned are natural people, they put their name in "SIGNED by ________". The witnesses write their name in "In the presence of ________". If the concerned are artificial people, they put their signatures in "SIGNED for and on behalf ________ of ________", followed by "In the presence of ________". Compared with Chinese contracts, Singaporean Contracts have "In the presence of ________" to sign the witnesses' names. Another difference is the date to sign is put in the opening paragraph rather than the end of the contract.

Attestation in Singapore has another way to express:

As Witness our Hands this ________ day of ________, in the year of our Lord Tow Thousand and One.

Signed, sealed, and delivered by the above named.

In the presence of

Signature

Address

Occupation

The above contract structure is typical as an English contract. Other contracts are similar in term of structure.

Example 2: U.S.A

APPOINTMENT AS CONTRACT FULL-TIME SENIOR CUSTOMS ADMINISTRATOR

AN AGREEMENT FOR SERVICES made the 1st day of September, 2000 between ________ of ________ (address)(hereinafter referred to as "the Company") as one part and Mr. ________ of ________ (address) (hereinafter referred to as the Contractor) of the other part.

WHEREBY IT IS AGREED AND DECLARED AS FOLLOWS:

1. THAT the Company shall...

2. This agreement shall commence on...

3.

4.

IN WITNESS WHEREOF, both parties set their hands on the date herein mentioned.
SIGNED BY.

Name:

Designation:

For and on behalf of: (signature)

Contractor:

Designation:

For and on behalf of: (signature)

This contract contains four parts without schedule. The structure is similar to the Singaporean contract. There is no predicate and complete sentence in the first paragraph. Besides, a few different phrases are used compared with the former contract. The inscribed is with designation or position.

Example 3: Hong Kong

CONTRACT

CONTACT NO.

SIGNING DATE/PLACE

THE BUYER: Name

Legal Address

Contact

THE SELLER: Name

Legal Address

Contact

This contract is made by and between the Buyer and the Seller.

Whereby the Buyer agrees o buy and the Seller agrees to sell the under-mentioned commodity according to the terms and conditions.

1. NAME OF COMMODITY AND SCOPE OF THE CONTRACT
2. PRICE
3. PAYMENT
4. PACKING
5.

IN WITNESS WHEREOF, this contract has been executed effective as of the date first above written.

THE BUYER	THE SELLER	THE END USER
________	________	________
By:______	By:______	By:______
Date:------------________	Date:------------________	Date: --------________

Compared with the former contracts, the differences are the opening has the contract number, the subscription date, and the concerned parties' names in brief forms. The Attestation is written in past perfect tense and passive sentence. The inscribed has the item of "the end user".

Example 4: Japanese

SERVICE AGREEMENT

This agreement is made and entered into on March 1st, 2001, by and between ______ LTD. (hereinafter referred to as "PARTY A"), and ______ CO., LTD. (hereinafter referred to as "PARTY B")

WITNESSETH:

WHEREAS, PARTY B has requested by PARTY A to dispatch its personal for the purpose of ______ to PARTY b; and

WHEREAS, (PARTY A is willing to dispatch its personnel PARTY B in response to such PARTY B's request)

NOW, THEREFORE, in consideration of the mutual promises and covenants herein contained, the parties hereto agree as follows:

1.
2.
3.

IN WITNESS WHEREOF, the parties hereto have caused this Agreement to be executed by their respective duly authorized officers as of the date first hereinabove written.

________ Ltd.	________ Co., Ltd.
(Signature)	(Signature)
MANAGING DIRECTOR	MANAGING DIRECTOR

This style is composed of four parts. The biggest difference is the new "WITNESSETH" part before the statement and no "SIGNED BY: item in the inscribed. The positions of the concerned people are typed below the signatures directly. Besides, the abbreviations of the concerned are all put in block letters.

Comparatively, English contracts are almost the same in terms of styles, sentence structures and choice of words. When an English contract is drafted, any one of the above is natural English expression and worth referring to.

5.2.2 The Verbal Characteristics of Contracts

The Verbal Characteristics of Contracts are Accurate, Formal and Professional.

1. Accurate Terms

"May", "shall", "must", "may not" (or shall not) should be used with deliberation. "May" is used to state the parties' rights; "shall" is used to describe the obligation; "must" is used to state the imperative obligations; "may not" or "shall not" is used to refer to prohibitive obligation. "May do" can be neither said to be "can do" nor "shall do". It cannot be said as "should do" or "ought to do". "May not do" can be replaced by "shall not do" in some American legal documents, but cannot be by"can not do" or "must not do". For example, when the methods to solve disputes are stipulated, we can say:

The parties hereto shall, first of all, settle any dispute arising from or in connection with the contract by friendly negotiations. Should such negotiations fail, such dispute may be referred to the People's Court having jurisdiction on such dispute for settlement in the absence of any arbitration clause in the disputed contract or in default of agreement reached after such dispute occurs.

2. Formal Terms

Contract English is of a serious style, which is a lot different from other English works, such as:

Formal Terms	Informal Terms
notwithstanding	despite/in spite of
prior to	before
as regards/ concerning/relating to	about
in effect	in fact
commencement	star/begin
cease to do	stop to do
convene a meeting	hold/call a meeting
at the close of the fiscal year	in the end of the fiscal year
miscellaneous	other matters/events
construe a contract/comprehend a contract	understand a contract"
deem	think/believe
intend to do/desire to do	want to do/wish to do

Some prepositions are typical and commonly used in contracts instead of phrases:

Formal Prepositions	Informal Phrases
hereafter	after this time
hereby	by means/reason of this
herein	in this
hereinafter	later in this contract
thereafter	afterwards
thereby	by that means
therein	from that
thereinafter	later in the same contract
whereby	by what; by which
wherein	in what; in which

3. Professional Terms

The contract is professional to ensure the accuracy. It usually has professional terms such as defect, remedy, force majuere/Act of God, jurisdiction and phrases such as hereinafter referred to as, whereas, in witness whereof, for and on behalf of, hereby, thereof. This is one of the typical features of contract English.

Professional Terms	Unprofessional Terms
indemnities	compensation
conveyance	transfer of real estate
wind up /cease a business	end/stop a business
pursuant to provisions contained herein/as provided herein	according to relevant terms and conditions in the contract
tenancy of houses/ lease of property	rent
neither party hereto may assign this contract	neither party to the contract

4. Sequence of Synonyms, Near Synonyms and Related Words

FOR value RECEIVED, the undersigned does hereby *sell*, *transfer*, *assign and set over* to ________ all his *right*, *tile and interest* in and to a certain contract dated ________, 19 ________ by and between the undersigned and ________, a copy of which is annexed hereto.

The sequent Synonyms, Near Synonyms such as sell, transfer, assign and set over, right, tile and interest in the above is quite common in English contract. This is out of deliberation and prevention of loopholes. Sometimes it is due to the fixed mode of contract words, for example:

This agreement is *made and entered into by and between* Party A and Party B.

For and in consideration of mutual covenants and agreements contained herein, the parties hereby *covenant and agree* as follows:

The parties have agreed to vary the Management *on the terms* and *subject to the conditions* contained herein.

Party A wishes to be *released* and *discharged* from agreement as from the effective date.

The following documents shall be deemed to form and be read and construed as an integral part of this Contract.

Other phrases include:

ships and vessels

support and maintenance

licenses and permits

charges, fees, costs and expenses

any and all

any duties, obligations or liabilities

the partners, their heirs, successors and assigns

control and management of the partnership

applicable laws, regulations, decrees, directives, and rules

5. Latin Words

In English contracts, Latin words are often used, for example, "pro rate tax rate" is more often used than "proportional tax rate"; "pro bono lawyer" is more often used than "lawyer engaged in charitable legal assistance", etc.

5.2.3 Samples of Contracts and Agreements

Example 1

Labor Contract

Employer:

Legal Representative:

Position: President

Address: Post code:

Employee:

Name: Gender:

Address: Nationality:

ID Card No.:

Date of Birth:

Education Degree:

This Contract is signed on a mutuality voluntary basis by and between the following Employer and Employee in accordance with the Labor Law of People's Republic of China.

1. Term of the Contract

The term of this contract is for ________ years and shall commence on ________, ________, and shall continue until ________, ________, unless earlier terminated pursuant to this Contract. The Employee shall undergo a probationary period of ________ months.

2. Job Description

The Employer agrees to employ Mr./Ms. ________ (name) as ________ (job title) in ________ Department, located in ________ (office location and city).

3. Remuneration of Labor

a. The salary of the Employee shall bimonthly paid by the Employer in accordance with applicable laws and regulations of PRC. It shall be paid by legal tender and not less than the standard minimum salary in Tianjin.

b. The salary of the Employee is RMB $ ________ per month in the probationary period and RMB $ ________ after the probationary period.

c. If the delay or default of salary takes place, the Employer shall pay the economic compensation except the salary itself in accordance with the relevant laws and regulations.

4. Working Hours & Rest & Vocation

a. The normal working hours of the Employee shall be eight hours each day, excluding meals and rest for an average of five days per week, for an average of forty hours per week.

b. The Employee is entitled to all legal holidays and other paid leaves of absence in accordance with the laws and regulations of the PRC and the company 's work rules.

c. The Employer may extend working hours due to the requirements of its production or business after consultation with the trade union and the Employee, but the extended working hour for a day shall generally not exceed one hour; If such extension is called for due to special reasons, the extended hours shall not exceed three hours a day. However, the total extension in a month shall not exceed thirty-six hours.

5. Social Security & Welfare

a. The Employer will pay for all mandatory social security programs such pension insurance, unemployment insurance, medical insurance of the Employee according to the relevant government and city regulations.

b. During the period of the Contract, the Employee's welfare shall be implemented accordance with the laws and relevant regulations of PRC.

6. Working Protection & Working Conditions

a. The Employer should provide the Employee with occupational safety and health conditions conforming to the provisions of the State and necessary articles of labor protection to guarantee the safety and health during the working process.

b. The Employer should provide the Employee with safety education and technique training; The Employee to be engaged in specialized operations should receive specialized training and acquire qualifications for such special operations.

c. The Employee should strictly abide by the rules of safe operation in the process of their work.

7. Labor Discipline

a. The Employer may draft bylaws and labor disciplines of the Company, According to which, the Employer shall have the right to give rewards or take disciplinary actions to the Employee;

b. The Employee shall comply with the management directions of the Employer and obey the bylaws and labor disciplines of the Employer.

c. The Employee shall undertake the obligation to keep and not to disclose the trade secret for the Employer during the period of this Contract; This obligation of confidentiality shall survive the termination of this Contract for a period of two (2) years.

8. Termination, Modification, Renew and Discharge of the Contract

a. The relevant clauses of the Contract may be modified by the parties:

i. The specific clause is required to be modified by the parties through consultation;

ii. Due to the force majeure, the Contract can not be executed;

iii. The relevant laws and regulations have been modified or abolished by the time of signing the Contract.

b. The Contract may be automatically terminated:

i) This Contract is not renewed at the expiration of this Contract;

ii) The Employer is legally announced to be bankruptcy, dismissed, or canceled;

iii) The death of the Employee occurs;

iv) The force majeure takes place;

v) The conditions of termination agreed in the Contract by the parties arise.

c. The Contract may be renewed at the expiration through consultation by the parties with the fulfillment of the procedure within 15 days to the expiration;

d. The Contract may be discharged through consultation by the parties;

e. The Contract may be discharged by the Employer with immediate effect and the Employee will not be compensated:

i. The Employee does not meet the job requirements during the probationary period;

ii. The Employee seriously violates disciplines or bylaws of the Employer;

iii. The Employee seriously neglects his duty, engages in malpractice for selfish ends and brings significant loss to the Employer;

iv. The Employee is being punished by physical labor for its misfeasance;

v. The Employee is being charged with criminal offences.

f. The Contract may be terminated by the Employer by giving notice in written form 30(thirty) days in advance:

i. The Employee fails ill or is injured to (other than due to work) and after completion of medical treatment, is not able to perform his previous function or any other function the Employer assigns to him;

ii. The Employee does not show satisfactory performance and after training and adjusting measures is still not able to perform satisfactorily;

iii. The circumstances have materially changed from the date this Contract was signed to the extent that it is impossible to execute the Contract provided, however, that the parties cannot reach an agreement to amend the contract to reflect the changed circumstances.

iv. The Employer is being consolidated in the legal consolidation period on the brink of bankruptcy or the situation of business is seriously in trouble, under such condition, it is required to reduce the employee. (in legal procedure)

g. The Employee shall not be dismissed:

i. The Contract has neither expired nor conformed to 8.d, 8.e, 8.f, 8.g;

ii. The Employee is ill with occupational disease or injured due to work and has been authenticated fully or partly disabled by the Labor Authentication Commission in Baodi County, Tianjin.

iii. The Employee is ill or injured (other than due to work) and is within the period of medical leave provided for by applicable PRC law and regulations and Company policy;

iv. The Employee is woman who is pregnant, on maternity leave, or nursing a baby under one year of age; or

iii. The applicable PRC laws and regulations otherwise prohibit the termination of this Contract.

h. The Contract may be discharged by the Employee by giving notice in written form 30(thirty) days in advance. However, the Employee may inform the Employer to discharge the Contract at random under the following occasions:

i. The Employee is still in the probationary period;

ii. The Employer force the Employee to work by violence, duress or illegal restriction to physical freedom;

iii. The Employer does not pay the remuneration of the Employee accordance with the relevant clause in the Contract;

iv. The Employer violates the relevant regulations of State or Tianjin for its terrible safe and health condition, which is harmful to the Employee's health.

i. The Contract can not be terminated by the Employee before the expiration if not conforming to 8.d, 8.h.

j. The Employer shall pay the economic compensation to the Employer if the Contract is terminated conforming to 8.d, 8.f, and 8.h.i-8.h.iv. Additional fee for medical allowance should be paid to the Employee if the Contract is terminated conforming to 8.f.i.

9. Breach Liabilities

a. Due to either party's fault, if breaching the Contract, that party shall undertake the breach liability according to the extent to the performance of the Contract; if the parties both breach the Contract, they shall undertake its separate liability according to the concrete situation.

b. Due to either party's fault, if breaching the Contract to damage the other party. The damage should be compensated by the faulty party accordance with the relevant laws and regulations of PRC.

c. Due to the force majeure, causing the non-performance or the damages to either party, the other party may not undertake the breach liability;

d. The Employee wants to resign and has received training provided by the Employer, the Employee shall compensate for the training cost. The method of compensation should be fixed according to the relevant company regulations as follows:

The Employee shall compensate RMB ________ within ________ year(s) in the Company if the Contract is terminated by the Employee at his cause;

The Employee shall compensate RMB ________ within ________ year(s) in the Company if the Contract is terminated by the Employee at his cause;

The Employee shall compensate RMB ________ within ________ year(s) in the Company if the Contract is terminated by the Employee at his cause;

10. Labor Disputes

Where a labor dispute between the parties takes place during the performance of this Contract, the parties concerned may seek for a settlement through consultation; or either party may apply to the labor dispute mediation committee of their unit for mediation; if the mediation fails and one of the parties requests for arbitration, that party may apply to the labor dispute arbitration committee for arbitration. Either party may also directly apply to the labor dispute arbitration committee for arbitration within 60 days starting from the date of the occurrence of a labor dispute. If one of the parties is not satisfied with the adjudication of arbitration, the party may bring the case to a people's court within 15 days of the date of receiving the ruling of arbitration

The verification of this Contract shall be made in Baodi Labor Bureau, Tianjin within 30 days after being signed by the parties.

Employer: (official stamp) Employee:

Representative:

Address: Address:

Date: July, 2003

It's verified herein that the Contract conforms to the relevant laws and regulations through examination and review.

Authority;

Clerk:

Example 2

Sales Contract

Date: Contract No.:

The Buyers: The Seller:

This contract is made by and between the Buyers and the Sellers; whereby the Buyers agree to buy and the Sellers agree to sell the under-mentioned goods subject to the terms and conditions as stipulated hereinafter:

(1) Name of Commodity:

(2) Quantity:

(3) Unit price:

(4) Total Value:

(5) Packing:

(6) Country of Origin:

(7) Terms of Payment:

(8) Insurance:

(9) Time of Shipment:

(10) Port of Lading:

(11) Port of Destination:

(12) Claims:

Within 45 days after the arrival of the goods at the destination, should the quality, Specifications or quantity be found not in conformity with the stipulations of the contract except those claims for which the insurance company or the owners of the vessel are liable, the Buyers shall, have the right on the strength of the inspection certificate issued by the C. C. I. C and the relative documents to claim for compensation to the Sellers.

(13) Force Majeure:

The sellers shall not be held responsible for the delay in shipment or non-deli-very of the goods due to Force Majeure, which might occur during the process of manufacturing or in the course of loading or transit. The sellers shall advise the Buyers immediately of the occurrence mentioned above the within fourteen days thereafter. The Sellers shall send by airmail to the Buyers for their acceptance a certificate of the accident. Under such circumstances the Sellers, however, are still under the obligation to take all necessary measures to hasten the delivery of the goods.

Example 3

Exclusive Patent License Agreement

This agreement is made and entered into between ________, a ________ established under ________ law (hereinafter called Licensor) having its principle office at ________, and ________ a for-profit corporation organized under the laws of ________ (hereinafter called Licensee), having its principle office at ________.

Witnesseth that:

1. whereas Licensor has the right to grant licenses under the licensed patent rights (as hereinafter defined), and wishes to have the inventions covered by the licensed patent rights in the public interest; and

2. whereas Licensee wishes to obtain a license under the licensed patent rights upon the terms & conditions hereinafter set forth:

Now, therefore, in consideration of the premises and the faithful performance of the covenants herein contained it is agreed as follows:

Article I - DEFINITIONS

For the purpose of this agreement, the following definitions shall apply:

1. **Licensed Patent Rights**: Shall mean:

a. Patent Application Serial No.. ________ filed ________ by ________.

Or

New Plant Variety registered and protected through ________.

b. Any and all improvements developed by Licensor, whether patentable or not, relating to the Licensed Patent Rights, which Licensor may now or may hereafter develop, own or control.

c. Any or all patents, which may issue on patent rights and improvements thereof, developed by Licensor and any and all divisions, continuations, continuations-in-part, reissues and extensions of such patents.

2. **Product(s)**: Shall mean any materials including plants and/or seeds, compositions, techniques, devices, methods or inventions relating to or based on the Licensed Patent Rights, developed on the date of this agreement or in the future.

3. **Gross Sales:** Shall mean total ________(Currency Unit) value(s) of Product(s) FOB manufactured based on the Licensed Patent Rights.

4. **Confidential Proprietary Information:** Shall mean with respect to any Party all scientific, business or financial information relating to such Party, its subsidiaries or affiliates or their respective businesses, except when such information:

a. Becomes known to the other Party prior to receipt from such first Party;

b. Becomes publicly known through sources other than such first Party;

c. Is lawfully received by such other Party from a party other than the first Party; or

d. Is approved for release by written authorization from such first Party.

5. **Exclusive License:** Shall mean a license, including the right to sublicense, whereby Licensee's rights are sole and entire and operate to exclude all others, including Licensor and its affiliates except as otherwise expressly provided herein.

6. **Know-how:** Shall mean any and all technical data, information, materials, trade secrets, technology, formulas, processes, and ideas, including any improvements thereto, in any form in which the foregoing may exist, now owned or co-owned by or exclusively, semi-exclusively or non-exclusively licensed to any party prior to the date of this Agreement or hereafter acquired by any party during the term of this agreement.

7. **Intellectual Property Rights:** Shall mean any and all inventions, materials, Know-how, trade secrets, technology, formulas, processes, ideas or other discoveries conceived or reduced to practices, whether patentable or not.

8. **Royalty (ies):** Shall mean revenues received in the form of cash and/or equity from holdings from Licensees as a result of licensing and using, selling, making, having made, sublicensing or leasing of Licensed Patent Rights.

ARTICLE Ⅱ - GRANT OF EXCLUSIVE LICENSE

1. Licensor hereby grants to Licensee the exclusive (worldwide, option) license with the right to sublicense others, to make, have made, use, sell and lease the Products described in the Licensed Patent Rights.

2. Licensor retains the right to continue to use Licensed Patent Rights in any way for non-commercial purposes.

3. It is understood by the Licensee that the Licensed Patent Rights were developed under ________ Grant No. ________. The ________ Government has a non-exclusive royalty free license for governmental purposes.

ARTICLE Ⅲ - LICENSE PAYMENTS

1. **Initial payment and royalty rate.** For the licensed herein granted:

a. Licensee agrees to pay a sign-up fee of ________ ( ).

b. Licensee shall pay on earned royalty of ________ percent (%) of Licensee's Gross Sales of Products and fifty percent (50%) of the sublicensing receipts.

c. Licensee shall pay an annual royalty of ________ ( ) for each leased Product.

2. **Sublicenses.** The granting and terms of all sublicenses is entirely at **Licensee's** discretion provided that all sublicenses shall be subjected to the terms and conditions of this agreement.

3. **Minimum royalty:** Licensee will pay Licensor, when submitting their royalty report a minimum royalty of ________ ( ) annually.

4. **When a sale is made:** A sale of Licensed Patent Rights shall be regarded as being made upon payment for Products made using Licensed Patent Rights.

5. **Payments:** All sums payable by Licensee hereunder shall be paid to Licensor in ______ (name of country) and in the currency of the ______ or in U.S. dollars.

6. **Interest:** In the event any royalties are not paid as specified herein, then a compound interest of eighteen percent (18%) shall be due in addition to the royalties accrued for the period of default.

Example 4

LEASE AGREEMENT

Contract No.:

This lease agreement (hereinafter referred to as this "***Agreement***") is executed in Shanghai, People's Republic of China ("PRC") by and between:

Landlord ("Party A"):
Address:
Legal Representative:
Postal Code:
Telephone:
Fax:
Business License No.:

Tenant ("Party B"):
Address:
Legal Representative:
Postcode:
Tel:
Fax:
Business License:

Pursuant to ***The Contract Law of People's Republic of China***, ***The Regulations on Lease of Real Estate in Shanghai***, on basis of equality, free-will, fairness and good faith, through consultation, Party A and Party B hereby enter into this Agreement on subject matter of leasing the premise by Party B from Party A as follows:

1. Legal Status of Parties and Certificates

1.1 Part A is a PRC legal person legally formed under license issued by PRC government, responsible for the development, construction and management of the in Shanghai.

1.2 Part B is a PRC legal person legally formed under license issued by PRC government.

1.3 Party B shall provide the copy of his business license to Party A.

2. Party's Acknowledgement and Warranties

2.1 Except as otherwise stipulated in this Agreement, both Party A and Party B acknowledge and warrant that:

(1) they have had the necessary power, capacity, authorization and ability for the execution and performance of this Agreement; they have been fully aware of and understood their respective rights, obligations and liabilities hereof and they are willing to exercise or perform foregoing rights, obligations and liabilities in strict compliance with the provisions of this Agreement, and either Party is entitled to claim damages against the other Party if the other Party breaches this Agreement.

(2) both Parties' internal approval formalities required for execution hereof have been completed.

(3) there is no contract signed with third party or any other maters, whatsoever, which will preclude the execution and performance of this Agreement.

2.2 Party A warrants that it has, up till the date of this Agreement, legally obtained the title certificate and/or presale certificate for the Premises (defined in Article 3.1) with serial numbers as follows:

The Title Certificate of Real Estate in Shanghai (________) or,

The Presale Certificate of Commodity Housing in Shanghai (_______) or,

(1) The certificate of Land Use Right (________) or the Approval of Land Construction (________) and,

(2) The Planning Certificate of Construction Project.

3. Conditions of Premises

3.1 The premises provided by Party A to Party B is located at ________(collectively "*Premises*"; separately "________") in ________. The type of the Premises is ________. The estimated construction area is approximately _______ square meters.

Party A and Party B agree to have the final construction areas of Premises measured and determined by authorized institute of Shanghai Real Estate Bureau; Accordingly, the total amount of year rental will accordingly be adjusted on the basis of the day rental agreed by two Parties in Article 6.1 hereof, and any overpayment shall be refunded and any deficiency should be made up by supplement payment.

3.2 Party A, as the owner of the Premises, hereby builds up the lease relationship with Party B. Before the execution hereof, Party A notified Party B that there was no mortgage of whatever kinds on the Premises.

3.3 The Premises have ferroconcrete structures, the pressure intensity load of the First Floor is ________ kg per square meter, and of the Second Floor and the rest floors above the Second floor is ________ kg per square meter. (or, the average loading capacity of the Premise is ________ kg/square meter).

3.4 The design electricity supply capacity for each floor in the Premise is ________ kW, single-loop electricity supply. If the electricity consumption exceeds ________ kW in each floor, then Party B shall apply to power supply administrative authority and bear relevant costs. (or, the electricity consumption of Party B shall not exceed the distributed supply capacity calculated on the base of the construction area).

4. Purpose of Lease

4.1 Party B undertakes to lease the Premises for conducting commercial activities within the approved scope stipulated in his business license and to comply with the relevant state and local laws and regulations in respect of property utilization as well as the rules of ________ with regards to the industry development, environment protection and property management.

4.2 Party B warrants not to change the purpose of lease specified in Article 4.1 during the Term (defined in Article 5.1) without Party A's written consent and approval by administrative authority (if necessary).

5. Handover Date and Lease Term

5.1 Both Parties agree that the lease term ("***Term***") for the Premises is from ________ to ________. The Rental commence date is ________ ("***Commence Date***").

5.2 Upon the expiry of the Term, Party A shall has the right to take back and Party B shall return the occupation of the Premises on due time. Any request for renewing the lease of the Premises by Party B shall be notified in writing to Party A three (3) months prior to the expiry hereof; and Party A shall give reply of agreeing or not within one (1) month upon receipt of such notice. If agree, both Parties shall enter into renewal agreement. Party A has the right to adjust the articles in the renewal agreement, such as articles in respect of rent. If no agreement be reach on articles in respect of rent, Party A has the right to terminate this Agreement and take back the occupation of the Premise upon the expiry of the Term.

6. Rent, Payment and Period

6.1 Party A and Party B agree that the charge rate of the rent for the Premises is RMB per square meter per day and the year rental amounts to RMB ________.

6.2 The rent of the Premise shall be paid in advance. Party B agrees to pay, before ________, the first installment of the period from ________ to ________ with the amount of RMB yuan(________ in words). Thereafter, in each year, the rent shall be paid in four installments on and before every following date: January 1, April 1, July 1 and October 1, with 25% of the year rental for each installment. If the last due date of each installment is Saturday, Sunday or any of other statutory holidays, the immediately subsequent working day shall be the last due date. For any delay in payment of the foregoing, a delay charge at 0.05% of the due rent per day shall be paid by Party B.

7. Deposit and Other Fees

7.1 Both Parties agree that, Party B shall pay a deposit for leasing the Premises equal to three (3) months rentals, i.e. RMB ________, within ten (10) days from the date as of the execution hereof ("***Deposit***"). Party A shall provide receipt to Party A after receiving the aforesaid Deposit.

During the Term, Party B shall not offset any rental payments with the Deposit. Upon expiry of the Term, Party B shall pay off all relevant fees and within ten (10) days after Party B completing all formalities in respect of returning the Premise, Party A shall return the Deposit without any interests to Party B. Party A may deduct from the Deposit any unpaid amount and such amount as equal to Party A's economic losses due to Party B's causes and return the rest to Party B without any interests.

7.2 During the Term, all relevant fees in respect of water, electricity, gas, communication, facilities for using the Premises shall be born by Party B.

7.3 Party B shall be solely responsible for applying to the relevant government authorities for the water and gas supply and electricity in the Premises, and bear all relevant costs.

7.4 Party B shall enter into relevant property management agreement with the property management company in the block where the Premises located before the Handover Date and pay the agreed management fee stipulated in such property management agreement. The current fee is RMB ________ per square meters (construction area) per month.

8. Requirements on Using of Premise and Maintenance Obligation

8.1 During the Term, if Party B finds any damages of the Premises or affiliated facilities due to nature causes, he shall immediately notify the property management company authorized by Party A to repair such damages. Party B shall actively assist and cooperate for the repair. Party B shall be responsible for consequences of any delayed repair due to his act or not acting.

8.2 During the Term, Party B shall reasonably use and protect the Premises and the affiliated facilities; Party B shall be responsible for repairing any man-made damages and faults and bearing the relevant costs.

8.3 During the Term, Party A shall ensure the Premises and affiliated facilities are under a normal, usable and secure condition. Party A may inspect and maintain the Premise and Party B shall cooperate with Party A. Party A shall reduce the impact on Party B's use of the Premises.

8.4 Except the fitments and facilities originally provided in the Premises, Party B may fit out or install other facilities affixed to the Premises subject to Party A's prior written consent and upon completion of relevant formalities with property management department and if required by any regulations, the approval from relevant government authorities in advance.

8.5 Upon the termination and release hereof, Party B shall be responsible for reinstate the Premises, to which alteration and added work have been done, to the original conditions except reasonable wear and tear. After Party A's inspection and acceptance of the Premises, Party B may complete other formalities in respect of returning the Premises.

9. Condition of Premises on Return

9.1 Excepted as being agreed by Party A for renewing the lease of the Premises by Party B and signing renewal agreement, Party B shall return the Premises upon the expiry of the Term or upon the release or termination hereof due to any reason; if Party B delays the return of the Premises without Party A's consent, Party B shall pay an amount equal to two (2) time of the day rental for each day of delay as a charge for occupying the Premise. Party B agrees that, if he delays return of the Premises on its original conditions for more than fifteen (15) days, Party A will have the right to enter into the Premises while Party B will be deemed as waiving his ownership or rights (whatsoever) to all fit-out, facilities, equipments and all other goods which has not been then dismantled or moved out of the Premise, including but not limited to facilities and goods which is regarded as belonging to Party B (in regardless of such facilities and goods in actual belonging to Party B or to third party), Party B may at his sole discretion dispose all the above and if any third party's legitimate right shall according affected, Party B shall be responsible for compensating such third party. Any costs for reinstate the Premise shall be born by Party B. The Premises shall be deemed as taken back as of the date on which Party A enters into the Premises.

9.2 Party B shall return the Premise on such conditions as being normally used. On return, the Premises shall be inspected and accepted by Party A and both Parties shall settle the relevant fee to be born by each Party respectively.

10. Sublease and Assignment

10.1 The tenant will have the right to sublease the whole or part of the premise to any of its subsidiaries or affiliated companies. Unless otherwise agreed by Party A in the supplementary terms of this Contract or in other written documents, Party B shall not sub-lease any part or all of the Premises to any third party within the lease term.

10.2 During the lease term, if Party A decides to sell the premise, Party A shall notify Party B in advance with a written notice. Party B shall have priority of purchasing of the premises under the same conditions.

11. Conditions of Early Termination

11.1 Both Parties agree that during the Term, this Agreement could be early terminated with no Party bears any (breach) liabilities against the other when any of the followings occur:

(1) The land use right to the site on which the Premises located shall be taken back in advance pursuant to laws;

(2) The Premises shall be expropriated for social and public welfare;

(3) The Premises shall fall into the scope of housing dismantlement and removal as need by urban construction;

(4) The Premises shall become damaged, destroyed or recognized as dangerous constructions.

11.2 Both Parties agree that, either Party may, by written notice to the other, terminate this Agreement if any of the followings occurs. The breaching Party shall pay to the other a damages equal to two (2) times of the monthly rental as decided according to the foregoing provisions; and if such damages is insufficient to cover the losses incurred on the other from the breach, the breaching Party shall also indemnify the insufficient part.

(1) Party A fails to deliver the Premises on time and the failure persists for ten days after Party B's notice of such failure;

(2) the Premises delivered by Party A does not conform to the provisions hereunder, preventing the fulfillment of the purpose of the lease;

(3) Party B alters the purpose of the Premises without Party A's prior written consent, resulting in damages to the Premises;

(4) The Premises are damaged for reason attributable to Party B;

(5) By infringing the stipulations of this contract, Party B arbitrarily sub-leases the Premises, assigns its right to any third party, as the lessee, to lease the Premises, or exchange the leased premises with any third party;

(6) Party B delays the payment of rent and such delay exceeds for over one (1) month;

(7) Party B uses the Premises for conducting illegal activities.

12. Breach

12.1 During the Term, Party A shall be responsible for compensating direct financial losses or personal injury incurred by Party B arising from the damages of the Premise due to Party A's delay in performing of his obligation of maintenance under this Agreement.

12.2 Party A shall not fit out or install facilities affixed to the Premises without or beyond the scope of Party A's written consent, otherwise Party A may require Party B to reinstate the Premise to the original condition and indemnify Party A's losses (if any).

12.3 During the Term, if Party A early terminates this Agreement in conditions other than those provided in this Agreement and takes back the occupation of the Premises, Party A shall pay the damages equal to half of rentals for the rest diays (but in no case exceeding three (3) months rentals). If the damages is not sufficient to cover Party B's losses, Party A shall be responsible for the insufficient part.

12.4 During the Term, if Party B early terminates the Term in conditions other than those provided in this Agreement, he shall pay the damages equal to half of rentals for the rest days (but in no case exceeding three (3) months rentals). If the damages is not sufficient to cover Party A's losses, Party B shall be responsible for the insufficient part. Party A may deduct the damages from the Deposit and Party B shall pay for any insufficient part (if any) for such deduction.

12.5 When a breach occurs, the non-breaching Party may select to terminate (subject to the conditions for early termination agreed in this Agreement) or continue the performance of this Agreement. If the non-breaching Party request to continue the performance hereof, the breaching Party must continue to perform this Agreement no matter whether he has paid the damages, indemnities or delay charges.

13. Miscellaneous

13.1 Any mortgage to be set on the Premises by Party A during the Term shall be notified to Party B in writing.

13.2 During the Term, Party B has the right to use the public corridor, stairs, elevators, lobby, public toilet and fire control facilities in addition to the Premises. Party B shall not have any flammable, explosive or poisonous goods deposited in the Premises or occupy any other place except those provided in this Agreement without due authorization. During the Term, Party B shall be solely responsible for his own asset and procure necessary insurances therefore with all relevant premiums born by Party B himself.

13.3 Any matters of Party B in connection with flammables, explosive, noise and "Three Kinds of Wastes" i.e. exhaust gas, waste water, waste residue and etc, shall be submitted for prior approvals by Developing Zone and relevant government authorities of Shanghai as meeting the safety and disposal criterion before starting-up. Party B shall start the work of second fit-out upon approvals by government authority administrating fire control.

13.4 If any Party hereto is prevented from performing any articles hereof due to war (regardless of such war has been declared or not), earthquake, typhoon, floods and fire, etc (collectively, "***Force Majeure***"), the affected Party shall immediately notify the other Party in writing and within fifteen (15) days provide the other Party with the detail information of Force Majeure, reasons for not performing or delay in performance of this Agreement, and effective supporting materials and documents.

Party A and Party B may consult and determine to terminate, release in part or delay the performance of this Agreement in light of the impact of the Force Majeure on the performance thereof.

13.5 This Agreement is governed by, and executed, construed and performed pursuant to PRC laws, regulations, local regulations and rules. Any disputes arising out of this Agreement shall be resolved pursuant to the foregoing PRC laws, regulations, local regulations and rules.

13.6 Any disputes arising out of or in connection with the performance hereof shall be resolved in the first instance though friendly consultation by both Parties; and if fail this, either Party may bring an action to the People's Court in Shanghai which has the jurisdiction. The court judgment shall be binding upon both Parties.

13.7 Shall there be anything not contained in this Agreement, both Parties may, through consultation, reach written agreement as an integral part of this Agreement, having the same effect herewith.

This Agreement may be amended by unanimous agreement of both Parties. No amendments shall come into effect unless being in written form and executed by the legal or authorized representatives of both parties. Before such amendments being effect, both Parties shall perform this Agreement pursuant to the provisions hereof.

13.8 Both Party A and Party B have complete civil right of conduct, are fully aware of and understand respective rights, obligations and liabilities, are willing to perform this Agreement in strict compliance with the provisions hereof. If one Party breaches this Agreement, the other Party is entitled to claim damages against such one Party.

13.9 All notices, documents and materials from one Party to the other in connection with the performance hereof shall be fax to the aforesaid number or delivering to the aforesaid address. If either Party changes his communicating address or telephone number, he shall notify the other Party in writing. Any notice so served by hand, fax or post shall be deemed to have been duly given:

(1) in the case of delivery by hand, when delivered and signed by the other Party;

(2) in the case of fax, at the time of completion of transmission;

(3) in the case of post, on the date of posting.

13.10 This Agreement shall come into effect as of the date on which the legal or authorized representatives of both Parties execute this Agreement.

13.11 This Agreement is made in two (2) originals with each Party holding one (1) original.

Party A:	Party B:
Legal/Authorized Representative	Legal/ Authorized Representative:
Signature:	Signature:
Date:	Date:
Bank:	Bank:
Bank Account:	Bank Account:

Section Two Language Handbook

Useful Words and Expressions

contract parties 合同当事人

contractual liability/obligation 合同规定的义务

expiration of contract 合同期满

renewal of contract 合同的续订

to make/ place /enter into/ sign a contract 签订合同

to draw up a contract 拟订合同

to draft a contract 起草合同

originals of the contract 合同正本

copies of the contract 合同副本

contract terms (or contract clause) 合同条款

contract provisions/stipulations 合同规定

contract period (or contract term) 合同期限

to be stipulated in the contract 在合同中予以规定

to be laid down in the contract 在合同中列明

to bring a contract into effect 使合同生效

to be stipulated in the contract 在合同中予以规定

to be laid down in the contract 在合同中列明

to bring a contract into effect 使合同生效

to come / go/enter into force 生效
to cease to be in effect/force 失效
to execute/implement/fulfill/perform /carry out a contract 执行合同
to honor the contract 尊重合同
to alter/modify the contract 修改合同
to approve the contract 审批合同
to abide by the contract 遵守合同
completion of contract 完成合同
interpretation of contract 解释合同
expiration of contract 合同期满
renewal of contract 合同的续订
to terminate the contract 解除合同
cancellation of contract 撤销合同
to annual the contract 废除合同
breach of contract 违反合同
to break the contract 毁约
to go back on one's words 反悔
agency agreement 代理协议
agreement on general terms and conditions on business 一般经营交易条件的协议
agreement on loan facilities up to a given amount 商定借款协议
agreement fixing price 共同定价协议
agreement on import licensing procedure 进口许可证手续协议
bilateral trade agreement 双边贸易协议
commercial agreement 商业协定
compensation trade agreement 补偿贸易协议
distributorship agreement 销售协议
exclusive distributorship agreement 独家销售协议
guarantee agreement 担保协议
international trade agreement 国际贸易协议
joint venture agreement 合营协议
licensing agreement 许可证协议
loan agreement 贷款协议
management agreement 经营管理协议
multilateral trade agreement 多边贸易协议
operating agreement 经营协议
partnership agreement 合伙契约
supply agreement 供货合同
agency contract 代理合同
barter contract 易货合同

compensation trade contact 补偿贸易合同
cross license contract 互换许可证合同
exclusive license contract 独家许可证合同
forward contract 期货合同

Useful Sentences

Any annex is the integral part of this contract. The annex and this contract are equally valid.

本合同附件是本合同的有效组成部分,与本合同具有同等法律效力。

There are 2 originals of this contract. Each party will hold 1 original(s).

本合同壹式贰份,甲、乙双方各执一份。

Other special terms will be listed bellows:

甲、乙双方如有特殊约定,可在本款另行约定:

Insurance: To be effected by buyers for 110% of full invoice value covering ________ up to ________ only.

保险:由卖方按发票全额110%投保至________为止的________险。

By confirmed, irrevocable, transferable and divisible L/C to be available by sight draft to reach the sellers before ________/________/________ and to remain

买方须于________年________月________日将保兑的、不可撤销的、可转让、可分割的即期信用证开到卖方。信用证议付有效期延至上列装运期后15天在中国到期,该信用证中必须注明允许分运及转运。

Either party shall not be held responsible for failure or delay to perform all or any part of this agreement due to flood, fire, earthquake, draught, war or any other events which could not be predicted, controlled, avoided or overcome by the relative party. However, the party affected by the event of Force Majeure shall inform the other party of its occurrence in writing as soon as possible and thereafter send a certificate of the event issued by the relevant authorities to the other party within 15 days after its occurrence.

由于水灾、火灾、地震、干旱、战争或协议一方无法预见、控制、避免和克服的其他事件导致不能或暂时不能全部或部分履行本协议,该方不负责任。但是,受不可抗力事件影响的一方须尽快将发生的事件通知另一方,并在不可抗力事件发生15天内将有关机构出具的不可抗力事件的证明寄交对方。

All disputes arising from the execution of this agreement shall be settled through friendly consultations. In case no settlement can be reached, the case in dispute shall then be submitted to the Foreign Trade Arbitration Commission of the China Council for the Promotion of International Trade for Arbitration in accordance with its Provisional Rules of Procedure. The decision made by this commission shall be regarded as final and binding upon both parties. Arbitration fees shall be borne by the losing party, unless otherwise awarded.

在履行协议过程中,如产生争议,双方应友好协商解决。若通过友好协商未能达成协议,则提交中国国际贸易促进委员会对外贸易仲裁委员会,根据该会仲裁程序暂行规定进行仲裁。该委员会决定是终局的，对双方均有约束力。仲裁费用，除另有规定外，由败诉一方负担。

This contract will be effective after being signed by both parties. Any party has no right to terminate this contract without another party's agreement. Anything not covered in this contract will be discussed separately by both parties

本合同一经双方签字后立即生效；未经双方同意，不得任意终止，如有未尽事宜，甲、乙双方可另行协商。

Exercises

Ⅰ. Write Contracts for the Following Reasons:

(1) Premises Lease
(2) Sales of International Trade
(3) Supply Agreement
(4) Agency Contract
(5) Barter Contract
(6) Compensation Trade Contract
(7) Exclusive License Contract
(8) Employment

Ⅱ. Write a Contract with the Following Information:

合同号码：PC0102325
卖方：美国 ABC 食品贸易公司
买方：中国粮油食品进出口公司
商品名称：大豆粗粉(soybean meals)
原产地：阿根廷或者巴西，由卖方选定。
规格：蛋白质(protein)最低含量 43.5%，脂肪(fat)最高含量 13%……
数量：50000 吨，10%溢短装由卖方选定。
单价：装运质量每吨 209 美元，成本加运费到天津新港。
总金额：1045 万美元
包装：散装
保险：由买方承担，按 GAFTA 规定从货物越过船舷时起。
装运港：美国旧金山
目的港：中国天津新港
唛头：由卖方选定
装运期：2005 年 10 月 20 日—11 月 20 日(含)期间不允许分装和转船。
付款方式：由 100% 合同价值的不可撤销的即期信用证付款。信用证保持在装运期后第 25 天美国议付有效。
签约地点、日期：纽约，2005 年 9 月 14 日

Ⅲ. Translate the English into Chinese for a Sales Contract.

(1) This contract is made by and between the Buyer and the Seller, whereby the Buyer agrees to buy and the Seller agrees to sell the under-mentioned commodity according to the terms and conditions stipulated below:

(2) Insurance: To be covered by the Sellers for 110% of invoice value against All Risks and War Risk as per the relevant Ocean Marine Cargo Clauses of the People's Insurance Company of China. If other coverage or an additional insurance amount is required, the Buyers must have the consent of the Sellers before shipment, and the additional premium is to be borne by the Buyers.

(3) Port of Shipment: Guangzhou, partial shipments are allowed.

(4) The Buyers shall open with a bank acceptable to the Sellers and Irrevocable Sight Letter of Credit to reach the Sellers 30 days before the month of shipment, valid for negotiation in China until the 15th day after the month of shipment.

(5) Any claim by the Buyers on the goods shipped shall be filed within 30 days after arrival of the goods at the port of destination and supported by a survey report issued by a surveyor approved by the Sellers. Claims in respect of matters within the responsibility of the insurance company or of the shipping company will not be considered or entertained by the Sellers.

(6) If shipment of the contracted goods is prevented or delayed in whole or in part due to Force Majeure, the Sellers shall not be liable for non-shipment or late shipment of the goods under this Contract. However, the Sellers shall notify the Buyers by fax or telex and furnish the latter within 15 days by registered airmail with a certificate issued by the competent authorities at the place of occurrence attesting such event or events.

(7) All disputes arising out of the performance of, or relating to this Contract, shall be settled amicably through negotiation. In case no settlement can be reached through negotiation, the case shall then be submitted to the China International Economic and Trade Arbitration Commission for arbitration in accordance with its arbitration rules. The arbitral award is final and binding upon both parties.

Chapter Six

Business Social Correspondence (Ⅰ)

Section One Business Writing

6.1 Introduction

Letters are important means of communication. Generally, there are two types of letters, business letters and personal letters. Business or Commercial English Correspondence includes letters, e-mails, telegraphs, telephones, faxes and cards.

6.2 Formats

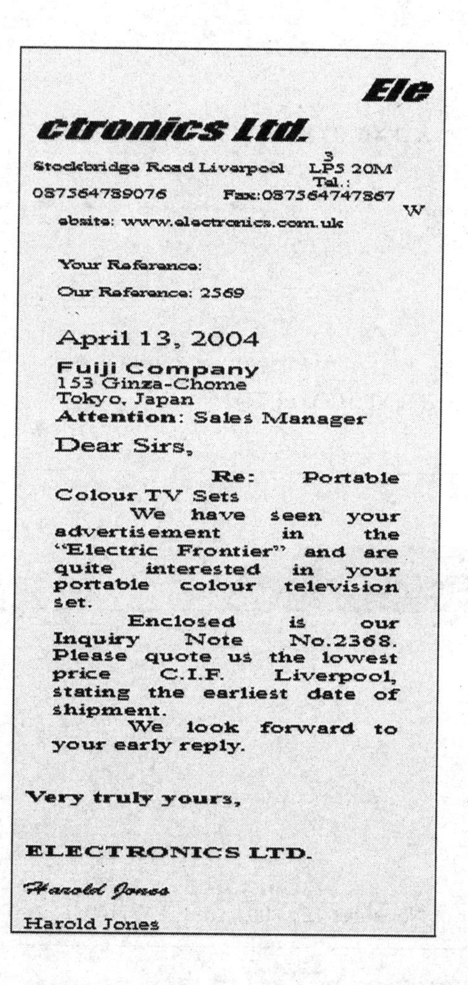

Ele
ctronics Ltd.

3
Stockbridge Road Liverpool LP5 20M
Tel.:
087364789076 Fax:087364747867
W
ebsite: www.electronics.com.uk

Your Reference:

Our Reference: 2569

April 13, 2004

Fuiji Company
153 Ginza-Chome
Tokyo, Japan
Attention: Sales Manager

Dear Sirs,

Re: Portable Colour TV Sets

We have seen your advertisement in the "Electric Frontier" and are quite interested in your portable colour television set.

Enclosed is our Inquiry Note No.2368. Please quote us the lowest price C.I.F. Liverpool, stating the earliest date of shipment.

We look forward to your early reply.

Very truly yours,

ELECTRONICS LTD.

Harold Jones

Harold Jones

1. Letterhead

Generally, a letterhead will include the company logo, company's name, address, telephone number, fax number and email address, and the web address if available.

Examples 1: the Formats of the Letterhead on the First Page

EASTERN TEXTILES IMP. & EXP. CO., LTD.
34297 Shangcheng Road, Shanghai, China
Tel: 6606811 Fax: 6507631
Http://will.nease.net
E-mail: bcxbcx@21cn.com

Examples 2: the Formats of the Letterhead on the Second Page

EASTERN TEXTILES IMP. & EXP. CO., LTD.
-2- April 16, 2004

Mr. Smith April 16, 2004, Page 2

Page 2 -
EASTERN TEXTILES IMP. & EXP. CO., LTD.
April 16, 2004

Mr. Smith
April 16, 2004
Page 2

EASTERN TEXTILES IMP. & EXP. CO., LTD.
-2- April 16, 2004

Examples 3: the Formats of Reference Number

Your ref: ALM
Our ref: 5511/ TL

Dear Sirs,
Your ref: ALM

Dear Sirs,
We refer to your letter of November 12, 2004, ref. TY 1160...

2. Date

Comparison for the Date 02/01/03

Year	Month	Day	Language
2002	1	3	Chinese way
2003	2	1	American way
2003	1	2	British way

To avoid confusion, it is a common practice to write months in words.

Examples 4: the Formats of Date

24th March, 2004
March 24th, 2004
24 March, 2004
March 24, 2004

3. Inside Address

Always include the recipient's name, address and postal code. Add job title if appropriate.

Examples 1: the Formats of Inside Address

Ms. Cecilia Green
Sales Manager
ABC Company
123 Berry Drive
Minneapolis, MN55106
U.S.A.

Vice President
Messrs. J. Harvey & Co.
66 High Street
Anytown, AY1 2BF

China National Machinery Import & Export Corp.
36, Jianshan Road
Dalian, 116023
People's Republic of China

Examples 2: the Formats of Particular Address or Attention Line

P & G Company
24 Madison Avenue
Columbus, OH 43004
U.S.A.
Attention of Pual Yang

Biddle, Sawyer & Co., Ltd.
Hadden House
Fitzroy Street
London, SW8 25DY, England
Attention of Export Department
Mr. H.A. Donnan, please

P & G John Morris & Co., Inc.
ATTENTION OF PURCHASING MANAGER
O' Sullivan Building
Baltimore, Maryland, 10026
U.S.A.

4. Salutation

If unsure to whom you should address a letter, you should use the following salutations:
Dear Sir or Madam,
When addressing a group of people, use one of the following salutations:

Ladies and Gentlemen: *Dear Sirs or Madams*,
Gentlemen:/*Dear Sirs*, (if all the readers are male)
Ladies:/*Dear Madams*, (if all the readers are female)

Examples 1: the Formats of Salutation and Corresponding Complementary Close

Salutation	Close
Dear Sirs, Dear Sir, Dear Madams, Dear Madam, Dear Sir or Madam,	Faithfully yours, Yours cordially, (formal)
Gentlemen:	Yours truly, Truly yours, (formal)

Sir, Madam,	Respectfully yours, Yours respectfully,
Dear Mr. Morgan: Dear John: Dear Miss Green: Dear Mrs. Smith: Dear Ms. White: Mmes. Stone: Messrs Shaw: My dear Mrs. (or Miss.) Bush:	Sincerely yours, Yours sincerely, (less formal)

Examples 2: the Formats of Subject Line or Caption

- Subject: Proposed delay of the delivery
- Re: Proposed delay of the delivery
- Proposed delay of the delivery
- In re: Invoice No. 1120
- SUBJECT: ACCOUNT NO. 689

5. Body of a Letter

The body of a business letter typically has three paragraphs:

- introductory paragraph
- one or more body paragraphs
- concluding paragraph

6. Signature

Example: the Formats of Signature

ELECTRONICS LTD.
Harold Jones
Harold Jones
Manager

Company's name
Your signature
Typed signature
(Job title)

Cathy Kurtz
Cathy Kurtz
Marketing Manager

Your signature
Typed signature
(Job title)

7. Endosure

Example: the Formats of Enclosure

Encls: 2 commercial invoices

1 Enc.

Enc: 1 B/L
1 certificate

Enc.

Attachments:2

1 Attachment

Enclosure as Stated

8. Carbon Copy Notation

Example: the format of Carbon Copy Notation

- C.C.: Dalian Branch
- C.C.: Jean Kipman
- B.C.C.: Mr. Brown (on the copy only)

6.3 styles

1. Indented Style

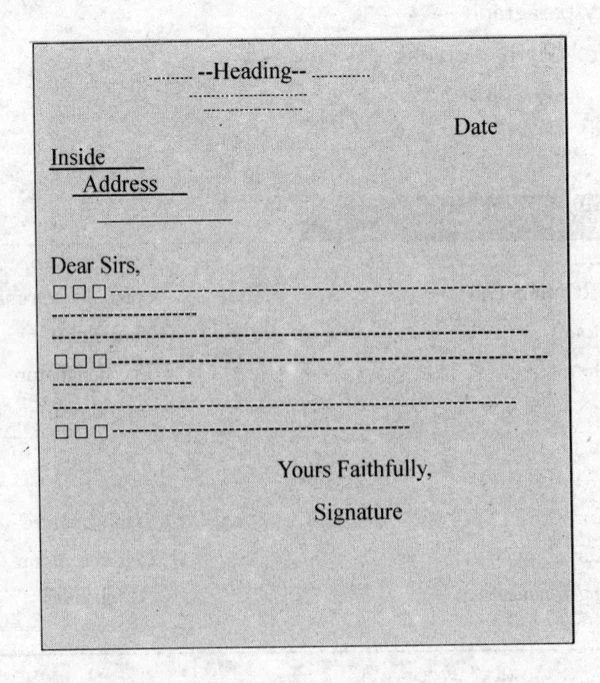

2. **Block Style**

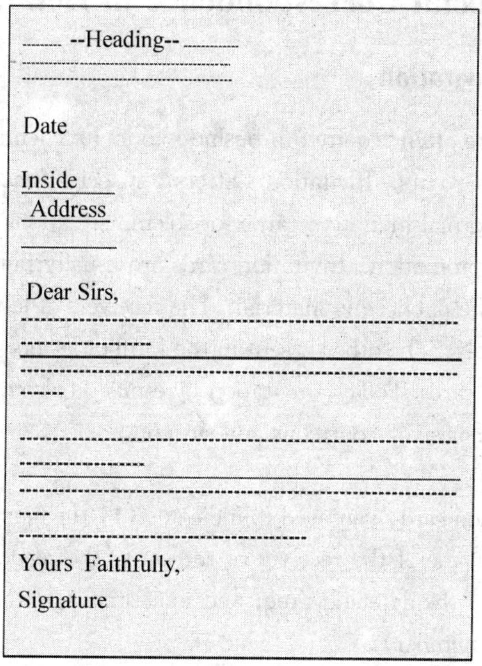

--Heading--

Date

Inside
Address

Dear Sirs,

Yours Faithfully,

Signature

3. **Semi-blocked Style**

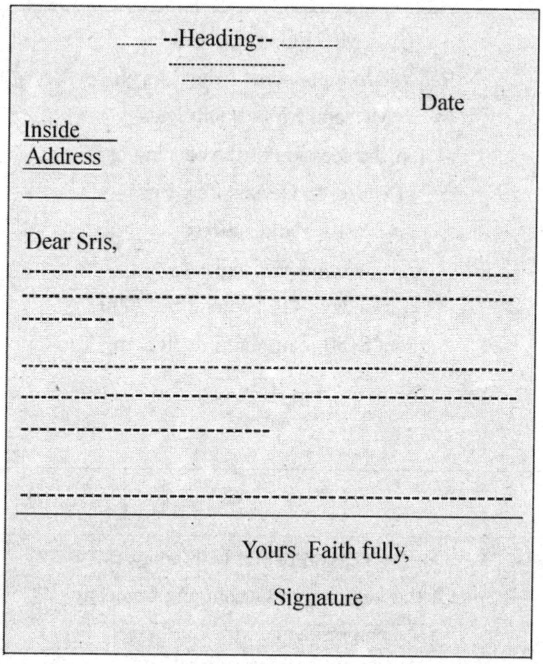

--Heading--

Date

Inside
Address

Dear Sris,

Yours Faith fully,

Signature

6.4 Punctuation Styles

Mixed Punctuation	Open Punctuation
Dear Mrs. Gasparian:	Dear Gasparian
Cordially yours,	Cordially yours

6.5 Business Social Correspondence in Details

6.5.1 Letters of Invitation

Invitation letters are often required in business to invite clients and/or customers to important conferences and events. Invitation Letters for social functions are categorized into two types. One is the formal invitation cards for solemn situations such as the opening ceremony and new product promotion. Invitation cards are usually put in specially designed envelopes, which is also the publicizing material. The receivers of letters, no matter accept the invitation or not, do reply. The other is sent in the form of letters. Such is not as formal and serious as the invitation card. Today, invitation by e-mail is also common. Invitation letters need to be short but persuasive, courteous and sincere.

1. Invitation Cards

In a formal invitation card, you need to indicate: (1) the name of the sender of the card (your name); (2) the name of the receiver of the card (the reader's name); (3) the occasion; (4) the place; (5) the date and time; and sometimes (6) the telephone number of the sender (your telephone number).

Example 1

Mr. Robert Devizes
Requests the pleasure of the company of
Mr. and Mrs. Philip Ross
On the occasion of the opening of
Devizes & Devizes Law Firm
10 Marker Street
London, England
On Monday, 4th September, 2000
From 8:30 a.m. until 9:30 a.m.

R. S. V. P.
Tel: 7654321

Example 2

On the occasion of the 15th anniversary
Of the founding of Guangming Company
The president, Mr. Lin Feng
Would like to invite Mr. Li Jiang
to a Reception at Orchid Hall, Garden Hotel
16 Marker Street
Beijing, China
On Saturday, June, 3, 2000
From 6:00 p.m. to 8:00 p.m.

Example 3

Mr. and Mrs. Alan Lee
Request the pleasure of
Mr. and Mrs. John Barrier's
Company for dinner
On Saturday, January 28, 2000
At six o'clock
At Sea Restaurant

Example 4

Mr. John Smith
President of ABC Company
requests the pleasure of
Mr. George Chan's company
at the official opening of
the new Causeway Bay Branch of ABC Company
in G/F, 123 Hennessy Road, Hong Kong
at 3 p.m. on Monday, 11 June, 2007

R.S.V.P.
Ms. Lam Tel: 1234 5678

Example 5

Mr. George Chan
You are cordially invited to
the official opening of
the new Causeway Bay Branch of ABC Company
in G/F, 123 Hennessy Road, Hong Kong
at 3 p.m. on Monday, 11 June, 2007
Mr. John Smith
President of ABC Company

R.S.V.P.
Ms. Lam Tel: 1234 5678

Example 6

Mr. and Mrs. Benjamin Rasool
cordially invite you to a reception
celebrating the engagement of
Mary Jane Rasool and Robert Yates
to be held Sunday, the sixth of June
at six o'clock
Pierre's Cafe
800 23rd Street NW
Washington, DC

RSVP Semi – Formal Dress
(202) 555 – 6908

From the above examples, we may see those invitation cards are used for various occasions, such as inviting somebody to an opening ceremony, to a celebration, or just to a dinner. If you want to make sure whether the person(s) will come, you may write "R. S. V. P." (an abbreviation for French that means "repondez s'il vous plait"—"Please Reply") at the lower left corner, as in the case of Example 1 and 4. Also, each line of the message should be written at the center. To show intimacy, "you" can be used as in Example 5.

2. Invitation Letters

In invitation letters, usually the invitation is made directly in the beginning. Then, the occasion, the reason for the invitation, the place, the date and time are introduced. The person and the telephone number to contact are often provided. Sometimes, a reply is requested in the end.

Example 1

Dear sir/madam:

The Fisheries company would very much like to have someone from your company speak at our conference on the Trend in Fisheries Export in 2008.

As you may be aware, the mission of our conference is to promote the trade and to provide an opportunity for fisheries companies to communicate. Many of our members are interested in the achievements your company has made in fisheries export. We'll highly appreciate if your company could attend the conference.

Enclosed is our preliminary schedule for the conference which will be reviewed in weeks. I'll call you on July, 3 to see who from your company would be willing to speak to us. I can assure you that we'll make everything convenient to the speaker.

Sincerely yours,
John Lee
Chief Manager

Example 2

Dear sir/madam:

We would like to invite you to an exclusive presentation of our new mobile car. The presentation will take place at Jia Xing Hotel, at 9 a.m. on May, 5. There will also be a reception at 11 a.m. We hope you and your colleagues will be able to attend.

Jason Company is a leading producer of high-quality. Our new models offer super quality and sophistication with economy, and their new features give them distinct advantages over similar products from other manufacturers.

We look forward to seeing you on May, 5. Just call our office at 666555 and we will be glad to secure a place for you.

Sincerely yours,
John Lee
Chief Manager

Example 3

Dear sir/madam:

On Aug. 10, we will host an evening of celebration in honor of the retirement of John Barrie, President of P&A Company. You are cordially invited to attend the celebration at Honor Hotel, Walnut Street, on Sept. 8 from 7 to 10 p.m.

John Barrie has been the President of P&A Company since 1989. During this period, P&A Company expanded its business from American market to global market. Now it's our opportunity to thank him for his years of exemplary leadership and wish him well for a happy retirement. Please join us to say Good-bye to John Barrie.

See you on Sept. 8.

Example 4

Dear Mr. /Ms,

We should like to invite you to attend the 2003 International Fair which will be held from April 29 to May 4 at Dalian Exhibition Center. Full details on the Fair will be sent in a week. We look forward to hearing from you soon, and hope that you will be able to attend.

If you have questions, please do not hesitate to contact us. Any questions regarding your attendance should be addressed to Mr. Devizes at 666555 from our company—the Exhibition Center.

Yours faithfully,

Example 5

Dear Mr. /Ms,

Thank you for your letter of March 20 inviting our corporation to participate in the 1997 International Fair. We are very pleased to accept and will plan to display our electrical appliances as we did in previous years.

Mr. Li will be in your city from April 2 to 7 to make specific arrangements and would very much appreciate your assistance.

Yours faithfully,

Example 6

Dear Mr. Chan,

ABC Company Annual Dinner 2007

Annual dinner is an occasion for us to thank our friends and supporters. Therefore, I write to invite you to attend our 2007 Annual Dinner on Monday, 18 June 2007 at the Ballroom of the ABC Hotel in (detailed address). Reception starts at 6:30 p.m. and dinner is to commence at 7:30 p.m.

I do hope you can join us for an evening of fun. With best wishes!

Yours sincerely,
John Smith
Chairman

R.S.V.P. by 2 June 2007
Ms. Amy Chan (Tel: 1234 5678, Fax: 8765 4321, E-mail: abc@abc.com)

Example 7

Dear Distinguished Guest:

We are greatly honored to invite you to attend the IT Summit in Liaoning 2006 to be held from October 23 – 28, 2006 (August 23 – 25 for tutorial, August 26 – 27 for conference, August 26 – 29 for Exhibition) at the Liaoning International Convention Center, Shenyang city, Liaoning province.

IT Summit in Liaoning 2006 will be held in conjunction with Liaoning International Telecom Show (August 26 – 29). These events create a one-stop exploring spot for the latest network and telecommunications technologies and trends. It is expected the total number of visitors in the week will outreach that of 2005, which was more than 65 thousands. Don't miss this great opportunity!

We believe that the IT Summit in Liaoning 2006 will provide a great opportunity for the whole IT community for learning and communication.

We hereby cordially invite you, a leading figure in this industry, to attend the IT Summit in Liaoning 2006. We are looking forward to your attendance and participation!

Sincerely,

When invitation letters are written, to show intimacy, the following sentences can be used:

We are having an informal dinner on Saturday, 12 May, at 6:30 p.m. at ABC Restaurant and

—Would you love to join us?

—We hope it will be possible for you to be with us.

—We would be happy if you come.

—We hope you can join us.

—We are looking forward to your joining us.

—Please phone to let me know if you can come.

3. Acceptance of the Invitation

If you accept the invitation, you can reply with reference to the following sentences:

—I accept with pleasure the kind invitation of Mr. Smith for the dinner at 6:30 p.m. on 12 May.

—Many thanks for your kind invitation to the Opening Ceremony. I am delighted to accept and look forward to seeing you on 9 June.

—Thank you for your kind invitation to the dinner you are giving on 9 June. I shall be very happy indeed to come, and look forward with pleasure to meeting you.

—Thank you so much for inviting me to dinner on 12 May. I will be there by seven.

—It is really very kind of you to include me in your event.

—I will be happy to be at your party on Saturday, 12 May, at 7:00 p.m.

—Thank you for including me.

Example

Dear Mr. White:

Many thanks for your kind invitation to dinner on September 23rd. David and I accept with pleasure.

Teresa

4. Declining the Invitation

If you cannot accept the invitation, you can decline with reference to the following:

—I am really happy to receive your invitation to the Annual Dinner. I regret that I am unable to accept because I have a prior engagement. Wish you have happy time.

—We regret that we are unable to accept the kind invitation of the party.

—I greatly regret that I am unable to join you next Friday. Hope you have happy time.

—I am really sorry that I couldn't make it. I hope you understand.

Example 1: Negative Response

Dear Mr. /Ms,

Thank you very much for your invitation to attend the 2007 International Fair. As we are going to open a repair shop in your city at that time, we are sorry that we shall not be able to come.

We hope to see you on some future occasion.

Yours faithfully,

Example 2: Negative Response

Dear Mr. Smith:

I am really happy to receive your invitation to the Annual Dinner. I regret that I am unable to accept because I have a prior engagement. I am really sorry that I couldn't make it. I hope you understand.

Wish you have happy time.

6.5.2 Letters of Apologies

1. Why an Apology Letter is So Important?

Writing an apology letter shortly after the offense can usually help save a relationship before a wound becomes a scar and the damage becomes irreparable.

(1) You can usually find forgiveness and understanding if you freely acknowledge what you did wrong and express sincere regret in your apology letter.

(2) Depending on the situation, if you offer the injured party the appropriate material restitution for whatever loss they incurred because of you, this will also help to repair your relationship.

(3) You can help to rebuild your credulity in your apology letter if you promise not to repeat the offense and assure the injured party that they will see a definite change in your behavior.

(4) You can use your apology letter to assure the injured party that you truly value their friendship and do not want to lose it.

(5) You may find that if you freely apologize and accept responsibility for what you did, the injured party may also accept some responsibility for the problem and apologize to you in return.

2. Write a Business Apology

You should write this letter as soon as possible after the incident. It should be clear, brief, and dignified. Focus on actions taken to rectify the situation rather than on any damage that resulted. A sincere, well-worded apology can be very effective in winning back disgruntled customers and business associates.

3. 7 Tips for Writing a Business Apology Letter

(1) When writing apology letters, acknowledge the nature of the complaint and its impact upon the individual. Offer your apology in the beginning of the letter and clearly state the problem: "Please accept my apology for being unable to give you a definitive answer at this time..." or "We apologize for whatever inconvenience this may cause you, but..."

(2) Briefly explain your perspective on the situation. Express your understanding of the situation. Empathize with the individual's concerns.

(3) Give some specific statements regarding the situation. This will show the reader that you really understand the matter at hand.

(4) Detail the positive actions you have taken to resolve the situation at hand. If necessary provide a date or time of resolution. Focus on what actions you are taking to rectify the problem: "We are happy to offer you a full refund..." or "We will be happy to notify you as soon as we receive the information you requested..."

(5) Provide a brief, concise overview of the situation. Include any explanations or reasons that may provide a better understanding to the individual. Give some explanation for what happened: "Our committee has not yet completed its investigation into..." or "In order to err on the side of caution, this toy has been recalled by the manufacturer..."

(6) Assure the reader that you have taken the necessary steps to ensure there is no reoccurrence of the situation.

(7) Remember: Say you are sorry as soon as wisdom dictates! You will find that an apology letter will not only help save your friendships and your business associates, it can also dissolve a small problem and keep it from snowballing into a big one!

Example 1

Apology for Discrepancies

Dear Mr. Turner,

We acknowledge that there are indeed discrepancies between the shipping instructions and the actual shipment. Consequently, there will be a shortage in your October shipment.

We are also very sorry for causing you so much trouble in regard to your monthly reports. New procedures have been adopted to eliminate the possibility of such problems happening again.

Your cooperation and patience in these respects would be greatly appreciated.

Sincerely yours,

Example 2

Apology for a Late Delivery

Dear Mr. Faulk,

We have received your letter of August 10, and ask you to accept our apologies fro the delay in sending your order for the leather shoes. The goods are in fact still with the forwarder. We assured you that your order has been attended to in strict rotation, but we should inform you that ordering has been particularly heavy over the past six months and it has been as much as we could do to meet the demand.

We have instructed the forwarders to treat your shipment with absolute priority, and we are given to understand that dispatch will be effected on the Evergreen due to arrive at London on the 10th of September. Owing to the increase in business, we are making a number of modifications to our organization which will ensure that such a delay will never occur again.

Example 3

Dear Mr. Clark,

I would like to express my apologies for not being able to keep our 10 o'clock appointment. I had a small accident to deal with. I will come over to your company the day after tomorrow—Monday, November 3, at 9 a.m., if that is convenient for you. Please call 123 - 456 if not. With many apologies.

Li Xia

Example 4

Dear Mr Al Capone,

Our merchandise is easy enough to replace, but your time and faith in us isn't. We apologize for your recent experience with the shipment of Tommy guns and we'll do our best to satisfy you on all counts.

We've received a number of complaints from other businesses on this same model. After speaking with the manufacturer, we've isolated the problem. We're prepared to take the guns back and replace it with new units. We apologize for the inconvenience and hope that this solution is satisfactory.

My direct line is 666-6666.

Sincerely,

Example 5

Dear Ms. Bunyan,

I am sorry I have given you so much trouble over finding Mr. John Eastman's address. I am very grateful to you for all you have done. Please do not worry about the matter any further.

Sincerely yours,

Liang Zuolin

Example 6

Henry,

I am sorry I shall be out of town on business on Nov. 8, so I am afraid I'll have to postpone our meeting to Thursday, Nov. 12 at the same hour. I do hope you can still come, and very much regret any inconvenience the postponement may cause you.

Sunny

Example 7

Dear Sir or Madam:

Thank you for your letter of 26 January. I apologize for the delivery problems you had with us last month. I have had a meeting with our production and shipping managers to work out a better system for handling your account. We know we made a mistake on your last order. Although we replaced it for you. we want to make sure it does not happen again. We have devised the enclosed checklist to use for each of your future order. It includes your firm's particular specifications, packing requirements and marking instructions. I believe can service your company better and help you operations run more smoothly with this safeguard. Please contact us if there are any additional points you would like us to include.

6.5.3 Letters of Thanks

Writing a thank you letter is not only extremely important but is also a common courtesy. Writing a thank you letter will always serve as a kind and conscientious gesture. To thank someone is one of the most important memos or letters you will write because it builds good will, respect, and cooperation. For people need to be congratulated on their accomplishments, and appreciated for doing a good job, a thank you letter demonstrates thoughtfulness, which is a characteristic many employers and people value. Since so few take the time to write a thank you letter, someone who does will indeed be remembered. Never underestimate the power of a sincere compliment. Extending congratulations and expressing appreciation will pay high dividends over the long term.

There are various times when writing a thank you letter is appropriate: to thank a business for good service, low prices, or professional courtesies; to thank for orders, payments; to thank employees for their well done jobs; to thank partners and customers for suggestions; to thank others for gifts, assistance, help, support, hospitality, condolence and greetings; thank after an employment interview, etc.

Your thank you letter does not need to be lengthy. Just a few kind words even, will show that you put some time and thought into your message. A brief letter acknowledging others' cooperation and endeavors reinforces a solid business relationship. More likely than not, the receipt of such a letter will ensure you future good service and relation.

When you write thank you letters, try to follow these hints:

(1) Express your appreciation sincerely, usually at the beginning;

(2) State what you want to thank the reader or elaborate on the compliment;

(3) Then add a final word of thanks;

(4) Be sure your letters are professional, for example: typed, no errors, on quality paper, etc;

(5) Keep your letters short and simple—usually one page is enough;

(6) Send your letter within one day—do not put if off!

Example 1

Dear Mr. / Ms,

Thank you for your letter of June 4, enclosing an account of the organization and work of your Chamber of Commerce and Industry.

We are very grateful for such a detailed account of your activities. This information is certain to help increase our future cooperation.

Yours faithfully

Example 2

We want you to know how much we appreciate the way you have cared for our lawns and flowers this year. I can't remember a time when our lawns have looked so nicely groomed and weed-free, or when the flowers have been more beautiful. Several visitors to the corporate headquarters have commented on how nice things look. Thank you for your excellent service.

Example 3

We want you to know that we are very pleased with the quality of service your company provides. We sincerely appreciate your responsiveness and the way you conduct business. We have recommended your company to others because of our satisfaction with your service. We look forward to doing business with you for years to come.

Example 4

Thank you for your prompt deliveries to our Doe Plant.

In our business we must get our products to the stores on a regular schedule. We rely on dependable service from suppliers like you to help us keep our schedule and satisfy our customers. We want you to know that we appreciate your efforts and look forward to continuing our business relationship.

Example 5

Thank you for the computer benchmarks produced by Springfield Computer Associates; they really are excellent!

Computer benchmarks produced by an independent third party such as your company provide a professional and unbiased standard that the industry relies on for making critical purchasing decisions. In addition, the software is easy to use and is updated regularly.

Thank you once again for your contribution to the industry.

Example 6

Dear Dr. Lector:

Our main office has just processed your order for Fresh Body Parts, which you will be receiving via priority mail as requested.

We would like to take this time to thank you for taking a chance on a "new company". We hope we have gained that trust with immediate, efficient service.

If there is any other service we can provide for you, please let us know.

Regards,

Example 7

Dear Mr. Singh,

I'm writing to express my appreciation of all that you did for me during my visit to your company in New Delhi.

Wang Cong

Example 8

Dear Mr. Bunny:

Thank you for your order of 20,000 tons of TNT from our factory. We are pleased that you are so happy with our products.

We look forward to a productive alliance between our companies. Feel free to call us with any concerns, requests or questions.

Cordially,

6.5.4 Card Writing

There are various types of cards, such as greeting cards, congratulation cards, business cards, and invitation cards.

Greeting cards are to greet anniversary, special accessions, festivals, success, job leaving, job promotion, job retirement.

As for the greeting card, it's something that is short, sweet, and to the point. Every word counts and it can be done in short spurts of time. You need to be aware of the types of cards that are out there. Greeting card categories include: Traditional Cards, Conversational Prose, Humorous Cards, and Alternative Cards.

(1) Traditional Cards: Traditional cards usually consist of a cover headline, such as Happy Birthday! Or For a Special Son, with rhymed metered verse inside. The buyer should always be able to tell what occasion the card is intended for either by the headline, or the cover illustration.

(2) Conversational Prose: These cards are exactly that—conversational. They use personal pronouns to make them very sender-recipient oriented. The writing is generally non-rhyming and should sound as if the sender is talking. Sometimes not more than a single sentence or phrase, the words always convey a warm, caring thought. Conversational Prose is sometimes called Contemporary Prose.

(3) Humorous Cards: Humorous cards may use puns, gags, and sometimes (but not often) even jokes in a timely, sarcastic, or risque fashion. Basically they present humorous statements on life as we see it. If humor is what you're good at, you will find it is much sought for greeting cards as well as the wide range of novelty items you can't help but notice while standing in the checkout lines at any book or card store.

(4) Alternative Cards: Alternative cards use both humor and contemporary prose in expressing thoughts for special or unusual circumstances, such as in a caring card for someone with cancer, or a humorous card for someone trying to quit smoking. These are cards that carry themes that were not available to shoppers years ago, which means card companies are expanding their lines "good news for freelancers".

1. Card Type

Example 1: Job-Leaving

Because you're leaving for pastures new,
We've collected together a quid or two,
A card and present, but more than that,
You leave us with all wishes glad.

Example 2: Job-Promotion

Your efforts have paid off!

Great going!

Cheers!

Congrats on your promotion!

Example 3: Job-Retirement (1)

Best wishes, now the fun starts!

Example 4: Job-Retirement (2)

You know you're getting old when: What works hurts and what doesn't hurt, doesn't work!

Enjoy!

Example 5: Job-Retirement (3)

You are retiring...
Time to indulge in your favorite pastime...

SNOOOOZZZZZING!

Example 6: Job-Retirement (4)

It is time for you to look back with pride and satisfaction on years well-lived, and look forward to all the things you're yet to enjoy! Congratulations & best wishes on your retirement!

Example 7: Job-Retirement (5)

You are no longer a colleague now, but the Boss...of your own time! Have fun! Happy Retirement!

Example 8: Job-New (1)

Hope you enjoy your job ×××!

Example 9: Job-New (2)

You're off to sail in new waters... Here's wishing your 'new job' is a great experience for you! Congratulations & wishing you luck & success today... and always!

Example 10: Job-New (3)

Congratulations on Your New Job!

Example 11: Farewell a Friend

Dear Richard,

May you have a bright career. We all miss you. Please don't forget to call us. You are our good friend and we are sure you will be our good friend too.

Goodbye.

Your friends,

Cindy, David, Raymond, Lily

Example 12: Business Cards

This part has been designed to provide you with some inspiration regarding the content and the layout. Remember that first impressions count and that your Business Card will not only provide contact details but will also convey a professional image of your company.

2. Useful Hints and Tips on Designing Business Cards

Some hints and tips to consider when designing Cards.

Company Logo-Adds color to business card and portrays a professional image of the company

- Content
- Company Logo
- Your Name
- Your Position (optional)
- Company Name
- Contact Details-Address, Telephone Numbers, Fax Number, Email address
- Web Address (Optional)
- Company Slogan or Tagline (Optional)
- Colors: keep the number of colors to a minimum to avoid a cluttered look - limit to three colors

Reverse of the card: Keep it simple. Put the most important information on the back such as the telephone number.

Example

Company Name
Your Name & Job Title
Address Details
Tel. Details
Fax Details & Email Address
Website Address：www.××××××.com

Section Two Language Handbook

Useful Words and Expressions

apologize to sb. for sth. 道歉
awfully 非常
excuse 借口
fault 错误
forgive 原谅
ignorant 无知
inconsiderateness 不顾及他人
inconvenience 不方便
make an apology 道歉
make up for it 弥补
misunderstanding 误解
negligent 疏忽的
offend 冒犯
overlook 忽略
regret 后悔
remedy 补救
remove 消除
shoulder the responsibility 承担责任
thoughtless 欠考虑的
beyond words 难以言表
convey/express one's appreciation 表示感激
cordial 衷心的
grateful 感谢
look forward to 期望
sincerest thanks 衷心的感谢
wholehearted appreciation 衷心的感激

please pass on my 请转达
thank everyone involved 感谢所有相关的人
how satisfied we have been 我们很满意

Useful Sentences

1. Invitation Letters

We are looking forward to seeing you then.
届时敬请光临。

We sincerely hope you can attend.
我们期待您的光临。

I hope you're not too busy to come.
我期望您会在百忙中出席。

May I have the honor of your company at dinner?
敬备菲酌,恭请光临。

It would be an honor to me if you would accept our invitation.
如您接受邀请,我将荣幸至极。

The favor of a reply is requested.
敬赐复函。

Thank you very much for your kind invitation.
感谢您的友好邀请。

It is with great pleasure that we shall come to your... at that time.
我们非常高兴届时能前去参加你们的……

I'm afraid that I can't attend (the party) because I have to...
恐怕我不能参加这个(聚会),因为我必须……

Please accept my sincere regrets for not being able to join you at your birthday party.
请接受我真诚的歉意,我不能前去参加您的生日庆祝会。

2. Letters of Thanks

We look forward to many more years of cooperation.
我们期望日后的长期合作。

I take this opportunity to express to you my deep appreciation for the assistance you rendered me.
借此机会,对贵方给予的协助致以我深深的谢意。

I wish there were a better word than "thanks" to express my appreciation for your generous help.
对于你的慷慨帮助,我的感激之情无以言表。

My appreciation to you for your help is beyond words. I wish I could repay it one day.
对于你的帮助,我的感激难以言表。但愿日后能够报答。

Please accept my most cordial thanks for your timely help, which I will always remember.

对你的及时帮助，请接受我最衷心的感谢，我将一直铭记在心。

Thank you from the bottom of my heart for your kind help.

由衷地感激你的好心帮助。

3. Letters of Apologies

Please accept my sincere apology.

请接受我诚心诚意的道歉。

I'm sorry to have caused you so much inconvenience.

给你造成诸多不便，我很抱歉。

I am awfully/terribly sorry for what I have done.

我对所做事情深感抱歉。

I am afraid what I have done has caused many inconveniences to you.

我担心所做之事为你带来诸多不便。

I regret to inform you that I am unable to do...

很抱歉告知你我不能……

Please accept my most cordial apologies for...

请接受我对……表示的最诚恳的道歉。

4. Card Writing

Best wishes for the year to come!

恭贺新禧！

Good luck in the year ahead!

祝吉星高照！

May you come into a good fortune!

恭喜发财！

Live long and proper!

多福多寿！

May many fortunes find their way to you!

祝财运亨通！

I want to wish you longevity and health!

愿你健康长寿！

Wishing you many future successes.

祝你今后获得更大成就。

On this special day I send you New Year's greetings and hope that some day soon we shall be together.

在这特殊的日子，向你致以新年的祝福，希望不久我们能相聚在一起。

I would like to wish you a joyous new year and express my hope for your happiness and good future.

祝新年快乐，并愿你幸福吉祥，前程似锦。

May the New Year bring many good things and rich blessings to you and all those you love!

愿新年带给你和你所爱的人许多美好的事物和无尽的祝福!

Rich blessings for health and longevity is my special wish for you in the coming year.

祝你在新的一年里身体健康,多福多寿。

Good luck, good health, hood cheer. I wish you a happy New Year.

祝好运、健康、佳肴伴你度过一个快乐新年。

With best wishes for a happy New Year!

祝新年快乐,并致以良好的祝福。

I hope you have a most happy and prosperous New Year.

谨祝新年快乐幸福,大吉大利。

Wishing you a song in your heart at Christmas and blessings all year long.

圣诞之际,祝你心中有首快乐的歌,新年快乐!

Wishing you peace, joy and happiness through Christmas and the coming year.

在圣诞和新年来临之际,祝福你平安、快乐、幸福!

Exercises

Ⅰ. Write a Formal Invitation Card for Your Client Asking Him or Her

- to attend the opening of your company
- to attend the reception at Blue Sky Hotel on the occasion of the 10th anniversay of the founding of your company
- to open an account
- to join an organization

Ⅱ. Translate the Following into English

亲爱的布尔先生:

很荣幸邀请您参加我们的年会,今年的会议将于8月20日到24日在诺丁汉大学举行。随信寄去会议的详细内容、住宿安排及业务活动计划。

去年您做了题为"学术标准及展望"的非常有趣的报告,如果您这次能就此专题的最新发展给我们做一发言,我们将非常感激。

如果您能在方便的时候尽快通知我们您能否出席此次会议,我们将不胜感激。

您忠诚的

菲利浦·卢伏特(会议组织者)

2002年6月24日

Ⅲ. Write an Apology Letter

- for employ termination
- for inadequate service
- for a detective product
- for a late payment

Ⅳ. Write a Letter

- to thank a business for professional courtesies
- to thank a customer for purchasing a product
- to thank someone for an inquiry
- to thank someone for media exposure

Ⅴ. Write Festival Cards Greeting Business Partners

- your friend's new job
- business success

Chapter Seven

Business Social Correspondence (Ⅱ)

Section One Business Writing

7.1 Letters of Praise and Appreciation

There is a variety of appreciation letters when you appreciate customers, clients, employees, government and media for honor/suggestion, services, products, etc.

There are many ways to state your appreciation. Writing a letter of appreciation is a simple way to recognize others for a job well done or you can go all the way and express your gratitude by presenting an award or bonus to the employee.

The following guidelines will help you come up with an effective letter of appreciation:

(1) Express a compliment or praise for good work done.

(2) Mention the "why to appreciate" in specific detail. The reader likes to know you learned of each specific effort and accomplishment.

(3) Express any positive feedback, results, or comments you received from others about the individual's or group's work.

(4) Be warm, and sincere.

(5) Write a note or letter of appreciation as soon as possible.

If you are giving an award or bonus:

(1) State what the award or bonus is.

(2) Elaborate specifically on what the person has done to earn the award or praise.

(3) Express what the award or bonus means in symbolic terms.

Example 1: Appreciation for an Employee's Endeavor

When John had his automobile accident last month, many of us offered to help while he was convalescing at home. Our efforts made a difference because you took the time to organize volunteers for specific tasks on specific days. I admire your willingness, energy, and organizational abilities. Everyone in the neighborhood joins with me in thanking you for what you did. Your example has been a great lesson for us.

Example 2: Appreciation with Bonus

Dear Sara:

Congratulations! Employee of the month! The plaque and bonus are tokens of our appreciation for your exemplary work.

I also want to extend my personal congratulations. Your hard work and positive attitude in the midst of this month's hiring crunch kept us all going. Volunteering to pitch in on Saturday to help us catch up is just one example of your willingness to go the extra mile.

You are a credit to our company.
Yours Truly,

Example 3: Compliment or Praise a Salesperson or a Sales Staff

Dear Mr. White,

Please convey these compliments to your entire staff for exceeding their goals for the last quarter of this year. It was truly a commendable performance. I know these things do not happen without a great deal of effort on the part of everyone, and I want you to know how much we appreciate your hard work. It appears that your emphasis on regular training sessions has paid dividends. Keep up the good work. We are proud of our entire team.

Example 4: Give Personal Compliments or Praise

Dear Laura,

My compliments on the way you conducted the division meeting this morning. I was surprised by the number of people who were opposed to the consolidation of our departments, but you handled the controversy remarkably well. You have an enviable ability to stay cool and help opposing parties reach agreement. It is a pleasure to work with you. Thanks for helping us all find the best solution.

Example 5: Compliment or Praise an Employee's Work Performance

I want you to know you have an exceptional employee, Jane Doe, in your support division. Her calm, patient manner was a great help to me when my frustration was at an all-time high. Her knowledge of the software and her remarkable problem-solving abilities are rare indeed. If the quality of a firm's employees is an indication of future success, then Doe Corporation has a very bright future.

Example 6: Compliment an Employee's Work Performance

As manager of our computer department, I commend your employee, John Doe, for the prompt and courteous service he gave us last week. He determined our cable needs and produced a fair written estimate very quickly. Once he started the work, he stayed on location until he had installed all additional computers. You can be certain that we shall ask for him personally to serve our future needs.

7.2 Congratulation Letter

Congratulation Letter is more often used in western countries. When there are events such like festivals and large activities, job promotion, job change, success of new products, opening of branch, people would write congratulation letters if they cannot go the site themselves.

In business, sending congratulation letters to each other have become a means to keep good public relationship. Congratulation letters are one of the most common ways to keep contact, promote friendship, and improve relation.

The following are the guidelines for writing congratulation letters:

- Explicit subject: emphasize on the readers' achievements and encouragement for them
- Proper evaluation: no exclamation and over praise
- Standard writing: proper salutation, brief and concise language
- Sincere feeling: expressing true happiness and sincere wishes; no apparent mention of the transaction and personal benefit
- Writing and sending promptly

Generally, congratulation letters are responded in letters.

Example 1: Congratulation Letter on Promotion

Dear Mr. Thomas,

Our heartiest congratulations on your promotion!

Your promotion to national marketing manager certainly came as no surprise to us in view of your brilliant record of achievements while you worked as the regional sales manager in the Central Region, and we always knew that you would become a great success someday.

You came to know us and our service well during the past five years, and you know that we stand ready to be of continued service to you in the days ahead.

We extend every good wish to you in this challenging task.

Sincerely yours,

Example 2: Congratulation Letter on Promotion

Dear Mr. Guy Grant,

Congratulations on your recent promotion to the vice presidency for international marketing at Dong'an Peanuts Company.

You truly deserve this promotion, and those who will work for you will be fortunate to have you as their immediate supervisor.

I have pleasure in recalling how much we've achieved by working with you over the past years, and am sure our pleasant business relationship will be going for the better under your executive presidency.

Sincerely yours,

Wang Ning

President, Huayin Co.

Example 3: Replying to Congratulation on Promotion

Dear Mr. Wang Ning,

Many thanks for your nice words about my promotion and for the good wishes.

The new job is going to be demanding, especially as I make the transition. I am going to give it my all, however. Your support and contribution will help ease the burden and open up a new era in our common interests.

Again I truly appreciate your thoughtfulness for my promotion. I am looking forward to more opportunities of working with you and wish you every success.

Cordially yours,

Guy Gran

Example 4: Congratulation Letter on Anniversary

Dear Mr. York,

We at HITEC congratulate you at ABC on your fifty years of business enterprise.

I read your anniversary folder with considerable interest. It is quite an accomplishment for a firm to change and grow with the times as yours has. We look forward to the continuing growth your company under your enlightened leadership.

Although we have been associated with you for only five years, we have found those five years to be helpful and profitable to us. It is hoped that the next five years of our relationship will be even closer.

Example 5: Congratulation Letter on Establishment of the Firm

Dear Mr. Johnson,

It was delightful news for me to learn of the establishment of your own advertising agency. Please accept our heartful congratulations.

With your brilliant background and long record of fine achievements, I'm sure the new agency will be a great success. I sincerely hope you will find in this new venture the happiness and satisfaction you so richly deserve.

Should there be any way in which we can be of assistance, please do not hesitate to contact me personally.

Yours sincerely,

Example 6: Congratulation Letter on Expansion

Dear Mr. York,

When we received your notice of expansion, we at (name of firm) were elated.

There are few firms that can boast of the success you have achieved over such a relatively short period of time. A great deal of that success, in our opinion, must be directly attributed to your strong leadership and the sense of direction that you provide.

Please accept our heartiest congratulations and best wishes for your continued success.

Example 7: Congratulation Letter On a Public Honor

Dear Mr. Burundi,

On reading through this morning's Times I came across your name in the "New Year Honor List" and hasten to add my congratulations to the many you will be receiving.

The award will give prove delightful to many people who know you and your work. I am happy that the many years service you have dedicated to global travel and marketing has been recognized and appreciated.

People working around me are deeply impressed by your work in our mutual business transactions over the past years. What you have done has been quite outstanding and it is very gratifying to know that these have now been so suitably rewarded.

We wish you ever success in the coming year and look forward to better cooperation with you in the future.

Warm regards and best wishes to you and your family!

Yours ever cordially,
Wang Fulin
Managing Director

Example 8: Replying to Congratulation on a Public Award

Dear Mr. Ge Yongming,

Thank you for your letter conveying congratulations to me on the award of the Who's Who honor.

I am of course happy that anything I may have done should be rewarded by an honor, but at the same time I regard the award as something of a tribute to the teamwork of my colleagues, rather than to me personally.

Indeed I have always enjoyed the willing help and support of many contributors, who include you, my sincere partner from the other side of the world.

May our pleasant relations continue to expand in future.

Yours truly,

Adam Adel

Example 9: Congratulations on a Job Well Done

Dear Miss. Rice,

The displays you created for the "Summer's Coming" promotion are just beautiful. Several of the sales personnel told me that they have received numerous compliments from the customers.

Congratulations on a job well done.

Example 10: Congratulations to New Owners

Dear Sir,

As the new owners of Cloud Restaurant, please accept our congratulations and very best wishes for your success.

Prosperous Company is a well established supplier of beef and provisions to many of the finer hotels and restaurants in Kansas and its vicinity. We specialize in choice and prime, portion controlled, pork, lamb, veal and western beef. We have enclosed a price list for your review, but would like to add that there are specific quantity discounts that are available.

Ross Stewart, our sales representative for your area would be pleased to come to the Cloud Restaurant at your convenience to show you the quality of our products and discuss our terms and prices with you.

Please call (phone) for an appointment.

7.3 Condolence Letters

To console is to comfort, to soothe, to provide solace, or allay sorrow or grief. A condolence letter or note is an expression of sympathy to a person who has experienced pain, grief or a misfortune; it may be one of the most meaningful acts of kindness and compassion you can give to a grieving person.

A simple condolence letter can be a great source of comfort and provide a gift of healing for anyone who is grieving a loss. Well-written condolences can help ease feelings of pain following the death of a love one.

A condolence letter or sympathy note may be one of the most challenging correspondences to write, but sending a message of compassion can also be a worthwhile experience. Bereaved people will acknowledge that condolence notes or sympathy letters from friends become some of their most meaningful mementos of a difficult time.

1. Purpose of a Condolence Letter or Sympathy Note

A condolence letter serves two main purposes:

(1) To offer tribute to the deceased.

(2) To be a source of comfort to the survivors.

2. Basic Guidelines for Writing Condolence to Business Associate upon Death of a Loved One

Express your regret over the death but avoid going into the details of the illness or tragedy, its consequences, or how you heard of the incident.

Honor the loved one by offering some specific praise. When you're unacquainted with the deceased, you may simply pass on complimentary remarks from others (even the recipient of the letter). Such comments help the reader to praise the loved one and to work through his own grief.

Offer any help you or the organization can provide, but be specific. General offers ("if there's anything I can do to help") sound insincere.

Mention any memorial you are making on behalf of the deceased such as flowers, a book, or monetary donations.

Handwrite your letter on personal stationery to add a warmer touch.

3. Components of a Condolence Letter

The authors of The Art of Condolence studied thousands of condolence letters to determine how they were organized. They identified seven key components to include when writing a condolence letter.

(1) Acknowledge the loss and the name of the deceased.

(2) Express your sympathy.

(3) Note special qualities of the deceased.

(4) Include a memory of the deceased.

(5) Remind the bereaved of their personal strengths or special qualities.

(6) Offer help, but make sure it is a specific offer.

(7) End the letter with a thoughtful word, a hope, a wish or expression of sympathy e. g. "You are in my thoughts and prayers." ("Sincerely," "love," or "fondly," may not be the best choices.)

The example of a condolence letter below provides a sample of how the components are used to help the writer organize a thoughtful condolence letter.

4. Sample of Condolence Letter

Example 1

Dear ____________________

[*Acknowledge the loss*]

I was deeply saddened to hear the news about the sudden death of ____________________.

[*Express your sympathy*]

My thoughts are with you and your family during this difficult time. We are all in a state of shock.

[*Note special qualities of the deceased*]

____________________ was such a funny, entertaining and supportive person to be around. She was often a bright spot in my day. I will miss seeing her on campus.

[*Include a memory about the deceased*]

I remember one time when ____________________.

[*Remind the bereaved of their personal strengths or special qualities*]

I know you will miss ____________________ greatly. During this difficult time, I know you will draw upon your own strength and the strength of loved ones that hold you in their thoughts.

[*Offer Assistance*]

You have my deepest sympathy. I will be in touch to see if you need help with the memorial service.

[*End with a thoughtful word or phrase*]

Remember the college is filled with people who care about you and are thinking about you in this difficult time of sorrow.

Your signature ____________________

Sincerely,

Example 2

I am writing to extend my deepest sympathies to you and your family. I was so very sad to hear about ________, he/she was such a wonderful woman/man.

I had the honor and the pleasure to know your husband/father/wife/sister and I was very sorry to hear about his/her passing away. I had the greatest respect for ________ and will miss working with him/ playing golf with him, his/her generous nature and sharing his/her remarkable sense of humor.

Please let me know whether there is anything I can do to help during this difficult time. You and your family are in my thoughts and prayers. I will light a candle for ________ tonight.

Example 3

> Heartful condolences in your great loss.
> We were shocked and deeply sorry to learn the passing away of Mr. B.
> Please accept our very sincere condolences in your great loss.

7.4 Letters of Recommendation

Although grade point averages and Graduate Record Exam (GRE) scores play a central role in graduate admissions and job opportunity, most graduate programs and employers do not base their decisions on numeric scores alone. In fact, highly competitive programs may simply use these scores as a screening device to reduce the size of their applicant pool. In such a situation, letters of recommendation can be extremely important.

1. References for Employment

You need to be sure that you are asking the appropriate people to write a letter of reference or to give you a verbal reference. You also need to know what the reference giver is going to say about you. The best way to approach this is to ask the reference writer if they would mind if you used them as a reference. Then review the type of positions you are applying for with the reference giver, so they can tailor their reference to fit your circumstances.

2. Who to Ask for a Reference

Former bosses, co-workers, customers, vendors, and colleagues all make good references. So do college professors. If you're just starting out in the workforce or if you haven't worked in a while you can use character or personal references from people who know your skills and attributes.

In general, the best letters of recommendation are from people who:

- have worked with you closely (e.g., a research supervisor)
- have known you long enough to write with authority (e.g., academic advisor)
- have relevant expertise (e.g., professors in the case of academic applications)
- are senior and well known (e.g., a departmental chair)
- have a positive opinion of you and your abilities
- have a warm and supportive personal style

3. Request a Reference Letter

Every time you change employment, make a point of asking for a reference letter from your supervisor or a co-worker. That way, you can create a file of recommendations from people you may not necessarily be able to track down years later.

4. Keep Your References Up-to-Date

Let your references know where your job search stands. Tell them who might be calling for a reference. When you get a new job, don't forget to send a thank you note to those who provided you with a reference.

Example 1: Employment Reference Written by an Employer

To whom it may concern:

I would like to recommend Sharon Doe as a candidate for a position with your organization. In her position as Staff Assistant, Sharon was employed in our office from 2002—2006. Sharon did an excellent job in this position and was an asset to our organization during her tenure with the office. She has excellent written and verbal communication skills, is extremely organized, can work independently and is able to follow through to ensure that the job gets done.

During her tenure with XXXX, Sharon was responsible for supervising the department office assistants. These assistants, under Sharon's management, were responsible for many of the office's basic administrative and clerical functions.

Sharon effectively scheduled and managed several assistants to maintain efficient office operations.

Sharon was always willing to offer her assistance and had an excellent rapport with the many constituents served by our office including clients, employers, and other professional organizations. She would be an asset to any employer and I recommend her for any endeavor she chooses to pursue.

Yours truly,

Example 2: Reference Letter for Explaining Lay-Off

To Whom It May Concern:

Mary Foley has been employed by Company, Inc. since June 1, 2007. During this period, she demonstrated all the qualities that employers seek in searching for promotable employees. She has an excellent capacity to quickly grasp new theories and applications, and has always seeked to gain additional responsibilities.

Mary's zeal to improve herself has been displayed by her attendance at evening school to complete her Master's Degree. Her competence is such that, in the absence of our Branch Manager, she was very capable of directing the entire work force to get the job done.

It is unfortunate for Company, Inc. that, due to economic constraints, we must reorganize our organization and lose valued employees such as Mary. I would highly recommend her for any position or career that she may now seek to pursue.

If you have any additional questions, please do not hesitate to call me.

George Evans
Title
Company
Address
Phone
Email

Example 3: Reference Letter from a Manager/Supervisor

To Whom It May Concern:

Jane Doe has worked for me as a Merchandiser Supervisor for the past two years. While under my supervision, her responsibilities have included hiring, training, and supervising store service personnel.

She has established an outstanding rapport with store managers and owners. Her ability to get work done through the service personnel has been outstanding. Jane is highly respected by the people who work under her supervision, she is organized, thorough in her paperwork, and is always on time.

Jane has done an excellent job and I would highly recommend her for a position with your organization.

Please let me know if I can provide you with any further information.

Respectfully,

John Smith
Title
Company
Address
Phone
Email

Example 4: Reference Letter from a Teacher

Attn: Julia M. Jones
Re: Katie Kingston

Dear Ms. Jones:

I am writing this reference at the request of Katie Kingston who is applying for Student Volunteer Program at St. Francis Hospital this summer.

I have known Katie for two years in my capacity as a teacher at Smithtown Middle School. Katie took English and Spanish from me and earned superior grades in those classes. Based on Katie's grades, attendance and class participation, I'd rate Katie's academic performance in my class as superior.

Katie has a number of strengths to offer an employer. Katie is always interested in supporting others.

For example, this year when we worked on our class community service project, Katie was helpful to me in collecting and organizing the food for the food pantry here in Smithtown.

In conclusion, I would highly recommend Katie Kingston. If her performance in my class is any indication of how she'd perform in your position, Katie will be a positive addition to your organization. If you should ever need any additional information you can feel free to contact me at 555 – 5555 or by email at e-mail@email.com anytime.

Sincerely,

Susan Samuels
Teacher, Smithtown Middle School

Example 5: Character Reference Letter Written by an Acquaintance, Rather than an Employer

I have known Jane Doe in a variety of capacities for many years. She has been my daughter's riding instructor for the past several years. In addition, she is my partner in a small business where she is responsible for writing and editing articles and website content.

Jane is organized, efficient, extremely competent, and has an excellent rapport with people of all ages. Her communication skills, both written and verbal, are excellent.

In summary, I highly recommend Jane for any position or endeavor that she may seek to pursue.

She will be a valuable asset for any organization.

If you have any questions, please do not hesitate to contact me.

Sincerely,

John Smith

Example 6: Personal Recommendation Letter

To Whom It May Concern

Dear Sir or Madam,

Recommendation *for Mr. John Smith*

I am writing this letter as a personal recommendation letter for Mr. *John Smith*.

I have known *John Smith* in a professional capacity, as his manager, for over ________ years and have found *him* to be honest, reliable, dedicated, conscientious and an excellent member of my team.

I have known *John Smith* in a social capacity for over ________ years and have found *him* to be honest, reliable, hard working, conscientious and courteous.

I trust that the information provided will be of assistance and will be happy to provide further information about *John*, if required Please just give me a call.

Yours faithfully,

Jean Brown
Customer Service Manager
Zzedro Inc.

Section Two Language Handbook

Useful Words and Expressions

accuracy 准确性
methodology 研究方法
imagination 想象力
creativity 创造力
industry/ diligence 勤勉
honesty/ integrity 诚实
sincerity 诚恳
cooperation 合作
enthusiasm 热诚
conscientiousness 自觉性
reliability/ dependability 可靠性
capacity for analytical thinking 分析思考能力
intellectual curiosity/ spirit of inquiry 好奇心
in response to 作为对……的答复
to whom it may concern 敬启者
native intellectual ability 天赋
capability for abstract reasoning 抽象推理的能力
potential as a researcher 研究的潜力
breadth of general knowledge 知识丰富
knowledge of literature in his field 本专业领域知识
continually impressed 十分欣赏
an outstanding performance 杰出的表现
congratulate you on your 恭贺
exceeded your quota 超额完成
extraordinary contribution you have made 超凡贡献
on behalf of management 代表管理层
sales expertise 销售技能
impeccable sales record 遥遥领先的销售记录
professional manner 专业风范

Useful Sentences

Rarely has a supplier given us such complete cooperation.
很少有供应商能提供给我们如此完善的合作。
We have always been able to rely on your flexibility and courteous service.
我们一贯信任你们灵活和周到的服务。

Your staff has consistently made extra efforts to assist us in completing our projects on time.

你们的员工一直非常努力地协助我们及时完成任务。

Your supporting work on the project did not go unnoticed.

我们十分感激你们在该项目中的鼎力支持。

We are proud to have such an outstanding design team work. You truly deserved the award for best performance of the year.

我们为你们杰出的团队设计工作感到骄傲。你们获得年度最佳业绩奖是名副其实的。

I wasn't at all surprised to hear that you were elected chairperson of our committee, but I was very pleased.

听说你获选委员会主席,我毫不意外,但是我还是十分高兴。

Congratulations on your promotion.

恭喜你升官。

His actions are a reflection of the courage and unselfishness.

他的行为反映出他的勇气和无私。

It is a tribute to your administrative talent and your hard work.

这归功于你的管理才能和辛勤工作。

What a pity we've lost such a great man!

我们为失去一个这么好的人而感到遗憾!

I sympathize with you.

我对您深表同情。

We have just learned with profound sorrow of the passing away of...

刚刚惊悉……不幸逝世,我们深感悲痛。

We wish to express our deep regret over the passing of...

对……的不幸逝世我们深感痛惜。

Please accept my sincerest condolences.

请接受我诚挚的哀悼。

Exercises

1. Write a letter to express appreciation to long-term customers.
2. Write a letter to compliment an employee's work performance.
3. Compliment or praise a service supplier.
4. Compliment or praise the media, an author, or an editor.
5. Congratulation someone on a speech.
6. Congratulate a associate on getting a new job.
7. Congratulate an employee on advancement.
8. Congratulation someone on the opening of a new business, store, or office.
9. Offer sympathy for loss or damage by a theft, vandalism, or natural disaster.

10. Offer sympathy for the loss of job.
11. Thank someone for expression of sympathy.
12. Write a get-well message to an employee or business associate suffering from illness or injury.
13. Recommend an acquaintant for a job.
14. Recommend a service or product.
15. Endorse or nominate a candidate for an award.

Chapter Eight

Trade Correspondence (Ⅰ)

Section One Business Writing

8.1 Introduction

Broadly speaking, the functions of trade correspondence letters may be said to be: (1) to ask for or to convey information, (2) to make or to accept an offer, (3) to deal with matters concerning business. A good trade correspondence letter is very essential and important for a businessman. While doing a business, it usually includes establishing business relations, inquires, offers, counteroffers, acceptance, orders and declining orders, terms of payments, packing and shipment, etc.

8.2 General Information and Samples of Trade Correspondence

8.2.1 Establishing Business Relations

In international trade, the importer is usually in one country and the exporter in another. They are separated sometimes by thousands of miles. Establishing business relations is the first step in a transaction in foreign trade.

Writing letters to new customers for the establishment of relations is a common practice in business communications. To establish business relations with prospective dealers is one of the vitally important measures either for a newly established firm or an old one that wishes to enlarge its business scope and turnover. There are several channels through which importers and exporters can get to know each other.

The Following are Channels Through Which Information Can be Obtained:

- chamber of Commerce both at home and abroad
- banks
- trade directories of various countries and regions
- commercial Counselor's Office
- exhibition and trade fairs
- internet
- trading fairs and exhibitions

• advertisements in the periodicals, magazines, and newspapers

• middlemen

Before writers correspond with a new customer, first, they should do credit investigation including:

• capital, financial condition

• capacity, business activity

• character, honesty integrity

In such cases, the writers usually put the following points in letters aiming at establishing business relations:

• the source of information

• the intention of writing the letter (to establish business relations)

• self-introduction (Generally, it includes two parts: the introduction of the company and its main products)

• expectation

• closing sentence

If the writers intend to buy for import, they may also make request for samples, price lists, booklet catalogues, credit reference, etc. On the contrary, if the writers hope to export, they possibly would like to supply documents. To close the letter, the writers usually express their expectation of cooperation and an early reply.

The first impressions count heavily. Make sure that the letter follows the standard format and that it is neatly typed and error-free.

Example 1

Dear Sirs or Madams,

We have obtained your name and address from the Ministry of Commerce of the People's Republic of China.

We were informed that you are one of the biggest importers of tea in UK and you are now in the market for tea. We take this opportunity to approach you in the hope of establishing business relations with you.

To give you a general idea of our products, we enclose herewith a copy of our brochure covering the main items available at present.

If you are interested in any of our products or have other products you would like to import, please contact us with your requirements. We look forward to providing you with high quality products, superior customer service and complete satisfaction.

Yours truly,

Example 2

Dear Sir:

On the recommendation of your Chamber of Commerce, we have learned with pleasure the name and address of your firm. We wish to inform you that we specialize in the export of Chinese textiles and shall be glad to enter into business relations with you on the basis of equality and mutual benefit.

To give you a general idea of our products, we are sending you under separate cover a catalogue together with a range of pamphlets for your reference.

Please let us have your specific enquiry if you are interested in any of the items listed in the catalogue. We shall make offers promptly.

We look forward to your early reply.

Yours faithfully,

Example 3

Dear sirs or madams:

Establish business relationship

We owe your name and address to the Commercial Counselor's Offices and British Embassy in Beijing, who have informed us that you are in the market for metal materials.

We avail of this opportunity to express our wish to establish business relations with you.

Our company, Metal Materials Co., Ltd. was established in 1965. As a state-owned company in china, its main business covers metal raw material and their finished products. We have good relations with many big manufactures in our country. So our products have competitive price and best, stable quality, we also have our own special-purpose line of railway to transport products and warehouse to store our goods. In 1993, our company was awarded "Enterprise Credit AAA Grade" by provincial and municipal commercial banks. Business volume is increasing fast. In 2002, annual sales amount of the company reaches 100 million dollars, sell material more than 150,000 tons of quantity, annual handling capacity of the storage is 500,000 tons.

We are now able to produce according to the customers' different needs. We sinceely hope to explore cooperation opportunities with clients both at home and abroad on the basis of mutual benefit and common development.

We are looking forward to your favorable reply.

Yours sincerely,

Metal Material. Co., Ltd
Import & export department
ZUO Quan (Mr.)

Example 4

Ladies and Gentlemen:

Hoping to establish direct business relationship.

We are a fireworks exporting company with our own factory, which is located in the international fireworks manufacturing base: Liuyang city. With many years of manufacturing experience, we can produce any kind of fireworks of good quality according to your specific requirements. Also we are sure we can offer you a competitive price.

Hope to cooperate with you to our mutual benefit.

Yours sincerely,

Example 5

Dear Sirs:

Re: Textile Materials

We get to know your corp. from CCPT company with which we have been in good business relations for many years, and that you are handling import and export of all textile materials.

We are one of the principal manufactures of wool sweater in U. S. A., and are interested in importing sweaters made of wool.

We shall be pleased to receive your details and prices of various sweaters with photos and specifications. We shall be glad to study the sales possibilities at our end.

Yours faithfully,

8.2.2 Inquiries

If the importer intends to purchase goods of a certain specification, he may make an inquiry. An inquiry is a request for information. In the international business the importer may send an inquiry to an exporter, inviting a quotation and or an offer for the goods he wishes to buy or simply asking for some general information about these goods.

Generally speaking, inquiries fall into two categories: a General Inquiry and a Specific Inquiry.

If the importer wants to have a general idea of the commodity, he may make a request for a pricelist, a catalogue, samples and other terms. This is a general inquiry. (Generally, it is also a first inquiry. That is an inquiry writing without first writing a letter to establish business relations.) In a specific inquiry, people can ask more conditions for the name of the commodity, the specifications, the quantity, the unit price FOB..., CIF..., the time of shipment, the terms of payment, etc.

The following structure may be referred to in writing an inquiry:

1. General inquiry

- the source of information and a brief self-introduction
- the intention of writing the letter. (ask for a catalogue, samples or a pricelist)
- stating the possibility of placing an order

2. Specific Inquiry

- expressing thanks for previous letters.
- the names and descriptions of the goods inquired for, including specifications, quantity, etc.
- asking whether there is a possibility of giving a special discount and what terms of payment and time of delivery you would expect
- stating the possibility of placing an order or expectation for favorable reply, etc.

Example 1

Dear Sirs,

We thank you for your letter of May 3 and shall be glad to enter into business relations with you.

We have seen your brochure and are interested in Green Tea Extract and Porcelain Tea Set No. TSM001. We shall be pleased if you will kindly send us samples and all the necessary information regarding these two products.

Truly yours,

Example 2

Dear Sirs,

We thank you for your letter of May 3 and shall be glad to enter into business relations with you.

We have seen your brochûre and are interested in Green Tea Extract and Porcelain Tea Set No. TSM001. We shall be pleased if you will kindly send us samples and all the necessary information regarding these two products.

Meanwhile, please quote us the lowest price, CIF Liverpool, stating the earliest date of shipment and the minimum quantity.

Should your price be competitive and date of shipment acceptable, we intend to place a large order with you.

Your early reply will be highly appreciated.

Truly yours,

Example 3

Dear Sirs:

Thank you for your letter of 25th, September.

As one of the largest dealers of garments, we are interested in ladies' dresses of all descriptions. We would be grateful if you would give us quotations per dozen of CIF Vancouver for those items as listed on the separate sheet. In the meantime, we would like you to send us samples of the various materials of which the dresses are made.

We are given to understand that you are a state-owned enterprise and we have confidence in the quality of Chinese products. If your prices are moderate, we believe there is a promising market for the above-mentioned articles in our area.

We look forward to hearing from you soon.

Yours faithfully,

Canadian Garment Co. Ltd.

Example 4

Gentlemen:

We have seen your advertisement in the Overseas Daily News concerning the new fabrics now available.

We should be obliged if you would send us your pattern books showing the complete range of these fabrics together with your price list.

Please note that we are in importer of quality clothing materials, and have large annual requirements for our many outlets throughout Hong Kong.

Yours faithfully,

Example 5

Dear Sirs:

Re: Tung Oil Bulk

We thank you for your letter dated July 2 informing us that you intend to develop business with us in the line of the captioned goods.

We have some plan using the half-container for carry the Tung Oil. Could you let us have your quotation for said goods at Ex. Works price for shipment in September, 1998. If you can supply it under this condition, our first order quantity will be 120 metric tons.

We look forward to receiving your favorable and prompt reply.

Yours faithfully,

Example 6

Dear Sirs:

We learn from Thomas H. Pennie of New York that you are producing hand-made gloves in a variety of artificial leathers. There is a steady demand here for gloves of high quality at moderate prices.

Will you please send me a copy of your glove catalogue, with details of your prices and terms of payment? I should find it most helpful if you could also supply samples of these gloves.

Yours faithfully,

8.2.3 Offers

Making a quotation or an offer is a most important step in negotiating an export transaction. A quotation is a reply to an inquiry. It is not an "offer" in the legal sense. It is just an indication of price without contractual obligation and subject to change without previous notice. An offer refers to a promise to supply goods on the terms and conditions stated, in which the seller not only quotes the terms of price but also indicates all necessary terms of sales for the buyer's consideration and acceptance. In addition, an offer may be classified into a firm offer and a non-firm offer.

A firm offer is a definite promise to sell goods at the stated prices, usually within a stated period of time. The terms stated in a firm offer is binding on the sellers if they are accepted by the buyers within its validity. Once it has been accepted it cannot be withdrawn. In a firm offer, an exact description of the goods, the time of shipment and the mode of payment should be included.

A non-firm offer is not binding upon the sellers. In other words, a non-firm offer can be withdrawn or changed by the sellers. Non-firm offers are usually made by means of sending catalogues, pricelist, and quotations. It can be considered as an inducement to business.

A satisfactory letter concerning an offer or quotation can be written in the following way:

(1) Open the letter by expressing thanks for the inquiry, if any.

(2) Explain the details of business conditions, such as name of commodities, quality, quantity, specifications, unit price, type of currency, packing condition, date of delivery, terms of payment, discount, etc.

(3) End the letter in the way that encourages the inquirers to place an order or give an early reply.

Example 1

Dear Mr. Brown

We are glad to know that you, one of the biggest suppliers of tea in the UK, are interested in our products. In order to establish a long friendly business relation with you, we are now making you a special offer.

For details, please see quotation sheet.

We are sending you under separate cover the samples of Green Tea Extract and Porcelain Tea Set for your reference. We are confident that you will be satisfied with both the quality of our products and their competitive prices.

We await your favorable news.

Yours very sincerely,

Example 2

Dear Mr. Jones:

We thank you for your email enquiry for both groundnuts and Walnut meat C&F Copenhagen dated February, 21.

In reply, we offer firm, subject to your reply reaching us on or before February 26 for 250 metric tons of groundnuts, handpicked, shelled and ungraded at RMB 2000 net per metric ton C&F Copenhagen and any other European Main Ports. Shipment is to be made within two months after receipt of your order payment by L/C payable by sight draft.

Please note that we have quoted our most favorable price and are unable to entertain any counter offer.

As you are aware that there has lately been a large demand for the above commodities, such growing demand will likely result in increased prices. However, you can secure these prices if you send us an immediate reply.

Sincerely,

Example 3

Dear Mr. Jones:

We thank you for your letter dated April 8 inquiring about our leather handbags. As requested, we take pleasure in offering you, subject to our final confirmation, 300 dozen deerskin handbags style No. MS190 at $124.00 per dozen CIF Hamburg. Shipment will be effected within 20 days after receipt of the relevant L/C issued by your first class bank in our favor upon signing Sales Contract.

We are manufacturing various kinds of leather purses and waist belts for exportation, and enclosed a brochure of products for your reference. We hope some of them meet your taste and needs.

If we can be of any further help, please feel free to let us know. Customers' inquiries are always meet with our careful attention.

Sincerely,

Example 4

Dear Sirs,

Re: SWC Sugar

We are in receipt of your letter of July 17, 2002 asking us to offer 10,000 metric tons of the subject sugar for shipment to Japan and appreciate very much your interest in our product.

To comply with your request, we are offering you the following:

1. Commodity: Qingdao Superior White Crystal Sugar.
2. Packing: To be packed in new gunny bag of 100kgs, each.
3. Quantity: Ten thousand (10000) metric tons.
4. Price: US dollars one hundred and five (US$105.00) per metric ton, FOB Qingdao.
5. Payment: 100% by irrevocable and confirmed Letter of Credit to be opened in our favor through A1 bank in Qingdao and to be drawn at sight.
6. Shipment: Three or four weeks after receipt of Letter of Credit by the first available boat sailing to Yokohama direct.

Please note that we do not have much ready stock on hand. Therefore, it is important that, in order to enable us to effect early shipment, your Letter of Credit should be opened in time if our price meets with your approval.

We are awaiting your reply.

Sincerely,

Example 5

Dear Ms. Dorrell:

Thank you for your recent inquiry concerning James Avery corporate gifts.

To help with your gift purchases, I have enclosed our most recent catalogs illustrating many of our popular items.

Because we design and manufacture our own jewelry, these catalogs can only represent a small portion of the more than 6,000 designs we make. Or, if you prefer, we can create a new design or modify an existing one especially for your corporation.

I've included these examples to let you see the breadth of our designs. I'll be in contact with you to see if the information I have provided is what you need and to answer any question you might have.

Please note that the prices on the enclosed information may not be current, however. I will be happy to provide special quantity prices on the specific items.

We appreciate your interest in James Avery Craftsman and look forward to helping you to select a very special gift.

Best regards,

Example 6

Dear Sir,

Thank you for your letter dated June 7.

We have pleasure in submitting the following quotation for your consideration. We confirm that the prices will remain valid for three months.

Description: headsets
Net Price: 12 U. S. D. Each

Packing charges and other duties and taxes are included in the price quoted above.

Since the equipment is breakable and expensive, we would strongly advise you to get it insured. If you agree, we shall do it for you at an extra charge of 1/2 per cent on the quoted price. The equipment will be sent by goods train within one month of the receipt of your order.

All items are guaranteed for three years. During this period, if necessary, we shall repair or replace any item at our cost.

We do not require any advance but would like the payment to be made by crossed cheque drawn on the City Bank, within 15 days of the receipt of equipment.

We look forward to receiving your order soon. If you need any further information, please do not hesitate to write to us.

Yours faithfully,

Example 7

Dear Sirs:

This is to confirm your telex of 16 May 2000, asking us to make you firm offers for rice and soybeans C&F Singapore.

We telexed you this morning offering you 300 metric tons of polished rice at A$2,400 per metric ton, C&F Singapore, for shipment during July/August 2000. This offer is firm, subject to the receipt of your reply before 10 June 2000.

Please note that we have quoted our most favourable price and are unable to entertain any counter offer.

With regard to soybeans, we advise you that the few lots we have at present are under offer elsewhere. If, however, you were to make us a suitable offer, there is a possibility of our supplying them.

As you know, of late, it has been a heavy demand for these commodities and this has resulted in increased prices. You may, however, take advantage of the strengthening market if you send an immediate reply.

Yours faithfully,

8.2.4 Counteroffers

When an offer is considered unacceptable, it may be rejected by a counter-offer, which much resembles bargaining over a product on the market. A counter-offer is virtually a partial rejection of the original offer stating his own terms instead. Then the original offer or seller becomes the offered. If he also disagrees with the relative terms in the counter-offer, he many send a counter counter-offer to the buyer. So a deal is usually concluded only after several cycles of bargaining. In other words, very often, it is only after the exchange of a number of letters and/or faxes that the two parties come entirely to terms.

Before making a counter-offer, you may thank the seller for his offer and express your regret for being unable to accept the offer and state the reason. For the sake of future business, there will be no harm for you to suggest that there should be other opportunities to do business together.

Letters including a counter-offer can be written in the following structure:

- thank the seller for his offer, mention briefly the content of the offer
- express regret at inability to accept (give the reasons for non-acceptance)
- make a counter-offer if, under the circumstances, it is appropriate
- hope the counter-offer will be accepted and there may be an opportunity to do business together

Example 1

Dear Mr. Jones,

We acknowledge receipt of both your offer of May 6 and the samples of Men's Shirts, and thank you for these.

While appreciating the good quality of your shirts, we find your price is rather too high for the market we wish to supply.

We have also to point out that the Men's Shirts are available in our market from several European manufacturers, all of them are at prices from 10% to 15% below the price you quoted.

Such being the case, we have to ask you to consider if you can make reduction in your price, say 10%. As our order would be worth around US$ 50,000, you may think it worthwhile to make a concession.

We are looking forward to your reply.

Sincerely,

Example 2

Dear Mr. Jones:

We confirm having received your telex No. LT/531 of May 17, asking us to make a 10% reduction in our price for Men's Shirts. Much to our regret, we are unable to comply with your request because we have given you the lowest possible price. We can assure you that the price quoted reflects the high quality of the products.

We still hope to have the opportunity to work with you and any further enquiry will receive our prompt attention.

Sincerely,

Example 3

Dear Mr. Zhang,

Re: Green Tea Extract and Porcelain Tea Set

We acknowledge with thanks receipt of your offer of May 8 for the subject goods.

In reply, we regret to say that we can't accept it. Your prices are rather on the high side and out of line with the world market. Information indicates that some parcels of Japanese make have been sold at a much lower level.

We have seen your samples and admit that they are of high quality, but there should not be such a big gap between your prices and those of other suppliers.

In order to conclude the transaction, we suggest that you reduce the prices of both products by, say 30%.

We hope you can accept the counteroffer and wait for your favorable reply.

Truly yours,

Global Tea Bags Ltd.

Example 4

Dear Sirs,

RE: COUNTER-OFFER FOR BICYCLES

Thank you for your letter about the offer for the captioned bicycles. Although we appreciate the quality of your bicycles, their price is too high to be acceptable. Referring to the Sales Confirmation No. 89SP-754, you will find that we ordered 1,000 bicycles with same brand as per the terms and conditions stipulated in that Sales Confirmation, but the price was 10% lower than your present price. Since we placed the last order, price for raw materials has been decreased considerablely. Retailing price for your bicycles here has also been reduced by 5%. Accepting your present price will mean great loss to us, let alone profit. We would like to place repeat orders with you if you could reduce your price at least by 1.5%. Otherwise, we have to shift to the other suppliers for our similar request. We hope you take our suggestion into serious consideration and give us your reply as soon as possible.

Yours truly,

Example 5

Dear Sirs:

Thank you for your letter of 20 May 2000. We are disappointed to hear that our price for Flame cigarette lighters is too high for you to work on. You mention that Japanese goods are being offered to you at a price approximately 10% lower than that quoted by us.

We accept what you say, but we are of the opinion that the quality of the other makes does not measure up to that of our products.

Although we are keen to do business with you, we regret that we cannot accept your counter offer or even meet you half way.

The best we can do is to reduce our previous quotation by 2%. We trust that this will meet with your approval.

We look forward to hearing from you.

Yours faithfully,

8.2.5 Acceptance, Orders and Declining Orders

When everything contained in an offer is accepted by the buyer unconditionally, an agreement should be finally reached between the two sides—the seller and the buyer, and once the offer is accepted it cannot be withdrawn.

Acceptance needs not always be direct and can, in certain circumstances, be implied by conduct. There are two common ways to inform the seller that the offer is accepted:

(1) Write or fax or e-mail to inform the seller your acceptance and repeat in writing the main conditions settled by both parties previously.

(2) Besides letter of fax acceptance, send an Agreement or a Sales Contract or a Purchase Contract to the other party for a Countersignature.

Example 1

Dear —,

In accordance with faxes exchanged, we are pleased to confirm having concluded with you an agreement for 200 dozen Ladies' Umbrellas.

Enclosed is our Sales Contract No. 568 in duplicate. Please countersign and return one copy for our file.

We assure you of our best attention to the execution of your order, and hope your L/C will arrive here in time so as to enable us to make early shipment.

Yours faithfully,

Example 2

Dear —,

Re: Contract No. AST 7681

We are enclosing herewith the captioned contract in two originals, of which please return one copy to us duly countersigned for our records.

We thank you for your kind cooperation.

Yours faithfully,

An order is a commercial document requesting the supply of a specific quantity of goods. It may result from the buyers' acceptance or confirmation of a firm offer made by the sellers or result from the sellers' acceptance or confirmation of a counter-offer made by the buyers. Order letters create one half of a contract.

The following structure can be for your reference in placing an order:

(1) Use direct language in the first paragraph to tell the seller of the buyer's intention to place an order.

(2) Describe what is being ordered in great detail. Indicate the catalog numbers, sizes, colors, prices (unit prices as well as total prices), specifications and all other relevant information that will enable the seller to fill the order without any further questions, such as terms of payment; mode of packing; time of transportation, port of destination and time of

shipment etc.

(3) Close the letter by expressing willingness to cooperate or suggesting future business dealings.

When confirming an order received, the following structure may be for your reference:

(1) Express appreciation for the order received.

(2) Assure the buyers that the goods they have ordered will be delivered in compliance with their request. It is also advisable for the sellers to take the opportunity to resell their products or to introduce their other products to the buyers.

(3) Close the letter by expressing willingness to cooperate or suggesting future business dealings.

Example 3

Gentlemen:

The price quotes contained in your E-mail of May 20,2002 gained favorable attention with us.

We would like to order the following items consisting of various colors, patterns and assortments:

Large 2000 dozen

Medium 4000 dozen

Small 2000 dozen

As the sales season is approaching, the total order quantity should be shipped in July. At that time an irrevocable L/C for the total purchase value will be opened.

Please confirm the order and E-mail a shipping schedule.

Sincerely,

Some times, the orders may not be able to be accepted for the following reasons:

(1) The goods required are not available;

(2) Prices and specifications have been changed;

(3) The buyers and the sellers cannot agree on some terms of the business;

(4) The buyer's credit is not in good standing;

(5) The manufacturer simply does not produce the goods ordered, etc.

The following organization can be for your reference in writing a letter declining an order:

A Positive Opening—It is sensible to open the letter in a positive way in order to place the message in its correct communication context. For example, appreciation or pleasure in receiving the order can be stated at the beginning of the letter.

Detailed explanations—When declining an order, detailed and sensible reasons should be provided in order to retain the reader's interest in the writer's products or services. In addition, in order to conclude a deal, the writer usually offers suitable substitutes, makes counter-offers and persuades the buyers to acceptable them.

A Positive Close—End the letter in the way that makes the reader aware of the writer's expectation for future business relations with him.

Example 4

Dear Sir,

Subject: Out of Stock

We thank you for your Order No. 222 received this morning for 8,000 dozen cotton shirts, but regret to have to disappoint you.

At present we have no stock of shirts in the size required and do not expect further deliveries for at least another five weeks. Before then you may have been to obtain the shirts elsewhere, but if not we will notify you immediately our new stocks come in.

Yours faithfully,

Section Two　Language Handbook

Useful Words and Expressions

to enter into business activities with 与建立业务联系
to build up business relations with 与建立业务联系
on the basis of equality and mutual benefit 在平等互利的基础上
catalog 目录,目录册
look forward to 盼望,期待
recommendation 推荐,介绍
Chamber of Commerce 商会
specialize in 专营
pamphlet 小册子
meet with great favor 受欢迎
financial position 财务状况
credit standing 信用地位
acknowledge 承认收到来信
to make an offer for 对……报盘(报价)
to offer for 对……报价

make/ send/ give/cable sb. quotation for sth. 对……报盘(报价)
firm (报盘等)确定的,有效的
non-firm offer 虚盘
subject to our final confirmation 以我方最后确认为准
without engagement 此报盘无约束力
conclude 达成,缔结(条约等)
valid 有效的
out of line 不合理的,不相符的
acceptance 接受
acceptable 可接受的
specification (多用复)规格
item 项目,商品,产品
in compliance with 按照,依照
trial order 试订单
bid 出价,递盘
approval 赞成,认可,批准
counter-offer 还盘
acknowledge 承认,告知收到
be desirous of sth. 想要某物
be desirous of doing sth. 渴望做某事
terms and conditions 条款
countersign 会签
stipulate 规定
send. . . under separate cover 另寄
together with 和,加之
regarding 关于
refer to 向……咨询,参阅
enclose 装入,放入套内,随函寄……
rest assured that. . . 确信无疑,放心
handle with 处理
commit 承担任务,接受订单,答应负责
stock 存货
market 推销,销售,在市场上出售
ceiling price 最高价,顶价
maximum price 最高价
minimum price 最低价
average price 平均价格
base price 底价
rockbottom price 最低价

bedrock price 最低价
priced catalogue 定价目录
price of commodities 物价
pricing cost 定价成本
pricing method 定价方法
price list 定价政策,价格目录,价格单
price current (p.c.) 市价表
market 市场,行市
come to the market 上市
find a market 找销路
a good (poor) market 畅销(滞销)
in the market for 要购买
an advancing market 市场上涨
a brisk market 市场活跃
a strong market 市场坚挺

Useful Sentences

1. Source of Information

We have learned from the website alibaba that you are in the market for textile.

我们从阿里巴巴网站上得知你方欲购买纺织品。

We have seen your toys displayed at the Guangzhou Trade Fair and are quite interested in item No. 123.

我们在广交会上看到你方展示的玩具,并对第123号商品感兴趣。

We understand from your advertisement in "Electric" that you are exporters of electric goods.

我们从你方在电子杂志中的广告得知你方是电子产品的出口商。

We've come to know your name and address from the Commercial Counselor's Office of the Chinese Embassy in London.

我们从中国驻伦敦大使馆的商务参赞处得知你们的名字和地址。

By the courtesy of Mr. Black, we are given to understand the name and address of your firm.

承蒙布莱克先生的介绍,我们得知贵公司的名称和地址。

Your firm has been introduced (recommended, passed on) to us by Maple Company.

枫叶公司向我方介绍了贵公司。

2. Introduction of the Products

Our products are not only attractive and durable but also complete in specification.

我们的产品不仅美观耐用而且规格齐全。

Our products are excellent in quality and low in price. They are the best-selling items in this line.

我们的产品物美价廉。它们是同类产品中卖得最好的。

Our products are very popular among the youth.

我们的产品很受年轻人的欢迎。

Our products enjoy high reputation in the world market.

我们的产品在国际市场上享有盛誉。

3. Introduction of the Company

We have been in the line of chemical for many years.

我们从事化工行业已经很多年了。

We are specialized in the export of textile.

我们专门从事纺织品的出口。

The item you inquired for comes within the frame of our business activities.

你们所询的商品正属于我们的业务经营范围。

We handle the import business of textiles.

我公司经营纺织品的进口业务。

We deal in Chinese textiles.

我们经营中国纺织品。

We are engaged in the exportation of chemicals.

我们经营化工产品的出口。

This shop trades in paper and stationery.

这商店经营文具纸张。

We are in the cotton piece goods business.

我们经营棉织品。

Cotton Piece Goods are our line.

棉布是我公司经营的产品。

Cotton Piece Goods are our main exports.

棉布是我们的主要进口商品。

4. Establishing Relations

We are willing to enter into business relations with your firm.

我们愿意与贵公司建立业务关系。

Our mutual understanding and cooperation will certainly result in important business.

我们之间的相互了解与合作必将促成今后重要的生意。

We express our desire to establish business relations with your firm.

我们愿和贵公司建立业务关系。

We shall be glad to enter into business relations with you.

我们很乐意同贵公司建立业务关系。

We now avail ourselves of this opportunity to write to you with a view to entering into business relations with you.

现在我们借此机会致函贵公司,希望和贵公司建立业务关系。

We are now writing you for the purpose of establishing business relations with you.

我们特此致函是想与贵方建立业务关系。

Your desire to establish business relations coincides with ours.

你方想同我方建立业务关系的愿望与我方是一致的。

We specialize in the export of Japanese Light Industrial Products and would like to trade with you in this line.

鉴于我方专营日本轻工业产品出口业务,我方愿与贵方在这方面开展贸易。

Your letter expressing the hope of establishing business connections with us has met with approval.

来函收悉,得知贵方愿与我方建立业务关系,我们表示同意。

In order to acquaint you with the textiles we handle, we take pleasure in sending you by air our latest catalogue for your perusal.

为了使贵方对我方经营的纺织品有所了解,特航寄我方最新目录,供细阅。

5. Inquiry

Please let us have your lowest quotation.

请报最低价。

Please make us your lowest quotation for Chinese Folding Fans.

请报中国折扇最低价。

Your quotation of Chinese Folding Fans is too high to be acceptable.

你方中国折扇报价太高,不能接受。

6. Offer

As requested, we are offering you the following subject to our final confirmation:

根据要求,现我方就如下货物向贵方报盘,以我方最后确认为准:

As recently the goods are in extremely short supply, we regret being unable to offer.

因近期货源紧张,很抱歉不能报盘。

It's a pleasure for us to offer you the goods as follows:

非常荣幸地向你方报盘如下:

Referring to your E-mail dated July 10 in which you inquired for shirts, we have pleasure in giving you an offer as follows:

关于贵方7月10日对衬衫的询盘,现报盘如下:

We can offer you a quotation based upon the international market.

我们可以按国际市场价格给您报价。

My offer was based on reasonable profit, not on wild speculations.

我的报价以合理利润为依据,不是漫天要价。

No other buyers have bid higher than this price.

没有别的买主的出价高于此价。

We can't accept your offer unless the price is reduced by 5%.

除非你们减价5%,否则我们无法接受报盘。

We'll give you the preference of our offer.

我们将优先向你们报盘。

This offer is based on an expanding market and is competitive.

此报盘着眼于扩大销路而且很有竞争性。

The offer holds good until 5 o'clock p.m. June 23,2007,Beijing time.

报价有效期到2007年6月22日下午5点,北京时间。

All prices in the price lists are subject to our confirmation.

报价单中所有价格以我方确认为准。

Our offers are for 3 days.

我们的报盘三天有效。

7. Counter-offer

Now we look forward to replying to our offer in the form of counter-offer.

现在我们希望你们能以还盘的形式对我方报盘予以答复。

our price is too high to interest buyers in counter-offer.

你的价格太高,买方没有兴趣还盘。

I'll respond to your counter-offer by reducing our price by three dollars.

我同意你们的还价,减价3元。

I appreciate your counter-offer but find it too low.

谢谢您的还价,可我觉得太低了。

The quality of the goods offered in your letter of... is not satisfactory. We would like to know if you could supply items of a better quality.

贵方××日来信所报货物的品质不能令人满意。我方想了解你方可否提供更好的品质。

If you could reduce the prices for your offer of... by 2%, we would be willing to accept your offer.

如果你方可以将报盘减价2%,我们便愿意接受报价。

Your payment conditions are not acceptable. We have to insist on payment by L/C.

你方所列付款条件无法接受。我方不得不坚持信用证付款。

We have to point out that the listed payment terms do not correspond to customary business practice.

我方不得不指出,所列付款条件不符合贸易惯例。

The shipping arrangements in your offer are not acceptable. We can accept your offer only if you adhere to our wishes regarding shipping.

你方报价所列装船安排无法接受。只有你方按照我方的意愿安排装运才能接受你方报价。

8. Replies to Enquiries and Offers

We are pleased to find your offer of... fits well into our sales program, and enclose our official order for the following:

我方很高兴的发现贵方报盘符合我方的销售计划,兹附上我方正式订单如下。

We regret having received your offer too late. We have already covered our needs elsewhere.

很遗憾,我方收到贵方报盘太迟,已经从别处订货(满足自己所需)。

Because your prices are higher than those of our previous suppliers, we cannot make use of your offer dated...

由于贵方价格高于我方以前的供货商,因此我方无法接受你方...日的报盘。

We would accept your offer of... if packing charges are included.

如果报价包括包装费,我们便接受你方报盘。

Your offer suits us. However, we must insist on delivery before the end of November.

你方报价对我方较适合,但我方坚持 11 月底前交货。

Due to the present price level, we are unable to change the price of our offer.

鉴于当前的价格水平,我方无法改变报价。

We are sorry not to adjust our offer according to your request.

很抱歉我方未能按照贵方要求调整报价。

We are sorry not to be able to comply with your request for a lower price, but we are in a position to send you a special offer.

很抱歉我方无法按照你方要求降价,但我方可以向你方报特价。

9. Reply to Letters

In answer to your favor of the 6th May, we inform you that we are unable to take the goods offered by you.

贵公司 5 月 6 日函悉,本公司无法承购贵公司开价的商品。此复。

In answer to your inquiry for bran, we offer you 20 tons of the same.

关于贵公司所询麦麸一事,现可提供该货 20 吨。

Answering to your letter, we state that the market remains quiet.

贵函收悉,此地商场仍保持平静。

Kindly excuse our not replying to your favor of the 8th May until today.

至今未复 5 月 8 日贵函,甚感歉疚,还望原谅。

In response to your letter of the 8th inst., I am pleased to say that Mr. × is a man of trustworthy character.

本月 8 日贵函敬悉,×先生是位诚实可靠的人,特此告知。

In response to your inquiry respecting Mr. H., we have pleasure in stating that he is a thoroughly reliable man.

关于所询 H.先生的情况,谨此高兴地告知,他是一位足以信赖的人。

We are glad to answer your inquiry concerning S. & Company.

关于 S.公司的情况,我们特此欣然函复。

Answering to your inquiry respecting Mr. J., we are pleased to say that we found him absolutely reliable.

关于 J.先生的情况,谨此高兴地告知,我们认为他是绝对可以信赖的人。

Replying to your letter of the 17th respecting the account, I will send you a cheque shortly.

17 日贵函关于结账一事,谨此告知,我们将很快寄去支票。

10. Acknowledgement of Letters

I acknowledge receipt of your letter of yesterday, and gratefully accept the appointment on the terms you mention.

您昨日来信已收悉,谨于此按您所约定的条件,接受此项任务。

We are pleased to acknowledge receipt of your favor of the 1st June.

6月1日贵函敬悉。

We acknowledge receipt of your letter of the 5th in this month.

本月5日来函敬悉。

Kindly acknowledge receipt, and have the goods sent by the last steamer in December.

本商品将于12月最后一班轮船付运,货到时请惠于告知。

We duly received your favor of the 15th May, contents of which we note with thanks.

我们如期收到您5月15日的信,信中所谈事宜尽悉。谢谢。

We are in possession of your favor of the 6th June, and regret having to inform you that it is impossible for us to deliver the goods.

6月6日来函收悉,我们无法交运该货,甚感遗撼。

We are in possession of your invoice of the 15th July.

7月15日寄来的货物发票收悉。

Your favor of the 7th July is at hand, and thank you for your order for:

7月7日的贵函收悉,感谢您订购下列货物:

Your favor of the 10th July came duly to hand.

7月10日来函敬悉。

Your favor of yesterday covering a cheque of $100 is duly to hand.

您昨天的信和所附来的100美元支票均已收悉。

We have to own with thanks the receipt of your favor of 5th June.

您6月5日的来函收悉,多谢。

11. Confirmation

We confirm our call of last week respecting our offers to you.

关于上周本公司通过电话给您的报价,我们特予以确认。

We confirm our respects of the 3rd May, and inform you that your consignment has duly arrived.

兹确认我们5月3日所发函并告知您发来的货物已如期到达。

I confirm the receipt of your shipment by m.s. "O", and now send you a cheque, valuing $550.

兹确认已收到"O"号轮船送来的货物,现寄去550美元的支票一张。请查取。

Confirming our letter of last week, we ask you to appoint an early interview with our representative.

兹确认我上星期致您函,请及早约定与我方代表面谈的日期。

Confirming ours of the 11th June, we now hand you enclosed B/L for 50 packages.

兹确认本公司6月11日的信,同函附上50包的提单。请查收。

We confirm our respects of yesterday, and have the pleasure to inform you that we have drawn this day on you.

兹确认昨天致您的信并欣告今天我们已给你们开出汇票。

We have much pleasure in confirming herewith the order which you kindly placed with us yesterday.

兹确认您昨天向我们提出的订单。承惠顾非常欣慰。

Kindly let us have confirmation of these orders by telegraph tomorrow by 3 p.m.

您对我公司所提订单,请务必于明天下午三时前来电确认。

In confirmation of my cable today, I regret to state that the factory was completely destroyed by fire last night.

谨确认今日电报,非常遗撼,该工厂于昨夜被毁于火。

Kindly give us an order sheet in confirmation of the message by telephone of this morning.

为确认今早电话中所订货物,请寄来订货单。

12. Pleasure

We have the pleasure to acknowledge your favour of yesterday advising 25 cases for Shanghai.

您昨日告知向上海发出25箱的信函我们已敬悉。

We have the pleasure of enclosing herewith the documents.

同函奉上有关文件。

We have pleasure in forwarding you a cheque for $50,000.

谨送上50000美元的支票一张。

We have pleasure in enclosing herewith a Bill of Lading covering 50 bales of cotton.

兹随信附去50包棉花的提单一张。

We have much pleasure of placing the following order with you:

我们愿向您提出下列订货:

We take pleasure in informing you that a parcel containing books and others has arrived for you from London.

我们高兴地通知您,从伦敦给您发来的书和其他东西的邮包已经到达。

We shall be pleased to enter your order at $900 per pound.

我们愿按每磅900美元接受您的订单。

We are glad to report on S. & Company, of this city.

兹报告本市的S.公司情况。

I Shall be glad if you will kindly give me a price for printing.

如蒙告知所需印刷费用,则不胜欣慰。

We are glad to answer your inquiry concerning S. & Company.

兹答复所询有关S.公司的情况。

13. Enclosure

We enclose for realization drafts as per the list at foot.

按照本函下列清单，附上应兑现的汇票。

Enclosed we hand you two Bills of lading for the goods, per S.S, "Shizuoka Maru" to Hong Kong.

今随信奉上由"静冈号"发往香港的货物提单两张。

Enclosed please find the invoice of 80 bales wool bought by your order.

依照您的订单同函奉上80包羊毛的发票，请查收。

Enclosed you will find an invoice of 50 cases goods.

随信附上50箱货物的发票，请查收。

Enclosed please find three orders for immediate attention.

随信附上订单三张，请立即安排。

A stamped envelope is enclosed for reply.

随信附上贴邮票的信封一个，静候回音。

An order form is enclosed. Fill it out and attach your check.

随函附上订单一张，请填妥后并附来支票为荷。

Enclosed we hand you an invoice, $5,000, for 10 cases goods.

同函附上10箱货物共价5,000美元的发票一张。

Exercises

Ⅰ. Fill in the Blanks

1. We are pleased to give you this order ________ the following items ________ the understanding that they will be supplied at the prices stated in your letter of last week.
2. We expect to find a good market ________ these cottons and hope to place further and larger orders ________ you ________ the near future.
3. All these items are ________ urgent need, and you are therefore requested to make delivery without delay.
4. Your letter of June 6, 2007 together with your order ________ bamboo ware has been received thanks.
5. We will arrange ________ the production in receipt of your order.
6. We are satisfied ________ the results of the negotiations held ________ the Spring Guangzhou Fair.
7. If the quality is ________ our expectation, we will place ________ you our further orders.
8. Your order is receiving our immediate attention and you can depend ________ us to effect delivery well ________ your time limit.
9. We are sending you our S/C No. 0024 ________ duplicate, one copy of which please sign and return us ________ our file.
10. Your alarm clocks are satisfactory ________ our customers and there is a possibility of their repeat orders ________ large quantities.

11. We note ________ your letter ________ October 5 that you are interested ________ Chinese Cotton Piece Goods.
12. The letter we sent last week is an inquiry ________ color TV sets.
13. We produce decorative fabrics ________ different kinds.
14. We would like to know something ________ the styles prevailing ________ your end.
15. We should be pleased to send you some samples of our shoes and hats on approval ________ our own expense.
16. We shall make a reduction ________ our price if you increase the quantity ________ 1,000 pcs.
17. We refer ________ your offer ________ 18th May.
18. I'd like to direct your attention ________ the quality ________ the goods which is superior ________ that of other makes.
19. Many of our clients requested us ________ approach you ________ offers.
20. Thank you ________ your quotation ________ September 5th ________ 500 pieces ________ the captioned goods.
21. We offer you ________ 200 TV sets ________ US$... ________ FOB New York basis ________ August shipment.
22. If you could make a reduction ________ 10% ________ quotation, we have confidence ________ securing large orders ________ you.
23. We rely ________ you to execute the order to the full expectation of our customers.
24. We regret our inability to comply ________ your request for shipping the goods by early November.
25. We take pleasure ________ sending you our Order No. 123 for 400 sets of Panasonic 2188 Color TV.

Ⅱ. Choice

1. Mr. Sidney has been our ________ salesperson. ( )
   A. poorest B. worst
   C. earliest D. most successful
2. We trust that you will find our goods ________. ( )
   A. to be attractive B. attractive
   C. attracting D. attract your attention
3. Our products enjoy ________ in world market. ( )
   A. good seller B. most popular
   C. great popularity D. selling fast
4. This offer is ________ your acceptance by E-mail on or before March 15. ( )
   A. effective of B. effective for
   C. effective to D. effectively for
5. If you are interested, we will send you a sample lot ________ charge. ( )

A. with B. in C. for D. free of

6. The exhibition has ________ to offer that you will find interesting. (　　)

A. many B. much C. more D. many a

7. This price is ________ of your 5% commission. (　　)

A. includes B. inclusive

C. covering D. including

8. ________ your request, we are sending you a catalog and a sample book for your reference. (　　)

A. According B. As

C. At D. About

9. On orders ________ 1,000 pieces or more we give a special discount of 5%. (　　)

A. on B. for C. at D. of

10. ________ the present market trend, we have to say that our price is really the best we can quote. (　　)

A. With B. On C. Because D. For

11. We are not in a position to make any reduction ________ price. (　　)

A. in B. of C. at D. on

12. We believe that there is a ready market ________ the goods in your place. (　　)

A. of B. about C. for D. with

13. With a view ________ the market at your end we have offered you our bottom price. (　　)

A. to promoting B. to promote

C. of promote D. into promoting

14. Our suggestion is that you ________ the similar article ________ what you request at a lower price than quoted owing to similarity in function. (　　)

A. recommend, as B. replace, by

C. take, into D. substitute, for

15. We agree to reduce your price ________ USD 160 per pair FOB Shanghai. (　　)

A. at B. to C. of D. for

16. We have decided to make a further concession ________ 5% per box in order to help you to increase the business with us. (　　)

A. to B. of C. on D. about

17. We regret that our low prices ________ narrow margin of profit. (　　)

A. leave us with B. include

C. earn D. give

18. We feel regretful that you ask us to allow you a commission ________ 10% on each sale. (　　)

A. of B. to C. on D. /

19. We place this order ________ the understanding that the goods will be shipped by April.

(　　)

A. based on　　B. with　　C. on　　D. through

20. Meanwhile we confirm ________ from you the following items. (　　)

A. to purchase　　B. purchase

C. having purchased　　D. to have purchased

21. you may ________ will always be carefully attended to. (　　)

A. place us　　B. place with us

C. make us　　D. make with us

22. ________ of our efforts, we have persuaded our clients to accept your offer. (　　)

A. Result in　　B. Result from

C. As a result of　　D. With the result in

23. We are pleased that we have booked ________ 2000 pcs bicycles. (　　)

A. your order　　B. with you

C. an order with you　　D. an order with you for

24. We suggest that shipment of our order ________ effected in May instead of June. (　　)

A. is　　B. will be　　C. is to be　　D. be

25. Following your order ________ 400 metric tons of rayon last year, we are pleased to receive your order No. 876 ________ the same quantity. (　　)

A. for, of　　B. of, of　　C. of, with　　D. of, for

Ⅲ. Translation

1. ________________(很遗憾地告知) we can't accept your offer for the cars.

2. It is regretful that ________________(你方报价与市价不符).

3. ________________(如果你方把报盘降价 2%), we will close the business.

4. You'd better lower your prices, ________________(由于市场不坚挺).

5. We would like to point out that the prices are our lowest level ________________(所获利润微薄).

6. The best we can do ________________(给你方 5 月底以前来的订单打 9%的折扣) as a special concession.

7. ________________(由于运输价格的上涨), we have to adjust our prices to cover the increasing cost.

8. We regret to say that ________________(我方的新价格于 5 月 6 日起使用).

9. Thank you for your letter of October 1 asking us to ________________

(你方报盘 500 个美的牌电饭锅)for May shipment.

10. For your information, ______________________(我们的报价中已包含你方百分之五的佣金).

11. As the price quoted by us is reasonable, ______________________(我们相信你方能够接受).

12. The prices listed in our proforma invoice ______________________(均为新港交货价).

13. ______________________(一旦获得进口许可证),please fax us so that we can get the goods ready.

14. ______________________(这是我方最优惠的报盘),which you can not obtain elsewhere.

15. In order to promote the development of our business, ______________________(我们决定按大连交货价向你方报盘).

16. Unless otherwise stated, the above offer ______________________(以先售为条件).

17. As requested, we are making you an offer as follows ______________________(每箱 84 美元 CIF 新港).

18. The commission on our shoes would be ______________________(以不少于 1000 箱的购买量).

19. Whenever you are in the market for the products, ______________________(请就你方的需求直接与我方联系).

20. ______________________(如果你方价格有竞争力),we are willing to place our first order for 1,200 dozen, i.e. 400 dozen of each type.

21. Only the goods which are fine in quality but low in price ______________________.(才能吸引我方客户).

22. Several of our customers have recently expressed interest in your products and ______________________.(现随函附上我方有关 1000 辆童车的询盘).

23. We should be obliged ______________________.(如蒙报给最低成本加运费、保险费美国纽约价)for the following goods.

Ⅳ. Translate the Following Sentences into English

1. 我们的价格和国际市场上的同类产品的价格相比一直是偏低的。
2. 由于原材料涨价,我们也不得不调整产品价格。
3. 产品的质量不一样,价格当然不一样。你要的是我们今年顶尖的产品,价钱当然不一样。
4. 我们双方若在价格问题上都坚持己见,那就很难谈下去了。
5. 你看这样行不行,你在发盘的基础上减 5%,我在还盘的基础上加 5%,怎么样?
6. 你同意多买 200 箱我们的产品,我们就可以按每箱 $ 138 新港离岸价成交。

7. 你若能保证我三个月内收到货,我现在就可以向你订货。
8. 如果你们同意分批交货的话,我们可以保证如数供应。
9. 我们两天之内就会将订货单寄去,而且也请贵公司加紧履行订单的工作。
10. 301号乌龙茶是高档茶。由于对健康有益,越来越受到欢迎。尤其是这几个月,国外订单不断地来,已经有些供不应求了。

Ⅴ. Write Letters with the Following Information

1. 我们从蒂科公司得知贵司商号与地址,特此来函,希望能同贵司发展商务关系。

多年来,本公司经营纺织品进口生意,目前想扩展业务范围。请惠寄商品目录与报价单。

如贵司产品价格合理,本公司必定向你方下定单。

恭候佳音。

2. 我方有客户对你方"天鹅"牌毛巾感兴趣,且让我方与你方联系报价和现可供出口的产品的样品。请报你方货号 AK-18 的 30000 打成本加运费的纽约最低价,指出可能最早装运时间及支付条件。

顺告你方,这里类似产品的竞争非常激烈。务请保证你方价格与现在市价相一致,这样使我们能够为你方争取更多订单。

盼尽快收到回信。

3. 感谢贵方6月6日来函。

按贵方要求,我方现报虚盘如下:

可立即装运 2000 桶"狮"牌油漆,上海离岸价每桶 12.5 美元。该报盘以我方最后确认为准。

随函附寄一些样品书及传单供贵方参考。

鉴于贵方是我方的老朋友,我方报最好价格,希望贵方接受并尽早传真确认。

4. 我们已收到贵方4月15日的信函及样品。

顺告贵方,我方对贵方样品测试很满意。但是非常抱歉告之贵方价格偏高并且已高出市场价格。有信息显示,贵方所报盘的品牌此地可以从其他供货地获得并且比贵价格低很多。我们不否认贵方产品的质量较好,然而,不论怎样,价格也不能差异太大。如贵方同意降低贵方限价,比方说5%,我们可能成交。我们希望贵方考虑我们最有利的还盘。

盼与贵方开始业务往来及尽快答复。

Chapter Nine

Trade Correspondence (Ⅱ)

Section One Business Writing

9.1 Packing and Shipment

9.1.1 Packing

Factors which influence the nature of packing: are value of the goods, nature of the transit, nature of the cargo, compliance with customers, or statutory requirements, resale value of packing materials, general fragility of cargo, variation in temperature during the course of the transit, ease of handling and stowage, insurance acceptance conditions and cost of packing.

There are two forms of packing: large packing/outer packing, i.e. packing for transportation and small packing/inner packing, i.e. packaging or sales packing.

Letters are written possibly for negotiation of the means of packing, packing materials, packing cost, marks and packing designs.

Three principal types of marking which may have to be done on export packages:

- the consignees' own distinctive marks
- any official mark required by authorities
- special directions or warnings

All the above are possible to create correspondence between the buyer and the seller.

The following are applicable structure in writing a letter concerning packing:

(1) Open the letter by pointing out the problem under discussion.

(2) The seller explains the packing arrangements and performance or the buyer makes packing instructions in great details. In case the writer wants the reader to change the packing method or to accept the changed packing method, detailed reasons should be provided.

(3) End the letter by asking for cooperation or expressing wishes for an early reply.

Example 1

Dear Sirs,

We have received your letter dated July 8. As for the shipping marks, we are now informing you of our requirements.

Please mark the bales with our initials, with the destination and contract number as follows:

KT
LONDON
250

This will apply to all shipments unless otherwise instructed. Please advise us by fax as soon as shipment is effected.

Yours faithfully,

Example 2

Dear Sirs,

The 12,000 cycles you ordered will be ready for dispatch by 17th December. Since you require them for onward shipment to Bahrain, Kuwait, Oman and Qatar, we are arranging for them to be packed in seaworthy containers.

Each bicycle is enclosed in a corrugated cardboard pack, and 20 are banned together and wrapped in sheet plastic. A container holds 240 cycles; the whole cargo would therefore comprise 50 containers, each weighing 8 tons. Dispatch can be made from our works by rail to be forwarded from Shanghai harbor. The freight charges from works to Shanghai are US $ 80 per container, totally US $ 4,000 for this consignments, excluding container hire, which will be charged to your account.

Please let us have your delivery instruction.

Yours faithfully,

Example 3

Dear Sir or Madam:

Your order No. 756

We are writing to inform you that we have today dispatched by road carrier one case containing the chinaware which you ordered on February 15.

All items were individually examined before being packed and we trust they will reach you in good condition. We should be glad if you would unpack and examine them as soon as possible after delivery.

In case of any breakage, please notify us as well as the carriers at once.

Your faithfully,

Example 4

subject: About the Packing

Dear Sir,

On 10 July, we received your consignment of 40 cardboard cartons of steel screws.

We regret to inform you that 10 cartons were delivered damaged and the contents had spilled, leading to some losses.

We accept that the damage was not your fault but feel that we must modify our packing requirement to avoid future losses.

We require that future packing be in wooden boxes of 20 kilos net.

each wooden box containing 40 cardboard packs of 500 grams net.

Please let us know whether these specifications can be met by you and whether they will lead to an increase in your prices.

We look forward to your early confirmation.

Sincerely yours,

9.1.2 Shipment

Letters regarding shipment are usually written for the following purposes:

- to send shipping instructions and urge an early shipment
- to amend shipping terms
- to give shipping advice

Before shipment, the buyers generally send their shipping requirements to the sellers, informing the packing, shipping mark, mode of transportation, etc., known as the shipping instructions. On the other hand, the sellers usually send a notice to the buyers immediately after the goods are loaded on board the ship, advising them of the shipment, especially under FOB or CFR terms. Such a notice is known as the shipping advice.

Foreign importer may arrange the cargo insurance on time based on the shipping advice (if buyer is to arrange the insurance). Moreover, importer may know when to receive the goods and arrange with a customs broker for the cargo clearance.

A shipping advice usually contains the following points:

- the date and number of bill of lading (B/L)
- the date and number of the contract
- the names of commodities and their quality and value
- the name of the carrying vessel
- the name of the shipping port/loading port
- the estimated time of departure (EDT)
- the name of the destination port
- the estimated time of arrival (ETA)
- a list of the relevant shipping documents
- thanks for patronage

The following are applicable structure in writing a letter concerning shipment:

(1) Open the letter in a positive way. Especially when negative information is conveyed, great care should be taken.

(2) Explain the problem in great detail to try to persuade the reader into accepting the request or to make the reader fully aware of the request.

(3) Close the letter by expressing good wishes to encourage the reader to cooperate.

Example 1

Dear Sirs,

With reference to our order No. 11579 for 5,000 pieces of Canvas Folding Chairs, we are glad to advise you that an L/C in your favor has been opened yesterday. We have booked shipping space on M. V. "East Wind", which is due to sail from London to New York around the end of this month. Please get the goods ready for shipment at an early date and make your efforts to ship them by that vessel without any delay.

We would like to remind you that the goods must be packed in cartons of one dozen each. At the same time, please make sure that the shipping marks indicated in our contract are to be printed on the cartons.

We hope that the above shipping instructions are clear enough. Thank you for your cooperation.

Yours faithfully,

Example 2

Dear Mr. Goodman:

Thank you for your fax of September 11. We are pleased to inform you that we have been able to secure the vessel you asked for.

She is the S. S. Bohai and is docked at present in Lianyungang. She has a cargo capacity of eight thousand tons, is a bulk carrier, and has a speed of 24 knots which will certainly be able to make the number of trips you mentioned.

Please fax us to confirm the charter and we will send you the charter party.

Yours sincerely,

Example 3

Dear sirs,

We wish to invite your attention to our Order No. 5781 covering 500 pieces Blue Woolen Serge, for which we sent to you about 30 days ago an irrevocable L/C expiration date 31st March.

As the season is rapidly approaching, our buyers are badly in need of the goods. We shall be very much obliged if you will effect shipment as soon as possible, thus enabling them to catch the brisk demand at the start of the season.

We would like to emphasize that any delay in shipping our booked order will undoubtedly involve us in no small difficulty.

We thank you in advance for your cooperation.

Yours faithfully,

9.2 Terms of Payment

An experienced exporting firm extends credit cautiously. It evaluates new customers with care and continuously monitors older accounts. Such a firm may wisely decide to decline a customer's request for open account credit if the risk is too great and propose instead payment on delivery terms through a documentary sight draft or irrevocable confirmed Letter of Credit or even payment in advance. On the other hand, for a fully creditworthy customer, the experienced exporter may decide to allow a month or two to pay, perhaps even on open account.

As being paid in full and on time is of the utmost concern to exporters, the level of risk in extending credit is a major consideration. There are several ways in which you can receive payment when selling your products abroad, depending on how trustworthy you consider the buyer to be. Typically with domestic sales, if the buyer has good credit, sales are made on open account; if not, cash in advance is required. For export sales, these ways are not the only common methods. Listed in order from most secure for the exporter to the least secure, the basic methods of payment are:

- cash in advance
- documentary Letter of Credit
- documentary collection or draft
- open account
- other payment mechanisms, such as consignment sales

1. Structure of the Letter Concerning Terms of Payment

(1) Put forward the problem of terms of payment.

(2) Present the desired terms of payment and explain why this mode of payment is preferred or why other terms of payment cannot be accepted.

(3) Close the letter by expressing expectations of an early reply or suggesting future business dealings.

Example 1

Dear Sir or Madam:

In the past, our purchases of Spinning Machine Parts from you have normally been paid by confirmed, irrevocable letters of credit.

This arragenment has cost us a great deal of money. From the moment we open the credit until our buyers pay us normally it ties up funds for about four months. This is currently a particularly serious problem for us in view of the difficult economic climate and the prevailing high interest rates.

If you could offer us easier payment terms, it would probably lead to an increase in business between our companies. We propose either cash against documents on arrival of goods, or drawing on us at three months' sight.

We hope our request will meet with your agreement and look forward to your early reply.

Sincerely yours,

Example 2

Dear Mr Grover,

Thank you for your letter of 10 March asking for a change in payment terms.

There is nothing unusual in our current arrangement. From the time you open credit until the shipment reaches your port it is normally about three months. In addition, your L/C is only opened when the goods are ready shipment.

We regret to say that we must adhere to our usual practice and sincerely hope that this will not affect our future business relations.

We will contact you as soon as supplies of the steel pipes you require come into stock.

Faithfully yours,

Example 3

Dear Mr James,

We refer to your Contract No. 375 covering lumber in the amount of \$ 800 and Contract No. 376 for iron pipes in the amount \$ 700.

Since both these contracts are less than U.S. \$ 1000 in value, we would like you to ship the goods to us on a cash against documents basis.

We trust that this arrangement will meet with your approval and look forward to your early reply.

Yours faithfully,

2. Letter of Credit

The exporter generally requires the importer to arrange for an L/C to enable the exporter to draw on a named bank when he presents the documents.

Here are the typical steps of an irrevocable Letter of Credit that has been confirmed by a

U.S. bank:

(1) After the exporter and buyer agree on the terms of a sale, the buyer arranges for its bank to open a Letter of Credit that specifies the documents needed for payment. The buyer determines which documents will be required.

(2) The buyer's bank issues, or opens, its irrevocable Letter of Credit includes all instructions to the seller relating to the shipment.

(3) The buyer's bank sends its irrevocable Letter of Credit to a U.S. bank and requests confirmation. The exporter may request that a particular U.S. bank be the confirming bank, or the foreign bank may select a U.S. correspondent bank.

(4) The U.S. bank prepares a letter of confirmation to forward to the exporter along with the irrevocable Letter of Credit.

(5) The exporter reviews carefully all conditions in the Letter of Credit. The exporter's freight forwarder is contacted to make sure that the shipping date can be met. If the exporter cannot comply with one or more of the conditions, the customer is alerted at once.

(6) The exporter arranges with the freight forwarder to deliver the goods to the appropriate port or airport.

(7) When the goods are loaded, the freight forwarder completes the necessary documentation.

(8) The exporter (or the freight forwarder) presents the documents, evidencing full compliance with the Letter of Credit terms, to the U.S. bank.

(9) The bank reviews the documents. If they are in order, the documents are sent to the buyer's bank for review and then transmitted to the buyer.

(10) The buyer (or the buyer's agent) uses the documents to claim the goods.

(11) A draft, which accompanies the Letter of Credit, is paid by the buyer's bank at the time specified or, if a time draft, may be discounted to the exporter's bank at an earlier date.

Care must be taken by the exporter in scrutinizing the L/C to see if all the terms and conditions in the credit can be complied with and if not, amendments should be made well in advance of shipment of the goods. Otherwise exporter may run the risk of his draft being dishonored by the bank.

Letters concerning L/C are written commonly for the following reasons: the seller urges the opening of the L/C; as the buyer informs of the establishment of the L/C, he possibly states expectation for of other terms, especially, the shipment date; the seller requires the buyer to amend the L/C terms; one party requires the extension of the L/C.

1) When Shall L/C be Opened?

It is the usual practice that the Letter of Credit is to be opened and to reach the sellers 30 days ahead of shipment so as to give the seller enough time to make preparation for shipment, such as making the goods ready and booking shipping space. For prompt shipment, it is advisable that the Letter of Credit be issued in good time.

2) Structure for Your Reference in Writing a Letter Urging Establishment of L/C

(1) Open the letter in a positive way. For example, in the first paragraph the seller usually informs the buyer that the goods are ready for dispatch or that the shipping space has already been booked.

(2) Politely push the buyers to open the L/C without delay, either by referring to the stipulations of the contract or by reminding the buyers of the seriousness of not opening the L/C in time.

(3) Express expectations and ask the buyers to take immediate action.

3) Principles of Writing Letters Urging Establishment of L/C

No suggestion of annoyance is allowed to be shown in the letter urging establishment of L/C. It is not advisable, except under special conditions, to start off too strongly by blaming the buyer for not executing the contract. The first message sent should therefore be a polite note saying that the goods ordered are ready but the relevant Letter of Credit has not yet be received. If the first message brings no reply, a second one will be sent. This one, though still restrained, will express disappointment and surprise.

4) Sample Letter of Urging Establishment of L/C

Example 1

Dear Sir:

We are very pleased to have signed Sales Contract NO. 5678 with you. But we have not received you L/C. We are writing you in the hope of inviting your attention to the terms about the arriving date of the L/C.

We do hope you will abide by the agreed articles and have the L/C opened before the stipulated time. On receipt of the L/C, we will make shipment immediately.

Yours Faithfully,

Example 2

Dear Mr. Johnson:

Our Sales Confirmation No. 518

Referring to the 5,000 pieces of Poplin under our Sales Confirmation No. 518, we wish to call your attention to the fact that the date of delivery is drawing near, but up till now, we have not received the covering Letter of Credit. Please do your utmost to expedite its establishment, so that we may execute the order within the prescribed time.

For your information, S.S. Peace is due to sail for your port around the middle of next month, according to the shipping company here. If we have your L/C before the end of this month, we might catch that steamer.

In order to avoid subsequent amendments, please see to it that the L/C stipulations are in strict conformity with the terms of the contract.

We look forward to receiving your favorable response at an early date.

Yours faithfully,

By cable:

S/C 518 POPLIN L/C UNRCVD PLS RUSH

By telex:

L/C FOR S/C 518 UNRCBC PLS EXPEDITE IT TO ENBL US SHIP YR ORDER WITH PRESCRIBED TIME ALSO PLS SEE THAT L/C STPULATNS R IN STRICT CONFORMITY WITH CONTRCT TERMS

Example 3

Dear Sirs,

With reference to our Sales Confirmation No. 220, we wish to draw your attention to the fact that the goods are ready for dispatch, but up to the present we have not received the covering L/C. Neither have we received any information from you about the above L/C.

To secure punctual fulfillment of the contract, please rush the L/C. We hope that the relevant L/C will reach us within 10 days, otherwise we shall not be able to deliver the goods on time.

We hope that you can understand our situation and give us close cooperation. We look forward to your early reply.

Yours faithfully,

5) Informing of the Establishment of L/C

Example 1

Dear Mr. Black:

We would like to draw your attention to our Order No. 321 for 500 pieces of Blue Woolen Serge.

On 3 April, we sent you an irrevocable Letter of Credit which expires on 30 June.

This is our busy season and our buyers urgently need the goods. We shall therefore be very grateful if you ship the goods as soon as possible.

We must stress that any delay in shipping the order will involve us in problems with our buyers, which could affect our future business.

Your earliest reply will be highly appreciated.

Yours faithfully,

Example 2

Dear Sirs:

Thank you for your letter of June 18 enclosing details of your terms. According to your request for opening an irrevocable L/C, we have instructed the Beijing City Commercial Bank to open a credit for US $ 50,000 in your favor, valid until Sep. 20.

Please advise us by fax when the order has been executed.

Sincerely Yours,

6) Amendment of the L/C

It is essential for the exporter to do so because a minor difference between the clauses of the L/C and the terms stipulated in the sales contract or sales confirmation, if not discovered or duly amended, may cause the seller much inconvenience because the negotiating bank will refuse to make the payment.

Letters to amend L/C are written in a polite way, sincerely stating reasons and expectation, or in a direct way asking for amendment.

Example 1

Dear Mr. Gray:

Your L/C No. 2233 issued by the Bank of Barclays has arrived.

On examination, we find that transshipment and partial shipment are not allowed.

As direct sailings to Liverpool are infrequent, we have to ship via London more often than not. As a result, transshipment may be necessary. With regard to partial shipment, it would speed matters up if we could ship immediately the goods we have in stock instead of waiting for the whole shipment to be completed.

With this in mind, we faxed you today, asking for the L/C to be amended to read: "partial shipment and transshipment allowed".

We trust this amendment will meet with your approval and you will fax us to that effect without delay.

Yours faithfully,

Example 2

Dear Mr. Quek:

We have received your L/C No. 8888 with thanks, but we are regretful to say that here are some discrepancies between your L/C and Sales Contract No. 0112. They are as follows:

Your L/C No. 8888:

1) Transshipment not allowed

2) Equal part shipment in March and in April

3) No more or less clause

The S/C no. 0112:

1) transshipment allowed

2) Shipment not later that April 1

3) 5% more or less allowed

In order to effect shipment smoothly, please make necessary amendment to your L/C with the least possible delay.

Yours faithfully,

Example 3

Dear Sirs:

L/C No. 8888 Amendment

Thank you for letter of April 4.

We could hardly believe at first that there should have been so many errors in the subject L/C. Only after checking up our records with your findings did we realize the errors, which had been caused by our negligence. We are sorry for this and meanwhile wish to tender our apologies for the trouble you have thus been cause. While approaching the opening bank immediately for an amendment to the L/C in question, we have adopted measures to avoid similar mistakes in future dealings.

It is expected that relative amendment will be reach you in a couple of days. We hope you will make shipment immediately.

We look forward to receiving your shipping advice.

Yours truly,

Example 4

Gentlemen:

We are sorry to report that in spite of our effort, we are unable to guarantee shipment by the agreed date due to a strike at our factory. We are afraid that your L/C will be expire before shipment. Therefore, please explain our situation to your customers and secure their consent to extend the L/C to Sept. 30.

Sincerely Yours,

7) Extension of the L/C

There are times when the exporter fails to get the goods or ship ready for the shipment in time or the importer requests that shipment be postponed for one reason or another. Under such circumstances, the exporter will have to ask for extension of the expiry date as well as the date of shipment of the L/C.

The following structure is for your reference in writing a letter asking for L/C amendment or extension:

(1) Acknowledge receipt of the L/C and thank the buyer for opening it.

(2) Point out the problem politely and ask the buyer to make the amendment accordingly. Usually, detailed and courteous explanations for such a request should be provided.

(3) End the letter in a way that encourages the buyer to take immediate action.

Example 1

Dear Mr. Green:

Thank you for your L/C covering your order for 30 metric tons of frozen chicken meat.

We regret to say that, owing to the delay on the part our suppliers, we will not be able to get the shipment ready before the end of this month. We faxed you earlier today to that effect.

We expect that the consignment will be ready for shipment in the early part of September. We are arranging to ship it on S.S. May Flower sailing from Boston on 3 September.

We are looking forward to receiving your faxed extension the L/C so that we can effect shipment of the goods.

We send our sincere apologies for the delay and trust that it will not unduly inconvenience you.

Example 2

Gentlemen:

The dressed you ordered under your Order No. 2255 are ready for shipment, but unfortunately, we found that the design of some dressed cannot match that of your samples. In order to ensure the quality of your products, we have to reproduce these goods.

In view of the above, we would like to request your to extend your shipment date fro April 15 to May 15, and validity from April 30 to May 30.

We hope you will understand our situation and let us have your amendment notice by return.

Yours faithfully,

Example 3

Dear Sirs:

RE: EXTENDING VALIDITY OF THE L/C

We regret to say that we have not received your L/C related to above mentioned sales Confirmation until today. It is stipulated clearly in the Sales Confirmation that the relevant L/C must reach to us not later than the end of Aug. Although the reaching time of the L/C is overdue, we would like still to ship your goods in view of long-standing friend relationship between us. However, we can not make shipment of your goods within the time stipulated in the Sales Confirmation owing to the delay of the L/C. Therefore, the L/C needs to be extended as follows:

(1) Time of shipment will be extended to the end of Oct.

(2) Validity of the L/C will be extended to NOV. 15,

Your kind attention is invited to the fact that we must receive your L/C amendment before Sept. 30. Otherwise, we will not be able to effect the shipment in time. Looking forward to receiving your L/C amendment early we remain.

Yours truly,

9.3 Insurance

To spread the financial losses of the insured members over the whole of the insuring community by compensating the misfortune few from the fund built up from the contributions of all members. Today, insurance is a form of intangible trade which helps our country to accumulate foreign exchange. Businessmen should have a thorough knowledge of it and the ability to handle its problems to win over the business of insurance.

Letters concerning insurance can be written in the following structure:

1. Put forward the problem of insurance in a positive way.
2. State which kind of insurance is desired and provide the reader with convincing and specific reasons.
3. Express expectations for an early reply or cooperation.

Example 1

Dear Sirs,

Re: Your Order No. 202, Our Sales Contract No. 70 Covering 400 Cases Pottery

We thank you for your letter of June 30, requesting us to effect insurance on the captioned shipment for your account.

We are pleased to confirm having covered the above shipment with the people's Insurance Company of China against All Risks for $ 3,000. The policy will be sent to you in a day or two together with our debit note for the premium.

For your information, this parcel will be shipped on S. S. "huoju", sailing on about the 28th this month.

Yours faithfully,

9.4 Complaints, Claims and Settlements

Complaints are usually made by the buyer, who suffers losses, against the seller. The reasons may be as follows:

- the seller's failure to make delivery as contracted
- the seller's delivery arriving damaged or too late
- part of the total quantity of the seller's deliveries being short shipped or missing

When writing a claim letter, be sure to:

(1) Remain courteous and respectful. Even if you feel you have been wronged, maintain a professional, though assertive, tone at all times.

(2) Send your claim letter within the prescribed time period so that the claim will be valid.

(3) If there are any necessary forms, etc., that you need to fill out or send, include them with your letter for faster approval.

(4) Clearly state what it is that you hope to accomplish in sending your claim letter.

A letter of a claim, whether made by the seller or the buyer, should be written as follows:

(1) Begin by regretting the need to claim.

(2) Mention the details of the delivery such as date, number of the order, date of delivery, the goods claimed on, and so on.

(3) State the reason (or reasons) for the claim.

(4) Suggest how the matter is expected to be settled or state the details of the claim.

Example 1

Dear Sir/Madam:

Please send us a correction on part of our order WP-11.

All the items we ordered arrived in excellent condition except for one model. It you refer to our original order (see the copy attached), you will note that we requested your fluorescent desk-lamps, Model 606. However, Model 608 reached us instead. For details, please see the inspection certificate issued by the Tianjin Commodity Inspection Bureau.

Will you kindly take back those you sent out and substitute them with an equal quantity (120 items) of Model 606? We would appreciate your attention to this matter promptly.

Yours faithfully,

Example 2

Dear Sirs:

We enclose Survey Report No. 6113 issued by the Shanghai Commodity Inspection Bureau certifying that the quality of the above-mentioned goods has been seriously damaged during transport. As the goods are entirely useless to us, you are requested to return the invoice value and the inspection charges involved, with the total of US $ 700.

We trust you will settle this claim promptly, to safeguard the goodwill of your company.

Yours faithfully,

Example 3

Dear Sirs:

We have recently received a number of complaints from customers about your fountain pens. The pens are clearly not giving satisfaction and in some cases we have had to refund the purchase price.

The pens complained about are part of the hatch of five hundred supplied to our order No 8562 of 28th March. This order was placed on the basis of a sample pen left by your representative. We have ourselves compared the performance of this sample with that of a number of the pens complained about. There is little doubt many of them are faulty; some of them leak and others fail to write.

The complaints received relate only to pens from the hatch referred to. Pens supplied before these have always been satisfactory. We are therefore writing to ask you to accept return of the unsold balance, amounting to 377 pens in all, and to replace them by pens of the quality our earlier dealings with you have led us to expect.

Yours faithfully,

Example 4

Dear Sirs,

Our Order No. 255 for Christmas gifts

The above goods reached here on January 2. We have to regret to tell you that we can't accept them, because of the late delivery. According to our agreement, the goods should have arrived before December 1 for the Christmas promotion.

Nevertheless, as you have sent us the goods, what we can do now is to accept them at a reduction of 30%.

It would be appreciated if you could give us a prompt answer to solve the problem.

Yours sincerely,

1. Acceptance of a Claim

The following structure is recommended in writing such a letter:

(1) A positive opening—No matter whose responsibility it is, it is not advisable for the writer to reject the complaint or claim promptly. Instead, the writer should open the letter by referring to the complaint or claim, expressing apologies or assuring the reader of his immediate attention to the matter in discussion.

(2) Explanation for how to settle the matter in discussion—If the writer admits his company is in error and is willing to take responsibility, he should express his willingness directly and inform the reader how he is planning to settle the problem. In case the writer cannot accept the complaint or claim for some reason, he should provide detailed reasons for his doing so and propose other alternatives to settle the problem.

(3) Close courteously and positively. —Usually, the writer chooses to end the letter by expressing his expectation for an early settlement of the complaint or claim or his willingness to cooperate.

Example 1

Dear Sirs

Please refer to your claim No. 202 for a short weight of 1,200 kg. Chemical Fertilizer, we wish to express our much regret over the unfortunate incident.

After a check-up by our staff, it was found that the packing bags of Some 30 bags were not strong enough, thus resulting in the breakage during transit, for which we render our apologies. In view of our long-standing friendly cooperation, we will make the payment by check for $ 3,300 into your account with the Bank of China, upon the receipt of your agreement.

We hope that the arrangement we have made will satisfy you and look forward to having your further orders.

Yours faithfully,

Example 2

Dear Mr. King:

We have received your letter of 16th. April, informing us that the sewing machines we shipped to you arrived in a damaged condition on account of imperfectness of our packing.

Upon receipt of your letter, we have given this matter our immediate attention. We have studied your surveyor's report very carefully.

We are convinced that the present damage was due to extraordinary circumstances under which they were transported to you. We are therefore not responsible for the damage, but as we do not think that it would be fair to have you bear the loss alone, we suggest that the loss be divided between both of us, to which we hope you will agree.

Example 3

Dear Ms. Leung:

Order NT－20717

Thank you for your fax of 17 January. We are extremely sorry to learn that an error was made in carton 13 of the above order.

The missing 9,000 ball pens were sent this morning by Cathay Airways and the documents have already been forwarded you.

We greatly regret the inconvenience caused by this and the previous two errors and offer our sincere apologies. We can assure you that every effect will be made to ensure that similar errors do not occur again.

Yours sincerely,

Example 4

Dear Sirs:

Damages on 25 Bags of Wheat

We have just received your letter of September 11 together with a copy of Survey Report No. 223 issued by the SCIB and have given it our prompt attention.

We are very regretful to learn that 25 of the total 80 bags wheat supplied to your order No. 477 arrived broken and seriously damaged by seawater. However, we are not the party to be blamed. According to the B/L, it is clearly noted that all the wheat were packed in perfect condition when they left here. Therefore, the breakage must be due to the rough handling in transit.

Under the circumstances, we are apparently not reliable for the damage and would suggest that you contact the shipping company or the insurance company concerned for settlement.

Anyhow, we thank you for placing this before us.

Section Two　Language Handbook

Useful Words and Expressions

packaging 包装方法
blister packing 起泡包装
neutral packing 中性包装
skin packing 吸塑包装
hanging packing 挂式包装

catch sb.'s eye 引某人注目
mark 唛头
unlabelled packing 无牌的包装
in bulk 散装
in loose packing 散装
nude packing 裸装
bulk pack 整批包装
consumer pack 零售包装
large packing 大包装
inner packing, external packing, end packing 小包装
shrunk packaging 压缩包装
foam-spray packaging 喷泡沫包装
gift-wrap 礼品包装
bag, sack 袋
jute bag 麻袋
polythelene bag, plastic bag 塑料袋
polythelene net 尼龙绳网袋
zippered bag 拉链袋
case, chest 箱
box 盒
wooden case 木箱
carton 纸箱
container 集装箱
rate 板条箱
fiber board case 纤维板箱
packing canvas 包装用的粗麻布
mark the centre of gravity with a red vertical line 用垂直红线标明重心
cord 绳子,绳索
second-hand case 用过的箱子
size of a case 箱子的尺寸
face plane side of a case 箱子的正面
waterproof envelope 防水信封
mark/ sign/ brand 商标,牌子,牌号,标志
special marking 专用(警告)标志,特殊标志
consignee's marking 收货人标志
instructions concerning marking 刷唛规定
mark, grade 涂刷唛头
marking 运输标志
up (此端)向上

gross weight 毛重,总重
net weight 净重,实重
in the form of a fraction 分数形式
denominator 分母
keep dry 保持干燥,切勿受潮
do not turn over 请勿倒置,请勿翻转
handle with care 小心轻放
water-repellent paint 防水油漆
indelible paint 不褪色的涂料,耐洗涂料
patter, template, templet, stencil 图案板
by pattern, by stencil 按图安板
in duplicate 一式两份
in triplicate 一式三份
in quadruplicate 一式四份
in quintuplicate 一式五份
draft 汇票
Promisory Note 本票
cheque 支票
clean bill 光票
documentary bill 跟单汇票
Sight Bill 即期汇票
Time Bill 远期汇票
Usance Bill 远期汇票
Commercial Bill 商业汇票
Commercial Acceptance Bill 商业承兑汇票
Bankers' Acceptance Bill 银行承兑汇票
invoice 发票
Performer Invoice 形式发票
At sight 即期,见票即付
at...days (month)after sight 付款人见票后若干天(月)付款
at...days sight 付款人见票后若干天即付款
at...days after date 出票后若干天付款
remittance 汇付
Mail transfer (M/T) 信汇
Demand Draft (D/D) 票汇
Telegraphic Transfer (T/T) 电汇
collection 托收
clean Bill for Collection 光票托收
Documentary Bill for Collection 跟单托收

Uniform Rules for Collection《托收统一规则》
Collection Advice 托收委托书
Advice of Clean Bill for Collection 光票托收委托书
copy 副本
original 正本
terms of validity 信用证效期
Expiry Date 有效期
date of issue 开证日期
to open by airmail 信开
to open by cable 电开
to amend L/C 修改信用证
Sight L/C 即期信用证
Usance L/C 远期信用证
Revocable L/C 可撤销的信用证
Irrevocable L/C 不可撤销的信用证
Confirmed L/C 保兑的信用证
Unconfirmed L/C 不保兑的信用证
Transferable L/C 可转让信用证
Untransferable L/C 不可转让信用证
Banker's Acceptance L/C 银行承兑信用证
Trade Acceptance L/C 商业承兑信用证
Credit payable by a trader 商业付款信用证
Credit payable by a bank 银行付款信用证
Uniform Customs and Practice for documentary Credits 跟单信用证统一惯例
without recourse 不受追索
Opening Bank's Name & Signature 开证行名称及签字
beneficiary 受益人
guarantor 保证人
Paying Bank 付款行,汇入行
Remitting Bank 汇出行
Opening/ Issuing Bank 开证行
Advising/ Notifying Bank 通知行
Negotiating Bank 议付行
Confirming Bank 保兑行
Presenting Bank 提示行
Transmitting Bank 转递行
Accepting Bank 承兑行
bearer 来人
consignee 受托人

consignor 委托人
drawer 出票人
principal 委托人
drawee 付款人
acceptor 承兑人
discount 贴现
endorsee 被背书人
endorse 背书
holder 持票人
endorsement 背书
payment against documents 凭单付款
payment against documents through collection 凭单托收付款
payment by acceptance 承兑付款
payment by bill 凭汇票付款
free from particular average (F. P. A.)平安险
with particular average (W. A.)水渍险(基本险)
all risks 一切险(综合险)
total loss only (T. L. O.) 全损险
war risk 战争险
cargo(extended cover)clauses 货物(扩展)条款
additional risk 附加险
from warehouse to warehouse clauses 仓至仓条款
theft, pilferage and nondelivery (T. P. N. D.)盗窃提货不着险
rain fresh water damage 淡水雨淋险
risk of shortage 短量险
risk of contamination 沾污险
risk of leakage 渗漏险
risk of clashing & breakage 碰损破碎险
risk of odour 串味险
damage caused by sweating and/or heating 受潮受热险
hook damage 钩损险
loss and/or damage caused by breakage of packing 包装破裂险
risk of rusting 锈损险
risk of mould 发霉险
strike, riots and civil commotion (S. R. C. C.) 罢工、暴动、民变险
risk of spontaneous combustion 自燃险
deterioration risk 腐烂变质险
inherent vice risk 内在缺陷险
risk of natural loss or normal loss 途耗或自然损耗险

special additional risk 特别附加险
failure to delivery 交货不到险
import duty 进口关税险
on deck 仓面险
rejection 拒收险
aflatoxin 黄曲霉素险
fire risk extension clause-for storage of cargo at destination Hongkong, including Kowloon, or Macao 出口货物到香港(包括九龙在内)或澳门存仓火险责任扩展条款
survey in customs risk 海关检验险
survey at jetty risk 码头检验险
overland transportation all risks 陆运综合险
air transportation risk 航空运输险
parcel post risk 邮包险
investment insurance(political risks) 投资保险(政治风险)
property insurance 财产保险
erection all risks 安装工程一切险
contractors all risks 建筑工程一切险
the stipulations for insurance 保险条款
marine insurance policy 海运保险单
specific policy 单独保险单
voyage policy 航程保险单
time policy 期限保险单
floating policy (or open policy) 流动保险单
ocean marine cargo clauses 海洋运输货物保险条款
claim against a person 向某人索赔
claim for sth. 因某事索赔
claim letter 索赔信
claim on account of damage 因损坏而索赔
claim on the goods 对该货提出索赔
raise/ file/ put in/ lodge /make/ issue/ lay/ register/ render/ enter/ bring up/ set up a claim against/ with/ on/ upon sb. for sth. 为某事向某人提出索赔
admit a claim 同意索赔
entertain a claim 受理索赔
dismiss a claim 驳回索赔
reject a claim 拒绝索赔
relinquish a claim 撤回索赔
settle a claim 解决索赔
waive a claim 放弃索赔
withdraw a claim 撤回索赔

an equitable settlement 公平解决
an impartial judgment 公正判断
bags torn 袋子撕破
bundles burst 捆带松散
a justified claim 有充分理由的索赔
conciliation 和解调停
to compensate partly 部分赔偿
to help one get out of the mess 帮助排除纠纷
to offset the difference 抵消差额
to raise an objection 提出抗议
to resort to arbitration 诉诸仲裁
to resort to litigation 打官司
to settle the case amicably 友好解决
to stretch a point 通融让步
to tackle the problem properly 适宜地处理问题
to view the matter in a proper light 正确地对待问题

Useful Sentences

Our usual way of payment is by confirmed and irrevocable Letter of Credit available by draft at sight for the full amount of the contracted goods to be established in our favour through a bank acceptable to the sellers.

我们的一般付款方式是保兑的、不可撤销的、以我公司为受益人的、足额信用证,见票即付。信用证应通过为卖方认可的银行开出。

For payment, we require 100% value, confirmed and irrevocable Letter of Credit with partial shipment and transhipment allowed clause, available by draft at sight, payable against surrendering the full set of shipping documents to the negotiating bank here.

我们要求用100%金额的、保兑的、不可撤销的信用证,并规定允许转船和分批装运,凭汇票向议付行交单即期付款。

The Letter of Credit should be established with its clauses in confirmation with the terms and conditions of the contract.

信用证所开条款,必须与合约条款相符。

We usually accept payment by L/C at sight draft or by T/T in advance, but never by C.O.D.

通常我们接受即期信用证付款或电汇。我们从不接受货到付款的办法。

We still intend to use Letter of Credit as the term of payment.

我们仍然想用信用证付款方式。

L/C at sight is normal for our exports to France.

我们向法国出口一般使用即期信用证付款。

Our terms of payment is confirmed and irrevocable Letter of Credit.

我们的付款条件是保兑的、不可撤销的信用证。

You must be aware that an irrevocable L/C gives the exporter the additional protection of banker's guarantee.

你必须意识到不可撤销信用证为出口商提供了银行担保。

For payment we require 100% value, irrevocable L/C in our favour with partial shipment allowed clause available by draft at sight.

我们要求用不可撤销的、允许分批装运、金额为全部货款并以我方为抬头人的信用证,凭即期汇票支付。

We have received your products we ordered, but regret to say they are very much inferior in quality to your samples.

我们今天收到我们的订货,但不得不遗憾地说:这些产品比贵方的样品质量低劣得多。

We shall lodge a claim against the Insurance Company for the goods damaged during transit.

对于货物在运输途中的损坏,我们将向保险公司提出索赔。

We file a claim against you for the short delivery of 145 lbs.

我们向你方提出短交145磅的索赔。

We regret to inform you that the goods are not in accordance with your samples.

我们遗憾地奉告:到货与样品不符。

We are obliged to ask you to make up for the heavy loss we have suffered by the damage of the goods.

因货品破损,我方蒙受了很大的经济损失,不得不请贵方赔偿。

It would be highly appreciated if you look into our order of May 8th for three cartons of personal computers, which should have reached our destination two months ago.

我方5月8日订单项下的三箱个人计算机应在两月前到货,请查询有关交货情况。

We regret to learn from your letter of May 8th that the goods sent to you arrived in a damaged condition.

从贵方5月8日来函得知,运送给贵方的货物到达时有破损,深感遗憾。

We have looked into the matter and found that your claim is perfectly justified.

我方已调查此事,发现贵方索赔完全正当。

Exercises

Ⅰ. Fill in the Blanks

1. In particular we wish to know whether you can issue a special rate ________ return ________ the promise of regular monthly shipment.
2. As shipment is due to begin ________ 14th March, please let us have your quotation by return.
3. ________ what terms will you be glad to arrange an all risks policy for us?

4. The invoiced value of the consignment, ________ the freight and commission, is $2,500.
5. We are pleased to note that you are ready to insure ________ us a shipment of Chinese porcelain from Shanghai to Sydney by sea.
6. If you find our rate acceptable, please present the details ________ your shipment so that we may issue our policy accordingly.
7. The terms you quote for an open policy of 1,200 covering all risks will apply ________ our consignment on the routes named.
8. We shall provide such ________ at your cost.
9. Please arrange to supply these and ________ to our account.
10. Our clients request their order to be ________ against all risks and war risk. Please arrange for the insurance cover accordingly.
11. Please hold us for the ________ referred to below.
12. We will ________ insurance coverage on your behalf.
13. Please insure at ________ value plus 10%.
14. We shall ________ insurance at this end under our Open Policy.
15. The coverage is for 110% of invoice value up to the port of ________.

Ⅱ. Translate the Following Sentences into English

1. 用纸箱可以减轻重量,节省运费;包装费也不用另外计算。
2. 我建议你们使用开窗包装,可以直接看到盒内的商品。
3. 在包装这些小瓶啤酒时,6 瓶为一盒,4 盒装一箱。
4. 这些盒子都需要里面内衬防震板,外加加固条。
5. 纸板箱应刷上“保持干燥”和“易碎品”之类指示性标志。
6. 7 月 14 日来函收悉,得知由“红旗”号轮所运的货物,其中两箱到达时已损坏,深表歉意。
7. 得悉发运给你方的订货中货物损坏颇多,令人失望,使你们失去一月份销售时机,致歉。
8. 由中国商品检验局出具的检验报告将作为最后依据,对双方都有约束力。
9. 今天航空邮出 3000 美元支票一张,以支付你方 500 磅短重索赔。
10. 你方 3 月 11 日电传中提到茶具到货受损,我们异常惊讶,因在发货前已像往常一样小心地予以包装。

Ⅲ. Choose the Best Answer

1. A 4% discount will be granted only ________ your order exceeds US$ 20,000.
   A. depends on　　B. for condition that
   C. on condition that　　D. subject to
2. An exporter cannot receive payment until the goods on consignment ________ sometime in the future.

A. have offered for sale　　B. are quoted

C. arrive at destination　　D. have been sold

3. We have made ________ that we would accept D/A at 60 days' sight for this order.

A. clear　B. it is clear　C. that clear　D. it clear

4. ________ an order for one hundred pieces or more we allow a special discount of 5% for payment by L/C.

A. At　B. In　C. On　D. From

5. We find your terms ________ and now send you our order for 2 sets of generators.

A. satisfied　　B. satisfaction

C. satisfactory　　D. of satisfaction

6. We have ________ at 30 days' sight for the contracted value.

A. written to you　　B. called on you

C. sent to you by air mail　　D. drawn on you

7. To our regret, your L/C was found not properly ________ on the following points in spite of our request.

A. amend　　B. to amend

C. amending　　D. amended

8. As arranged, we have effected insurance ________ the goods ________ 110% of the invoice value ________ all risks.

A. of, at, with　　B. for, in, against

C. on, for, against　　D. to, at, over

9. It is important that your client ________ the relevant L/C not later than April 15, 2004.

A. must open　B. had to open　C. open　D. opens

10. The goods ________ shipped already if your L/C had arrived by the end of December last.

A. would be　　B. must have been

C. had been　　D. would have been

Ⅳ. Write Letters According to the Following Information

1. 5月20日要求提早装运第954号合约的来信收到。

我们已经联系了船运公司,得知4月5日前开往贵公司港口的船只已没有剩余货位。因此,很抱歉我们无法满足你们的要求。

但请你们放心,我们一定会尽我们最大的努力,保证按时交货。

2. 感谢贵方7月16日的订单。得知你方想在贵地试销我们的水果罐头,我们非常高兴。

我们感谢贵方的好意,但是,很遗憾,我们无法接受你方用60天期承兑交单方式付款的要求。因为我们通常要求以不可撤销的即期信用证付款,我们无法做出与通常做法相反的安排,特别是对一个新客户。我们建议你我先使用信用证进行交易,以后再讨论这个问题。

希望贵方能够接受我方的建议,并盼望早日得到你方确认。

3. 你方9月29日来电收悉。在来电中,你方要求将7796号信用证延期2周,因为你方无法在规定日期内装运。

收到你方来电后,我们联络了我们的客户。但是,他们说自己急需这些货物,不可能允许延期交货。所以,展证是不可能的。

因此,我们要求你方尽力按原计划装运。如果你方不能照办,我们将要求你方赔偿我们的所有损失。

盼早复。

Chapter Ten

Netiquette in Business Communication

Section One Business Writing

10.1 Introduction

What is Netiquette? Simply stated, Netiquette is network etiquette—that is, the etiquette of cyberspace. And "etiquette" means "the forms required by good breeding or prescribed by authority to be required in social or official life." In other words, Netiquette is a set of rules for behaving properly online.

When you enter any new culture—and cyberspace has its own culture—you're liable to commit a few social blunders. You might offend people without meaning to. Or you might misunderstand what others say and take offense when it's not intended. To make matters worse, something about cyberspace makes it easy to forget that you're interacting with other real people—not just ASCII characters on a screen, but live human characters.

Management at many organizations has the uncomfortable feeling that its employees are representing the company out there in cyberspace. So, your netiquette represents your company's business etiquette. However, partly as a result of forgetting that people online are still real, and partly because they don't know the conventions, especially new ones, make all kinds of mistakes.

10.2 Netiquette in Details

Email has revolutionized the way that we communicate with others. It has given us the ability to process work and information faster and cheaper. Sending documents across multiple sites is instantaneous. We are able to stay in communication via a laptop, phone or PDA anywhere; giving us the ability to be far more productive. It's almost hard to believe how businesses functioned without E-mail. According to Lydia Ramsey, author of *Manners that Sell: Adding the Polish that Builds Profits*, E-mail has become one of the most popular and efficient means of communication in the business world.

1. The Effects of E-mail on the Working World

Email has made a number of major changes in the way business functions:

(1) Since many executives read their own email, rather than having it screened like their paper mail and phone calls, it's often possible to contact powerful people directly.

(2) Many systems make it easy to send mail out to everyone at the site or everyone at the company.

(3) Email overload: Some people receive dozens of messages per day. Others don't actually receive that much mail, but can't seem to handle it anyway.

(4) Snail-mail ignorers: Other people get so used to doing everything over the wires that they forget—or don't bother—to read their paper mail.

2. E-mail Etiquette

E-mail, although lacking "real" physical stationery do present an outward manifestation of the sender innate character and attitude. There should be no reason for the recipient to find the sender lacking in manners and good taste.

Unfortunately, because of its ease and convenience, there is a great deal of misuse and abuse associated with it. It's easy to lapse into the habit of writing informal, poorly structured e-mails. It's equally easy to assume that just because you can get someone's e-mail address, you are free to use it haphazardly.

People are increasingly tired of receiving e-mail from merchants and marketers who fail to respect their privacy or time, and likewise fail to treat them professionally and courteously. So you should be very careful about the privacy of your readers. Be sure to send e-mail only to people that have indicated a desire to hear from you. Such discretion will not only reduce your costs but also help preserve your reputation.

Next, treat e-mail like any other form of business correspondence. According to Jacqueline Whitmore, Founder and Director of The Protocol School of Palm Beach, "nothing irritates us more than receiving e-mails riddled with misspellings and poor grammar, and devoid of punctuation." A business e-mail should be treated simply as a business letter.

Experts also suggest the following tips for making the most of your e-mail communications:

(1) Reply as promptly to an e-mail as you would a phone call—never more than 24 to 48 hours later.

(2) Where possible, limit e-mails to 20 lines or less.

(3) Use the subject line as a "hook" and keep it specific and interesting.

(4) Include the text of earlier messages in replies for added convenience.

(5) Avoid using jargon, slang, abbreviations, profanity, or colloquialisms.

(6) Never use all capitals, the electronic equivalent of shouting, or all lower-case letters, which equates to whispering.

(7) Ensure that your e-mail includes a proper salutation, closing, and signature.

(8) Spell and grammar-check your e-mails so that they are as professional as any other form of business correspondence.

(9) Remember that there is no such thing as a confidential e-mail—post on the Internet only what you would post on your company bulletin board.

(10) Construct your copy list on a need-to-know basis. Be careful in using large distri-

bution lists for highly focused topics.

(11) Use formal language (with complete sentences, business letter formats and correct spelling) and a well-thought-out structure when communicating with senior management or customers. Remember, an e-mail message helps to create an image of you and your company.

(12) Avoid large attachments if at all possible. Background documents of interest to a subset of the recipients can be put on your intranet.

(13) Be prompt in responding to action items. Acknowledge an accepted action item with an e-mail response even if you can't get to it for a while.

(14) Avoid e-mail wars. Take personal conflicts offline, and handle them privately.

(15) Use auto response messages to notify correspondents if you are out of the office or on vacation and won't be able to read messages.

(16) Put meaningful data in the subject field. Many users are responding to information overload with filters and rules-based agents.

(17) Don't use e-mail to highlight negative thoughts about senior management. It can be too easily forwarded or misaddressed.

(18) Observe common practices within your organization. Every organization has a unique culture, and this also applies to E-mail etiquette.

3. Attachment Netiquette

Do not send any e-mail with attached document, graphics or images from whatever programs you are using. You may be using a program or special formatting that the recipient may not be using, hence, the recipient may receive gibberish and unable to view your attachment. Do not send any (large size) HTML designer e-mail.

The most important consideration is that your recipient doesn't want to open your attachment due to the possibility of virus.

Many recipient will also be upset by having to waste time downloading a "large" attachment without advance notification.

The attachment may even overload the recipient allocated storage space and cause all their important incoming mails to be returned "bounced"—and will really upset any recipient and sour a relationship before it even begins.

If you want to send any attachment, seek permission first, and inform the recipient why you are sending it and what program is needed to view it, as well as the file "size".

Most recipient would prefer that you to copy and paste; the text contents of your intended attachment into the body of your e-mail as part and parcel of the message.

Further more, sending any e-mail message HTML or TEXT with or without attachment, without permission is considered SPAM and the recipient may "retaliate" with "nasty" consequences for the sender and may even start a "Flam" war.

4. Fax

Fax is also electronic mail. The fact is that sending Fax will usually get a faster response because, many companies accept it as a "standard" form of communication, with management procedures already being used for years.

They can "physically" and visually judge the quality of your faxed message, "the way" it is written. The fact that, since the sender is willing to pay a "higher" price to fax the message—automatically increases the perceived commercial value of such faxed business message.

Example 1

Dear Sam,

I am writing to set up a two-hour meeting in Beijing from 9:00 to 11:00 on April 12.

The subject of meeting is Better E-Business Communication & Coordination Between all AIA Subsidiaries. Mr. Smith, our E-business Department Head, will come to Beijing to host the meeting and also make a presentation on the subject.

If any of your staff, you feel, will benefit from the presentation and would like to attend it, please send me their names and phone numbers.

Also please confirm whether you are available on the date and times suggested. I am looking forward to your prompt reply.

Best regards,

Jack Lee,
AIA

Example 2

Dear Mr. Ho,

Thank you for your suggestions for our products, and we are happy to know that you find them really useful. We would like to confirm the following with you:

First, the inclusion of business terms is an excellent idea, and we shall develop it.

Second, we assure you that our new model, launched in March 2005, includes 3 more languages.

Third, the inclusion of a leather case would add to the price of our machines and may not be necessary as the casing is very strong.

Finally, we are sending you 300 language translators by the end of this month.

Thank you for your valuable suggestions. We are looking forward to your new orders.

Kind regards,

Peter Wang,

Sales Manager

Example 3

Dear Mr. Burton,

Further to our phone call on July 20, I am writing to confirm our meeting on July 22 and request the following favors from you.

Would you please arrange for somebody to pick me up in the Paris International Airport at 11 pm on July 21?

Could you please book a standard room for me in a four-star hotel from July 21 to 23? Would you mind booking a ticket for my return trip in the afternoon of July 24?

I would like to thank you for your help. I am looking forward to your early reply.

Kind regards,

Jack Peterson
Sales Manager

Example 4

Subject: An order

Gentlemen:

The price quotes contained in your E-mail of May 20, 2002 gained favorable attention with us. We would like to order the following items consisting of various colors, patterns and assortments:

Large 2,000 dozen
Medium 4,000 dozen
Small 2,000 dozen

As the sales season is approaching, the total order quantity should be shipped in July. At that time an irrevocable L/C for the total purchase value will be opened.

Please confirm the order and E-mail a shipping schedule.

Sincerely,
×××

Section Two Language Handbook

Useful Words and Expressions

approximately	approx.	接近
et alia (and others)	et al.	以及其他人

et cetera (and so forth)	etc.	等
as soon as possible	ASAP	急件
blind carbon copy	Bcc	密件抄送
building	bldg.	大厦
calendar year	CY	公历年
carbon copy to	Cc	抄送
cash on delivery	C. O. D.	货到付款
company	Co.	公司
corporation	Corp.	公司
department	dept.	部门
doing business as	DBA	职业或公司名称
each	ea.	各
end of month	e. o. m	月底
fiscal year	FY	会计年度
for your information	FYI	通知
government	govt.	政府
incorporated	Inc.	公司
limited	Ltd.	有限公司
manufacturing	mfg.	制造公司
merchandise	mdse.	商品
month	mo.	月
videlicet (namely)	viz.	亦即
numero (number)	no.	号码
post meridiem (post noon)	p. m.	下午
postscript	PS	又及
quarter	qtr.	季度
very important person	VIP	重要人物

Useful Sentences

1. Date and Expiry 期满到期

I received in due course your letter of the 30th July.

我们如期收到您 7 月 30 日的来信。

The steamer will due in Yokohama on the morning of the 5th May.

该轮将于 5 月 5 日晨,如期到达横滨港。

The bill falls due on September 1.

这张票据将于 9 月 1 日到期。

The discount rates have failed to come down below 2 sen per diem, even in the middle of the month.

甚至到本月中旬,折扣率也未下降到日率 2 分以下。

We have duly received your valued favour of the 10th June.

我们如期收到您6月10日的贵函。

2. Apology and Regret 抱歉遗憾

Meanwhile, I can only ask you to accept my apologies.

此时,我只能请您接受我的歉意。

We are sorry to learn from your letter of the 10th May that your customer is still dissatisfied with the condition.

从你们5月10日信中得知,你方客户仍对该条件不表满意,甚为遗憾。

We are sorry that we have taken the liverty in writing you prematurely on the subject.

在时机尚未成熟以前,我们就冒昧地写信谈及此事,对此甚表遗憾。

I am regretted to have to inform you that two cases of them are so bad in quality.

我们遗憾地告诉您,其中两箱,质量极为差劣。

We regret to inform you that our premises at 15 R.C. were partly destroyed by fire yesterday afternoon

我们遗憾地告诉您,本公司在R.C. 15的房产,因昨日下午失火,已部分烧毁。

Please accept our apologies for the inconvenience this matter has given you.

对此事给您带来的不便,请接受我们的歉意。

3. Honor 荣幸

Today, we feel very much honoured to have Prof. M. Wilson with us.

今天,我们感到很荣幸能和M. 威尔森教授欢聚一堂。

We feel speially honoured to be given this opportunity to meet such a nice group of distinguished people like you.

特别使我们感到荣幸的是能有机会遇到你们各位知名人士。

To have the honour of doing/ To have the honour to do...

对于……甚感荣幸。

4. Appreciation 感谢

We appreciate your telling us about the defective sets, and are glad to make things right.

承蒙告知该若干套不合格产品,我方愿妥善处理不误。

While thanking you for your valued support, I wish to ask for a continuance of your confidence in the new company.

在感谢您过去惠予支持的同时,希望对我新公司也继续给予信赖。

We take this opportunity to thank our patrons and friends for the liberal support extended to us during our business career.

藉此机会,让我们对凡在业务发展方面给予有力支持的朋友、客户表示感谢。

We take this opportunity of thanking you for your past valued support, and of assuring you that your orders will continue to receive our best personal attention.

藉此机会,让我们对您过去珍贵的支持表示感谢,对您今后的订单,我们将保证继续格外关照。

We can confidently assert that any business with which you may favour us will be transacted in such a manner as will afford you the fullest satisfaction.

我们满怀信心的向您保证,您所给予我们任何的业务,我们都会以完全使您满意的方式去执行。

5. Offer Service 提供服务

We are always pleased to serve you at any time.

我们随时乐意为您服务。

We thank you for the opportunity to be of service to you.

如有机会为您服务,我们将非常感谢。

In the meantime, please be assured of our most cordial good wishes and of our desire to be of service.

同时,请牢记我们最诚挚的心愿和为您服务的热望。

We wish to assure you that we appreciate an opportunity afforded us for service.

请相信,我们将非常感谢您能为我们提供服务机会。

We are anxious to be able to sever you.

我们渴望为您服务。

6. Signatures 留意签名

We would ask you kindly to note our respective signatures given below.

惠请留意我们每个人在下面的签名。

Below you will find a facsimile of his signature, which I ask you to regard as my own.

下面是他的签名传真件,请惠予留意,该签名效果与我的相同。

Have the kindness to take note of my signature.

惠请留意我的签名。

I request your attention to his signature, appended below.

请留意附在下面的签名。

7. Response 回信

A return envelope that requires no postage is enclosed for your convenience in replying.

为供您回信方便,随信附去免贴邮票的信封一个。

Make out your check for $20, put it in the enclosed envelope, and start it on its way to us now.

请开20美元的支票一张,放在所附信封里,立即寄给我们。

A postcard is enclosed for your convenience in requesting further information

为了使您从我们这里取得更进一步的信息,随信附去明信片一张备用。

Exercises

E-mail Writing:

1. You are the training manager of a company which has won a large export order. You have been asked to organize foreign language training for some of your staff. Send your staff an

email explaining the schedule.

2. Your company exports to a number of countries around the owrld. As the Export Sales Manager, send an e-mail to a forwarding agent discussing international transport.
3. Selected staffs of your company are to receive a questionnaire requesting feedback on their views about the company. Write an email to the selected members of staff who will receive the questionnaire. You should state the purpose of issuing the questionnaire, then say how staff opinions count.
4. Send e-mails to the employees in the Customer Service Section Aiming to improve customer satisfaction.
5. You work for a company which is going to buy a set of equipment from China. You are asked to translate a lot of specifications and instructions within four months, which is impossible.

   Therefore you decide to advertise for two experienced translators as soon as possible. Write an e-mail to Mr. Max Remington, the Public Relation's manager. Ask for an advertisement for two translators:

   (1) Explain the reason.

   (2) Mention your urgency.

Appendix

1. Sales Contract

Whole Doc. No.
Date:
For Account of:
Indent No.
This contract is made by and between the Sellers and the Buyers; Whereby the Sellers agree to sell and the Buyers agree to buy the undermentioned goods according to the terms and conditions stipulated below and overleaf:
(1) Names of commodity (ies) and specification(s)
(2) Quantity
(3) Unit price
(4) Amount
TOTAL:
_______% more or less allowed
(5) Packing:
(6) Port of Loading:
(7) Port of Destination:
(8) Shipping Marks:
(9) Time of Shipment: Within _________________ days after receipt of L/C, allowing transhipment and partial shipment.
(10) Terms of Payment: By 100% Confirmed, Irrevocable and Sight Letter of Credit to remain valid for negotiation in China until the 15th day after shipment.
(11) Insurance: Covers all risks and war risks only as per the Clauses of the Peoples Insurance Company of China for 110% of the invoice value.
To be effected by the Buyer.
(12) The Buyer shall establish the covering Letter of Credit before _______; failing which, the Seller reserves the right to rescind this Sales Contract without further notice, or to accept whole or any part of this Sales Contract, non-fulfilled by the Buyer, of to lodge claim for direct losses sustained, if any.
(13) Documents: The Sellers shall present to the negotiating bank, Clean On Board Bill of Lading, Invoice, Quality Certificate issued by the China Commodity Inspection Bureau or the Manufacturers, Survey Report on Quantity/Weight issued by the China Com-

modity Inspection Bureau, and Transferable Insurance policy or Insurance Certificate when this contract is made on CIF basis.

(14) For this contract signed on CIF basis, the premium should be 110% of invoice value. All risks insured should be included within this contract. If the Buyer asks to increase the insurance premium or scope of risks, he should get the permission of the Seller before time of loading, and all the charges thus incurred should be borne by the Buyer.

(15) Quality/Quantity Discrepancy; In case of quality discrepancy, claim should be filed by the Buyer within 30 days after the arrival of the goods at port of destination; While for quantity discrepancy, claim should be filed by the Buyer within 15 days after the arrival of the goods at port of destination. It is understood that the Seller shall not be liable for any discrepancy of the goods shipped due to causes for which the Insurance Company, Shipping Company, other transportation organizations and/or Post Office are liable.

(16) The Seller shall not be held liable for failure or delay in delivery of the entire lot or a portion of the goods under this Sales Contract in consequence of any Force Majeure incidents.

(17) Arbitration: All disputes in connection with this contract or the execution thereof shall be settled friendly through negotiations. In case no settlement can be reached, the case may then be submitted for arbitration to China International Economic And Trade Arbitration Commission in accordance with the provisional Rules of Procedures promulgated by the said Arbitration Commission. The arbitration shall take place in Beijing and the decision of the Arbitration Commission shall be final and binding upon both parties; neither party shall seek recourse to a law court nor other authorities to appeal for revision of the decision. Arbitration fee shall be borne by the losing party. Or arbitration may be settled in the third country mutually agreed upon by both parties.

(18) The Buyer is requested always to quote THE NUMBER OF THE SALES CONTRACT in the Letter of Credit to be opened in favour of the Seller.

(19) Other Conditions:

Seller: Buyer:

2. Sales Confirmation

SELLER:		NO.:	
		DATE:	
		SIGNED IN:	
BUYER:			

This contract is made by and agreed between the BUYER and SELLER, in accordance with the terms and conditions stipulated below.

Art No.	Commodity & Specification	Quantity	Unit Price & Trade Terms	Amount
	Total:			

With more or less of shipment allowed at the sellers' option:

Total Value:
Packing:
Shipping:
Marks:
Time of Shipment & Means of Transportation:
Port of Loading & Destination:
Insurance of Terms:
Payment:
Remarks:

The Buyer	The Seller

3. Certificate of Origin

<table>
<tr><td colspan="2">1. Exporter</td><td colspan="3">Certificate No.</td></tr>
<tr><td colspan="2"></td><td colspan="3" rowspan="3">CERTIFICATE OF ORIGIN
OF
THE PEOPLE'S REPUBLIC OF CHINA</td></tr>
<tr><td colspan="2">2. Consignee</td></tr>
<tr><td colspan="2"></td></tr>
<tr><td colspan="2">3. Means of transport and route</td><td colspan="3">5. For certifying authority use only</td></tr>
<tr><td colspan="2"></td><td colspan="3" rowspan="3"></td></tr>
<tr><td colspan="2">4. Country / region of destination</td></tr>
<tr><td colspan="2"></td></tr>
<tr><td>6. Marksand numbers</td><td>7. Number and kind of packages; description of goods</td><td>8. H. S. Code</td><td>9. Quantity</td><td>10. Number and date of invoices</td></tr>
<tr><td></td><td></td><td></td><td></td><td></td></tr>
<tr><td colspan="2">11. Declaration by the exporter
The undersigned hereby declares that the above details and statements are correct, that all the goods were produced in China and that they comply with the Rules of Origin of the People's Republic of China.

....
Place and date, signature and stamp of authorized signatory</td><td colspan="3">12. Certification
It is hereby certified that the declaration by the exporter is correct.

....
Place and date, signature and stamp of certifying authority</td></tr>
</table>

4. Commercial Invoice

ISSUER	COMMERCIAL INVOICE			
TO	NO.		DATE	
TRANSPORT DETAILS	S/C NO.		L/C NO.	
	TERMS OF PAYMENT			
Marks and Numbers	Number and Kind of Package Description of Goods	Quantity	Unit Price	Amount
Total:				
SAY TOTAL:				

5. Praforma Invoice

<table>
<tr><td colspan="2">ISSUER</td><td colspan="3" rowspan="2">形式发票
PROFORMA INVOICE</td></tr>
<tr><td colspan="2" rowspan="2">TO</td></tr>
<tr><td colspan="2">NO.</td><td>DATE</td></tr>
<tr><td colspan="2" rowspan="2">TRANSPORT DETAILS</td><td colspan="2">S/C NO.</td><td>L/C NO.</td></tr>
<tr><td colspan="3">TERMS OF PAYMENT</td></tr>
<tr><td>Marks and Numbers</td><td>Number and Kind of Package
Description of Doods</td><td>Quantity</td><td>Unit Price</td><td>Amount</td></tr>
<tr><td></td><td></td><td></td><td></td><td></td></tr>
<tr><td colspan="5">Total:</td></tr>
<tr><td colspan="5">SAY TOTAL:</td></tr>
<tr><td colspan="5">PORT TO LOADING:
PORT OF DESTINATION:
TIME OF DELIVERY:
INSURANCE:
VALIDITY:

BENEFICIARY
ADVISING BANK:
NEGOTIATING BANK:</td></tr>
</table>

6. Bill of Lading

Shipper		BILL OF LADING B/L No.:	
Consignee		COSCO	
Notify Party		中国远洋运输公司	
* Pre carriage by	* Place of Receipt	CHINA OCEAN SHIPPING	
Ocean Vessel Voy. No.	Port of Loading	ORIGINAL	
Port of discharge	* Final destination	Freight payable at	Number original Bs/L

Marks and Numbers	Number and kind of packages; Description	Gross weight	Measurement (m^3)

TOTAL PACKAGES(IN WORDS)	
Freight and charges	
	Place and date of issue
	Signed for the Carrier

* Applicable only when document used as a Through Bill of Loading

7. Draft

凭 信用证

Drawn under .... L/C NO ....

日期

Dated .... 支取 Payable with interest @........%......按.......息....... 付款

号码 汇票金额 宁波

No .... Exchange for Ningbo,................

见票.......................................日后(本汇票之副本未付)付交

AT.........................sight of this FIRST of Exchange(Second of Exchange being unpaid)

Pay to the order of the sum of

款已收讫

Value received ....

....

此致

TO: ....

....

....

....

8. Inspection Certificate

中华人民共和国上海进出口商品检验局
SHANGHAL IMPORT & EXPORT COMMODITY INSPECTION BUREAU OF THE PEOPLES REPUBLIC OF CHINA

地址：上海市中山一路13号
ADDRESS: 13, ZHONGSHAN YI RORD, SHANGHAI
TEL: 215529

质量检验证书
INSPECTION CERTIFICATE OF QUALITY

NO.:
DATE:

发货人：
Consignor:
受货人：
Consignee:
品名：
Commodity:
标记及号码：
MARKS & NO.:

检验数量/重量：
Quantity/Weight Declared:
检验结果：
Results of Inspection:

We hereby certify that the goods are of the above-mentioned quantiry And of sound quality.

9. Packing List

ISSUER	PACKING LIST					
TO	INVOICE NO.	DATE				
Marks and Numbers	Number and kind of package Description of goods	Quantity	PACKAGE	G. W	N. W	Meas.
	Total:					
SAY TOTAL:						

10. Collection Order

CABLE: CHUNGKUO
TELEX: 33062 BOCSH E CN
SWIFT: BKCHCMBJ300
FAX: 63232071

Collection Order

Date:____________

<table>
<tr><td>Principal: (Full name, Company ID and Email address)</td><td>Payer: (Full name, Company ID and Email address)</td></tr>
<tr><td>Amount: (in words, specifying the currency)</td><td>Terms: (marked with "X")
(　　) D/P　　at　　days' sight
(　　) D/A　　at　　days' sight</td></tr>
<tr><td colspan="2">We hereby entrust you with proceeds collection under ____________
(Contract No.)

(Signature)</td></tr>
<tr><td colspan="2">Documents attached:</td></tr>
</table>

11. Letter of Credit, Irrevocable Documentary

Bank A London, International Division

Address:

Tel: Telex: Date:

Irrevocable Letter of Credit Credit number:

Advising bank Applicant

Bank of china Guangzhou Joseph Smith & Sons 52×× Street, Southampton

Beneficiary Amount

Guang Arts & Crafts Corporation US $ 2000(US Dollars Two Thousand Only)

Guangzhou, China

Expiry: 31 May 1986

Dear Sirs

We hereby issue in your favour this Irrevocable Letter of Credit which is available by you drafts at...... sight drawn on us

For 100%...... of invoice value accompanies by the following documents:

Signed Invoice in three copies certifying that goods are in accordance with Contract No. GA/JS-453

Insurance certifieate for invoice amount plus 10%

Clean shipped Bills of lading in complete set issued to order and blank endorsed marked "Freight paid"

Packing list

Covering: 250 Cartons Porcelain Figures (CIF Southampton)

Despatch/Shipment from China port to Southampton, Britain

Partal Shipments Permitted

Transhipment Permitted

Special conditions:

We hereby engage that payment will be duly made against documents presented in conformity with the terms of this credit.

Yours faithfully

Bank A, London, International Division Countersigned

Advising Bank's notification

We hereby advise this credit without any engagement on our part

Bank of China, Beijing

(signed)

20 April 1986

12. Marine Cargo Transportation Insurance Policy

Invoice No. Policy No.

This policy of Insurance withesses that the People's Insurance (Property) Company of China (here-inafter called "The Company"), at the Request of _ _ _ _ _ _ _ _ _ _ (hereinafter called the "insured") and in consideration of the agreed premium being paid to the company by the Insured, undertakes to insure the undermentioned goods in transportation subject to the conditions of this policy as per the Clauses printed overleaf and other special Clauses attached hereon.

_ _

Marks & Nos.	Quantity	Description of Goods	Amount Insured

Total Amount Insured _ _ _ _ _

Premium as arranged Rate as arranged per conveyance

Slg. on or abt. _ _ _ _ _ from _ _ _ _ _ to _ _ _ _ _ _ _

Conditions

In the event of loss or damage which may result in a claim under this Policy, immediate notice must be given to the Company's Agent as mentioned hereunder. Claims, if any, one of the Original Policy which has been issued in One Original together with the relevant documents shall be surrendered to the Company.

_ _ _ _ Insurance Company

Claim payable at _ _ _ _ _

Address of Issuing Office _ _ _ _ _ _ _

13. English Abbreviations in Business

A accepted 承兑
AA Auditing Administration （中国）审计署
AAA 最佳等级
abs. abstract 摘要
a/c, A/C account 账户,账目
a/c, A/C account current 往来账户,活期存款账户
A&C addenda and corrigenda 补遗和勘误
Acc. acceptance or accepted 承兑
Accrd. Int accrued interest 应计利息
Acct. account 账户,账目
Acct. accountant 会计师,会计员
Acct. accounting 会计,会计学
Acct. No. account number 账户编号,账号
Acct. Tit. account title 账户名称,会计科目
ACN air consignment 航空托运单
a/c no. account number 账户编号,账号
Acpt. acceptance or accepted 承兑
A/CS Pay. accounts payable 应付账款
A/CS Rec. accounts receivable 应收账款
ACT advance corporation tax 预扣公司税
ACU Asia Currency Unit 亚洲货币单位
A. C. V actual cash value 实际现金价值
a. d., a/d after date 开票后,出票后
ADRS asset depreciation range system 固定资产分组折旧法
Adv. advance 预付款
ad. val., A/V ad valorem to (according value) 从价
Agt. agent 代理人
Agt. agreement 协议,契约
AJE adjusting journal entries 调整分录
Amt. amount 金额,总数
Ann. annuity 年金
A/P account paid 已付账款
A/P account payable 应付账款
A/P accounting period 会计期间
A/P advise and pay 付款通知
A/R account receivable 应收账款
A/R at the rate of 以……比例
a/r all risks （保险）全险
Arr. arrivals, arrived 到货,到船
A/S, a/s after sight 见票即付
A/S, acc/s account sales 承销账,承销清单,售货清单
ASAP as soon as possible 尽快
ASR acceptance summary report 验收总结报告
ass. assessment 估征,征税
assimt. assignment 转让,让与
ATC average total cost 平均总成本
ATM at the money 仅付成本钱
ATM Automatic Teller Machine 自动取款机(柜员机)
ATS automated trade system 自动交易系统
ATS automatic transfer service 自动转移服务
Attn. attention 注意
Atty. attorney 代理人
auct. auction 拍卖
Aud. auditor 审计员,审计师
Av. average 平均值
a. w. all wool 纯羊毛
A/W air waybill 空运提单
A/W actual weight 实际重量
BA bank acceptance 银行承兑汇票
bal. balance 余额,差额
banky. bankruptcy 破产,倒闭
Bat battery 电池
b. b. bearer bond 不记名债券
B. B., B/B bill book 出纳簿
B/B bill bought 买入票据,买入汇票
b&b bed & breakfast 住宿费和早餐费
b. c. blind copy 密送的副本
BC buyer credit 买方信贷
B/C bills for collection 托收汇票
B. C. bank clearing 银行清算
b/d brought down 转下页
Bd. bond 债券
B/D bills discounted 已贴现票据
B/D bank draft 银行汇票
b. d. i. both dates inclusive, both days inclusive 包括头尾两天
B/E bill of entry 报关单

b. e., B/E bill of exchange 汇票
BEP breakeven point 保本点,盈亏临界点
b/f brought forward 承前
BF bonded factory 保税工厂
Bfcy. Beneficiary 受益人
B/G, b/g bonded goods 保税货物
BHC Bank Holding Company 银行控股公司
BIS Bank of International Settlements 国际清算银行
bit binary digit 两位数
Bk. bank 银行
Bk. book 账册
b. l., B/L bill of lading 提货单
B/L original bill of lading original 提货单正本
bldg. building 大厦
BMP bank master policy 银行统一保险
BN bank note 钞票
BO branch office 分支营业处
BO buyer's option 买者选择交割期的远期合同
BOM beginning of month 月初
b. o. m. bill of materials 用料清单
BOO build-operate-own 建造—运营—拥有
BOOM build-operate-own-maintain 建造—运营—拥有—维护
BOOT build-operate-own- transfer 建造—运营—拥有—转让
b. o. p. balance of payments 收支差额
BOT balance of trade 贸易余额
BOY beginning of year 年初
b. p., B/P bills payable 应付票据
Br. branch 分支机构
BR bank rate 银行贴现率
b. r., B/R bills receivable 应收票据
Brok. broker or brokerage 经纪人或经纪人佣金
b. s., BS, B/S balance sheet 资产负债表
B/S bill of sales 卖据,出货单
B. T. T. bank telegraphic transfer 银行电汇
BV book value 票面价值
c. cents 分
C cash; coupon; currency 现金;息票;通货
C centigrade 摄氏(温度)
C. A. chartered accountant; chief accountant 特许会计师;主任(主管)会计师
C. A. commercial agent 商业代理、代理商
C. A. consumers' association 消费者协会
C/A capital account 资本账户
C/A current account 往来账
C/A current assets 流动资产
C. A. D cash against document 交单付款
can. cancelled 注销
cap. capital 资本
CAPM capital asset pricing model 固定资产计价模式
C. A. S. cost accounting standards 成本会计标准
c. b., C. B. cash book 现金簿
CBD cash before delivery 先付款后交货
C. C. cashier's check 银行本票
C. C contra credit 贷方对销
c/d carried down 过次页,结转下期
CD certificate of deposit 存单
c/f carry forward 过次页,结转
CG capital gain 资本利得
CG capital goods 生产资料,资本货物
C. H. custom house 海关
C. H. clearing house 票据交换所
Chgs charges 费用
Chq. cheque 支票
C/I certificate of insurance 保险凭证
CIA certified internal auditor 注册内部审计员
c. i. f., C. I. F. cost, insurance and freight 到岸价,货价+保险+运费
C. I. T. comprehensive income tax 综合所得税
Ck. check 支票
C. L. call loan 短期拆放
C / L current liabilities 流动负债
C. M. A. certificated management accountant 注册管理会计师
CML capital market line 资本市场线性
CMO Collateralised Mortgage Obligations 担保抵押贷款债务
CMV current market value 现时市场价值
CN consignment note 铁路运单
CN credit note 贷方通知书
c/o carried over 结转后期
C. O., C/O cash order 现金汇票,现金订货

C. O. certificate of origin 产地证明书
Co. company 公司
c. o. d, C. O. D. cash on delivery 货到付款
Col. column 账栏
Coll. collateral 担保,抵押物
Coll. collection 托收
Com., comm. commission 佣金
cont. container 集装箱
cont., contr. contract 契约,合同
conv., cv., cvt. convertible 可转换的,可兑换的
Cor. corpus 本金
Cor. correspodent 代理行
Corp. corporation 公司
CP. commercial paper 商业票据
C. P. A Certified Public Accountant 注册公共会计师
CPB China Patent Bureau 中国专利局
CPI consumer price index 消费者价格指数
CPM cost per thousand 每一千个为单位的成本
CPP current purchasing power 现行购买力
Cps. coupons 息票
CPT carriage paid to 运费付至……
C/R company's risk 企业风险
Cr. credit 贷记,贷方
CR carrier's risk 承运人风险
CR current rate 当日汇率、现行汇率
CR cash receipts 现金收入
CR class rate 分级运费率
CS civil servant, civil service 公务员,文职机关
CS convertible securities 可转换证券
C. S. capital stock 股本
CSI customer satisfaction index 顾客满意指数
csk. cask 木桶
CT corporate treasurer 公司财务主管
CT cable transfer 电汇
ct crate 板条箱
ctge cartage 货运费,搬运费,车费
Cts. cents 分
CTT capital transfer tax 资本转移税
cu cubic 立方
CU customs unions 关税联盟
cu. cm. cubic centimeter 立方厘米
cu. in. cubic inch 立方英寸
cu. m. cubic meter 立方米
cu. yd. cubic yard 立方码
cum. pref. cumulative preference (share) 累积优先(股)
cur. curr. current 本月、当月
CV convertible security 可转换债券
CVD countervailing duties 抵消关税,反倾销税
C. V. P. analysis Cost Volume Profit analysis 本—量—利分析
C. W. O. cash with order 订货付款
Cy. currency 货币
CY calendar year 日历年
CY container 整装货柜
CY container yard 货柜堆场、货柜集散场
D degree; draft 度;汇票
D/A deposit account 存款账户
D/A document against acceptance 承兑交单
d/a days after acceptance 承兑后……日(付款)
D. A. debit advice 欠款报单
D. B day book 日记账、流水账
DB method declining balance (depreciation) method 递减余额折旧法
D. C. F. method discounted cash flow method 现金流量贴现法
D/D documentary draft 跟单汇票
D. D., D/D demand draft 即期汇票
D/d, d/d days after date 出票后……日(付款)
d. d. dry dock 干船坞
DDB method double declining balance (depreciation) method 双倍递减余额折旧法
D. D. D deadline delivery date 交易最后日期
def. deficit 赤字,亏损
dem. demurrage 滞期费
Depr. depreciation 折旧
d. f, D. F., d. frt. dead freight 空舱费
D. G dangerous goods 危险货物
diff. difference 差额
Dis. discount 折扣,贴现
dish'd, dishd dishonored 不名誉,拒付
D. I. T double income-tax (relief) 双重所得税(免征)
div., divd dividend 红利,股息

D-J Dow Jones & Co. 美国道—琼斯公司
DJIA Dow Jones Industrial Average (Stock Index) 道—琼斯工业股票指数
DJTA Dow Jones Transportation Average 道—琼斯运输平均数
DJUA Dow Jones Utility Average 道—琼斯公用事业平均数
DK Don't know 不知道
DL direct loan 直接贷款
DL discretionary limit 无条件限制
DLD deadline date 最后时限
Dls., Dol(s), Doll(s) dollars 元
DM Deutsche Mark, D-mark, Deutschmark 德国马克
DMCs developing member countries 发展中国家
DN date number 日期号
DN, D/N debit note 借记通知单
DNR do not reduce 不减少
do., dto. ditto 同上,同前
D/O delivery order 发货单
Doc(s) documents 凭证、单据、文件
doc. att. documents attached 附单据、附件
Doc. code document code 凭证(单据)编号
D. O. G. days of grace 宽限日数
DOR date of request 要求日
DP, D/P document against payment 交单付款
DPI disposable personal income 个人可支配收入
DPOB date and place of birth 出生时间和地点
DPP damp proofing 防潮的
Dr. debit 借记,借方
D. R., DR discount rate 贴现率、折扣率
Dr debtor 债务人
DR deposit receipt 存单,存款收据
dr. drawer 借方
DS, d/s days after sight(days' sight) 见票后……日(付款)
ds., d's days 日
dstn. destination 目的地(港)
DTC Deposit taking company 接受存款公司
DTC Deposit Trust Company 储蓄信托公司
dup., dupl., dupte. duplicate 副本
DVP delivery versus payment 付款交货
dy., d/y day; delivery 日,交货
dz dozen 一打
E. exchange, export 交易所,输出
E. & O. E. errors and omissions excepted 如有错漏,可加更正
e. a. o. n. except as otherwise noted 除非另有说明
EAT earnings after tax 税后收益
EB ex budgetary 预算外
EBIT earnings before interest and tax 扣除利息和税金前收益
EBS Electronic Broking Service 电子经纪服务系统
EBT earning before taxation 税前盈利
EC European Community, European Commission 欧洲共同体,欧洲委员会
EC export credit 出口信贷
EC error corrected 错误更正
Ec. exemple causa 例如
Ec. ex coupon 无息票
ECA export credit agency 出口信贷机构
ECAFE Economic Commission for Asia and the Far East 亚洲及远东经济委员会
ECE Economic Commission for Europe 欧洲经济委员会
ECG Export Credit Guarantee 出口信用担保
ECI export credit insurance 出口信用保险
ECR export credit refinancing 出口信贷再融资
ECT estimated completion time 估计竣工时间
ECU European Currency Unit 欧洲货币单位
E/D export declaration 出口申报单
ED ex dividend 无红利,除息,股利除外
EDD estimated delivery date 预计交割日
EDI electronic data interchange 电子数据交换
EDOC effective date of change 有效更改日期
EDP Electronic Data Processing 电子数据自理
E. E., e. e errors excepted 如有错误,可加更正
EERI Effective Exchange Rate Indexes of Hong Kong 港汇指数
EET East European Time 东欧时间
EF export finance 出口融资
EF Exchange Fund 外汇基金
EFT electronic funds transfer 电子资金转账
EFTA European Free Trade Area (Association)

欧洲自由贸易区(协会)
EGM Extraordinary General Meeting 特别股东大会
EIB Export-Import Bank 进出口银行
EL export license 出口许可证
ELI extra low impurity 极少杂质
EMF European Monetary Fund 欧洲货币基金
EMIP equivalent mean investment period 等值平均投资期
EMP end-of month payment 月末付款
EMP European main ports 欧洲主要港口
EMS European Monetary System 欧洲货币体系
EMS express mail service 邮政特快专递
EMU European Monetary Union 欧洲货币联盟
enc enclosed 停业
encl(s). enclosure 附件
encd. enclosed 附件
End., end. endorsement 背书
Entd. entered 登记人
EOA effective on or about 大约在……生效
EOD every other day 每隔一日
EOE European Options Exchange 欧洲期权交易
EOM end of month 月底
EOQ economic order quantity 最底订货量
EOS end of season 季末
EOU export-oriented unit 出口型单位
EOY end of year 年终
EPD earliest possible date 最早可能日期
EPN export promissory note 出口汇票
EPOS electronic point of sale 电子销售点
EPR earnings price ratio 收益价格比率
EPR effective protection rate 有效保护率
EPS earnings per share 每股收益额、每股盈利额
E. P. T excess profit tax 超额利润税
EPVI excess present value index 超现值指数
EPZ export processing zone 出口加工区
ERM exchange rate mechanism 汇率机制
ERS Export Refinance Scheme 出口再融资计划
ESOP Employee Stock Ownership Plan 职工持股计划
Est. estate 财产,遗产
EST Eastern Standard Time 美国东部标准时间
et seq. et sequents 以下
ETA estimated time of arrival 预计到达时间
ETD estimated item of departure 预计出发时间
ETDZ Economic and Technological Development Zone 经济技术开发区
ETLT equal to or less than 等于或少于
ETS estimated time of sailing 预计启航时间
EU European Union 欧盟
EUA European Units of Account 欧洲记账单位
ex., exch exchange 汇兑,兑换
ex cont. from contract 从合同
ex cp. ex coupon 无息票
ex div. ex dividend 无股息
excl. exclusive 另外,不在内
Exp. export 出口
Extd. extend 展期
EXW ex works 工厂交货价
F dealt in flat 无息交易的
f. following (page) 接下页
f. fairs 定期集市
F. A. face amount 票面金额
F. A. fixed assets 固定资产
F. A freight agent 货运代理行
FA free alongside 启运港船边交货
FBAAA Fellow of the British Association of Accountants and Auditors 英国会计师和审计师协会会员
FAC facility 设施,设备
f. a. c. fast as can 尽快
FACT factor analysis chart technique 因素分析图解法
fad. free delivery (discharge, dispatch) 免费送货
F. A. F. free at factory 工厂交货
FAIA Fellow of the Association of International Accountants 国际会计协会会员
F. A. Q fair average quality (货品)中等平均质量
F. A. S. free alongside ship 发运地船边交货价
FASB Financial Accounting Standards Boards 财务会计标准委员会
FAT fixed asset transfer 固定资产转移
FAT factory acceptance test 工厂验收试验
FB foreign bank 外国银行
F. B. E. foreign bill of exchange 外国汇票

F. C. fixed capital 固定资本
F. C. fixed charges 固定费用
F. C. future contract 远期合同
fc. franc 法郎
FCA Fellow of the Institute of Chartered Accountants 特许会计师学会会员
FCG foreign currency guarantee 外币担保
FCL full container load 整货柜装载
FCL/LCL full container load/less (than) full container load 整装/分卸
FCR forwarder's cargo receipt 货运代理行收据
FCT forwarding agent's certificate of transport 货运代理行领货证
fd. fund 资金
FDB method fixed rate on declining balance method 定率递减余额折旧法
FDI foreign direct investment 外商直接投资
FDIC Federal Deposit Insurance Corporation 联邦储蓄保险公司
FE foreign exchange 外汇
FE future exchange 远期外汇
FF French franc 法国法郎
fib free into barge 驳船上的交货价
FIBC financial institution buyer credit policy 金融机构买方信贷险
FIFO first in, first out 先进先出法
fin. stadg. (stndg.) financial standing 资信状况
fin. stat. (F/S) financial statement 财务报表
fin. yr. financial year 财政年度
FINA following items not available 以下项目不可获得
FIO free in and out 自由进出
F. I. T free of income tax 免交所得税
fl. florin 盾
FLG finance lease guarantee 金融租赁担保
flt. flat 无利息
FMV fair market value 合理市价
FO free out 包括卸货费在内的运费
fo. folio 对折,页码
FOB free on board (启运港)船上交货、离岸价格
FOBST free on board stowed and trimming 包括清理及平仓的离岸价格
F. O. C. free of charge 免费
FOCUS Financial and Operations Combined Uniform Single Report 财务经营综合报告
FOK fill or kill 要么买进或卖出,要么取消
FOR free on rail (or road) 铁路或(公路)上交货价
for'd., fwd forward, forwarded 转递
FOREX foreign exchange 外汇
FOS free on steamer 蒸汽船上交货(价)
FOUO for official use only 仅用于公事
FOW, f. o. w. free on wagon (启运站)火车上交货(价)
FOX Futures and Options Exchange 期货和期权交易所
FP floating policy 浮动政策
FP fully paid 已全付的
FRA forward rate agreement 远期利率协议
FRCD floating rate certificate of deposit 浮动利率存单
frt., frgt. forward 期货,远期合约
FREF fixed rate export finance 固定利率出口融资
frt. & grat. freight and gratuity 运费及酬金
Frt. fwd freight forward 运费待付
Frt. ppd freight prepaid 运费已付
FS final settlement 最后结算
FSR feasibility study report 可行性研究报告
FTW free trade wharf 码头交易
FTZ free trade zone 自由贸易区
fut. futures 期货,将来
FV face value 面值
FVA fair value accounting 合理价值法
FWD forward (exchange) contract 远期合约
F. X. foreign exchange 外汇
FX broker foreign exchange broker 外汇经纪人
fxd fixed 固定的
FXRN fixed rate note 定息票据
FY fiscal year (financial year) 财政(务)年度
fy. pd. fully paid 全部付讫
FYI for your information 供您参考
g gallon; grain; gram (s); gold 加仑;格令;克;金
G. A. general agent 总代理商,总代理人
GA go ahead 办理,可行
GAAP General Accepted Accounting Principles 通

用会计准则
GAAS　Generally Accepted Auditing Standard　通用审计标准
GAC　General Administration of Customs　海关总署
gas.　gasoline　汽油
GATT　General Agreement on Tariffs and Trade　关税及贸易总协定
GCL　government concessional loan　政府优惠贷款
GDP　gross domestic product　国内生产总值
gds.　goods　商品,货物
GJ　general journal　普通日记账
GL　general ledger　总分类账
gm.　gram(s)　克
GMP　graduated payment mortgage　递增付款按揭
GND　gross national demand　国民总需求
GNE　gross national expenditures　国民支出总额
GNP　gross national product　国民生产总值
GOFO　gold forward rate　黄金远期利率
GP　gross profit　毛利
GPP　general purchasing power　总购买能力
gr.(grs.) wt.　gross weight　毛重
GR　gross revenue　毛收入
GS　gross sales　销售总额
GSP　generalised system of preferences　普惠制
GTM　good this month　本月有效
GTW　good this week　本星期有效
HAB　house air bill　航空托运单
HAWB　house air waybill　航空托运单
HCA　historical cost accounting　历史成本会计
hdqrs.　headquarters　总部
HIBOR　Hong Kong Interbank Offered Rate　香港银行同业拆借利率
hifo　highest-in, first-out　高入先出法
H. in D. C.　holder in due course　正当持票人
Hi-Q　high quality　高质量
HIRCS　high interest rate currencies　高利率货币
hi-tech　high technology　高技术
HKD　Hong Kong dollar　香港元
HKI　Hong Kong Index　香港指数
hl. hectoliter　百升
hldg.　holding　控股
Hon'd　honored　如期支付的
HSCPI　Hang Seng Consumer Price Index　恒生消费价格指数
HSI　Hang Seng Index　恒生指数
hwevr.　however　无论如何
I. A.　intangible assets　无形资产
I & A inventory and allocations　库存和分配
IAS　International Accounting Standard　国际会计标准
IB　investment banking　投资银行(业)
I. B.　invoice book　发票簿
IBA　International Bank Association　国际银行家协会
IBBR　interbank bid rate　银行间报价利率
I. B. I　invoice book inward　购货发票簿
IBNR　incurred but not reported　已发生未报告
I. B. O.　invoice book outward　销货发票簿
IBOR　inter-bank offered rate　银行间的拆借利率
ICB　international competitive bidding　国际竞标
ICIA　International Credit Insurance Association　国际信用保险协会
ICJ　International Court of Justice　国际法庭
ICM　international capital market　国际资本市场
ICONs　index currency option notes　指数货币期权票据
ICOR　incremental capital-output ratio　资本一产出增量比
I. C. U.　International Code Used　国际使用的电码
IDB　industrial development bond　工业发展债券
IDB　Inter-American Development Bank　泛美开发银行
IDB　inter-dealer broker　交易商之间经纪人
IDC　intangible development cost　无形开发成本
IDR　international depositary receipt　国际寄存单据
IE　indirect export　间接出口
I. F.　insufficient fund　存款不足
IFB　invitation for bids　招标邀请
I. G.　imperial gallon　英制加仑
IL, I/L　import licence　进口许可证
ILC　irrevocable letter of credit　不可撤销信用证
IMF　International Monetary Fund　国际货币基金组织
imp.　import　进口,输入

Inc. incorporated 注册(有限)公司
incl. inclusive 包括在内
incldd. included 已包含在内
incldg. including 包含
inl. haul inland haulage 内陆运输费用
INLO in lieu of 代替
Ins, ins. insurance 保险
inst. instant 即期,分期付款
Instal., instal. installment 分期付款
Int., int. interest 利息
inv., Inv. invoice 发票,付款通知
in trans (I. T.) in transit. 在(运输)途中
inv. doc. /attach. invoice with document attached 附提货单的发票
Inv't., invt. inventory 存货
I-O input-output 输入—输出
IOU I owe you 借据
IOV inter-office voucher 内部传票
IPN industrial promissory note 工业汇票
IPO initial public offering 首次发售股票
IQ import quota 进口配额
IR Inland Revenue 国内税收
I. R. inward remittance 汇入款项
IRA individual retirement account 个人退休金账户
IRA interest rate agreement 利率协议
IRR interest rate risk 利率风险
IRR internal rate of return 内部收益率
irred. irredeemable 不可赎回的
IRS interest rate swap 利率调期
IS International System 公制度量衡
ISIC International Standard Industrial Classification 国际标准产业分类
IT information technology 信息技术
IT international tolerance 国际允许误差
I/T income tax 所得税
ITC investment tax credit 投资税收抵免
ITO International Trade Organization 国际贸易组织
ITS intermarket trading system 跨市场交易系统
IV investment value 投资价值
J., Jour. journal 日记账
J. A., J/A joint account 联合(共管)账簿
J. D. B. journal day-book 分类日记账
J/F, j/f journal folio 日记账页数
J. V. joint venture 合资经营企业
J. V. journal voucher 分录凭单
JVC joint venture company 合资公司
K. D. knocked down 拆散
K. D. knocked down price 成交价格
L listed (securities) (证券)上市
L., (Led.) ledger 分类账
L. A., L/A letter of authority 授权书
L. A. liquid assets 流动资产
L. B. letter book 书信备查簿
LB licensed bank 许可银行
LC, L/C letter of credit 信用证
LCL/FCL less than container load/full container load 拼装/整拆
LCL/LCL less than container load/less than container load 拼装/拼拆
L. & D. loans and discounts 放款及贴现
L&D loss and damage 损失和损坏
ldg. loading 装(卸)货
L/F ledger folio 分类账页数
LG letter of guarantee 保函
Li. liability 负债
LI letter of interest (intent) 意向书
lifo, LIFO last in, first out 后进先出法
L. I. P., LIP life insurance policy 人寿保险单
LIRCs low interest rate currencies 低利率货币
L/M list of materials 材料清单
LMT local mean time 当地标准时间
LRP limited recourse project 有限追索项目
LRPF limited recourse project financing 有限追索项目融资
i. s. lump sum 一次付款总额
i. s. t. local standard time 当地标准时间
LT long term 长期
Ltd. limited 有限(公司)
M matured bond 到期的债券
M&A merger & acquisition 兼并收购
MA my account 本人账户
Mat. maturity 到期日
Max., max maximum 最大量
M. B. memorandum book 备忘录

MBB　mortgage-backed bonds　抵押支持的债券
MBO　management by objectives　目标管理
M/C　marginal credit　信贷限额
m/c　metallic currency　金属货币
MCA　mutual currency account　共同货币账户
MCP　mixed credit program　混合信贷计划
M/d　months after deposit　出票后……月
M. D.　maturity date　到期日
M. D., M/D　memorandum of deposit　存款(放)单
M. D.　malicious damage　恶意损坏
mdse.　merchandise　商品
MEI　marginal efficiency of investment　投资的边际效率
mem.　memorandum　备忘录
MERM　multilateral exchange rate model　多边汇率模型
M. F.　mutual funds　共同基金
MF　mezzanine financing　过渡融资
mfg.　manufacturing　制造的
MFN　most favoured nations　最惠国
mfrs.　manufacturers　制造商
M/I　marine insurance　海险
min　minimum　最低值,最小量
MIP　monthly investment plan　月度投资计划
Mk　mark　马克
mks.　marks　商标
mkt.　market　市场
MLR　minimum lending rate　最低贷款利率
MLTG　medium-and-long-term guarantee　中长期担保
M. M.　money market　货币市场
MMDA　money market deposit account　货币市场存款账户
MMI　major market index　主要市场指数
MNC　multinational corporation　跨(多)国公司
MNE　multinational enterprise　跨国公司
MO, M. O.　money order　汇票
mo.　month　月
MOS　management operating system　经营管理制度
Mos.　months　月
MP　market price　市价
M/P　months after payment　付款后……月
MPC　marginal propensity to consume　边际消费倾向
Mrge. (mtg.)　mortgage　抵押
MRJ　materials requisition journal　领料日记账
MRO　maintenance, repair and operation　维护、修理及操作
MRP　manufacturer's recommended price　厂商推荐价格
MRP　material requirement planning　原料需求计划
MRP　monthly report of progress　进度月报
MRR　maintenance, repair and replace　维护、修理和替换
M/s　months of sight　见票后……月
msg　message　留言
MT　medium term　中期
M/T mail transfer　信汇
mthly　monthly　每月
MTI　medium-term insurance　中期保险
MTN　medium-term note　中期票据
MTU　metric unit　米制单位
n.　net　净值
N. A.　net assets　净资产
n. a　not available　暂缺
N. A.　non-acceptance　不承兑
NA　not applicable　不可行
N. B.　nota bene　(拉丁)注意
NC　no charge　免费
N/C　net capital　净资本
n. d.　no date　无日期
n. d.　non-delivery　未能到达
N. D.　net debt　净债务
ND　next day delivery　第二天交割
NDA　net domestic asset　国内资产净值
N. E.　net earnings　净收益
n. e.　no effects　无效
n. e.　not enough　不足
negb.　negotiable　可转让的,可流通的
Neg. Inst., N. I.　negotiable instruments　流通票据
nego.　negotiate　谈判
N. E. S.　not elsewhere specified　未另作说明

net. p.　net proceeds　净收入
N/F　no fund　无存款
NFD　no fixed date　无固定日期
NFS　not for sale　非卖品
N. G.　net gain　纯收益
NH　not held　不追索委托
N. I.　net income　净收益
N. I.　net interest　净利息
NIAT　net income after tax　税后净收益
NIFO　next in, first out　次进先出法
nil　nothing　无
NIM　net interest margin　净息差
NIT　negative income tax　负所得税
N. L.　net loss　净损失
NL　no load　无佣金
NM　no marks　无标记
N. N.　no name　无签名
NNP　net national product　国民生产净值
NO., no.　number　编号,号数
no a/c　no account　无此账户
NOP　net open position　净开头寸
NOW　a/c negotiable order of withdrawal a ccount　可转让存单账户
N/P　net profit　净利
NP　no protest　免作拒付证书
N. P.　notes payable　应付票据
NPC　nominal protection coefficient　名义保护系数
NPL　non-performing loan　不良贷款
NPV　method　net present value method　净现值法
N. Q. A.　net quick assets　速动资产净额
NQB　no qualified bidders　无合格投标人
NR　no rated　(信用)未分等级
N/R　no responsibility　无责任
N. R.　notes receivable　应收票据
N. S. F., NSF　no sufficient fund　存款不足
NSF　check no sufficient fund check　存款不足支票
nt. wt.　net weight　净重
NTA　net tangible assets　有形资产净值
NTBs　non-tariffs barriers　非关税壁垒
ntl　no time lost　立即
NTS　not to scale　不按比例
NU　name unknown　无名
N. W.　net worth　净值
NWC　net working capital　净流动资本
NX　not exceeding　不超过
N. Y.　net yield　净收益
NZ $　New Zealand dollar　新西兰元
o　order　订单
o., O.　offer　发盘、报价
OA　open account　赊账,往来账
o/a　on account of　记入……账户
o. a.　overall　全面的,综合的
OAAS　operational accounting and analysis system　经营会计分析制
OB　other budgetary　其他预算
O. B.　ordinary business　普通业务
O. B., O/B　order book　订货簿
OB/OS　index overbought/oversold index　超买超卖指数
OBV　on-balance volume　持平数量法
o. c.　over charge　收费过多
OC　open cover　预约保险
o/d, o. d., O. D.　overdrawn　透支
OD　overdraft　透支
O/d　on demand　见票即付
O. E., o. e.　omission excepted　遗漏除外
O. F.　ocean freight　海运费
OFC　open for cover　预约保险
O. G.　ordinary goods　中等品
O. G. L.　Open General License　不限额进口许可证
OI　original issue　原始发行
OII　overseas investment insurance　海外投资保险
ok.　all correct　全部正确
o. m. s.　output per manshift　每人每班产量
O. P.　old price　原价格
O. P.　open policy　不定额保险单
opp　opposite　对方
opt.　optional　可选择的
ord.　ordinary　普通的
OS　out of stock　无现货
O/s　outstanding　未清偿,未收回的
O. T.　overtime　加班

OTC　over-the -counter market　市场外交易市场

OVA　overhead variance analysis　间接费用差异分析

OW　offer wanted　寻购启示

OWE　optimum working efficiency　最佳工作效率

ozws.　otherwise　否则

p　penny;pence; per　便士;便士;每

P　paid this year　该年(红利)已付

P.A.　particular average, power of attorney　单独海损,委托书

P.A.　personal account, private account　个人账户,私人账户

p.a.,per ann.　per annum　每年

P&A　professional and administrative　职业的和管理的

P&I clause　protection and indemnity clause　保障与赔偿条款

P&L　profit and loss　盈亏,损益

P/A　payment of arrival　货到付款

P/C　price catalog, price current　价格目录,现行价格

P/E　price/earning　市盈率

P/H　pier-to-house　从码头到仓库

P/N　promissory note　期票,本票

P/P　posted price　(股票等)的牌价

PAC　put and call　卖出和买入期权

pat.　patent　专利

PAYE　pay as you earn　所得税预扣法

PAYE　pay as you enter　进入时支付

PBT　profit before taxation　税前利润

pc　piece; prices　片,块;价格

pcl.　parcel　包裹

pd　paid　已付

per pro.　per procurationem　(拉丁)由…代理

PF　project finance　项目融资

PFD　preferred stock　优先股

PMO　postal money order　邮政汇票

P.O.C.　port of call　寄航港,停靠地

P.O.D.　place of delivery　交货地点

P.O.D.　port of destination, port of discharge　目的港,卸货港

P.O.R.　payable on receipt　货到付款

P.P.　payback period　(投资的)回收期

P.P.I.　policy proof of interest　凭保证单证明的保险利益

POE　port of entry　报关港口

POP advertising　point-of-purchase advertising　购物点广告

POR　pay on return　收益

PR　payment received　付款收讫

PS　postscript　又及

PV　par value; present value　面值;现值

q.　quarto　四开,四开本

Q.　quantity　数量

QB　qualified buyers　合格的购买者

QC　quality control　质量控制

QI　quarterly index　季度指数

qr.　quarter　四分之一,一刻钟

QT　questioned trade　有问题交易

QTIB　Qualified Terminal Interest Property Trust　附带可终止权益的财产信托

quad.　quadruplicate　一式四份中的一份

quotn.　quotation　报价

q.v.　quod vide (which see)　参阅

q.y.　query　查核

R　option not traded　没有进行交易的期权

R.　response; registered; return　答复;已注册;收益

r.　rate; rupee; ruble　比率;卢比;卢布

RAD　research and development　研究和开发

RAM　diverse annuity mortgage　逆向年金抵押

RAN　revenue anticipation note　收入预期债券

R&A　rail and air　铁路及航空运输

R&D　research and development　研究与开发

R&T　rail and truck　铁路及卡车运输

R&W　rail and water　铁路及水路运输

R/A　refer to acceptor　洽询(汇票)承兑人

R/D　refer to drawer　(银行)洽询出票人

RB　regular budget　经常预算

RCA　relative comparative advantage　相对比较优势

RCMM　registered competitive market maker　注册的竞争市场自营商

rcvd.　received　已收到

r.d.　running days=consecutive days　连续日

RDTC　registered deposit taking company　注册接

受存款公司

Re. subject 主题

re. with reference to 关于

RECEIVED B/L received for shipment bill of lading 待装提单

REER real effective exchange rate 实效汇率

ref. referee; reference; refer(red) 仲裁者;裁判;参考

REO real estate owned 拥有的不动产

REP import replacement 进口替代

REP Office Representative Office 代办处,代表处

REPO, repu, RP Repurchase Agreement 再回购协议

req. requisition 要货单,请求

REVOLVER revolving letter of credit 循环信用证

REWR read and write 读和写

RIEs recognized investment exchanges 认可的投资交易(所)

Rl roll 卷

RLB restricted license bank 有限制牌照银行

RM remittance 汇款

rm room 房间

RMB RENMINBI 人民币,中国货币

RMS Royal Mail Steamer 皇家邮轮

RMSD Royal Mail Special Delivery 皇家邮政专递

RMT Rail and Maritime Transport Union 铁路海运联盟

ROA return on asset 资产回报率

ROC return on capital 资本收益率

ROE return on equity 股本回报率

ROI return on investment 投资收益

ROP registered option principal 记名期权本金

ro-ro roll-on/roll-off vessel 滚装船

ROS return on sales 销售收益率

RPB Recognized Professional Body 认可职业(投资)机构

RPI retail price index 零售物价指数

RPM resale price maintenance 零售价格维持措施(计划)

rpt. repeat 重复

RRA Reverse Repurchase Agreement 逆回购协议

RSL rate sensitive liability 利率敏感性债务

RSVP please reply 请回复

RT Royalty Trust 特权信托

RTM registered trade mark 注册商标

Rto ratio 比率

RTO round trip operation 往返作业

RTS rate of technical substitution 技术替代率

RTW right to work 工作权利

RUF revolving underwriting facility 循环式包销安排

RYL referring to your letter 参照你方来信

RYT referring to your telex 参照你方电传

S no option offered 无期权出售

S split or stock divided 拆股或股息

S signed 已签字

s second; shilling 秒,第二;先令

SA semi-annual payment 半年支付

SA South Africa 南非

SAA special arbitrage account 特别套作账户

SAB special assessment bond 特别估价债券

sae stamped addressed envelope 已贴邮票,写好地址的信封

SAFE State Administration of Foreign Exchange 国家外汇管理局

SAIC State Administration for Industry and Commerce (中国)国家工商行政管理局 SAP Statement of Auditing Procedure 《审计程序汇编》

SAR Special Administrative Region 特别行政区

SAS Statement of Auditing Standard 《审计准则汇编》

SASE self-addressed stamped envelope 邮资已付、有回邮地址的信封

SAT (China) State Administration of Taxation (中国)国家税务局

SATCOM satellite communication 卫星通信

SB short bill 短期国库券,短期汇票

SB sales book; saving bond; savings bank 售货簿;储蓄债券;储蓄银行

SBC Swiss Bank Corp. 瑞士银行公司

SBIC Small Business Investment Corporation 小企业投资公司

SBIP small business insurance policy 小型企业保险单
SBLI Savings Bank Life Insurance 储蓄银行人寿保险
SBN Standard Book Number 标准图书号
SC sales contract 销售合同
sc,SC; supplier credit 卖方信贷
SCF supplier credit finance 卖方信贷融资
Sch schilling (奥地利)先令
SCIRR special CIRR 特别商业参考利率
SCL security characteristic line 证券特征线
SCORE special claim on residual equity 对剩余财产净值的特别要求权
SD standard deduction 标准扣除额
SDB special district bond 特区债券
SDBL sight draft, bill of lading attached 即期汇票,附带提货单
SDH synchronous digital hierarchy 同步数字系统
SDR straight discount rate 直线贴现率
SDRs special drawing rights 特别提款权
SE shareholders' equity 股东产权
SE Stock Exchange 股票交易所
SEA Single European Act 《单一欧洲法案》
SEAF Stock Exchange Automatic Exchange Facility 股票交易所自动交易措施
SEATO Southeast Asia Treaty Organization 东南亚公约组织
sec second(ary); secretary 第二,次级;秘书
sect. section 部分
Sen senator 参议院
Sept. September 九月
SET selective employment tax 单一税率工资税
SEC special economic zone 经济特区
SF sinking fund 偿债基金
Sfr Swiss Frank 瑞士法郎
SFS Summary Financial Statements 财务报表概要
sgd. signed 已签署
SHEX Sundays and holidays excepted 星期日和假日除外
SHINC Sundays and holidays included 星期日和假日包括在内
shpd. shipped 已装运
shpg. shipping 正装运
shpt. shipment 装运,船货
SI Statutory Instrument; System of Units 有效立法;国际量制
SIC Standard Industrial Classification 标准产业分类
SIP structured insurance products 结构保险产品
SITC Standard International Trade Classification 国际贸易标准分类
sk sack 袋,包
SKD separate knock-known 部分散件
SLC standby LC 备用信用证
SMA special miscellaneous account 特别杂项账户
SMEs small and medium-sized enterprises 中小型企业
SMI Swiss Market Index 瑞士市场指数
SML security market line 证券市场线
SMTP supplemental medium term policy 辅助中期保险
SN stock number 股票编号
Snafu Situation Normal, All Fouled Up 情况还是一样,只是都乱了
SOE state-owned enterprises 国有企业
SOF State Ownership Fund 国家所有权基金
sola sola bill, sola draft, sola of exchange (拉丁)单张汇票
sov. sovereign 金镑=20 先令
SOYD sum of the year's digits method 年数加总折旧法
spec. specification 规格,尺寸
SPF spare parts financing 零部件融资
SPQR small profits, quick returns 薄利多销
SPS special purpose securities 特设证券
Sq. square 平方,结清
SRM standard repair manual 标准维修手册
SRP Salary Reduction Plan 薪水折扣计划
SRT Spousal Remainder Trust 配偶幸存者信托
ss semis, one half 一半
SS social security 社会福利
ST short term 短期
ST special treatment (listed stock) 特别措施(对有问题的上市股票)
St. Dft. sight draft 即期汇票

STB special tax bond 特别税债务
STIP short-term insurance policy 短期保险单
sub subscription; substitute 订阅,签署,捐助;代替
Sun. Sunday 星期日
sund. sundries 杂货,杂费
sup. supply 供应,供货
t time; temperature 时间;温度
T. tare 包装重量,皮重
TA telegraphic address = cable address 电报挂号
TA total asset 全部资产,资产
TA trade acceptance 商业承兑票据
TA transfer agent 过户转账代理人
TAB tax anticipation bill (美国)预期抵税国库券
TACPF tied aid capital projects fund 援助联系的资本项目基金
TAF tied aid financing 援助性融资
TAL traffic and accident loss (保险)交通和意外事故损失
TAT truck-air-truck 陆空联运
TB treasury bond, treasury bill 国库券,国库债券
T.B. trial balance 试算表
t.b.a. to be advised; to be agreed; to be announced; to be arranged 待通知;待同意;待宣布;待安排
t.b.d. to be determined 待(决定)
TBD policy to be declared policy 预保单,待报保险单
TBL through bill of lading 联运提单,直达提单
TBV trust borrower vehicle 信托借款人工具(公司)
TBW Thompson Bankwatch, a rating agent 托马逊银行评估公司
TC tariff circular 关税通报
TC telegraph collation 校对电报
T.C. traveler's check 旅行支票
TCI trade credit insurance 贸易信用保险
TCIC technical credit insurance consultants 技术信用保险顾问
TCM traditional Chinese medicine 中国传统医学,中医
TD time deposit 定期存款
TD Treasury Department (美国)财政部
TDA Trade Development Authority 贸易发展当局
TDC technical development corporation 技术开发公司
TDC Trade Development Council (香港)贸易发展局
TDR Treasury Deposit Receipt 国库券存据
Tech technical 技术的
Tel. telephone number 电话号码
telecom telecommunications 通信
temp temperature; temporary (secretary) 温度;临时(秘书)
TESSA Tax Exempt Special Savings Account 免税特别储蓄账户
TEU twenty-foot-equipment unit (货柜、集装箱)20英尺当量单位
TF trade finance 贸易融资
t.f. till forbid 直到取消为止
tgm. telegram 电报
three T's type, terms, technique 交易三要素(交易类型,交易条件,销售技术)
thro., thru. through 经由,通过
Thu. Thursday 星期四
TIP to insure promptness 确保迅速
TIR carnet Transports Internationaux Routier (法国)国际公路运输证
tks. thanks 致谢,感谢
tkt ticket 票
TL time loan; total loss; trade-last 定期贷款;总损失;最后交易
TLO, T.L.O. total loss only = free from/of all average 全损赔偿险
TLX telex = teleprinter/teletypewriter exchange 电传
TM trademark 商标
TM telegram with multiple addresses 分送电报
TMA Terminal Market Association 最终市场协会
TMO telegraph money order 电汇单
TN treasury note 国库券
TNC transnational/multinational company 跨国公司

TOD time of delivery 发货时间
Tonn. tonnage 吨位(数)
TOP Trade Opportunities Program (美国)贸易机会计划
T.O.P. turn over, please 请翻转
TPM total productive maintenance 总生产维修(护)制
TPND theft, pilerage, and non-delivery 偷窃及不能送达险
tpo telephoto 电传照片,传真
TQ tariff quota 关税配额
T.Q., t.q. tale quale (拉丁)按现状,现状条件
TQC total quality control 全面质量控制
TR telegram restante; trust receipt 留交电报;信托收据
T.R. tons registered (船舶)注册吨位
Tr. transfer 过户,转让
trans translated 译本
treas treasurer 会计,出纳,库管,司库
Trip. triplicate 一式三份中的一份
TRS terminal receiving system 港外待运仓收货制度
TRT Trademark Registration Treaty 商标注册条约
TSP Total Suspended Particle 总空中悬浮物(污染指标)
TST test 检查,检测
TT Testamentary Trust 遗嘱信托
TT, T/T telegraphic transfer 电汇
T.T.B. telegraphic transfer bought 买入电汇
T.T.S. telegraphic transfer sold 卖出电汇
TTY teletypewriter 电报打字员
TU Trade Union 工会,职工协会
Tue.,Tues. Tuesday 星期二
TV terminal value; television 最终价值;电视
TW transit warehouse 转口仓库
TWI training within industry 业内训练
txt. text 课文,电文,正文
Ty. territory 领土,(推销员的)推销区域
T&E Card travel and entertainment card 旅行和娱乐信用卡
T&H temperature and humidity 温度和湿度
T&M time and material 时间和材料
T/C time charter 定期租船,计时租船
U union; upper; fashionable; polite 联盟;上等;时髦;礼貌
U, U. unit; United 单位;联合的,联合(公司)
U.A. unit of account 记账单位,记价单位
U.K./Cont. United Kingdom or Continent 英国或欧洲大陆(港口)
U.K.f.o. United Kingdom for orders 英国沿岸的指定港口
U.L.C.C. ultra large crude carrier 超大型油轮
U/A underwriting account 保险账户
u/c. undercharge 不足的价钱,少讨的价钱
U/M unscheduled maintenance 计划外维护
U/W, UW underwriters 保险公司,承销人
UAE the Union of Arab Emirates (阿拉伯联合酋长国)阿联酋
UBR uniform business rate 统一商业税率
UBS Union Bank of Switzerland 瑞士联合银行
UCP Uniform Customs and Practice (for Documentary Credit) (跟单信用证)统一惯例与事物
UGT, ugt urgent (电报用语)急电,加急
UHF ultra high frequency 超高频
UIT Unit Investment Trust 单位投资信托
UITF Urgent Issue Task Force (财务报表)紧急补救解释处
Ull. ullage 缺量,损耗
ult. ultimo (拉丁)(商业函电)上月的
UN United Nations 联合国
undelvd. undelivered 未装运的
Univ university 大学
unkwn. unknown. 未知的
unrevd. unreceived 未收到的
UNSYM unsymmetrical 不对称的
UOS unless otherwise specified 除非有特别说明
UPC Uniform Practice Code 《统一作法法典》
UPR unearned premiums reserve 未获得保险金储备
ur. your 你的
US United States; unlisted securities 美国;未上市证券
USD United States dollar 美元
USG United States gallon 美国加仑
USIT Unit Share Investment Trust 单位股投资

信托

USM Unlisted Securities Market 为挂牌(上市)证券市场

UT universal time 世界标准时间,格林尼治时间

UUE use until exhausted 用完为止

UV under voltage; ultraviolet 电压不足;紫外线

v refer to 参见

v., vs versus (拉丁)对

V Roman 5; victory; volt (罗马数字)5;胜利;(电压)伏

V.A. value analysis 价值分析

VAB vertical assembly building 垂直装配建筑物

vac vacation 假期

vac. vacant (职位)空缺,(旅馆、公寓)空房间

VAT value added tax 增值税

VC Vice Chairman; Vice Chancellor; Vice Consul 副主席,副首相;副总理;副领事

VD volume deleted 勾销的数量

VE value engineering 价值工程

Veep Vice President 副总裁

VER voluntary export restraint 自愿出口限制

Ves. vessel 船舶

via. through, by way of 经由,通过

vid vide (see) (拉丁)参看,请看

VIP Very Important Person 贵宾

vis major (拉丁)不可抗力

viz. videlicet, namely (拉丁)即,也就是

VL value line investment survey 价值线投资概览法

V-mail video-mail 声像电子邮讯系统

VOD video on demand 交互电视技术系统

vol. volume 量,额,本,卷,容积

voy. voyage 航海,航程

VQA vendor quality assurance 售主质量保证

VQC vendor quality certification 售主质量确认

VQD vendor quality defect 售主质量缺陷

VRM variable rate mortgage 可变利率抵押

VS/N vendor serial number 售主系列号

VSI vendor shipping instruction 售主船运说明

VSO Voluntary Service Overseas 海外义务服务

VSQ very special quality 特级质量

VSSP vendor standard settlement program 售主标准程序结算

VTC Voting Trust Certificate 股东投票权信托证书

VTP vendor test program 售主检测计划

VTR video tape record 录像带录像

W winter mark for load line; won (船舶)冬季装载线标记;(韩国)元

W., w. warehouse; weight; width; week 仓库;重量;宽;星期

W.A. with average 水渍险,单独海损险

W.A.C.C.C. Worldwide Air Cargo Commodity Classification 全球空运商品分类

W.A.I.O.P. W.A. irrespective of percentage 单独海损不计免赔率,单独海损全赔

WAEC West African Economic Community 西非经济共同体

WAG wagon 卡车

WAN Wide Area Networks 泛区网络

WASH Washington; washer 华盛顿;洗衣机

WB, W.B. waybill 运送单

WB EIL WB Economic Integration Loan 世界银行经济一体化贷款

WB World Bank 世界银行

W.B. water ballast (以)水压载,水压舱

W.B.S. without benefit to/of salvage 不享有获救财产的利益

w.c., W.C. without charge; water closet 免费;洗手间

WCG working capital guarantee 流动资金担保

WCO World Customs Organization 世界海关组织

WD when distributed (股票)发售时交割

wd. warrented (品质)保证的

wdth. width 广度,宽度

Wed. Wednesday 星期三

WEF World Economic Forum 世界经济论坛

W.E.T. Western European Time 西欧时间(格林尼治时间)

wf. wharf 码头

WFOE wholly foreign owned enterprises 外资独资企业

W.G., w.g. weight guaranteed 保证质量

WHO World Health Organization 世界卫生组织

whs, whse. warehouse 仓库

whsle wholesale 批发

WI when issued (股票)发行时交割

WIP work in progress = goods in progress 在制品
wk week; work 星期;工作
Wky. weekly 每星期的,周刊
wmk watermark 水印
Wmk. water mark 水位标记
WOC without compensation 无补偿
WP weather permitting; word processing 天气允许;文字处理
W.P. without prejudice 不损害(当事人)权利
W.P.A. with particular average = with average 水渍险
W.P.M. words per minute (电传)每分钟字数
W.P.P. waterproof paper packing 防潮纸包装
W.R. war risk 战争险
W.R. = W.W. warehouse receipt = warehouse warrant 仓单,仓库收据
Wrap worldwide receivables assurance protection 全球应收账款担保措施
WT warrant (股票)认证股
WT watertight (包、盒)不漏水的,防水的
WT, W/T wireless telegraphy, wireless telephone 无线电报;无线电话
wt., wgt. weight 重量
WTO World Trade Organization 世界贸易组织
W/Tax withholding tax 预扣税
WW warehouse warrant; with warrants 仓库保证;附认股权
w/w wall-to-wall 覆盖全部地面的(地毯)
W/W warehouse-to-warehouse 仓至仓
W/W clause warehouse-to-warehouse clause 仓至仓条款
www worldwide web 万维网,全球计算机网
X ten dollars (美国俚语)10美元
X ex-interest 无利息
X. out of 在外
x.a. ex all 无所有权益
x.b., xb, XB ex bonus; extra budgetary 不附(本期)红利;预算外的
X.C., X. cp. ex coupon 无息债券
x.d. ex distribution 不包括(下期股息或红利)分配
X-Dis ex-distribution 无分销
X. d., X. div. ex dividend 未付红利
XI, X. in, X. int. ex interest 利息除外
XL extra large; extra long 特大;特长
Xm., X'mas Christmas 圣诞节
X-mark a signature "X"符号签字(盲人或受伤的人可以画"X"作为签字)
Xn Christian 基督的
XN, XW ex-warrant 除证
X.n., X. new ex new 无权要求新股
X.P. extra message paid 额外通讯费付讫
XR, x.r. ex-right 无优惠权认购新股,除权
XS extra small 特小
Xtry. extraordinary 非常的,临时的
XXX international emergency signal 国际紧急信号
Y ex-dividend and sales in full 不计红利,全数出售
Y Yen 元(日本货币单位)
Y Yuan 元(中国货币单位)
y yard; year; yen 码(三英尺);年;日元
Y.A.R. York-Antwerp Rules 约克—安特卫普规则(海险)
YB, yrbk yearbook 年报,年鉴
y'day, yest. yesterday 昨天
YLD yield 收益
YOB year of birth 出生年份
YOD year of death 死亡年份
YOM year of marriage 结婚年份
yr year; your 年;你的
YTB yield to broker 经济商收益
YTC yield to (first) call 至通知赎回时收益
YTM yield to maturity 全期收益,到期收益
z zero; zone 零;区
ZBA zero bracket amount 零基数预算好量
ZBB zero-based budgeting 零基数预算法,免税金额,免征点
ZDD zero defect program 无缺陷计划
Z. P. G. zero population growth 人口零增长
ZR zero coupon issue 零息发行
zswk this week 本周
ZT zone time 区时
Z-Time Zebra time = GMT 格林尼治时间

References

[1] Anderson P V. Technical Writing: A Reader-Centered Approach. 2nd ed. New York: Jovanovich Publishers, 1991.
[2] Ding Wangdao. A Handbook of Writing. Beijing: Foreign Language Teaching and Research Press, 1994.
[3] Fan Hong. Business English Writing Course. Beijing: Tsinghua University Press, 2000.
[4] Hu Yingkun. Contemporary Business Writing. Dalian: Dalian University of Technology Press, 2000.
[5] Li Xiahui. Practical Auditing English. Beijing: China Modern Eoconomic Publishing House, 2002.
[6] Safina S N. Topics and Procedures for Teaching Formal Reports. Cincinnati: South-Western College Publishing. 2000.
[7] Shea V. Netiquette. New York: Albion Books, 1994.
[8] Wu, Baixiang. Business Writing. Beijing: Tsinghua University Press, 2005.
[9] Yu Sumei. Business English Basic Writing. Beijing: Higher Education Press, 2000.
[10] Lian Xian. Business English Wring. Beijing: Foreign Language Press, 2002.
[11] Beijing King&PARTNERS. Labour Contract . http://www.gaotonglaw.com/english/lssw.asp.
[12] Horne, Jerry. Report Topics. http://members.shaw.ca/horne/cmns/.
[13] UCLES. Cambridge BEC Test. Beijing: People's Post Press, 2006.